Prey No More

The In-Between Series: Book I

Stevi Mager

Mager-Lightfoot Publishing

STEVI MAGER

PREY NO MORE

BOOK 1

Mager-Lightfoot Books; www.stevimager.com

Book Cover by Amanda S. Dumky

Map Copyright Stevi Mager, 2024

Developmental Editing by Callista Morgen

Line Editing and Copy Editing by SML Editorial

Proofreading by Callista Morgen

Paperback ISBN: 979-8-3304-6150-9

Hardback ISBN: 979-8-9888254-1-8

Ebook ISBN: 979-8-9888254-2-5

1st edition 2024

Published in 2024 by Bookvault Publishing, Peterborough, United Kingdom. An environmentally friendly book printed and bound in England by Bookvault, powered by printondemand-worldwide.

To everyone who has ever pulled themselves out of the darkness
and found their light among the shadows.

Author's Note

The story behind this book was inspired by a recurring nightmare I experienced for over seven years as a response to trauma. The same nightmare, over and over and over again. Until one day, it changed. Something courageous happened. Something brave. Something I never thought myself capable of—not even my dream-self.

I couldn't get this change of events out of my head. So, naturally, I wrote it down. What began as the reaction to one nightmare stemmed into creating an entire world, lore, history, and characters, and the story that they would tell. The words on the page gave me an opportunity to rewrite my nightmare—to rewrite my story.

I never could have predicted that a repeated nightmare could lead to me fulfilling a lifelong dream.

Thank you for picking up this book, and for making that dream a reality. If you feel so inclined, please consider leaving a review of this book once you've finished. Reviews on sites such as Amazon, Goodreads, and Storygraph help authors like me reach the people who might resonate with their stories.

Thank you for reading Evenia and Kalland's story.

Thank you for reading my story.

P.s. For content warnings, please see the next page.

Content Warnings

Please examine this list carefully before reading further. As much as I appreciate you for wanting to read and experience the world that lies within the pages of Prey No More, your mental health and wellbeing mean more to me.

Beyond this point, please be advised of the following trigger warnings: PTSD, mental health (panic attacks; depression; anxiety), and trauma representation; nightmares (from PTSD); implied sexual assault (no detailed recounts or memories); grief of family members; violence; graphic death; torture; explicit language; explicit sexual content; discrimination; abandonment.

If you're looking for a closed-door romance, then this book is not for you.

Pronunciation Guide

1. Evenia Raldir ("Eee-ven-eee-uh" "Rall-deer")

2. Kalland Sothenas ("Call-lend" "Soth-uh-nay-ss")

3. Alekze ("Uh-leck-zee")

4. Andira ("And-deer-uh")

5. Aesthï ("Aye-ess-tee")

6. Duloar ("Dew-lore")

7. Duolvain ("Dew-all-vin")

8. Émeriah ("Ay-mare-ree-uh")

9. Enacor ("Enn-uh-core")

10. Gathéla ("Guh-thay-luh")

11. Gauiel ("Guy-elle")

12. Gunarakz ("Goon-uh-racks")

13. Huymi ("Hugh-my")

14. Inojk'l ("inn-oh-kull")

15. Irenz ("Eye-wren-z")

16. Jushelk ("Joo-shell-k")

17. Kajarnas (Kuh-jar-nus")

18. Lunrea ("lune-ray")

19. Marensha ("Muh-wren-shuh")

20. Mircha ("Meer-cha")

21. Neladrie ("Nuh-lod-dree")

22. Nioma ("Nye-oh-muh")

23. Nishara ("Knee-shar-uh")

24. Nulhe ("Null-hee")

25. Parveuri ("Paarv-yur-eee")

26. Qelena ("Kell-lean-uh")

27. Selaria ("Suh-laar-ree-uh")

28. Siersha ("See-air-shuh")

29. Taszarin ("Tas-zar-rin")

30. Thaïselle ("tie-ees-elle")

31. Urur ("Urr-urr")

32. Valoreg ("Vuh-lore-rig")

33. Vhi-aiorhi ("Vee-ay-ore-eee")

34. Xelfrina ("Zell-free-nuh")

STEVI MAGER

PREY NO MORE

BOOK 1

I

Evenia

L eaves rustled in the wind, singing a song of their own for any who dared to stop and listen, while the faint sound of a wolf's howl reverberated off the mountainside in the distance. But Evenia didn't notice any of that. All she could hear was the sound of her own heartbeat pounding in her ears as she ran.

Just a little farther, she told herself.

She had no idea where "a little farther" would get her, and she didn't know how long she had been saying it to herself. She just knew she had to keep going, because stopping now was not an option.

Before she fled from that helhole—whatever that place had been—the old timeteller above the door of her dank cell had read three-thirty a.m. She didn't know what time it was now, or how long before it would be safe for her to stop. *If* it would be safe for her to stop.

Just a little farther.

There were patches of moss and soil adorned with moonlight shining through where the branches parted ways overhead, casting rays of silvery light in various spots throughout the woods. She steered clear of the moonlit paths, even if it meant it was so dark that she could barely detect her own foggy breath from the chilled night. As much as she didn't want to be in the darkness again, the lit paths would make it easier for her to be seen, caught, and dragged back to wherever she just escaped from.

No, the dark was better. *Except when it isn't.* Her body shuddered and she shook the thought from her head.

Darkness had quickly become Evenia's greatest fear. In a twisted turn of events, it seemed it was to be her salvation tonight.

Focus.

But it was getting increasingly more difficult to do so. Her head felt heavy on her shoulders. Her eyes were shuddering, struggling to focus on anything. Her feet felt like lead pounding the ground, getting harder to lift with each step.

Still, her catlike eyesight was sharp enough to keep her from tripping over the tree roots, fallen branches, and anything else that might obstruct her path. As much as she despised that side of her, she found herself thankful for being a shifter for the first time in her life.

Just shift, a voice inside her head screamed at her. *You'll be faster if you would just shift!*

Even in her groggy, humanoid state, Evenia was faster than most humans and duolvain—someone who was part fae, part human. A fact that had kept her from joining any festival activities back home. So, she always told herself she didn't need to shift to be faster. It was safer, better not to.

Ignoring that pesky voice, she kept going.

Based on the chill, she was no longer in Enacor. Where, then? Akvar? Valoreg? Urur?

A shudder ran down her spine before she blinked away the thoughts. No, she couldn't think of anywhere, not even home right now. Of her cousin and aunt waiting for her in Enacor. Were they searching for her? How long was she away from them? Did they know where she was now? Were they worried?

Would she ever see them again?

A stinging in her nose stretched to her eyes, but she blinked away the annoying sensation. This was not the time. Not now.

Just a little farther.

And then, she felt them...the shadows of The Darkness creeping up behind her. The already chilly night suddenly became almost unbearable with an icy coldness sinking straight into her bones. The closer he crept, the clearer her breath glowed in front of her. It cut through the night as she exhaled with each desperate stride.

She tried to quicken her pace, but The Darkness was almost overpowering her now. The frigid cold seeping from his shadows threatened to strike the very breath from her lungs.

And then came that deep, hair-raising laugh, as if this had all been a tease. As if she'd never stood a chance of escaping. As if he thought he'd won and was going to haul her back.

Like hel, she thought to herself.

But her chest was heaving, and her lungs were burning from running. Her heart pounded harder as she realized she was struggling to keep going.

Not like this. Please, not like this, she pleaded to the air, to the trees, to the Moon herself.

And that was when she heard it: laughter. *Real* laughter. Her ears perked up when it sounded again.

He must have heard it, too, because the shadows' presence eased a bit, no longer nipping right at her heels. Her heart fluttered. If it was enough to scare him, then it was enough for her to risk it. She abruptly switched directions and ran toward that hopeful sound.

A low, warning growl emanated behind her.

Good. She'd have smiled if there was enough strength to. The fact that she felt the urge to was proof that there was some fight—some hope—left in her. She clung to that fleck of hope, embracing the onset of adrenaline-induced strength it gave her, and ran faster.

The distance between her and the trees' edge was closing with each step. There was no way to know where it led to—what laid beyond—but it was her only shot. The closer she got to the edge of the tree line, the more that fleck of hope grew. She could see light from torches somewhere below. It had to be the source of the laughter.

She could make it. She had to make it.

"NO!" his animalistic growl echoed into the air behind her. The roar was followed by the cawing and flapping of birds fleeing the treetops above her at the predatory sound.

She felt the panic and anger growing from the shadows, which were a few feet behind her now. It only fueled her more. She embraced the sudden adrenaline rush coursing through her, giving her the strength to keep going. It was going to happen. She was so close to the tree line—to the edge. So close to freedom. A few more steps, and she'd be there.

Just a little farther. The moonlight was caressing her skin through the trees already. The taste of freedom was practically at her fingertips.

Just a little farther. The hope inside of her grew like fire on the wind. An unbelieving breath fell from her lips, and a small smile escaped with it.

And then, his shadows struck.

Her small smile vanished the second she felt the cold, shadowed hand graze her shins as her feet were pulled out from beneath her, her upper body quickly falling forward from the contact. With a glance down and just past the tree's edge, she realized that her fall over the hillside was inevitable, but she wasn't going to give him the satisfaction of catching her again. *Never* again. This wasn't going to be how she went out. *Not like this.* Not without a fight.

There was a mere split-second to decide what to do, but her gut told her there was only one choice. As she fell, she stretched her body as far forward as she could, reaching for where the line of trees ended and the light shone from below.

With a leap, her upper body stretched toward the glow at the same time she twisted and reached her hands out to the unnaturally large, umbra figure racing toward her. Using every last bit of her strength, she summoned the power of Light to her fingertips, and shot the brightest beam of Light she could muster out at the shadows chasing her.

A beacon of Light. *Just like Mother.* She smiled at the realization. But this time, she intended to blind the beast.

With a screech, The Darkness dropped his hold on her leg. His shadows shrank back as he covered his yellow eyes with both his clawed hands and his swirling shadows.

There was no chance to celebrate before she felt the presence of the ground fast approaching. She attempted to twist her body back facing forward, holding her hands out to brace for the impact. But it was too late.

Her hand crunched under her when her body met the ground, and kept meeting it. Still, she reached for that light—that laughter—while rolling straight down a hillside.

Would the one whose laughter had saved her notice her falling? She tried to yell for help, but the air was ripped from her body as she landed hard on her back, and then continued rolling.

Was she even breathing? It didn't matter because the farther she rolled down that hill, the less she felt The Darkness's presence.

That was enough for Evenia.

It was enough to know that she had made it. That if she was to die tonight, at least she would die free.

With that thought, she closed her eyes and let the Fates take control.

2

 Kalland

K alland was trying and failing to listen to Neladrie's recount of her recent visit home to Gathéla. His mind was elsewhere. Despite her attempt at light conversation, there was no joy to be felt on this dark path. Even the Light from their floating torches seemed to be dimmer than normal.

The patrol of the Gunarakz Forest—the border separating Mircha from the Urur Mountains—was every Mirchan sentry's least favorite patrol. Unfortunately, it could not be ignored with the numerous reports of foul creatures spotted near the edges of the mountain passes. No one knew what all lurked beyond in the unknown of the Urur Mountains, and all with a pulse knew to not go searching for answers. Yet here they were.

They were a few sentries short of their normal party, but they were where they were meant to be. They all were, even if many in the company appeared on edge. Conversation and laughter felt strained tonight, which was unusual since most everyone in the company liked one another. *Most* everyone.

Tension was rising among the group—even from himself—as much as he hated to admit it. It was those damned mountains. But the Mirchan sentries could only do so much about the creatures lurking in the mountains without the risk of wiping out their entire region's sentries and angering the gods.

No, some things were better left alone.

Neladrie abruptly stopped talking when a wolf howled in the distance, echoing off a mountainside past the cliff's edge above. In his peripheral vision, Kalland saw Alekze tense, straining against the urge to keep his body relaxed from the sound.

Kalland didn't react to his friend's change in body language, but he made a silent note of it. After all, it was a full moon, which meant there'd be more than just natural wolves roaming these mountains tonight.

"Friend of yours?" Emilzorn asked from behind Kalland.

Alekze let out a low growl, and Kalland didn't need to look to know that Emil was smirking.

"That was a mourning cry," Alekze finally said about the howl they heard. His shoulders were still slightly tense from hearing the pained sound, but his sharp-featured face remained unreadable, as usual.

Kalland shot Emilzorn a warning look before the sentry could respond with a retort. Emilzorn's mouth snapped shut just as quickly as it had opened, and his eyes darted forward again as he stood a little straighter in his saddle.

Kalland casually glanced once more at his friend, whose pale features appeared more lupine than normal as a result of the night's full moon calling him to shift. The only thing that kept the half-werewolf from doing so was the elven blood coursing through his veins. It allowed him to shift at will and resist when the Moon's Call filled him, urging him to answer her like a siren luring a human deep into the sea's depths.

Kalland could tell the howl had affected Alekze more than he would ever willingly admit. However, if his friend did not believe it to be an indicator of an immediate threat, then now was not the time to discuss it.

Instead, he looked back to the tree line and the ominous cliffs looming above. It was darker than it should have been with a full moon high in the night sky. Yet another comforting feature courtesy of the Urur Mountains.

As if to fill the sudden awkward silence, Neladrie continued talking about Gathéla and her family. He couldn't concentrate on her words, but he made a point to smile and muster a small laugh in response when she laughed. He wasn't even sure exactly what was so funny—something about her little brother and mud during one of their Nature elf training sessions.

He tried, he really did, but his gaze couldn't stay away from the tree line for long. The Urur Mountains always stirred something inside of him—a part of him he tried his best to keep buried deep, deep down. Especially while working. He could not afford to let his emotions control him in a place like this. No, that would be a mistake that would undoubtedly lead to death—whether his or another's.

He was absentmindedly scanning the tree line when a flock of birds shooting out of the trees above caught his attention. The startled caws made a few horses within the company whinny but not stop entirely. His own horse was calm, but he was not. The ominous sight had the hair on the back of his neck standing up. As he tapped into his elven sight to find what disturbed the birds, a flash of light illuminated the trees above and—

Something was flying out of the shadows just past the tree line and off the cliff's edge. It was accompanied by a scent he recognized all too well. His heart stopped. So much for keeping it all buried. His horse, ever loyal, had stopped moving in response to his distress, but Kalland's mind was racing too much to notice.

Before he could process what he saw and smelled, the hill started tumbling down in front of them. Tangled in the mess of dirt and rocks was golden hair and pale limbs.

"Landslide!" Emilzorn yelled behind him.

No shit, Kalland wanted to yell back.

General Andira Elsvarin shouted orders to Neladrie and her twin, Kaj, the company's two Huymi—Nature elves—but they had already run off to tend to the land. In all the chaos, Kalland's eyes never left the pale, tumbling woman who reeked of darkness and...death.

Andira shouted for Alekze, a command Kalland knew was made to care for the mystery woman. He wasn't about to lose his chance to find out where that unfortunately familiar scent had come from. To find out if she was the key he was searching for all these years.

"I've got her!" he shouted as he jumped off his horse and ran for her in the still-unstable land. The words came out sharper than he'd meant them to, but fuck it.

He reached the bottom of the hillside, but he could go no farther. The land was too unstable for him to safely approach her. The woman was no longer falling thanks to Kaj, who created a platform of dirt for her to rest on and a protective barrier to shield her from any debris while Neladrie worked to right the land.

Kalland could only stand there and wait.

As talented as Neladrie was, she was taking far too long to stabilize the ground and restore it to its original state. Kalland resisted the urge to pace or, worse, snap at his friend to hurry. As that would likely draw too much attention—and cause a well-deserved verbal beating from both Neladrie and Andira—he opted for balling his hands into fists at his sides as he impatiently waited.

It was a matter of seconds before his knuckles turned bone white and half-moon indentations appeared in his palms. So deep that they almost drew blood.

He eased the pressure in his palms and distracted his thoughts by honing into his elven sight and taking in every detail of the woman in front of him. The gold he saw fly out of the shadowed trees was her long blonde hair. Her skin was an unhealthy pale, as though she hadn't seen the sun in months.

Examining her face further, he saw her cheeks were sunken in and void of color, but there was a visible marking on her eyes. A sharp black streak adorned the crease of each of her eyes. The markings had not been smudged, as if they were part of her skin. Still, they were not free of dirt and ichor.

In fact, there was blood all over her body—both fresh and dried. Most of her exposed skin was covered in it and caked-on muck. He took note of a few open wounds he could see, and some others that looked as if they had been healing and were partially re-irritated. No doubt a result of her tumble.

He tensed when he was finished taking in just how much blood was on this woman, attracting only gods knew what from the mountains. The most visible injury was her right arm bending in the wrong direction.

He grimaced at the sight before silently cursing at himself for allowing the reaction to slip through. Kalland immediately willed his face back into the unreadable expression that had been instilled in him at a young age from his training as both a soldier and a royal member of Valoreg's Court—the Wind Realm.

He lifted his nose an inch as he honed his senses on her, taking in her scent again. He recoiled and the hairs on the back of his neck raised. She reeked of that scent—that *darkness*—but it was commingled with her own.

He felt a pang to the chest as he realized it wasn't actually *her* scent, and to his surprise, he also felt a small wave of relief. This mystery woman might not be the source of the scent, but it was the closest he'd ever come to finding answers about that night. About their deaths.

Was that a seed of hope he felt? He shoved down the feeling. He couldn't endure any more false hope or dead ends after all these years.

A heat rose deep down as his eyes landed on her wrists. There were indentations—clean, even lines—around the entirety of her too-thin wrists. Shackled, then. A prisoner. But of what?

He glanced once more at the tree line, toward the Urur Mountains, and then back at the woman. Was it to keep the outside world from her as punishment—a true prisoner—or to keep her from the outside world because she was a threat?

It was obvious she was a fighter, for she had endured all these injuries and the landslide and still breathed before him. Perhaps even escaped, by the smell of the fear emanating off her.

"She is not the enemy you seek," a voice on the Wind whispered to him. He resisted the urge to shudder, but his defenses went up.

"Who are you?" he asked the Wind, but there was no cold breeze, no visible current of communication, and no unrecognizable voice in response. Wind whispering was meant to be a warm sensation for the recipient. But this... This had been something entirely different than he'd ever heard or felt before.

His eyes narrowed. She might not be The Darkness, but *he* would decide if she was an enemy, not some voice on the wind.

As if she, too, had heard the voice, the woman cracked open her eyes. Granted, they were mere slits as she peered out of them, taking in the two Huymi in front of her, and then finally landing on him. It looked like she was straining against the pain from opening her eyes just that little amount.

His heartbeat faltered a moment, not knowing what he should say or do. After only a few seconds, she closed her eyes once more and sank back into the dirt mound she was being held in as Kaj brought it closer.

Once she was within arm's reach, Kalland wasted no time in gently wrapping his gloved hands around the woman. He lifted her from the dirt, being careful of her injuries—both old and new. It was shocking how small and frail she seemed in his arms.

Her lips were blue, and she was shivering against him. Pulling her in closer to his body, he enveloped her in warm Wind as he turned and walked toward his horse, Xelfrina. He grabbed the spare faux fur cloak that was draped along the saddle and wrapped it around the woman.

At the touch of the blanket, her eyes opened again, growing slightly wider as they settled on him. It felt like she was looking through him rather than at him. Her eyes were a striking light blue. At least, one eye—her right—was. Her left eye was that same blue on top, but it was split diagonally in the middle, with the pale blue bleeding into a light green on the bottom.

The sight reminded him of a lakeshore meeting the edge of grass. The blades of grass trying to reach toward the lake while the water was attempting to seep into the land. They bled into one another where they intersected. It was as if they were fighting for the right to claim her eye. He'd never seen anything like it in all his years.

The woman slowly blinked, bringing his attention back to her. Fear radiated off her, and he felt an overwhelming need to take that fear away.

"I've got you," he Wind whispered, sending the message on a warm breeze straight to her ears so that only she could hear. *"You're safe."*

Their eyes briefly met then. Her lips slowly parted half an inch, the effort causing her eyes to shudder. Although no sound passed her lips, he understood the meaning.

Not knowing what more he could say to assure her, he held his breath for her reaction. It didn't take long before her eyes slowly closed and her body began to relax in his arms. He pulled her in tightly to his chest with his right arm and willed his body heat to warm her as he mounted Xelfrina, settling into the saddle.

Kalland nodded at Andira, whose eyes he knew were upon him throughout the whole encounter. The general didn't return the nod, but briefly looked down at the woman and then again at the cliff's edge. He didn't even have time to instruct Xelfrina before she had started gliding toward the general, simply knowing what it was he wanted.

"Do we know who she is?" Andira asked when he reached her side, but her gaze remained on the elevated tree line above. The dimly lit torch floating above her head was highlighting her sharp cheekbones.

"I'm not sure. She's too weak to speak," Kalland said, resisting the urge to look down at the woman resting in his arms. She had finally stopped shivering. "She's in need of a healer."

"Esral and Nishara are scouting the source of the landslide. They have not finished yet." Translation: *The healer can wait.*

He didn't even realize that the two sentries had left. Esral was a Nulhen hawk shifter, making their abilities and very essence a product of the Moon, which meant that they thrived in the moonlight. And Nishara was one of the most powerful Lunrae—a Moon elf—that Kalland had ever met. There would be no one better to search in the dark than the two of them, the Moon's energy fueling their powers.

Still, a muscle ticked in Kalland's jaw as his impatience grew. "I request permission to take her to the Capital." Kalland willed his face to remain still, to not reveal the flicker of hope he felt in his chest at this mystery woman's sudden appearance. He only hoped his eyes did not betray him. Not that Andira was looking at him, anyway. Her eyes were glued to the cliff's edge.

"We will all continue our journey to Fort Norlon once Esral and Nishara have returned." Andira's voice was stern—the voice of a commander. She still had not so much as glanced in his direction. In fact, she looked a little angry and...unsettled. Kalland had never seen his general like this.

He followed her gaze to the tree line. Seeing nothing, he looked back at her.

"Andira," he Wind whispered so that the nosey sentries behind him could not hear. The Wind current was acknowledged with a subtle side eye in his direction. His throat bobbed. *"She has the scent on her."* The words would have come out as a whisper, with or without the Wind's power flowing through him.

Andira looked at him now. *Really* looked at him, before she glanced at the woman, understanding flooding through her as she made the connection of what the mystery woman meant to him. He could tell she was making a note of the scents for her own mental catalog.

Her eyes flickered back to his face as she regarded him once more.

"Very well," she finally said. "You may take your leave."

No further instruction was required as he nodded and whispered a command in his natural tongue to Xelfrina: *"Inojk'l."*

The horse responded by turning toward the open path before them, releasing her grey wings, and taking off as fast as the wind itself.

He was going to find out who she was and what she knew. He was going to find The Darkness.

He tried his best to fight it, but that flicker of hope was flaming inside of him now.

3

Kalland

"I found the remains of a werewolf when I scouted the Gunarakz Forest four nights ago," Nishara said from her spot around the oval conference table.

Kalland's eyes instinctively flew to Alekze, who suddenly sat stiff as a board in his seat.

"He was...hardly recognizable as a wolf, due to the injuries he sustained," Nishara continued, but Kalland kept his eyes on his friend, who was keeping his emotions closed off. "If it was not for his companion being there, I wouldn't have known the sight was a wolf at all."

"Do we have access to this 'companion' to question them about the night's events? And are we certain they did not kill the werewolf themselves?" Marensha asked.

Nishara nodded. "Yes, she is staying here in Mircha for a couple days now that she's fully transitioned back after the full moon. She was in shock from...everything. Per Thaïselle's instructions, we gave her a couple days to recover from the transition back to her human form." Her hand waved toward the healer sitting at the other end of the table.

Dropping her arm, she continued. "Esral and I plan to question her later this morning about what happened and who—or what—killed the other werewolf from that night."

That was a mourning cry, Alekze's words from the night of the full moon played through Kalland's head. Alekze did not show signs of any immediate threat when he'd first heard the howl, so Kalland thought nothing of it at the time. Then, they'd been so preoccupied by the landslide that he completely forgot about it.

It had been four nights since the full moon made her descent from the sky, and four nights since the mystery woman made her own descent down the cliff's edge. The same cliff that Kalland later learned had housed The Darkness, even if for a brief second.

He wished Andira had told him the truth of why she was so rattled that night. Told him the truth that she'd seen The Darkness's yellow eyes and felt his presence watching them. If he'd known, he would have tossed the mystery woman to Alekze and hunted the beast down himself.

But his stubborn ass felt pulled to this woman who fell, and he insisted on following this lead from the scent on her. Now, she was his *only* lead. The only chance he had of finding the truth. Because helping the mystery woman ruined his chances of finding The Darkness himself. Could she have been a distraction for The Darkness to get away from the sentries ascending on the forest? Kalland's fists clenched at the thought of falling right into the demon's plans.

Nishara hesitated before clearing her throat, prompting Kalland to look at her. "As for if this companion killed the werewolf, I do not believe so. Wolves are predatory animals, yes," in the corner of his eye, Kalland saw Alekze tense again, "but the deceased wolf was...torn, limb by limb. There was also a foul stench I could neither identify nor shake. But it felt...otherworldly." Her throat bobbed at the last word.

Kalland's heart stopped. *Torn, limb by limb ... a foul stench ... otherworldly.*

Images flashed in Kalland's mind of the night he discovered his parents' bodies in the Urur Mountains. Twenty-five years ago, Lystheria and Daestor Sothenas went on a mission as sentries for the Wind Realm of Valoreg—the place Kalland called home—to investigate reports of missing shifters native to the realm.

At least, that was what his aunt, Queen Eleftrine of Valoreg, had told Kalland. Nothing he found since suggested otherwise, but there also wasn't much information available on their mission for him to review. Something he always found strange, and one of the reasons he'd never been able to let it go. He was missing something. No, he wasn't just missing it; it was being withheld from him. And he'd figure it out someday.

Even so, there was likely some truth to the mission. For over a century now, shifters were considered an endangered species. Their animal forms typically appeared at twice the size of a normal animal, making them desirable among sport hunters and traders. After receiving reports that some shifters from Valoreg's ranks went missing in the Urur Mountains, Kalland's parents went to investigate a lead on one of the missing shifters.

What should have been only a four-day mission turned into almost ten days without word from their party.

After his parents missed their return-home-by date by six days, his aunt finally gave Kalland permission to send a search party to find them. But when he and the Valoreg Sentries finally tracked down his parents' scents in the snow-covered mountains, they'd been too late. His mother—

Torn, limb by limb. A foul stench. Otherworldly.

A wave of nausea overwhelmed him as the usually repressed images flooded his mind. That was the day Kalland learned of The Darkness and what he was capable of. And it was the day Kalland swore to hunt the bastard down and send him back to Hel.

Six days. It took six days to convince anyone to let him search for his parents. He often wondered if he went out on his own instead of waiting for permission, if he would have made it in time. If he could have saved them. If...

He took a deep breath and released it. He shoved the mental images and grief down, visualizing a box to contain them in that he could nail shut. Hopefully, forever. There was no use in dwelling in "what ifs," only "what now?"

Right now, he planned to take this lead that practically fell at their feet and shake her down until she revealed her connection to The Darkness and how Kalland could get to him. He'd finally get his revenge, because now, he had the key to it all.

His fingers twitched at his sides, itching for the chance to move...to act.

Soon, he thought to himself.

He took another deep breath and exhaled slowly as Nishara's words sounded muffled under the intensity of his thoughts. Sitting through the formality of this meeting was proving to be worse than having to listen to Tasz try to sing when he was drunk on Elndish wine. And Elndion—the Sun Realm—was well known for its strong wine.

Kalland's pointed ears perked at the mention of a new topic, bringing him back out of his thoughts.

"Now that it's settled who will talk with the companion from that night," Marensha said, gesturing in the direction of Nishara, "do we know who will get to question the hill rider?"

The moment he was waiting for. He stiffened in his seat, because he'd be damned if anyone else got to talk to her.

His lead. His key. *His.*

"She's mine."

4

Kalland

"And there it is," Marensha said, dragging out the *and* in her ever-so-dramatic fashion. Granted, he practically growled his right to be the one to question the woman.

Marensha rolled her eyes and shook her head, her long, fiery red hair swaying side to side against her sun-kissed cheeks. He resisted the urge to flip her off, seeing as how they were in a work meeting, and that would be highly unprofessional.

"Oh, so he speaks?" Nishara teased, but Kalland wasn't in the mood. He held her gaze while she got comfortable in her chair. "Right, yes, anyone else?"

"You mean, anyone else to *accompany* me?" he asked.

"No, I meant, anyone *other* than the one person who is not-so-secretly wanting to bombard our patient. We're here to discuss who gets to talk with her, not who *wants* to talk with her," Nishara countered. Her hands rested on the tabletop, fingers interlaced with one another, while her lavender-colored eyes were locked on his grey ones.

Almost all eyes were on them, as he looked around the table to each sentry among General Andira Elsvarin's most trusted circle. There was a tight-lipped Alekze, his dirty blonde hair tied back in a bun. Neladrie seemed both nervous and concerned. For whom, he did not know; it was just in Neladrie's nature to worry about others. Tasz casually leaned back in his chair, with his golden eyes staring off into the distance, looking like he was daydreaming.

On the opposite side of the table, Marensha's hazel eyes glanced back and forth between Nishara and Kalland. At the far end, Gauiel, the Vice President of Mircha, sat next to Andira, and next to him was his brother and assistant, Jushelk, his face looking like he just swallowed a lemon. Then again, that was how he always looked.

Finally, his gaze fell on his general. Andira was silently observing in her spot across the table. Thaïselle sat on the other side of her, looking like she was waiting her turn to butt in.

When in this room and around this oval table, they were all equals. Title, rank, experience, age, species—none of it mattered here. They'd all earned their spot at the table in one way or another.

Ordinarily, he would be honored to be among so many brave, courageous sentries. The people who had become his family here in Mircha. But today, he only saw them as obstacles to getting answers. He was the only one with the biggest stake in questioning her, and he wasn't backing down from this.

"Who said I would 'bombard' her? I simply want to ask her questions, same as everyone else here," he said, hoping that he was able to mask the anxiety and eagerness overwhelming him.

"Kalland..." Nishara's tone was gentle, concerned. Her lavender eyes softened on him. "We understand. We just need to make sure we aren't...hasty in our decision here."

He understood to a degree, but could she really blame him for wanting to be the one to talk to this woman? To find out why she held The Darkness's scent? To learn if it was because she was fleeing from the beast or because she was associated with him? Worked alongside him? Did his bidding? Killed—

An anxious tapping of his foot started as his thoughts spiraled. This was someone who not only held *the* scent but had somehow been found near where they suspected the beast had killed that night. But could they be certain it was The Darkness who had been on the murderous rampage? How did they know it wasn't this mystery woman who was killing for the beast?

With a deep inhale, he shifted in his seat. *Enough.* That was enough. He would get answers. Answers to questions that *he* would ask. Because this woman—this woman, who had quite literally fallen at his feet—was the closest he had ever come to answers about what happened that night.

He stood up and turned away from his people, choosing to face a wall. The downward spiral of thoughts and emotions was becoming overwhelming. A muscle in his jaw ticked and his eyes involuntarily shut as the memories flooded in for the second time during this meeting.

His closed eyes squeezed tighter at the flashing images, as if he could push them out of his mind—block them from plaguing him further. But it was useless.

He remembered what it had been like, finding his mother and father in the Urur Mountains. His sweet, loving mother, who used to read to him at night and hold him when his fear of monsters became too much as a child. His brave father, who never passed up the opportunity to wrestle or tell a joke that only he laughed at.

If he had not been able to identify their personal scents, the auburn hair of his mother, or the chestnut hair of his father, Kalland wouldn't have known the carnage he walked upon that day was the very elves who used to tuck him in at night. The ones who used to read him bedtime stories. Who would cook with him or throw snowballs at him.

His shoulders fell.

Once upon a time, he loved the snow. The way it shimmered in the sunlight like diamonds, or the way it resembled a starry night when the moonlight hit it just right. Building snow creatures with his little sister and all the snowball fights they used to have after their lessons. But after finding his parents in the snow, Kalland found he did not particularly care for the cold, white substance anymore.

It was no longer a joyous experience to detect the scent of snow in the air because it now reminded him of the rancid smell of dead bodies mixed with that foul creature's essence. He could no longer hear snow crunching under his boots without instantly being taken back to that moment. To the scream that escaped his sister's throat when they found what was left of their parents.

He could no longer feel the sensation of a snowflake landing on his cheek without being reminded of the tears he shed when he saw his mother's lifeless body—or at least, part of it scattered in the snow. He would never again be able to feel the iciness of the cold on the wind without being reminded of the numb feeling that overtook him for years after in his grief.

Something he once found beautiful and peaceful now made him feel numb and murderous at the same time.

So, could Nishara really blame him for wanting answers? Could any of them blame him for wanting to be the one to talk to the first person who came along in the twenty-five years since their deaths?

Shaking the memories off, he turned and met Nishara's gaze. "What's there to be hasty about?" he asked, the stress of the moment getting to him. "She had The Darkness's scent on her. I am the only one among us to have also encountered that monster. What more is there to discuss?" He looked around, daring anyone to object. Yes, his emotions were definitely getting the best of him, but he didn't give a damn.

"Kal, we know what she means to you," Alekze said. "But they're right; you don't get to just assume you're the one who gets to talk to her." His deep voice was calm.

"Oh, I'm sorry, I didn't realize this was even up for debate," Kalland sneered.

"Of course, you didn't," Marensha huffed at him. Fire burned in her eyes as her anger rose. "Sit down before you make me act on the urge to throw you out that window." She was sitting back in her chair, rocking it on its two back legs. He glared at her, and she halted the rocking motion as she narrowed her fiery eyes right back at him. A silent warning.

Marensha was a Fire Elemental witch—a mortal fae—and the only non-elven sentry sitting around the table. Granted, some were only part elven. Everyone but Marensha had some elven blood—and magic—coursing through their veins.

The human witch certainly earned her spot in Andira's circle, but gods, she had a temper on her. One that rivaled Kalland's. He'd be lying if he said it wasn't what made them such good sparring partners, but the two were constantly butting heads as a result.

"What makes you think she'll even want to talk to you?" Alekze asked, pulling Kalland's attention back to his best friend. "Especially when you go busting down her door like a blood-thirsty lunatic?"

The tapping motion of his foot stopped and his lips parted a fraction at his friends' objections.

"He's right," Nishara agreed. "She was alone in the middle of the night in the Urur Mountains, produced Light that rivals Tasz's Sun magic, and survived what would have been a fatal landslide, had we not been there. I mean no offense, Kalland, but I don't think this is one you can intimidate into talking to you."

Tasz's ears perked up at the mention of his name, breaking him from his daydream, but he still didn't speak. Neither for nor against Kalland's argument.

Kalland looked around the room at everyone he trusted, had fought next to many times, and would instantly forfeit his own life for. They were fighting him on this now—his chance to figure out what the hel happened to his parents.

Could they not see how desperate he was for the truth? To find out what all this woman knew?

He never thought he'd see the day that his people would question his motives or prevent him from fulfilling his only purpose. If they thought so little of him, that he would intimidate someone who was innocent, then they didn't know him at all.

Shit, he might actually do just that—intimidate her with everything he had. Part of him wouldn't believe that someone who carried that scent as strongly as she did could possibly be innocent. But if he did interrogate her, they need not know about it. Right?

No. He knew how to be discreet. Knew how to communicate with her without anyone knowing.

"Who said anything about intimidating her?" he snapped back.

Alekze's eyes narrowed. "You've been irritable and angry ever since we found her. You will lose that very thin grasp you have on your patience if she refuses to talk with you. Whether you mean to or not, you intimidating her is inevitable."

Kalland scoffed as he sat down again. Something told him this mystery woman wasn't one to scare easily. Hel, like Nishara pointed out, she clearly had a backbone and a strong will to live. Surely, being questioned by Kalland wouldn't be the worst thing she'd experienced in the past week.

He thought back to her broken and battered body. To the broken bones, all the dried blood, and the injuries and wounds that were improperly healed. Something twisted in his gut at the reminder. No, being interrogated by him definitely wouldn't be the worst thing she'd experienced in *months*.

But this woman was dragged into this revenge-filled war the second she associated herself with The Darkness. She had secrets, and he was going to learn them one by one.

He'd be damned if his own people were going to keep him from finding out exactly what she knew. Because she had to know something. He could feel it deep in his bones. Why couldn't they see it?

"Is no one else fucking curious why she has the scent on her? Why am I the only one who seems to give a damn that this fucker is back out there, doing only the gods know what? And hurting gods know who? Who's next? It could have been her laying dead if we hadn't been patrolling that night. Nishara finding that wolf is proof enough."

The room fell silent. *Good.* Only, that was all assuming she was not working with The Darkness.

An internal groan threatened to escape his lips as he realized Alekze was somewhat right. Kalland wasn't used to being so angry and irritable all the time. Normally, he was relatively calm-natured. Unless someone he cared about was in trouble, or if someone was being treated unfairly. Especially women, children, and animals. Then, all bets were off.

Ever since finding the mystery woman, he'd been an absolute fucking mess. What occurred over the last four days was proving to be worse than the mood swings he had experienced as an elven teen. And that was saying something, considering those lasted *decades* longer than a human teen's, thanks to elven longevity.

His fists balled and uncurled under the table. Electricity zinged at his fingertips and the Wind gently caressed his hair, both responding to his heightened emotions. He sighed out of frustration at the response of his powers and connection to the Elements.

Godsdamn it. Alekze really was right; he was losing his cool. It was causing the Wind and Storm Elements in his blood to respond to his emotions, and that couldn't happen.

Frustration caused the backs of his eyelids to replace the sight of the sentries around him. It didn't take long for a memory of the woman that night to flash in his mind. A moment that made him question everything.

When he held her in his arms that night, she looked at him. The sight of her eyes—that pale blue mixed with green—nearly stole his breath, and he'd wondered if she was not the enemy. If she... If she was actually fleeing from The Darkness.

But then, the wind picked up while they were flying on Xelfrina, and he couldn't deny that *smell*. It was so strong that he'd nearly gagged. Every pore of hers practically oozed the beast's odor. There was no other explanation for why that would be, except that she was working with him. She had to be. She just had to be.

He slowly breathed in and out, composing his breath and body.

The lightning left his fingertips as Neladrie's soft voice helped save him from his spiraling thoughts. "I don't think anyone who saw her injuries can say that she didn't have the hardest part in all of this. She fought for the right to be here right now, and she won.

"She is owed our respect and patience as she acquaints herself with our home and chooses what to tell us and what not to as we work to reacquaint her with *her* home," she said, breaking her silence on the matter.

"She's right, Kalland," Gaiuel said in his calm, gentle voice.

Gaiuel was one of the few old men in Mircha who Kalland liked and respected. He didn't act like a politician or like he owned the world, not like his brother, Jushelk. Unlike his brother, Gaiuel was a peacemaker and someone who wished they could offer the world to everyone. He was everything that Mircha was supposed to represent, and that was exactly why he was the Vice President of Mircha.

"I don't disagree, sir." The words managed to slither out of his lips. Were they the truth? He didn't know. All he knew was that at this point, he was willing to say whatever he needed to in order to gain access to the interrogation.

"I don't know what will happen when we speak with her, but I can say I do not wish to intimidate her. I simply want to know what she knows, and I want to be there to hear it all from her lips."

There. If that didn't satisfy them, then nothing would. His breath halted as he waited.

Andira eyed Kalland warily, as if she could read his thoughts. He raised his chin and met her stare to show her he had nothing to hide.

After a few moments, Andira finally nodded. "It is settled, then. Thaïselle, Kalland, and I will meet with our guest when she wakes. Let us wait and see what she has to say." Andira's voice was assertive.

No one objected or dared to question the general's decision.

Fighting the urge to smile at his sudden victory, Kalland slowly breathed out through his nose. Only the gods and the deepest part of his mind knew he was going to be a wolf in sheep's clothing. He would act the part of the Mirchan sentry—a peacekeeper—someone who didn't need anything from her, and only wanted to help.

The smile broke through because, from now on, that was far from the truth. He was going to get his answers. One way or another, he'd get everything from her.

5

Evenia

*I*t was cold. So cold.

Evenia moved to wrap her arms around her body to stay warm, but there was a sharp pain in both hands as her wrists were jolted back and away from her body. Her eyelids were fighting her, and her head felt so very heavy. Still, she was determined to see why her arms wouldn't budge.

She blinked once. Twice. Three times. Finally, she slowly opened her eyes to see why her wrists suddenly felt weighted down. Her lashes shuddering from the alarming heaviness weighing on them, it took a second for her vision to clear in the dark. Once they adjusted, she realized she was in a cold, lightless room with straw strewn out over the floor.

Blink.

Around her wrists were large, cold cuffs shackled to the wall by a chain link. By the feel of it, the metal of the chains was the width of three of her fingers put together.

Blink.

No windows.

Blink.

There was a dim light flickering under the massive metal door—the only exit in the entire room. It offered little light.

Blink.

A bloodcurdling scream from someone. She didn't know where it came from.

Blink.

The pounding of footsteps sounded like they were coming straight for her.

Blink. Blink.

A fear-filled scream built in her chest, but nothing came out—not even a breath. Her wrists were burning under the cuffs now as she tried to move, tried to sit up. She winced at the feel of a sharp sting on her right wrist. Instantly smelling blood, she didn't need to open her eyes to know that she'd cut herself deeply.

That was the least of her worries, for someone had opened the door and crossed the threshold into the dark of the room. She couldn't see them, but she felt their presence.

Her heart stopped.

The room was suddenly full of a different kind of darkness, and she screamed as it swallowed her.

6

Evenia

The sound of voices pulled Evenia from her sleep. Her hand went to wipe her closed eyes but was met with resistance. As if she'd been hit in the stomach, all the air left her lungs as reality hit her.

Not again. She didn't want to open her eyes—didn't want to see that it had all been for nothing. Squeezing her eyes closed even tighter, she fought back the tears threatening to surface.

I didn't make it. I—

Wait. There was no screaming. No weight of chains around her wrists. No foul stench. No presence of an endless void. With a deep breath, then another, she risked opening one eye.

Oh. Both eyes opened now, and a small sound of surprise passed her lips.

Daylight.

Sunshine.

Warmth.

She wasn't back in that helhole. This room was too well-lit and nicely decorated to be called that. She didn't know where she was, but she knew what she felt. It was warm and bright and—

Her eyes drifted to the closed door and the voices beyond that were gradually growing louder. One sounded familiar, but she couldn't figure out why, because she certainly didn't recognize this place.

Forcing herself to calm her breathing, she focused her attention on listening to the voices.

Breathe in... Breathe out...

Nothing. A few deep breaths in before she held her breath, hoping that would make a difference. Held it until her cheeks puffed and her head felt like it might explode from the pressure. Still, nothing. Whomever was behind the door, they were talking too quietly for her to understand.

"Good for nothing half-elf ears," she muttered.

When she attempted to sit up, her body protested, and not in the kind of way that meant she was just sore. There was no indication from her body that it was going to move at her insistence.

Not a single muscle below her neck moved. Fortunately for her, she recognized this resistance. Eyes focused upward, they landed on the healing bubble humming lightly around her, working to heal her wounds as she laid there. Her eyes rolled in annoyance.

It was impossible to break a healing bubble without causing great harm, hence the temporary paralysis to prevent a disaster. The last time she'd tried to escape one, she'd ended up right back in it as her left leg had been sliced open, exposing bone from the impact of the bubble popping. No, that was one fight she wasn't sure she wanted to pick in her current state.

With eyes closed, she tried to remember what had happened and how she got here. Wherever "here" was.

Deep breath in.

She was running—no, escaping—*through the woods. Her hands reached for that small, flickering light, when a cold, soulless hand grabbed at her legs and she went tumbling down and down. But not before she used her mother's Elemental power of Light to free the shadows' grip from her legs.*

A sorrowful smile graced her face at the memory. Her mother would have been proud. Wouldn't she? A part of her tried her best to connect with her mother through their shared Element.

Another deep breath in as she shook the thoughts away and focused again on what she could remember.

The ground beneath her was moving, and she was rolling right along with it. She winced at the memory of it. *The land hummed underneath her, but she wasn't falling anymore. No, she had started moving* with *the ground. How was that possible?*

It took all her strength at the time to simply open her eyes to see what was happening. Although, she couldn't open them wide as she took in what she could of her surroundings.

Blurry figures in armor stood in front of her. Sentries. One of them had his arms outstretched, moving in a sort of rhythm—reaching toward her, then back to his chest. The same motion repeated over and over. A Huymi—a Nature elf. That was why she had been moving with the ground.

She tried to speak, to cry for help, to say her name. To say anything. But when she finally mustered the strength to part her lips, nothing came out.

The last thing she remembered seeing was a face with a pair of pale grey eyes and brown hair. Then, someone's hands wrapped around her body, lifted her up, and surrounded her in...warmth.

No darkness. No yellow eyes. No shadows in sight.

Evenia sighed. She'd made it. She'd found the laughter that night. Found the light.

There was a stinging in her eyes, but she blinked it away as she focused on taking in her surroundings. The healing bubble was well-constructed. The ones she was used to being around in her Aunt Siersha's healing quarters usually had a slight tint to them, if not a full color, courtesy of the healer's own power thrumming through the bubble.

It was said that moragainks—master healers—could create an undetectable healing bubble. Well, undetectable to the eye. While humans had no way of noticing a difference, a fae's nose could easily detect who had created the bubble if they knew what they were looking for.

This one had no color—just a clear coating around her as she laid in bed. It was obviously done by a moragaink. Its creator was almost undetectable. *Almost.* Evenia smirked.

Based on the mild dirt scent emanating off the healing bubble, she'd guessed it had been a skilled Nature fae who created it. While she could tell where their magic originated from based on the scent, it was difficult to tell what species of fae they were. They could be an elf, a witch, a dryad, or a species she'd never met before. Any fae with magic could be a healer if they wanted.

Evenia was impressed. It would probably be impossible to break through. A grimace crossed her face as she realized that was probably on purpose. So, was she to be a prisoner again?

Looking around, she examined her new "prison." The bed was nice and looked large enough to fit at least four people. It was a four-poster—

Wait, *a bed.* It was a real bed—in a room—not in a prison cell. Not in a dungeon. Not even in healing quarters. Where was she? She looked down at her trapped body again. Her wounds were healing, and she didn't look nearly as thin as she had remembered being before.

That was when she noticed her battered, torn slip had been replaced with a short-sleeved, cream gown—a similar style worn by patients in her aunt's clinic. Who had changed her? Her cheeks blushed as she remembered those pale grey eyes and the massive hands that wrapped around her.

No, surely someone else had removed her filthy, shredded garment and dressed her in this clean gown. Probably an assistant to the healer who had placed the bubble around her. Yes, professionals. No, *sentries.*

Her eyes scanned the room again. There was a tall, oak armoire to her left, and thick, cream-colored curtains adorned on each floor-to-ceiling window. They looked like they might actually be real velvet. She wanted to run her hands across the fabric to see if she was right. Not that she could, anyway. Behind the fabric were glass doors leading out to a balcony. It was all so lovely and lavish.

What was this place? she asked herself. It was almost too good to be true. Like a dream. A better one than the nightmare she had before waking.

Her eyes fell upon a cream tapestry on the wall opposite her. A golden emblem outlined in white on the tapestry was nearly a diamond shape. It donned scroll-like designs intertwined throughout with a symbol representing each realm's Element: a snowflake for the Ice Realm of Akvar; a flame for the Fire Realm of Caburh; a sun with wavy rays for the Sun Realm of Elndion; a two-headed hammer for Enacor, which did not have a designated Element; a leaf for the Nature Realm of Gathéla; a water droplet for the Water Realm of Ketiskali; a crescent moon for the Moon Realm of Nulhe; and four wavy lines for the Wind Realm of Valoreg.

Her stomach dropped. The emblem was that of Mircha. The ones who claimed to be the Land of Peace, serving all and none. Evenia had witnessed how "peaceful" they were, and the only ones they appeared to serve were themselves.

They were responsible for her uncle's death...

She had traded one monster for another.

Her brow started dripping with sweat. Casting a spell to tear through the healing bubble crossed her mind, but the voices beyond the door suddenly grew louder. Even if she could have escaped the bubble, it was now too late to act.

Panic rose within when the giant wooden door to the room opened and her eyes fell on the Mirchans in the doorway.

There was a short, round man with slightly pointed ears—a duolvain by the looks of it—who entered the room first. At least that meant she wasn't the only one in Mircha.

Duolvain were part human, part fae. They were most often identified by any sort of visible fae physical characteristics—like having only slightly pointed elven ears, a shifter's birthmark, or even fairy wings. When the ears were rounded or physical characteristics were well hidden, it was often harder to detect a duolvain. Many looked human, while hiding undetectable magical abilities and oftentimes their age, thanks to inherited fae longevity.

Duolvain were fae, simply because anyone with an ounce of magical blood would be considered fae. Ever since the Peacekeeping Realm of Mircha was created, it was more common than ever to see duolvain. However, there were many in the world who proceeded with caution around them because of their human lineage. Humans and fae lived together peacefully now, but that was not always the case. So, humans who were seemingly "hiding" behind fae appearances were not easily trusted.

On the other hand, humans often didn't trust the fae abilities of duolvain. Witches, like Evenia and her family, arguably had the easiest time fitting into human territories, but that was because of their created communities—covens.

This elder duolvain's tipped ears peeked out under his salt and pepper hair. The cream robes wrapped around his round frame were the finest she'd ever seen. The collar of the robe framed a face that was surprisingly pleasant, with a white chest-length beard and kind eyes.

Next to him stood a tall, lean warrior. Her dark brown hair was pinned half up, showcasing her elven ears, which were the sharpest Evenia had ever seen. Those cheekbones looked equally as sharp. Her eyes were soft as they took in Evenia. A stark contrast to the sharp features.

The elf was stunning. There was also no mistaking her for anything but a warrior, as she was armed from head to toe with knives, daggers, and a beautiful, arced blade strapped to her side.

Behind them were three others, one of whom wore the universal healer emblem in the staple Mirchan cream. The healer walked toward the bed, followed by another short duolvain. Evenia ignored them both as her eyes immediately fell on the tall elf with red-brown hair in the doorway. It wasn't necessary to tap into her shifter eyesight to know he had pale grey eyes.

I've got you... You're safe. Butterflies fluttered in her stomach at the memory of his words on the Wind, caressing her cheeks and the tips of her ears. So, that part had been real. It hadn't all been a dream.

You're safe. The memory repeated in her head. Could it be true? Was she really safe?

He lingered in the doorway while the healer, who introduced herself as Thaïselle, examined the status of the healing bubble. She tutted at the look of some of the deeper wounds on Evenia's body that weren't healing as quickly as others, but Evenia thought she looked better than she had before. Sure, some wounds weren't fully healed, but she at least wasn't bleeding anymore. Just how terrible had her injuries been?

The healer placed her hands over the healing bubble as she worked to reinforce it.

"She's about to put you to sleep to spare you from having to talk," came a voice on the Wind. She felt the familiar Element envelop her as the words flitted around her ears.

Evenia's gaze shot back up to the doorway, where the elf with grey eyes stood, waiting. He was Wind whispering to her from the other side of the room. Part of her wanted to panic and another part of her wanted to yell about being held against her will in Mircha of all places.

However, his voice—the voice that insisted she was safe—was strangely soothing. Not to mention that they were healing her, not hurting her. But why? What motive did they have to help her? What did they want in return? There was always a price for "peace."

"In case you didn't catch their names, the healer is Thaïselle. The fierce elf to the right of you who looks like she could kill someone with a single glare—because she can—is Andira." Evenia's eyes flicked from one to the other, suddenly even more on edge. *"The relatively harmless old man is called Gauiel, among other things. The puny old man with the nasally voice...is not worth mentioning."*

Evenia managed to resist a laugh as she glanced at the short, slender duolvain who couldn't seem to stop inserting himself. He really did have an annoying voice.

"And my name is Kalland Sothenas." He gave her a small half wave, with his arms still folded against his chest. *"Are you willing to tell me your name?"*

There was a gentle vibration of magic as the healer, Thaïselle, worked to reinforce the healing bubble and make it stronger. Evenia slowly opened her mouth, but she wasn't sure if she should answer. Yes, he helped her that night, but that didn't mean she had to tell him her name. Not to mention that she had no idea how to whisper on the Wind.

He seemed to realize her lack of Wind whispering ability as the corner of his lip ticked up. *"Ah, yes, Wind whispering. Visually hold on to this current of Wind as it closes in on your ears. Hold it clear as day in your mind, and when you're ready, say whatever it is you'd like to."*

She paid extra close attention to the Wind current this time as it caressed her ears, carrying the elf's softened voice for only her to hear. With eyes closed, she imagined that current as a visible line of connection between herself and the elf.

When she envisioned that line between them becoming clearer, almost a solid form in-between them, she clung to it and opened her eyes.

"Didn't you just say your healer is trying to spare me from having to talk?" Her eyes widened as she felt the current of Wind slowly leave her body with the faintest sound she'd ever heard escape her lips.

The grey-eyed elf gave a quick, wry smile before saying, *"Just say the word, and you can talk to all five of us. Or...you could just talk to me."*

Her eyes rolled, because that sounded like a grand time, with his condescending tone even while whispering. The rest of them probably would be just as welcoming as him. She sneered as she glanced from one sentry to another hovering around the bed as they conversed with each other and not her. No, she wasn't interested in talking to any of them.

"Why would I tell you anything?" she snapped back down the line.

With arms still crossed, he shifted on his feet and a muscle in his jaw ticked. *"Because I'm the one who peeled your body away from that landslide and flew you back to a healer. That healer to be exact."* His chin jutted out in the direction of the woman to the left of her.

Her attention remained on him as his words registered. *Flew?* The sound of wings beating in the air and the wind whooshing through her hair flashed through Evenia's head. She squinted at him, but he didn't appear to have wings.

"Given the current state of affairs..." she glanced from Thaïselle to the short man with a nasally voice nearly yelling at the healer. *"I don't think I can offer you my gratitude."*

He chuckled and leaned against the door frame. *"I can't say I blame you. Too much. If you don't want to give me your name, is there something I can call you besides 'mystery woman'? Or, as the other sentries are calling you, 'Hillrider.'"*

Hillrider? She felt a twinge of embarrassment at the thought of anyone calling her that. She shook the thought, focusing instead on his words and trying to figure out his intentions. She didn't know why they chose to heal her or place her in a room instead of a cell or healing quarters. But this much she knew: he wanted her name, and she wasn't about to give him anything.

She smirked. *"I don't know. I quite like the sound of Hillrider."*

"Hillrider it is." He offered her a tight-lipped smile.

"Why do you care?" She looked from the elves surrounding her and back to him. *"What do you want with me?"*

It was several seconds before he responded, *"To help."* How convincing. She started to roll her eyes. *"And to find out why you were commingling with The Darkness."* Mid-eye roll, her eyes flew back to him. All the breath in her lungs seized in her chest, forming a lump.

A fire was brimming inside of her. *Commingling?* How could this stranger dare accuse her of being involved with the very being who kidnapped and tortured her? The heat of her anger only grew when she saw how unrelenting his stare was.

"Fuck you," she breathed.

"Notice how you're not denying it." There was a bite in his tone that she didn't feel she deserved.

What had she done to deserve this? To deserve being accused of consorting with that beast. To be accused of working with the one who tortured her day in and day out for gods only knew how long.

If she could move, her hands would be at this elf's throat. She already hated this guy.

"Go. To. Hel." She bared her teeth at him.

He bared his teeth right back. *"A little too late for that."* His eyes suddenly went to something above her. *"Fortunately for you, she's about to put you back to sleep,"* he said, looking at her once more. *"Nice meeting you, Hillrider."* But his tone said otherwise.

She started to reply with the exact opposite sentiment, but her eyes began shuddering. It was getting difficult to listen to the older duolvain, Gaiuel. What was he saying? Was he telling her what he was going to do with her? No, she really didn't want to talk, but why was the healer, Thaïselle, putting her back to sleep? She was tired of sleeping. Tired of dreaming. Tired of what she saw when she closed her eyes.

Her heart pounded as she realized she was losing control of her mind and body from the magically induced fatigue taking over.

She wanted to ask what they wanted with her. To hear how they found her and why they were keeping her in Mircha.

Before she could, everything went black, and darkness waited for her on the other side.

7

Kalland

"Did you truly find it necessary to place her back into this deep sleep?" Jushelk asked Thaïselle, his annoyance clear as day in his tone.

"I truly did, *sir*." Thaïselle spoke the last word so quickly, as if she had forgotten who she was talking with. Forgotten what kind of temper he had on him. She didn't so much as look up at Jushelk, whose eyes flickered to the healer.

It was known that Thaïselle Guérisald didn't respond well to being questioned about her healing practices—not that it happened often. Part of Kalland wondered if she put the girl back to sleep in spite of the orders Gauiel and Jushelk gave in the hallway about keeping her awake long enough to talk.

In fact, putting her to sleep out of spite for refusing to listen to her professional opinion sounded exactly like something that Andira's personal healer and longtime friend would do. Kalland fought the urge to smile at Thaïselle's boldness.

Except, she robbed him of the chance to get more information from *Hillrider*.

He, himself, was playing their game. He pretended he had listened and took in every word his found family said to him earlier that afternoon. As if he had miraculously healed enough in two hours to keep his cool while they questioned the woman. Acted like he wouldn't say a word, just observe as they worked.

And now, he was going to pretend to befriend this *Hillrider*, to be someone she could trust, so that he could get some answers. It was all a game, and he'd be damned if he didn't play it right. Although, he might have just blown it with that temper of his. He'd tried. But all resolve left him the moment he smelled The Darkness on her again.

His attention was pulled back to the conversation happening on the other side of the room.

Andira's chin raised at Thaïselle's words, but there was some humor dancing in her eyes. She must have had the same realization as Kalland about Thaïselle not taking kindly to being told what to do when it came to her own healing practices.

"And why is that?" The puny man asked as he placed a pale, scrawny hand on his hip. His eyes were scanning the mystery woman. "She appears fine to me."

Quietly observing, Gauiel looked from Jushelk to Thaïselle as he rested his pale, wrinkled hands on his round belly.

"Yes, she *appears* to be in good health." Thaïselle's hands remained over the healing bubble, although Kalland could no longer sense her using magic. "But looks can often be deceiving. I could feel she still had some internal bleeding. I know the plan was for you four to speak with her, but I'd rather be safe than sorry. Sir." Not a true apology, but she didn't owe him one.

Before Jushelk could respond, Gauiel nodded and said, "Very well, Moragaink Guérisald. Please notify us when you feel she is well enough to speak." He turned to leave, with Andira and an irritated Jushelk following on his heels.

Thaïselle nodded, never looking up from her "work."

Kalland stepped out of the doorway and into the room so they could pass, but Andira stopped in front of him.

"Will you be staying?" she asked. Gauiel turned in the doorway at the sound of her voice.

"Yes, I think I will," Kalland said. He avoided her gaze, knowing she was looking for any insight into his thoughts and feelings, and he wasn't about to give it to her. Or to Jushelk, for that matter. "I cleared my afternoon for this. So, I might as well stay for a bit."

The truth was, if Andira came back to talk with the Hillrider, he didn't want to miss out on another opportunity to find out more about who she was and what she was doing with The Darkness.

"Very well." She nodded and stepped out of the room with the two duolvain.

He heard Jushelk grunt to get him from the west wing if the woman woke. Kalland resisted the urge to laugh because absolutely *no one* would be rushing to tell him when she did.

Neither he nor Thaïselle moved until they could no longer hear their footsteps and voices.

"I thought they'd never make it down that hallway." Thaïselle let out a sigh and lowered her hands. "Forgive me." Her eyes raised to Kalland's. "I know you wanted to talk with her, but it's only been four days. Healing bubble or not, she deserves to rest."

Kalland walked toward the four-poster bed, stopping just short of the footboard, and nodded. "I agree."

"You do?" Her eyebrows raised in surprise, and he couldn't blame her, considering his earlier actions. Or the impatience growing with each hour that passed.

"Of course. She looks as though she requires nourishment and rest, both of which your healing bubble can offer her. Who are we to deny anyone that kind of help?" Way deep down, part of him believed the words coming out of his mouth. Internally, his oath as a loyal sentry was warring with his responsibility as a dutiful son to avenge his parents.

Thaïselle let out a sigh of relief, and Kalland peeled his eyes away from the mystery woman to look at the healer.

"Thank you." She raised her arms, as if her point had been made. "Why is it *he* couldn't see that?" One hand casually waved toward the now-empty hallway. Kalland didn't need to ask to know who she was talking about. "It's almost like he has more of a desire to talk with her than you do, and that just doesn't make sense to me."

"Doubtful," Kalland grunted. "But we're just anxious for some answers." An understatement.

"Yes. Yes, I understand that," Thaïselle said, straightening her healer uniform and removing specks of lint invisible to his eye. "But..." She slowly looked at the young duolvain. "She's so young."

He looked at the mystery woman, who had been feisty, unafraid. She was neither weak nor a child. "She looks grown enough to me. Young, yes, but an adult, nonetheless."

"Sure, yes, but she still looks young. Li–like someone's daughter. Like..." Her voice trailed off.

Kalland's eyebrows rose as the tone registered with him. It suddenly all made sense now why Thaïselle was defending this woman relentlessly, even against him.

"She reminds you of your daughter." Kalland's voice was soft. *Bryelin.*

Thaïselle bowed her head and nodded slowly.

Memories of the healer sobbing in Andira's arms flashed in Kalland's mind. Andira's legs had given way, and both elves slid down the wall to the floor. Not even Andira could hide her emotions that day at the loss of her non-blood-related niece. It had only been twelve years—what could feel like a mere blink of an eye in the life of an elf. Not nearly long enough to heal and grieve such a loss.

"She was only fifty-three." Thaïselle's voice was hoarse. "She was determined to be a sentry, like her Aunt Andira. I begged her not to. We both did. We asked her to look into being a healer, a fisher, a carpenter—anything but a sentry." Her hand flew to her chest.

Kalland walked to her side and gently laid his hand on her shoulder. "You could not have stopped her then anymore than Jushelk could have stopped you just now." He nodded his head toward the woman resting in Thaïselle's reinforced healing bubble. The patient she stuck her neck out for only minutes before.

She followed his gaze and let out a breathy laugh. "I suppose not." Her smile didn't reach her eyes.

He gently squeezed her shoulder before removing his hand. "She was a brave girl, Thaïselle."

"Bravery doesn't keep you safe." She wrapped her arms around herself. "If she had let me keep her safe, she would still be alive."

Kalland paused for a moment. "Perhaps. But would she have been happy not following her passion? Being safe doesn't always mean you're living."

She met his gaze for a moment, half nodded, and then looked to the ground again.

"I should go," she said, wringing her hands.

"The markings on her eyes…" He nodded in the direction of the woman sleeping. He was determined to not end the conversation that way, forcing Thaïselle to go off on her own while she silently crawled back into her inner shell of grief. "They're the only markings I see on her still."

The change of topic might have been intended to distract Thaïselle, but he was also curious about the black marks in the creases of the woman's eyes. They pointedly winged away from her eyes. Yes, they looked a bit like small black wings. Didn't they?

"Hmm, yes." Thaïselle's chin raised a little. "Vorelna—she'll be assigned to her rooms—helped in bathing her. She said that no matter how much she tried, those markings wouldn't come off. I believe they're a birthmark of sorts."

He nodded, thinking the same thing. Back home in Valoreg, Kalland had seen similar markings on a shifter named Ailnarde. The markings on Ailnarde were lighter, with a light brown wing in the crease of his eyes extending to the top and bottom of his eyelids. Ailnarde's other form was an eagle.

To Kalland's knowledge, every shifter had some sort of marking, similar to either a birthmark or a tattoo. Sometimes they appeared at birth, and other times they appeared the first time someone shifted. Not all markings were visible to the eye—whether they were faint or somewhere that you'd have to get lucky to see. There was also no telling if he was right in his assumption that she was one. However, his gut was telling him he was right about this.

So, were these the markings of a flying shifter? Or something else entirely?

"You spoke with her." Not a question. He looked at Thaïselle, who was studying his face. "You did. I knew it! I felt a brush of Wind while I was reinforcing the bubble. It felt weird." She chuckled and gave him a sly grin. "It's why I took so long 'reinforcing' the bubble." She motioned air quotations as she spoke the word *reinforcing*. "What did she say?"

He laughed. *Of course.* "Nothing I can say without breaking her confidence." He offered Thaïselle a small smile, knowing that she—a healer—would never press the topic of a private conversation. Even though there really was nothing to share... His jaw ticked as the interaction replayed in his head.

Thaïselle laughed. "Whatever she said got under your skin."

His eyes flew to hers. "No."

"You're a terrible liar." She grinned, but it quickly fell as she narrowed her eyes at him. "Were you at least kind to her? Controlled?" The tone of her voice caused a pang in his chest as it made him think of his own mother. How he missed her.

"Of course. Despite what everyone thinks, I'm not a total jerk." He rolled his eyes, but he smiled.

"I know." She patted his arm. "And it's what how *everyone* thinks. If I had thought for even a second that you might have blown up on my patient, I wouldn't have let you within one hundred feet of this room." She gave him a stern look.

"But I am glad she felt well enough to speak with someone. Although, I am curious what she said that has your feathers so ruffled." The corner of her mouth curved upward, but her eyes seemed sad as she looked at the woman once more and then down at her own hands. "I really should be going."

He watched her for a few moments. Watched how she hadn't moved an inch toward the door.

He cleared his throat. "You're a moragaink. I'm sure no one would question if you were held up for a minute or two helping a patient in need."

Surely not. A moragaink was the title given to the top healers from the Nature Realm of Gathéla. A moragaink's healing powers were not limited to that of a body, extending to the trees, plants, and to the ground itself. They were rare, and as such, treated like royalty.

Moragainks were often also in charge of other healers in a realm. Thaïselle was in charge of the entire hospital in Mircha, which was another reason why Jushelk questioning her professional opinion about *her* patient was laughable. Then again…this patient was different. It was why she was assigned to Thaïselle's care and not one of her healers.

"No, I suppose they wouldn't question it." Her mouth curled up farther on one side.

He smiled back and motioned to two chairs positioned to overlook the chambers' balcony. With the flick of his wrist, currents of Wind wrapped around the chairs' legs, lifted them in the air, and gently placed them at the foot of the bed. They were facing the door so as to give their still-healing guest some privacy.

"Care to join me?" he asked, motioning toward the chairs. She looked from the chair to the door and back at the chair again.

"I suppose I can spare a few minutes," she said, a mischievous smile growing on her face. "But only a few minutes."

"Only a few minutes," he repeated, gesturing to the seat. "I think the hospital could spare you for a bit." She harrumphed at that as she sat down.

After only a minute, she began fidgeting with her hands once more. He sat down in the chair next to her and attempted not to notice. There were few ways he knew of to get Thaïselle to relax, and it was only a matter of time before allowing a moment to herself during the middle of the day would get to her conscience.

He lifted his hand in the air and waved it once again, this time in the direction of Thaïselle.

"Oh!" she exclaimed as a book gently plopped onto her lap. Eyes wide, she wrapped one hand around the book's spine and quickly placed her other hand over the cover.

Keeping his smile to himself, he pretended not to have noticed the author, Vardith Viniusauf, before she'd managed to cover it. Vardith Viniusauf was a famous author of passionate love stories. In fact, she was one of his favorite authors.

"But ho—how did you know?" She looked at him, her eyes still wide.

He paused before answering. "I asked your office door what book lay on your desk that you picked up last. It showed me the book's silhouette for me to send to you. Is it the correct one?"

"I… You asked my door what I was reading?"

"In a way, yes." The truth was, he'd asked the Wind, who traveled through her office door, to see. Whatever the Wind power thrumming in his veins sensed in order to know it was the last book she touched was beyond his comprehension.

"You mean to tell me that you talk to doors?"

He hesitated. He always did when it came to revealing the secret, heightened Wind powers his royal blood allowed him. "Sure, among other things." He pretended to look out the bedroom windows, trying to brush off the conversation.

"What does that even mean?" She scoffed, but he only shrugged in response, not wanting to give away all his secrets. "You royals and your hidden talents." There was a hint of amusement in her voice, and he could see her head shaking in his peripheral vision. "Well, thank you. You're a good kid. Strange, but good." She patted his knee.

Normally, it would be weird to be called a kid by someone who looked only a few years older than you, but not for elves. He was considered a baby at one hundred six years old, and since Thaïselle was Andira's longtime friend, she had to be at least three hundred fifty years older than him.

It was no secret that elves rarely looked their age. He knew someone who was just starting to get a little salt and pepper in his beard at eight hundred seventy-nine years old. How one hundred six years old was considered ancient to humans but a mere child to elves always seemed an odd truth to him.

"You're welcome." He looked at her and smiled.

She opened the book and began to read, a real smile growing on her face. He whispered to the Wind to quietly shut the door, and it obeyed, as it always did to a Dueri—a Wind elf—like him.

⁂

Kalland and Thaïselle remained in companionable silence for the next half hour. It was spent with Thaïselle reading her book and Kalland lost in his thoughts about what the intermingled dark scent—now barely detectable on the woman—could mean. As well as the memories it brought up that he was struggling to shove down once more, and what to ask her in order to get the answers he so desperately wanted.

No, the answers he *needed*.

And he needed to know her name. Where she came from, how long she'd been with The Darkness, what her purpose was, what—

His jaw tensed. He would check the missing person's board again tonight for any physical descriptions that matched the woman's.

Kalland was lost in thought when he heard a quiet knock at the door. Thaïselle quickly stood and hid her book behind her back on the chair before a head of mousy brown hair and semi-pointed ears poked into the room. A shy voice reported that Thaïselle's head nurse, Jasine, needed her.

"Please tell her I'll be there in a moment, Molhom," she told the messenger, who quickly bowed his head and looked grateful to be leaving with his task completed.

Once the door clicked shut behind the boy, Thaïselle turned and looked at Kalland. "Thank you for this."

"I've done nothing but sit here in silence." Kalland shrugged.

"Exactly." She smiled at him. Her eyes fell on the book laying in her chair. "Would you mind…" She gestured to the book. "I mean, it's just, I don't wish to be lugging it around the rest of the day."

"Of course." He waved his hand and sent it back to her room. She blinked at the movement.

"Thank you. Again," she said, still staring at the spot where the book disappeared from before smiling at him.

"It was nothing." He smiled back.

"Keep telling yourself that," she said as she slipped out of the room and closed the door behind her.

Silence, once again, save for the faint humming of the healing bubble behind him. He usually enjoyed silence, but when his thoughts were as unpredictable as they were now, it made him more uncomfortable than he wanted to admit.

Because the silence forced him to think about that scent. That deplorable scent that reminded him of his greatest loss and failure. Of the months spent searching the Urur Mountains for answers about his parents' deaths, and coming up empty-handed each time.

His aunt had finally begged him to stop searching after five years—to stop "wasting life," as she'd put it. He didn't see it as a waste, and he'd resented her words at the time. However, she'd been right. As always. He rolled his eyes and smiled at the thought of her smirk if he ever spoke those words aloud. But he wasn't wasting his life now. This was a sign to keep going. To not give up.

The sound of a heart pounding brought him back from his thoughts. It sounded like someone's heart was about to burst straight out of their chest. He turned toward the sound and saw the mystery woman's face twitching in her sleep. It looked like she was having a nightmare.

He stepped to the side of her bed and went to lay a hand on her shoulder, but the healing bubble stopped him just a few inches away. He glanced at the door. Should he call for Thaïselle to return? Seeing how it was no longer a restful sleep, he wondered if the bubble needed to be reinforced to include dreamless sleep. Was that even possible?

He glanced back at the healing bubble, which looked just as strong as it had when the healer reinforced it. At least, he thought so. He hated to admit that he didn't know a damned thing about healing bubbles, besides the fact that you shouldn't try to escape one. A fact he learned at a young age after a pathetic attempt to fly off the roof like the winged fighters he grew up with in Valoreg.

"Hey..." He resisted the urge to swear because he wished she'd told him her name. "You're okay." The words came out a little harsher than he'd meant them to, and he recoiled. He was normally so in control. So restrained. He hadn't felt this way in years, and he didn't like it.

Her eyes were closed and her heart was still pounding, but her partially pointed ears had twitched, as if she'd heard him in her sleep. That was all the assurance he needed.

"Focus on my voice, Hillrider," he spoke quietly on the Wind, which successfully weaved its way through the healing bubble to her ears once more. *"No one is going to hurt you here. You. Are. Safe."*

Her face was relaxing now. He waited until her heart had slowed to a steady beat again before leaving her side. He needed to leave the room, but what if she had another nightmare? It'd be weird to stay here all day like a watchdog... He also didn't have that kind of time to spare.

His eyes searched the woman's now calm face as the temptation to stay near her overwhelmed him. He shook his head. No, that wasn't an option. At least not until she was ready to talk. Not to mention that he wasn't exactly the nicest to her earlier, which was clearly a mistake since she immediately shut him down. He needed to try harder to keep a handle on his emotions for their next interaction. His eyes briefly roamed the face of the woman who held secrets he was desperate to uncover. And he would. In time.

Opening the nightstand drawer, he withdrew a piece of paper and an ink pen to write a note to Thaïselle about the nightmares. When he finished, he placed the note on the bedside table and pinned a corner down with a candlestick so that it wouldn't blow away.

He looked at the woman's face once more and found himself wondering what her true voice sounded like—not just a whisper. What it might be like to see her smile, to hear her laugh.

Get a grip, Kalland. He rolled his eyes at himself and shook the thoughts away. He had to keep a rational head where she was concerned.

It was clear that this woman had escaped The Darkness, but it still wasn't clear to Kalland *why* she was with him to begin with. Was she always a captive, or had her usefulness run out and she escaped before death befell her?

Until he had an answer, she was not to be trusted.

She is not your enemy. He stilled at the memory of the Wind whisper on the night they'd first met. It wasn't this woman's voice he'd heard. So, whose voice had it been? It belonged to no one he'd ever spoken with before. In fact, it was like nothing he'd ever heard before. The voice sounded as if it were strung along a musical instrument on the wind, strumming a beautiful melody with each word spoken.

It sounded unreal, and not of this world. But what did that even mean?

Resisting the urge to take one last look at the woman, he turned and walked to the door without looking back.

8

Evenia

The healing bubble was gone when Evenia woke before the sun. She'd wiped a hand down her face and flinched when her skin actually connected with her face. When she opened her eyes, there was no faint humming, no mild earthy scent, and her body was no longer immobile. Since then, she hadn't stopped moving.

When she first got up, she immediately checked the mobility in her wrists, arms, legs—everywhere—to see if there were any unhealed injuries. She needed to know what her weak points would be if she was presented with the opportunity to run. *Again.*

On wobbly legs, she ventured into the attached bath and found a floor-length mirror on the far wall. Everything looked to be mostly healed, beyond some mild bruising on her ribs and a few once open wounds along her abdomen and legs that looked to be healing well now. It was unknown where these ones had come from, or how many she received from—

Thump. Thump. Thump.

Evenia froze in front of the mirror. Someone was knocking on the door of the bed-chambers. She peeked her head around the still-open bathroom doorway, listening intently.

"Miss?" asked a voice through the bedroom door. Evenia put her hand to her mouth, muffling the sound of her breath. "My name is Vorelna. I've been assigned to your room to assist with anything you may need."

Evenia's eyes flew to the balcony doors. She'd already looked earlier and saw she was three stories up. There was no way out. She silently cursed and let her breath go. They knew she was in here. So, holding her breath was foolish.

"Do you mind if I come in?" the voice—Vorelna—asked.

Looking around, she found a nail file in the top drawer of the bathroom cabinet. Evenia grabbed the nail file and hid it in her palm, then took a deep breath in and out.

"Sure, come in." She tried to keep her voice steady as she walked out of the bathroom.

Evenia braced herself as the bedroom door slowly opened and a short woman walked into the room. Her grey hair was pinned up, showing partially pointed ears. In her hands was a basket full of pale fabrics and stopper bottles.

The woman smiled and dipped her chin at Evenia. The wrinkles in the corners of her eyes crinkled with the facial movement. "My name is Vorelna," she said again.

Evenia dipped her chin back, gripping the nail file harder in her palm to make sure it was well hidden. Just in case.

"I assist our moragaink. I'll show you how to run the bath, and then I'll dress your still-healing wounds. If that's all right?" The woman pulled her basket up a smidge, gesturing to the fabrics and ointments in it.

"Thanks," Evenia mumbled. She nearly knocked over a chair as she stepped aside when the woman walked toward the bathroom.

Vorelna stopped advancing at the sudden movement and Evenia's nervous action.

"Apologies, Miss. My intent is not to scare you." Her voice was soft, kind. "I'm just here to help." Evenia studied the woman's face, and seeing no ill intentions in her eyes, she let out a deep breath and nodded. "How are you feeling today?"

Evenia looked down at herself, and then back at the woman. "Fine."

"Pleased to hear it." The woman gave her another small smile as she headed to the bath with the basket in hand. A few seconds later, Evenia heard rushing water and the aroma of lavender hit her.

"By the way..." Vorelna's voice echoed from the bathroom. "You can put the nail file down." Evenia's lips parted as Vorelna popped her head out of the bathroom door, a sheepish grin causing the corners of her eyes to wrinkle. "I might be old, but this half-elf still has a sharp sight." She winked as Evenia dropped the nail file to the floor.

It'd be a lie if she said a bath with lavender wasn't exactly what she needed. The hot water eased her muscles inch by inch. Before Evenia got in, Vorelna placed a magical bubble around her still-healing wounds so that she could fully submerge and relax.

She would have sat in the tub until her skin pruned if Vorelna wasn't still there, waiting in the bedroom to dress Evenia's remaining wounds. The older duolvain was starting to grow on her. She reminded Evenia of her Grandma Meyaral. Except...Vorelna was much nicer than Grandma Meyaral.

When she'd dressed and stepped into the bedroom, Vorelna grabbed the basket of ointments with a kind smile. Releasing the magic bubbles around her open wounds, she got to work.

"I'm wrapping here to offer your ribs more support, and to keep the salve from rubbing off onto your clothing," Vorelna said. With the healing salve applied, she was now wrapping a particularly nasty bruise on Evenia's ribs.

"I'm sorry for what you've been through," Vorelna said, her tone soft. Evenia tensed. "Whatever happened, I hope you heal well during your time here, Miss."

"Evenia." Vorelna paused and made eye contact with her. "You can call me Evenia." The older duolvain smiled and dipped her chin. "And it looks like I'm already healing well."

Vorelna's gaze fell back down to her work at hand. Several seconds passed before she spoke again. "There's more than one type of healing that needs to be done after an event like this, Mi— Evenia." Evenia flinched, and it wasn't because of how tight Vorelna was making the wrap. "Remember to give yourself grace during this time." She offered Evenia a small nod as she tied off the wrap.

Stepping away, Vorelna walked to her basket sitting on a chair at the foot of the bed. "I've left the lavender in the bathroom for you, and this," she held up an amber bottle, "is for any discomfort you may feel in the days to come. Just take a drop as needed." She placed the bottle on the nightstand.

Evenia picked it up and sniffed it. She smiled at the familiar smell. "Olojbi." It was an herb native to her home realm of Enacor. Her aunt carried it in her shop.

"I'm impressed. Are you a healer?" Vorelna's eyebrows raised.

"No, my aunt is, but I often help her." Evenia smiled as she placed the bottle back down.

The older woman picked up the basket. "We could always use an extra hand in the hospital if you're interested."

Evenia's head whipped up. She'd never seen an actual hospital before, but she didn't know if healing was her calling. Especially…here, helping Mirchan sentries, no less. "I'll think about it. Thank you."

Vorelna nodded as a knock sounded at the door. Evenia quickly stood on her feet. "It's just our moragaink and General Elsvarin." Vorelna offered an encouraging smile. "Would you like me to stay?"

"No, it's fine. I'll be fine," Evenia said, though she wasn't sure how much she believed the words.

Vorelna hesitated before she opened the door and greeted the healer and general. "Good morning, Moragaink Guérisald, General Elsvarin."

Both smiled and nodded at Vorelna before looking at Evenia, who was surprised she recognized those sharp cheekbones and the arced blade attached to the elven warrior's back.

"Good morning, Elna," the healer said.

"Hello, Vorelna," the taller elf said, briefly looking at the older woman before facing Evenia again. "I'm General Andira Elsvarin. We met briefly before. Although, it is fair if you do not recall our introduction," said the tall elf with long brown hair.

Evenia remembered the grey-eyed elf mentioning the names of the others surrounding her the day she woke up in the healing bubble. This fierce warrior before her was one of them. There were fewer weapons strapped to her today, but she was still armed with the beautiful, curved blade that Evenia wasn't soon to forget. It had silver and gold metal wrapped around the hilt in a vine-like design, the leaves etched so perfectly into the hilt that it looked like they might actually feel real.

"And I'm Thaïselle, the healer at your service," the other brown-haired elf pulled Evenia's gaze from the blade. She was shorter than the general, and her eyes pulled Evenia in. They were full of warmth and…sorrow. Grief. Evenia looked away because she recognized those emotions on a level she didn't want to feel at that moment.

She hesitated but decided the secret was already out with Vorelna. "I'm Evenia."

"It is nice to meet you, Evenia," the general said, the smile heard in her voice. "Do you have a surname?"

Evenia almost bit back that she didn't, but what good would being sarcastic to a freaking general do for her? Plus, now that they'd seen her face, it wouldn't be hard for a *general* to discover her true identity. "It's Raldir, ma'am. Evenia Raldir." The words came out reluctantly, and there was a bitter taste in her mouth. Vorelna might have been growing on her, but that didn't mean she had to like talking to all Mirchan sentries…

The healer smiled at her. "How are you feeling today, Evenia?" Thaïselle's right foot and hand moved, as if she planned to take a step forward, but Evenia took a step back at the movement. The healer stopped. "Sorry, I just want to check on you." She offered a half smile, but Evenia only stood there, her eyes aware of every movement.

"I already wrapped her still-healing bruises, ma'am," Vorelna cut in. She winked at Evenia, who realized the older woman was helping her to feel less bombarded by strangers. "I'm sorry. I should have known you'd want to give them a look."

Thaïselle stopped herself from going any farther into the room. "Yes. Yes, of course, Vorelna. That's perfectly fine. I trust your judgment." She gave the duolvain a genuine smile. "Are there any wounds that need any further mending? Did the healing bubble do its job?"

"I'm fine," Evenia said, not liking that she felt they were talking about her as if she wasn't standing right in front of them. "Vorelna gave me some Olojbi to use, and I'll be fine. I've been through worse." She paused, not wanting to risk angering anyone from Mircha until she knew more. "But thank you for your help."

The healer's eyes softened. "Of course, you will be fine." Her eyes lit up suddenly. "Oh! You pronounced it properly. Most people don't. Does that mean you're familiar with Olojbi?"

Evenia nodded. "My aunt is a healer in Enacor, in a small town called Poultom. I've helped her out a time or two."

"Poultom…" Thaïselle paused for a moment, as if deep in thought. "Is she blonde? Average height?" Evenia slowly nodded. "Ah, Siersha, is it? Yes. Yes, I quite like her. She's a skilled Water witch healer, if I'm not mistaken?"

"Yes, how did you know that?" Evenia grinned thinking about her aunt, but her brows furrowed.

"It's part of my continued training as a moragaink to visit each realm to learn from and train other healers, as well as treat patients of different species. Your aunt was one of my favorite healers in Enacor I had the pleasure of working with."

A moragaink? Evenia looked toward the elf in front of her, her jaw threatening to spring open. The term hadn't registered when Vorelna mentioned it before opening the door while Evenia was silently panicking, and Thaïselle had introduced herself as merely a healer. What an understatement.

Moragainks were some of the best trained healers in the world. Their healing abilities stretched to nature itself, even being able to heal charred grass or sick trees.

Evenia had met many healers in her life, her coven being full of them, but it was an honor to meet a moragaink. So, what was someone as experienced as Thaïselle doing checking on someone like her?

Thaïselle shifted on her feet, and the movement pulled Evenia back to the topic at hand.

Right, Aunt Siersha. Poultom. Healing.

"Really? When was this?" Evenia finally asked.

"Oh, gods. Now you're making me think." Thaïselle laughed. "Poultom... Hmm... Maybe three decades ago?"

Evenia's heart skipped a beat. "Was it just my aunt there?"

"No, there were other witches in her coven working in the shop, but your aunt is the only one I remember well. We worked together the most because she was the best trained healer there, but I still tried to pass on a bit of my knowledge to everyone there." She smiled.

Evenia nodded and tried her best not to show the disappointment on her face.

"Is your mother a healer alongside your aunt?" General Elsvarin asked, as if she'd picked up on what Evenia was thinking.

Evenia shifted from one foot to the other. "No." She cleared her throat while Thaïselle and the general stood there, patiently waiting for more. "She went missing when I was a baby." Her voice was void of emotion, though her heart was breaking thinking about how her mother had left her with her aunt and uncle one night, never to return. There was no explanation for why she was left on her aunt and uncle's doorstep, and not a single word since.

"Oh, that's awful," Thaïselle said, her tone soft and comforting. "What is her name?"

Evenia looked from one elf to the other, contemplating telling the truth. But these were sentries she was talking to. What if they recognized her mother's name? What if they knew something and could tell her? Her throat bobbed.

Studying their faces, she said, "Nioma Brohn."

Neither elf reacted to the name, and Evenia felt her heart sink into her stomach. She should have known better.

"And your father, is he also a healer?" General Elsvarin asked.

Her back went rigid and she felt her jaw clench so hard her teeth ground together. It took great effort to relax her jaw as she said, "He's dead."

"Oh, you poor thing," Thaïselle said. She looked like she wanted to hug Evenia but thought better of it.

The truth was the man who raised her and was like a father to her for all those years—her uncle—was dead. Murdered at the hands of Mirchan sentries.

As for her biological father? She didn't actually know if he still lived, for her mother never revealed her father's identity to her aunt. As far as Evenia was concerned, he was dead to her. It didn't matter if he still breathed life in this world, because to her, he never existed. The man never came looking for her, and she no longer held the desire to go looking for him.

General Elsvarin cleared her throat, breaking Evenia from her thoughts. "Since we now know where home is for you, I will make contact with your aunt. Depending on how quickly the message is received and when she can leave to come here, we could likely get her here within the next week."

A week. Evenia knew that it took around three days to travel to the Mirchan border from her aunt and uncle's house in Poultom, Enacor. However, she hadn't realized how deep into Mircha the Capital building was. A week until she could see her family again. It was unclear which emotion she felt more: excitement over seeing her aunt and cousin again or fear over having to explain what had happened to her.

Her breathing became erratic.

Did she want to talk with her family? Of course. However, she also wasn't ready to have to relive those memories. Those thoughts. Those fears. Those moments where she felt helpless and alone.

What was said to her.

What she felt.

What she didn't feel.

What she couldn't remember.

Because the truth was, she barely remembered what had happened to her or how she ended up there. She remembered claws and shadows and the unmistakable taste of blood and fear. She had been drugged most of the time, unsure of what was going on, where she was, what was happening to her.

Until the light—

There was a light that broke through the darkness. A light that separated the shadows. Separated the dark thoughts, the dark words. It helped her escape. It showed her the way out.

Where did that come from? Her eyes squinted, attempting to make the mental image clearer, but the memory grew hazy.

"Unless you would rather we wait a little longer?" The general's question pulled Evenia's attention back. She looked up at the elf and almost flinched under the intensity of General Elsvarin's stare. It was as though the elf could see right into her soul. "I can ask the sentries stationed at Fort Knowlton to delay the messengers by a day or two. Or perhaps...even delay your aunt."

Evenia's mind whirred, trying to remember the map of Mircha she studied day after day when her uncle was away for work, wondering what route he would be taking on his way home.

Oh! Knowlton was a fort just past the border of Mircha. She remembered the map showing small, half-circle landmarks, marking high hills that weren't quite mountainous, but potentially difficult to travel along.

Should she ask for more time? How much time was enough time before she saw them again and had to explain what happened? Had to explain the night she was kidnapped and what happened to her since. What he—

She shook her head, not wanting to go down that mental spiral again. "No, that feels wrong to ask of them. They must be worried."

The general studied her for a moment before nodding. "Very well." She started to walk toward the door but stopped in the doorway and half turned toward Evenia. "If you would, take the night to think about it and let me know your decision in the morning."

Evenia nodded. "Thank you, General."

"Please, call me Andira." She smiled before walking out the door, with Vorelna following behind her.

Closing the door, Evenia sighed, relieved to be alone with her own thoughts again.

A throat cleared and Evenia tensed.

She wasn't alone.

9

Evenia

venia found herself suddenly wishing she had the nail file once more as she whirled on the stranger in her room. Her shoulders relaxed a little when she realized it was only the moragaink.

"I thought you were gone." Evenia took in a few deep breaths to calm herself.

"No, I'm sorry! I didn't mean to startle you. I thought you knew I was still here." The moragaink's hands were raised in a submissive way. "I just wanted to make sure you were truly okay. You know, without an audience?" A dainty hand gestured toward the door, where the general and the healer's assistant walked out just seconds before.

"Oh, yeah, I'm fine. I don't make for a great patient. So, doting over me won't fare well for either one of us. You can ask my aunt when you see her." Evenia paused. Because she'd be able to ask her soon. So soon. Her stomach both fluttered and sank at the thought. She wasn't ready.

Thaïselle laughed. "I completely understand. I'm a moragaink, for crying out loud, but if you try to give me so much as a shot, I'll stick that syringe in your neck." Evenia looked at her with furrowed brows. The healer shrugged. "What? It only happened once."

Evenia blinked several times before she realized the healer wasn't joking, and she laughed at the image of this elf stabbing someone with a syringe over a shot. Really laughed for the first time since being here. So hard that her stomach hurt.

Except, the laugh wouldn't stop. It just kept going, until her attempts at sucking in air in between laughs turned into deep sobs and tears streamed down her face. She collapsed against the side of the bed, hugging her arms around herself. What was wrong with her?

"Shh. Shhh. You're okay. You're going to be just fine, okay? You're safe now." Thaïselle's arms suddenly wrapped around Evenia, who only sobbed harder at the words. "It's just you here—a safe space. So, just let it out, all right?"

Several minutes went by before the sobs stopped and Evenia realized Thaïselle was hugging her closely to her chest. But she didn't care. She welcomed the comfort—something that became foreign to her in the past... However long it was.

The sobs subsided and she sucked in a deep breath that was cut short as her stomach grumbled. Her hand clutched her stomach.

"I'd say you're feeling well enough to eat real food today." Thaïselle chuckled and pulled away, making sure Evenia was okay before releasing her and standing to fix her cream coat.

Evenia resisted the urge to grab her stomach as it grumbled again.

"You should go to the chow hall for breakfast this morning. It has a wide variety of food from all over to cater to everyone's homeland dishes."

"Where is it?" Evenia asked, looking out into the hallway as she wiped her eyes and cheeks dry.

Thaïselle smiled and gestured toward the door. "I'm going in that direction. So, I can walk you there." The healer half-turned, smiling back at her.

Evenia dipped her chin as they walked out of the room. "Thanks."

They walked in silence down two hallways and a set of stairs, with Evenia's newly healed body quickly getting used to the movements and balance of walking again. The entire time, Evenia could sense Thaïselle wanted to say something but was holding back.

"What is it?" Evenia finally asked.

Thaïselle looked up at her, and let out a small laugh. "I've always been terrible at hiding my thoughts." She started fidgeting with her hands. "It's just, I'm curious how you're *really* feeling. This is a lot, I'm sure. So, how are you doing?"

Evenia's eyes shuttered, thinking about the breakdown she just had. "Oh, I–I'm okay...I think. I haven't really had the chance to process it all." Evenia's hand flew to the hem of the sweater Vorelna gave her, picking at a loose thread.

The truth was, she wasn't sure how to feel. Nothing had happened to her since she'd been here. No unnatural shadows. No unbearable coldness. No torture. In fact, she'd mostly only experienced kindness and acceptance since she'd been there.

Mostly.

Her mind flashed to a certain grey-eyed elf. She didn't know which was worse: a plain threat or a hidden one.

"I'm here, and I'm...okay," she managed to say.

Thaïselle offered her a small smile. "I can say from experience that there are worse places to heal than here." The moragaink raised the sleeve of her cream coat and Evenia's eyes widened as she saw a deep scar nearly the length of her arm. Was that the wound she was healing from when she attacked someone with the syringe?

Voices rose from down the hall as Thaïselle rolled her sleeve back down. "That doesn't mean it's not going to take some time. I just hope that you find some peace while you're here."

Peace. Interesting choice of words for the supposed Peacekeeping Realm. Evenia bit back a retort because Thaïselle had been kind to her so far, and as much as she didn't want to admit it, she kind of reminded Evenia of her Aunt Siersha.

The realization sent a pang through Evenia's chest.

"Moragaink Guérisald!" yelled a voice at the end of the hall behind them.

Thaïselle halted and sighed before turning. "Yes, Molhom?" Evenia followed her gaze to a scrawny, brown-haired boy fidgeting his hands and standing at the end of the hall.

"Your presence has been requested in the west wing, ma'am."

Thaïselle grimaced. "Very well. Thank you. I'll be there in a moment." The mousy-haired young man bowed and ran off around the corner. "I hate the west wing," she huffed.

Her gaze softened as she made eye contact with Evenia again. "I'm sorry, I have to go. If you continue down this hall, the chow hall will be around the corner on your right. Just follow the voices. Oh! As you're walking, think about what you'd like to eat and it'll appear the second you sit down." Evenia stared at her in confusion. "You'll see what I mean." She winked.

Evenia nodded, but she was more confused than ever, and not at all certain of what she'd be met with when she made it to the hall. "Thanks," she managed to say.

Thaïselle looked like there was something more she wanted to say. Instead, she just smiled and nodded before following in the direction the brown-haired boy disappeared moments before.

Taking a deep breath, Evenia followed the voices down the hall. As the sounds got louder, her footsteps grew slower. But then, the most delicious smells wafted down the hall, and she couldn't resist walking faster as her stomach growled with more intensity.

When she turned the corner, there were open double doors, revealing a room full of tables. Different mouth-watering smells and the sounds of spoken languages she wasn't familiar with hit her the second she stepped in the doorway.

Enacor was full of duolvain and humans. So, Evenia was used to seeing all sorts of beings back home. However, it never occurred to her that she might see so many together in one room in Mircha. Elves of all Elements scattered around. Some duolvain all about, from what she could tell of their ears and markings. A few dwarves huddled around one table. A couple centaurs chugging mugs. A fairy with translucent wings walking by her. The list kept going, including some fae she did not recognize the species of.

Not a single table was empty. Her heart pounded in her ears. Being around so many people—so many *sentries*—spiked her anxiety as she attempted to calm her racing mind and heart. But she was hungry...

Before she could second-guess whether this was a good idea, a raised hand to the right caught her attention.

"Good morning!" said a tall elf with long, brown hair and tanned skin.

Evenia paused, looking around and behind her before realizing the elf was talking to her. With slow footsteps, she cautiously approached the nearly full table the elf with the friendly smile was waving her over to. It felt like trying to make friends at her coven's school all over again, and Evenia instinctively wanted to run away. But there was something in that smile that pulled her in.

"Hi! I'm Neladrie," the elf said, sticking her hand out when Evenia reached the table.

Evenia hesitated before gripping her forearm, and Neladrie gripped Evenia's in return in greeting. If she thought the elf had a friendly smile before, it was even bigger now, reaching to her bright, copper-colored eyes. She couldn't stop herself from smiling back at her.

Evenia cleared her throat and lifted her chin, straightening her back in the process. "I'm Evenia," she nodded as they released each other's arms.

"Lovely to meet you, Evenia," Neladrie said, and Evenia was surprised to feel the elf actually meant it. Taking her seat once more, Neladrie pointed to her right at an elf with hair black as night and skin the color of smoky quartz. "This is Nishara."

Nishara stood and greeted Evenia the same way Neladrie had, with her arm reaching over the table. There was something that felt almost...familiar about the elf that made Evenia not hesitate this time to accept the greeting as she took hold of Nishara's forearm. It felt like they'd met before.

"Nice to meet you, Evenia." Nishara said, her lavender-colored eyes full of warmth. "It's good to see you walking and looking better."

Evenia felt a small pang of embarrassment at the thought of so many of them knowing she was...incapacitated. "Thanks," she managed to say.

Neladrie pointed to the male to her left. "This is Taszarin—Tasz, for short."

The male elf lifted his chin to meet Evenia's eyes, his long, thick locs shifting with the movement of his head. Striking gold eyes, like melted pools of gold, momentarily mesmerized her. He nodded once, and then looked back down to finish eating. Part of her wished she was doing the same. It looked like he was eating some sort of egg scramble, and Evenia was just thankful her stomach didn't growl again.

"And that's my twin brother, Kajarnas," Neladrie said, pointing across from her to an elf with brown hair sitting a couple feet from where Evenia stood.

"You can just call me Kaj." He gave her that same kind smile Neladrie had. Besides the similar smile, hair color, and eye color, they looked different from one another. So, not identical twins, then.

Still sitting, Kaj put out his hand in greeting, and the motion suddenly caused a disjointed memory of arms moving back and forth to flash in her mind.

Blinking her way back to the present moment, to the brown-haired elf before her, Evenia hesitated before taking his arm. "Hi," she spoke slowly. "Do–do I know you?" she asked.

"Ah, perhaps." His face changed to a gentle smile as he released her forearm. "I was there...you know, that night."

Evenia nodded. *Of course.* Was she ever going to meet someone in this place who didn't see her tumble or look broken? Her cheeks grew pink.

"Neladrie and I are from Gathéla. We're Huymi." *Nature elves.* He waved his empty fork toward his sister, who sat across the table from him. "Drie handled righting the landslide to keep it from hurting anyone and causing further damage to the hill, while

I created a platform for you to hover on until it was all clear. It's possible you may have seen me then." He placed his fork back down on his tray, to a meal Evenia wasn't familiar with but that smelled amazing.

Yes, she'd remembered at least one Huymi that night, but she hadn't realized there were two.

"Thank you." She dipped her chin at him, and then looked to Neladrie. "Both of you."

Neladrie smiled and Kaj simply shrugged.

"Don't mention it," he said, plopping a roll in his mouth. He patted the seat next to him for Evenia to join them.

She looked from him to the empty seat before sitting down. The second she sat, a tray of fluffy eggs, bacon, and brown sugar oatmeal suddenly appeared in front of her. There was barely enough time to blink before a gold goblet appeared next to the tray. She paused before picking it up to examine its contents.

"What's your poison?" Nishara asked.

Evenia's eyes went wide, the hand holding the cup in it stopping mid-air. *Poison?* Was this it? Were they finally showing their true colors?

Nishara gestured to the cup. "In the cup. What'd you pick?"

Evenia's eyes went to the goblet once more, finally pulling it the rest of the way to her nose. She paused before sniffing once, and her mouth watered.

"Chocolate milk," she said, her cheeks growing pink again.

Nishara smiled but Evenia's attention was pulled to the other side of Neladrie as Tasz chuckled. Evenia's eyebrows raised when a second gold goblet appeared next to Tasz's tray and first goblet. His large hand went to reach for it and briefly paused when he realized everyone's eyes were now on him. He grabbed the goblet and took a sip. As he pulled away, there was a milky chocolate film on his top lip.

Shrugging at the stares, he wiped his sleeve over his lip. "What? It sounded good."

Evenia grinned. As she took a sip from her own goblet, she nearly moaned at the richness of the chocolate. She dug into her eggs next, before her stomach could growl again.

"So, where are you from?" Kaj asked through a mouthful of food. Evenia hesitated.

"Don't worry, it's a normal question in Mircha. Everyone's from everywhere here," Neladrie said, smiling at her. "Kaj and I were born and raised in Gathéla. Tasz, our grumpy Soluxen, is from Elndion." Evenia started. She'd never met a Soluxen—a Sun elf. "And Nishara is a Lunrea from Nulhe." Nishara, the Lunrea—a Moon elf—smiled at Evenia.

Two Huymi, a Lunrea, and a Soluxen sat around a table. That sounded like the start to a bad joke. Elves representing Mother Nature, the Sun, and the Moon. It never occurred to her that elves of so many backgrounds would swear an oath to Mircha.

She'd never met a Sun elf before. Light elves and witches couldn't produce heat, just bright light. They were also natural healers. The difference between Light magic and Sun magic was the same as daylight—pure, bright light—vs. Sunlight—harsh, damaging light. That wasn't to say that Light couldn't be as deadly as Sun if wielded properly.

Wielders of Sun magic produced heated rays that were almost as dangerous as the Sun itself. Sunburns and actual burning of skin were only a couple of many potential injuries. Whereas Light could be blinding in brightness, a Sun wielder's power could actually blind another, similarly to how Sunlight could. Whether temporarily or permanently.

"You don't have to share if you don't want to," Neladrie said, her voice sympathetic. Having been lost in thought, the words brought Evenia back to the present moment.

"My family lives in Poultom," Evenia finally said, before digging into the oatmeal. Everything was delicious.

"Ah, Enacor. Poultom's a small town, isn't it?" Kaj asked. Evenia nodded as she took another bite. "I think there's a nice healer in that town. She's patched Tasz and me up a time or two." Kaj waved a hand at Tasz, but his attention was on a smiling Neladrie, who looked like she was waiting for a moment to jump in. Evenia smiled. You'd have to be a fool to not notice he was smitten by her.

"That had to have been my Aunt Siersha," Evenia said, smiling.

Kaj paused for a moment, eyebrows pinched together as if he was thinking hard. He didn't seem to hear her, lost in his memories. "She was tall and had dirty blonde hair."

Smiling, she nodded at the mental image of her aunt that popped in her head. Looking back down at her nearly empty plate, she was shocked at how delicious it all was. Aunt Siersha was a great cook, but Evenia had never tasted such good food before. Or maybe she was just really hungry.

"It's been years, but I think it was her and her sister that patched us up the last time," Kaj said.

Evenia froze, a forkful of eggs hovering inches from her mouth. She nearly dropped the fork. "What? Are you sure?" Evenia asked, turning to him.

Kaj looked at Tasz. "Am I remembering wrong? The sister was petite and had lighter blonde hair." Tasz's gaze fell on Evenia, and Kaj's eyes followed. He lazily gestured to Evenia. "Ah, yes, similarly to that blonde." He looked back at the Sun elf. "Good catch."

With a deep and soothing voice, Tasz said, "I vaguely remember two witch healers in Poultom. One had the power of Water, and the other—"

"Light?" Evenia interrupted. Her heart was pounding. Tasz met her gaze, his eyes searching her face for the first time.

Kaj snapped his fingers, as if a memory suddenly locked into place for him. "Yes! Water and Light! They healed us a few times after some unpleasant patrols along the Urur border there, but it was mostly the taller sister there when we went. I think the other woman was there the last time. Actually, now that I'm thinking about it, it seemed weird between them."

Evenia stopped breathing. Weird? Weird how? She'd always heard they were close.

"Kaj..." Neladrie tried to grab his attention, but he was too focused on remembering the sisters. Her aunt and... It couldn't be.

He looked at Tasz again, who hadn't looked away from Evenia. "Tasz, what were their names? Sielle? Sierrin?" His fingers snapped again. "Siersha! And...hmm. Nori? Naomi?"

"Nioma," Evenia said quietly. Her heart had stopped. They'd met her mother. They'd actually met her. They knew her and she didn't. Kaj finally looked at her then. "How long ago was this?"

"Oh, I'm not sure." He glanced at Tasz. His tone had changed, as if he'd finally returned from memory lane and realized what everyone else at the table had already appeared to pick up on. "What, thirty years ago now?" Tasz slowly nodded. "Give or take a year or two." Kaj's tone hitched, as if the elf was suddenly uncomfortable with the topic.

"If you said the current healer is your aunt," Neladrie's voice was soft, "does that make her sister your mother?"

Evenia met her gaze. She could hear her heartbeat in her ears. Her eyes flashed from Kaj to Tasz. "Whatwasshelike?" It all came out at once; she couldn't speak the words fast enough.

Kaj shifted in his seat. "She, um... She was a good healer?" Kaj's voice went up an octave, clearly uncomfortable. His twin glared at him from across the table.

Tasz laid his large hand on the tabletop, pulling Evenia's attention toward him. "I remember her being polite. She was never anything but kind to us over the years we required healing in that area," Tasz's calm voice broke through to Evenia's racing thoughts.

He paused briefly, as if dredging up old memories. "Yes, a skilled healer, though she once told me she wanted to be an alchemist but fell into healing because of her sister's practice. She was smart, too." Neladrie squeezed his shoulder, a small, proud smile on her face, but he didn't break his eye contact with Evenia.

Kind. Skilled. Smart. She'd heard it all before, but her mother wanting to be an alchemist instead of a healer was news to her. This Mirchan sentry seemed to know more about her mother than she did.

Evenia felt a stinging in her eyes. A loss of appetite hit her hard as she laid her fork down on her tray.

"Light..." Neladrie's voice was soft. "We saw your Light in the woods that night. Didn't we? Are you a Light witch like your mother?"

Evenia slowly nodded. She'd lied about her abilities since she was young, but it didn't mean it was an easy thing to do. However, pretending to *only* be a Light Elemental witch helped keep her alive all these years.

Feeling uncomfortable and vulnerable, she looked away from the table to blink back the tears and catch her breath after the revelation about her mother. Instead of a moment of peace to recover, when she turned her head, her breath hitched as she saw a certain grey-eyed elf enter the room. That fiery anger was brimming to the surface again, but there was something else there... Curiosity. As infuriating as he had been, she couldn't deny he was attractive, which only made her more irritated.

He made eye contact with her from the doorway, and she refused to be the first to look away.

"Do you know him?" Nishara asked after a moment.

"Unfortunately," Evenia cleared her throat, breaking away the lump that had formed. "We've talked briefly."

A minotaur bumped into him from behind, making him break eye contact. She peeled her eyes from the doorway and faced the table once more. The fiery anger instantly extinguished. Everyone suddenly seemed very tense, either looking at her or at Kalland.

"What?" she asked, her eyes flicking from one face to another.

"Nothing," Neladrie said quickly. "But...what did he say to you?"

Evenia's gaze briefly flew back to the doorway, to the elf who was now walking their way. His eyes were on her, and all she could think about was him accusing her of *commingling* with The Darkness.

Evenia sneered. "He was just being an ass, if I'm honest," she said, turning back toward the table. Neladrie and Nishara made eye contact, and Evenia felt on the outs as they clearly passed an unspoken message between them.

"Hey, I'm headed to the training grounds," Nishara said, rising from the table. She looked right at Evenia as she spoke. "Care to join me?" Evenia looked from Nishara to Kalland, who was only four tables away now.

Without responding, Evenia shot up from her seat. She looked down at her tray, and both the tray and goblet vanished before her eyes. Her head shook in amazement at the magic before she quickly said her farewells and turned to leave. Side by side with Nishara, she walked across the room to a side exit a few tables away and in the opposite direction of Kalland.

As Evenia stepped over the doorway that appeared to lead to another long hallway in this never-ending maze of a place, she looked back once, her eyes locking on Kalland's. A mixture of emotions came from him as she saw his jaw tick and release in almost the same breath, his eyes softening slightly with the movement.

An opportunity for fight-or-flight, and her body once again chose flight. The swinging door closed before Evenia could question whether running had been the right thing to do this time.

10

Evenia

N ow that they were nearing the training grounds, Evenia was having second thoughts. Her palms dampened the closer they got to the sounds of swords clashing and grunts in the distance. Panic set in, and her steps faltered.

Nishara stopped a few paces ahead of her. "Are you all right?" she asked, studying Evenia's face.

Evenia breathed in and out, and then finally nodded. "Yes, I think I just need to rest a bit instead."

Her eyes darted from sentry to sentry training in the distance. The need to get away from here was overwhelming her. She needed to stay away from the sharp weapons wielded by the very people responsible for her uncle's death.

She glanced at Nishara, at her kind eyes full of genuine concern and her nonthreatening stance. How could someone who seemed so polite be associated with murderers?

Evenia took a step back. A step away from the Mirchan sentries. A step away from Nishara. A step away from danger. Her breath seemed to stall.

"Of course, you must still be exhausted." Nishara nodded. "Do you want me to take you back to your room?"

Did she? Evenia looked behind her, toward the Mirchan palace, with Nishara still in her peripheral vision. Just in case. The castle was massive. The exterior stood tall in beige stone and dark brown details, including the shutters, balconies, and columns. At least, the ones Evenia could see before her.

There were so many windows and so many details to examine. The sheer size of it was intimidating, and she wasn't sure she'd be able to successfully navigate it. Was it worth trying alone? Worth the risk of getting lost in enemy territory?

She turned back toward Nishara, who looked harmless enough, and even so, she stood only a few inches taller than herself. Evenia didn't have her full physical strength back *yet*, but now that her body was mostly healed, she knew she could take her with her magic if she had to.

So, she nodded. "Please."

Nishara smiled and led the way with Evenia at her back, watching every shadow and observing everyone they passed. She wasn't going to get caught off guard or led into another trap.

⁂

Before they approached Evenia's temporary room, they passed the hallway where they met and ate not long ago. There was laughter and conversation streaming down the corridor, and it only confused Evenia more. She'd spent the past ten years thinking these people were monsters—*murderers*. They'd taken the only father figure in her life, the man who raised her.

Except, seeing them all now—*living* amongst them—they seemed so...normal.

"I'll talk with Neladrie and a few others about making sure you have enough clothes during your time here," Nishara said over her shoulder as they walked up the steps leading to the hall of her rooms.

"Oh, that's not necessary. I shouldn't be here much longer," Evenia said.

"Even so, it's better to have options."

Options? What more did one need than a pair of trousers and a sweater? But she nodded anyway.

When they turned onto the hallway that housed her room, Evenia saw Vorelna walking down the hall toward them. There were beige fabrics draped on one arm and a basket full of tonics hanging from her other arm.

"Good morning, Elna," Nishara said in a sweet tone. Evenia could hear by her tone that Nishara was clearly fond of the woman.

"Morning, Nisha. Tell my favorite Soluxen that I have a gift for him later," Vorelna said as she winked at Nishara, who laughed in response.

Soluxen? Could that be Tasz—the Sun elf—from breakfast? She found herself wondering how many different types of elves lived in Mircha and *why*.

"He'll be glad to hear it," Nishara said.

Vorelna smiled at the Moon elf and turned her gaze to Evenia, offering a warm smile. "Hello, dear. Do let me know if you need anything." She dipped her chin, and Evenia did the same in return. She wasn't sure what to say, nor was she sure how to reach Vorelna if she *did* need help.

Vorelna passed by them, and before Evenia knew it, they'd made it to her door. Nishara stood a few feet away from the threshold, as if she was trying to make it clear she didn't plan to enter.

Evenia faced her. "Thank you."

"Anytime." Nishara smiled at her. "This place takes some getting used to."

"I can tell," Evenia said. She was trying to be nice, but she didn't plan to stick around to find out just how long it took to get used to it. The first instance she could take to run, she would. Right out the front door if she had to. Well...wherever the front door was, she'd find it and walk right out of it.

She turned to enter her room but paused when she saw Nishara shuffle awkwardly in her peripheral vision.

Evenia faced her. *She's nervous,* Evenia thought to herself. Whatever for?

The Lunrea reached down to one of the daggers attached to her thigh and Evenia froze for a split second before she braced herself. This was it. With her training as a child, she was prepared for anything. Prepared to finally see Mircha's people for what they really were.

Evenia's palms started to dampen as Nishara unhooked the holster of a black dagger, wrapping her hand around the hilt.

As if picking up on Evenia's sudden change in body language, Nishara's eyes went wide and she put her hands up. The dagger was still in its thigh holster and clasped in her left hand. "Don't worry, I won't hurt you. It's for you—a gift—so that you can feel safe here."

Evenia stood still. Was this a trick?

"It occurred to me that if we had gone to the training grounds, you wouldn't have any weapon of your own. You'd be able to use some of the weapons at the training grounds, sure, but it's nothing like having your own." She slowly lowered her hand holding the dagger and held it out for Evenia, with the hilt facing Evenia and the blade in the holster facing herself. A nonthreatening action.

"So, this is for you. To defend yourself, so you hopefully feel safe in this unfamiliar place, and...just in case."

Because they didn't know what was after her. Evenia understood the unspoken words, filling in the blanks herself.

Her eyes went from Nishara's hand to her face multiple times before finally putting her hand out, palm up. The Lunrea gently laid the dagger in Evenia's hand and backed away, hands still up.

Gaze locked on the dagger now in her hand, she slowly removed it from the holster. It was stunning. The phases of the moon were etched in silver along the black hilt, and the decorative sheath matched the design. As she unsheathed it, she saw that the blade itself was a lavender color.

Evenia picked up the dagger, examining it in the light coming through the windows at the end of the hall. When the sunlight touched the blade, she noticed the lavender had an accent of silver to it, shining like the moon and stars each time the light hit it. The beauty of it took her breath away.

"It was made by one of the best blacksmiths in Nulhe, my home. Duloar, the blacksmith, is truly an artist," Nishara said. There was pride and warmth in her voice.

Evenia looked from her to the blade, and back again. "This is too nice of a gift. I can't take it." She started to hand the dagger back to Nishara, who was shaking her head.

"It's rude to refuse a gift, Evenia," she said in a playful tone, with a smile on her face. "Take it. Please. It will make me feel better knowing that you are armed." She paused, her smile faltering a little. "You do know how to use a dagger, don't you?"

Evenia bit back her smile, keeping her face as serious as she could. "Of course."

"Good," Nishara said. "I'll leave it to you, then." She nodded and walked away.

Rooted to the spot, Evenia watched her walk down the hallway. It wasn't until Nishara turned the corner before Evenia opened the door and walked into the empty room. She shut and locked it. The laughter from down the hall was but a memory now.

Leaning against the door, she examined the dagger once more. It really was a beautiful and thoughtful gift.

This is for you. To defend yourself. To feel safe.

It wouldn't be enough to protect her from the monster that hunted her...

Evenia's breath stalled at the thought. There was nothing that could save her from The Darkness that plagued these lands. Or even from the darkness that lurked within her for that matter.

Vorelna's words suddenly popped in her head—that there would be wounds Evenia must heal from not just physically. She lived in a constant state of fear for gods only knew how long.

Now, she couldn't believe she was free. It was like her body, her mind, her very soul still didn't believe it. Evenia felt panicked every time she saw a flickering shadow, or a quick movement from someone simply walking by. It was something she realized while she stood in the doorway of the chow hall, waiting, assessing, before Neladrie pulled her from her thoughts. And again, just now, as Nishara escorted her through the castle.

These sentries were not at all what she expected...

Neladrie, who had been warm and welcoming to her. Kaj, who helped save her and reminded her how much she enjoyed helping her aunt back home. Tasz, who made her feel less foolish for wanting chocolate milk and gave her a glimpse into what her mother had been like. And Nishara, who gave Evenia an escape from the grey-eyed elf, and then gifted her with such a special weapon.

A weapon. She *armed* Evenia.

But why? The sudden urge to toss the dagger in a drawer and never lay eyes on it again hit her. These people—these sentries—they were responsible for her uncle's death.

Well, not these specific sentries. Otherwise, she would have asked the chow hall for a knife and gutted them where they stood. No, theirs weren't the faces she saw that day. But the men who murdered her uncle had the Mirchan crest upon their breastplates when they attacked him.

She couldn't stop it before she was pulled into a memory—one she tried so hard to forget over the years.

It was late summer, right before Aunt Siersha's birthday. Evenia and Émeriah went out to the hidden berry patch on the outskirts of town—the one her aunt kept telling them not to visit. They went to gather ferynmin berries to make a pie for Aunt Siersha's birthday.

No one had ever explained to them why it was dangerous to go there, but the ferynmin berries were fresh and too good to pass up sneaking some. Plus, it wasn't like they were stealing from anyone since that land didn't belong to anyone.

That day, they learned why it was dangerous. And her uncle paid the ultimate price for it.

He'd come, knowing exactly where his girls had run off to. Having come straight to his daughter and niece when his patrol ended, he wore his typical dark brown armor that signaled he was a sentry for Enacor. He tried to sneak up on Evenia and Émeriah, but he'd trained them too well.

Evenia heard the twig snap behind her and Émeriah, which set her on alert. She casually looked to her cousin, pretending to talk, and spied the shadow of a man inching toward them.

Evenia discreetly unsheathed the dagger at her hip, as she made small talk with her cousin, and waited to strike. Just as the figure's shadow came closer, she whirled on him, knocking his feet out from under him. When she pointed the dagger at his familiar face, she smiled, and pride filled her.

"Nice try, Uncle Ensel," Evenia said, while Émeriah was in a giggle fit over seeing her father knocked on his back.

He cleared his throat as he sat up on his elbows, pretending like she hadn't just knocked every last breath from his lungs with that fall. "Just trying to keep you on your toes," he croaked as he attempted to catch his breath again.

Laughing, she offered him her hand.

Regaining his composure, he asked, "So, how many have we got?" A jut of his chin gestured to the basket full of berries hanging from Émeriah's arm.

Émeriah lifted the basket. "Plenty to eat." Evenia cleared her throat and narrowed her eyes at her cousin. "Oh, and some for Ma." She tried to wipe away the mess the berries had left on her hands from eating them as she picked. The evidence of how much she already consumed being wiped away.

"Don't you think she'll be angry with you lot for coming here and picking the berries?" Uncle Ensel asked, a teasing tone in his voice.

"How will she know? It's not like we're going to tell her," Émeriah said, sticking out her tongue at her father. A silent dare to not be a snitch.

He grinned. "I think the name 'ferynmin pie' gives away that you came here and snuck some ferynmin berries, Mer." Émeriah looked from him to the basket, and shrugged, before she continued picking more berries.

Evenia's face mirrored her uncle's. When his grin fell and his gaze scanned over the woods around the berry patch, she turned her head to follow.

Yards ahead were four gruff-looking males wearing the emblem of Mircha. All four had beards and two of them were round in the belly, with one's tunic rising up slightly because of the fit. It was hard to know if the sentries had noticed them, since their voices couldn't be heard as they weaved through the trees of the woods bordering the berry patch.

Why were they in the middle of the woods? Mirchan sentries typically traveled into town, gathering reports from the Enacoran sentries and townsfolk about anything mysterious from the border of the Urur Mountains. The sentries in Enacor typically handled daily disputes between townsfolk, and sentries from Mircha tended to the Urur Mountains' borders. The place that actually was full of danger, and where Evenia doubted there were fresh berries.

Just as she was about to turn fully toward them to ask if they were lost, her uncle stopped her. Pulling her attention to his face, he lifted his finger to his mouth—a signal to stay quiet—before he pointed at Émeriah and gestured to the direction of home. A silent message that he wanted Evenia to take her cousin and go. Without him.

She started to shake her head no, but he gave her the look, and she nodded. He kissed her on her forehead and silently nudged her along.

She went up to Émeriah and whispered, "All right, Mer, I think that's plenty for now. We'll have enough to make her a birthday pie, and still have lots left to eat later."

Émeriah groaned but gave in and started walking with Evenia. Her cousin was about to turn around to look for her father—who was now inching closer to the woods—but Evenia stopped her. "I'll race you home!" She took off for home, knowing Mer would follow, and it would ensure she could make it back to her uncle quicker.

But she didn't make it in time. She failed him that day. And every day since.

She mentally shook her head, shoving those memories deep, deep down, where they belonged. No, these were not the same sentries she met today. Still, they still wore the same emblem, and it was possible they knew the men who murdered her uncle. What if it was an order to kill him? No, that couldn't be. Her uncle was well-loved. He was *good*.

The men were likely corrupt. And because they were sentries, she'd bet what little money she had that they were protected by the very people who now offered her shelter.

Her hand wrapped around the dagger's hilt as her anger rose. Stomping toward the balcony doors, she threw them open with a force she wasn't aware she was capable of. Once in the threshold, she held the dagger up, ready to be tossed out into the land below.

Right as she went to toss it, the sun reflected off the blade, catching her eye, and Evenia stopped herself. She tilted the dagger, examining where the sun hit it. As she did, she noticed that when the light hit it in the right spot, a reflection appeared on the floor just inside the threshold of the room. Like a ray of light, it created some sort of blur on the floor.

She messed with the angle of the dagger, until the blur cleared, and—

Oh! It looked like a painting, with strokes of lavender, silver, and black throughout, twinkling in the sun's light. When she looked closer, she realized there was a pattern. An image she recognized. It was a map of the stars somehow hidden in the lavender blade.

Duloar, the blacksmith, is truly an artist, Nishara had said. And she wasn't lying. How could anyone create such a masterpiece in a blade? Was it spelled?

She admired the painting of the stars through the blade's reflection a few more moments before she finally lowered the dagger and reentered the room. Face contorting in a grimace, she was flooded with guilt and shame. How could she be about to throw away such a precious gift? But on the other hand, how could she accept something from those responsible for Uncle Ensel's death?

This is for you. To defend yourself. To feel safe.

She held the dagger a little closer to her chest, as Nishara's words rang through her head again. But the elf hadn't specified who Evenia needed to defend herself from.

II

Evenia

S he needed to get out of this room. If she stayed any longer, Evenia was certain she'd lose her godsdamn mind. Her soul was in desperate need of some fresh air and to feel the grass between her toes.

Part of her regretted not continuing the journey to the training grounds with Nishara earlier that day. However, the other part of her patted herself on the back for not placing herself in unnecessary danger. Although, she was upset for letting her anxiety get the best of her and not making a mental map of the Mirchan palace when she had the chance. That would change now.

Lunch and dinner were spent in her room. After each meal, she impatiently waited until the Moon made Her ascent. Once the sky turned from a blend of fuchsia and orange to navy mixed with silvery moonlight, she could wait no longer.

It was finally time.

After rewrapping her ribs, Evenia searched through the chest filled with clothes for her that Nishara and Neladrie brought while on their lunch breaks. Even if she still wasn't sure of their motive or if she could trust them, she couldn't deny that it was nice of them to bring clothes for her.

As she sifted through them, she started to feel a little overwhelmed. There were so many clothes of different colors and fabrics. Some were perfect for the chilly night, and others... Well, she wasn't sure what occasion she'd wear them to.

One garment caught her eye as she pulled it out. Why would someone need a short, glittery dress with such a low back? Although, she couldn't deny it was pretty. There was also that beautiful, deep blue gown hanging in the armoire, along with a few other nicer dresses. It was silky soft and had shined in the room's candlelight.

Why would she need beautiful dresses while staying in Mircha? She never had much choice in the way of fashion back home in Enacor, and she wasn't sure where to start now.

As she continued to search through the generous amount of clothing, she opted for a pair of black leggings with a floral pattern and a matching belted cardigan. She pulled out a pair of black lace-up boots and thick wool socks after quickly realizing the boots were a size too big for her.

The pants and sweater she'd been wearing were now on the floor as she changed into the clothes she picked out. The belted cardigan was oversized, but it only made her feel all the more comfortable wearing it.

Walking over to the nightstand, she attached the thigh holster to her right leg before unsheathing the dagger that Nishara gave her. It was almost like it became more beautiful the more times she laid eyes on it. Her fingers traced the black as night hilt adorned with the most intricate design of each moon phase cascading in a crescent-like shape. Subtle hints of silver and lavender were intertwined in the design.

She unsheathed it to view the lavender-painted stars on the blade. It took her breath away each and every time she looked at it. Sheathing it once more, she attached the dagger to the thigh holster Nishara had handed it to her in and made sure the oversized sweater covered it.

Grabbing the hair ties from around her wrist, she quickly parted her hair down the middle and braided it in a double plait. The use of a mirror to braid hadn't been necessary since her and Émeriah were young girls. Doing Mer's hair always made Evenia feel like they were more like sisters than cousins. She smiled at the thought of her sister-cousin, and felt a small pang in her chest.

A small smile graced her lips after she successfully braided her long hair in less than four minutes. She always enjoyed doing her own hair. While she liked to switch it up every once in a while, braids were her go-to style when she was in a pinch for time. Or when she didn't feel like sitting in front of a mirror, like now.

She double-checked that the dagger was secured to her thigh and then stepped in front of the door. Pressing her ear to it, she honed into her duolvain hearing to make sure no one was on the other side. Several silent minutes passed before she opened the chamber door and prowled out into the night.

Unexpectedly, her senses were filled with bergamot and patchouli, and a hint of something else she couldn't place. In the same breath, she ran straight into a tall, hard body right outside the doorframe. Almost stumbling backward on impact, she quickly recovered and instinct took over.

Unsheathing the Nulhe dagger at her waist, she pinned the lurking stranger to the wall. In the same movement, her right foot hooked behind their left knee, widening their stance and bringing them eye level to her.

When she saw who it was standing before her, she shoved the dagger to their waistline. Just as her hand inched toward their groin—a slice that would surely cause blood to fall...or something else—a large, tanned hand grabbed her wrist, stopping her from drawing any blood.

Adrenaline pumped as she looked up into the face of the annoying male himself: Kalland Sothenas. She wasn't soon to forget the name of the male who accused her of *commingling* with The Darkness. Her teeth bared at the memory of the accusation.

His grey eyes were slightly wide, but there was a shadow of a smile on his face. She looked down at his hand around her wrist. It was tanned with nicks and scars all over it. The hands of a warrior. However, the hold on her wrist said otherwise, with only a gentle pressure keeping her from piercing through sensitive skin, almost as if to let her know she could strike if she wanted to. A strange thought, considering where it was aimed.

She looked back up at his face to see he was eyeing her wrist. Eyes narrowing at him, she said, "You're not even trying to hold me back. Why?"

He pulled his eyes from the dagger at his groin to look at her face. "I'm a firm believer in allowing one to arm themselves. If this makes you feel safe, then fine." He shrugged.

"And you'd be okay if I killed you now? Or worse?" She tested his hold and switched gears, suddenly holding the knife to his throat. His hand never left her wrist, but it didn't increase the pressure either.

She applied more pressure to his neck, but he only smirked in response to the tip of the dagger touching his throat, causing the skin there to whiten. Just the smallest bit more, and she'd draw blood.

"You might regret it," he said, briefly glancing down to the area her knife was seconds before. Slowly, those grey eyes trailed up her body and to her face.

She sneered in response, and he raised an eyebrow, clearly amused.

"However, if killing me makes you feel safe, then yes." He shrugged again, and this time, she found the movement and his nonchalant attitude mildly annoying. "But...I don't think you will."

The pressure to his neck increased under the weight of her hand. She smirked as she smelled that familiar copper scent fill the air, and a small part of her suddenly wished she hadn't moved the knife from its previous spot.

He chuckled, which only irked her more. "You misunderstand me." He gently squeezed her wrist for the first time, pulling her attention, and she noticed his eyes had grown dark. "I'm not underestimating your strength, but I am crediting your sense. You won't kill me because of who I am and where you are now." The words were firm but not cold as his free hand gestured to the hallway—to all of Mircha.

"If you kill me, you'll have a lot of explaining to do. Unless, of course, you struck me down and were immediately prepared to run. In which case..." He slowly looked her up and down, and her lip curled. "I'd say you have a fighting chance of making it out alive."

They stared at each other for a few long moments, before she reluctantly released her dagger. "Luckily for you, I've done my fair share of running recently."

"Yes, you have." His eyes narrowed at her.

What happened next occurred within the blink of an eye. As she started to lower her dagger from his neck, Kalland's hand on her wrist suddenly tightened to a painful grip. It forced her to loosen her hold on the dagger. He took it from her, and in what felt like the same breath, pinned her against the wall. With one hand, he restrained both her wrists above her head, the other hand holding her new dagger to her throat.

She squirmed, but she could barely move an inch. The beast within her was stirring, growling, ready to tear his throat out. Her claws were beginning to peek out and heat rose, as if her magic was ready to light his ass on fire.

But she tamped it all down before it was too late. It wouldn't be smart to reveal all of her secrets to the enemy. And this snake was certainly the enemy. She cursed herself for silently letting her guard down in front of him.

"What the hel are you doing?" she growled.

"Showing you how to properly pin your enemy."

"Fuck you," she breathed out, fuming. She attempted to move again, kicking out. In response, he moved his leg between hers, making it nearly impossible for her to move. Nearly, but not entirely impossible.

"How are you so fast?" she grunted. "Are you a vampire, or what?"

He smiled, not showing his full teeth. "Like I'd reveal my secrets to you." Her eyes narrowed at his barely exposed teeth.

"But it's not a secret you have a problem with me," she said. He smirked in response, and she had the urge to claw it right off his face. She breathed in and out, releasing that urge with each breath. For now. "Then tell me what your fucking problem is."

"You threatened me first, remember?" he said, quickly glancing from the dagger—*her* dagger—back to her.

"You know what I mean. You've had a problem with me since I woke up." *Almost...* She just needed him to move another inch... "You don't even know me. So, why?"

"That's my business, not yours." His eyes were searing into her now.

"It's my business when it involves me," she growled. "Try again."

His nostrils flared and the pressure on the dagger at her throat increased slightly. But after a second, he sighed and slowly pulled away. Just an inch. Just enough. That was all the opening she needed.

Her right leg reached out toward his. If he was paying attention, he would see that her short leg never actually reached his long one, but she was too fast to get caught. As always, the Wind came forth when she asked. In the blink of an eye, he was lying on the floor with his left side down. She smiled and mentally thanked the Wind for the gust that knocked his feet out from under him.

To his credit, and to her annoyance, he hadn't dropped the dagger.

His mouth was parted, eyes wide. With a smirk, she kicked up at his hand, dislodging the dagger from it. She caught the knife by the handle midair.

"What the *fuck!*" he growled, pulling his kicked hand close to his chest, which only made her smile harder.

"As it turns out, I can't hurt you, and you won't hurt me." He glared at her, and she raised one eyebrow, daring him to deny her suspicions based on his hesitation. There was no verbal response. So, she sheathed the dagger. "Consider this a truce...for now."

Not knowing what compelled her to do so, she held her hand out to him. His eyes glanced from her hand to her face. After a few seconds, she rolled her eyes and began to pull her hand back right as he placed his hand in hers. A gasp escaped her lips when she felt a jolt of electricity the second their hands connected.

Great. I offer kindness and almost get electrocuted for it, she thought to herself.

She looked down to see his eyes were equally as wide. Her eyes narrowed on him. "Was that you?" It certainly hadn't been her because she'd been extra careful not to let her anger affect her magic.

He narrowed his eyes right back, but there was a hint of amusement within them. "If it was me, you'd know."

"Whatever," she mumbled.

She braced herself, expecting to be pulled down as she pulled on his hand to help him up, but he didn't fight her on it. He gracefully rose to his feet, as if nothing had happened, and she immediately regretted helping. He was standing tall in front of her now. *Right* in front of her. Too close to her.

He was so tall that she was eye level with his chest. If she took a deep breath, she'd imagine her breasts would brush against the top of his abs. His very defined, very toned abs she could see through the outline of his shirt.

Slowly looking up, his broad shoulders drew her eye. She blinked once, twice, before her eyes trailed up again to a strong jaw with a trimmed reddish-brown beard. She liked a bit of facial hair. None at all made some grown men look like teenagers, and too much made her question how it would feel against her body.

Her eyes caught on his lips, where she glimpsed the left corner of his mouth twitching. The slightest movement she would have missed had she so much as blinked.

Up. There were faint freckles on his cheeks and nose.

Up, and up, until their eyes met. Those beautiful grey eyes. Her breath hitched at the intensity in them. So much anger. So much...pain. What had caused those strong, unmistakable emotions? What secrets was he hiding? And what the hel did she have to do with it all?

That mouth twitched again. "Enjoying the view?" he asked.

Bastard. He was like a beautiful, poisonous flower: exotic and mesmerizing on the outside, but really a calculated trap to lure its prey in.

Her lip curled in annoyance. "Not much to see, I'm afraid."

"Your eyes say otherwise."

"Yeah, yours speak volumes, too. Another one of your secrets?" she snapped back.

His eyes narrowed as a vein popped in his neck.

Oh, she hit a nerve. *Good.*

However, he wasn't backing away, wasn't backing down. Neither would she. They stood there, silently staring at one another, until Evenia felt the sudden urge to sit. She tried to fight it. Tried to stay strong and still. But she felt her eyes shutter and her body waver in its stance.

She started to lose her balance, but a strong hand at her elbow steadied her. Knowing who was on the other end of that offered support, she refused to lean into his strength. Although, she did allow her body to benefit just enough to be able to stand steadily on her own two feet, while still keeping her distance from the elven male in front of her.

Someone was talking, but she couldn't understand a single thing they said. It was like her head was plunged under water—deep, deep under the surface.

Her eyes blinked a few times, until her vision was less blurry. Blinked until her head stopped feeling like it was sinking. Blinked until her eyelids felt less heavy and the action went from difficult and slow to involuntary and rapid.

The voice was slightly clearer now. She looked up. Kalland's mouth was moving, but the movement didn't match when his actual voice met her ears. It was delayed by several seconds, which only made her panic a bit more. What was wrong with her?

"Are you okay?" She saw his lips mouth, and then heard him say several seconds later.

She didn't know how many times he'd asked it, but she could tell by his tone that he was concerned. Genuine concern. Her brows furrowed. That must be a first. The corner of her mouth raised at the thought. Hey, at least she hadn't lost her sense of humor.

A rough, calloused hand grazed her cheek. His fingers hooked under her chin, gently pulling her chin up to look into his eyes. Those beautiful grey eyes that were... Her breath caught in her throat. His eyes were swirling in a mesmerizing mixture of grey and silver like a tornado. *Swirling*? That couldn't be. It meant he was using his magic at that moment.

That was when she felt a warm gust of Wind against her back. One supported her upright and kept her from swaying in place. Something fluttered in her stomach but instantly halted as he slowly let go of her elbow. There was an urge to glance down at the movement, but his hand on her cheek kept her head from dipping down to look.

He was looking into her eyes, and she couldn't read a single thought as that tornado whirled in them. It wasn't lost on her that he used his magic to *help* her. But why?

His hand left her face next, but she could still feel the lingering warmth of it against her cheek. It felt like sunshine kissing her cheeks as she stepped outside. Her chest warmed at the thought of being outdoors. She loved that feeling and was craving it right now. Yes, it was a shame he had removed his hand.

"Are you okay?" he asked again.

Her eyes shuttered as the words registered with her and she realized she had silently wished for him to place his hand back on her face. That she had wanted him to touch her intimately. Her head shook, which caused her whole body to sway. The warm Wind caught her, but he grabbed her elbow once more for added support.

"Easy," he said softly. "No sudden movements, because you look like you're about to fall over."

Instinctively, her eyes closed at the pressure of her chest falling as she breathed out.

"Feeling better?" he asked. Eyes still closed, she slowly nodded. "Good." He removed his hand from her elbow. "What happened?"

Her eyes flew open. What *had* happened? She shook her head once, but only a small movement to prevent herself from swaying once more from the motion. "I don't know. I just felt so...weak all of a sudden."

Those pretty grey eyes searched her face. For what, she didn't know.

Finally, he shook his head and rolled his eyes in response. "Of course, you did. You're still healing. Bubble or not, your body is still adjusting and healing itself. You've probably done too much today. You should be in bed."

She grimaced at the thought of more bedrest. Although that made sense, she still didn't like it. She didn't like feeling weak. Didn't like feeling like she had to depend on anyone. Didn't like feeling as though she didn't have control over herself or her body. No, that would never happen again. Not now that she was finally free.

"Maybe you should sit down." He jerked his head in the direction of the door to her room, which was only a few feet to her right. She glanced from him to the door, and back at him. "Don't worry, I'm not inviting myself in. I have better things to do." Her eyes narrowed, and he winked. "I just think it might do you some good to rest."

"All I've been doing is resting," she countered.

He studied her for a moment again. "Considering everything you've been through, more rest is probably exactly what your body needs."

"Considering I don't give a damn what you think," her eyes narrowed at him, "I disrespectfully decline the command to rest."

His eyes narrowed right back at her. The pleasant demeanor he'd shown since her body first swayed was gone, replaced by a mask of anger. "See if I give a damn. It's your death wish." He shrugged and started to walk away.

"Wait!" she said before she could stop herself. He paused but didn't turn to face her. She stared at his back as she asked, "Is there anywhere here that I can take a walk?"

He still hadn't turned, but she could see his fingers flexing at his sides.

A minute went by before he said, "You almost just fell over, and now you want to walk." Not a question. "Are you *trying* to kill yourself?"

"I need to get out of here. I need some fresh air. I need to see something other than four walls and the assholes that mysteriously lurk in them, standing behind doors at night," she rambled.

"I wasn't lurking," he snapped as he looked at her over his shoulder, but he didn't deny the 'asshole' part. "You ran into me, remember?" She took a page out of his book and shrugged. He faced forward again for a minute before he responded, "Follow me." His voice was gruff once more.

She hadn't expected him to walk her anywhere. She just wanted to be alone, free. "What, you can't just point me in the direction? You're not going to lead me into a trap, are you?" she joked, and he finally turned to glance at her.

"If I was leading you into a trap, trust me when I say you would have no idea," he said with a straight face before he continued walking.

"Whatever." She rolled her eyes but followed him, because why would he help her from falling over just now if he was planning on leading her into a deadly trap? Why not let her fall and walk away? In fact, why not cut her throat when he had the knife against her, like he did minutes ago?

No, as much as he clearly despised her, he was keeping her alive for some reason. Something told her it wasn't because of his duty as a sentry. No, her instinct told her he needed her alive, and she was going to find out what for.

So, she trailed him but kept her distance, warily watching his every move. Just in case. She wasn't going to let herself become someone's prey again.

12

Evenia

Without being too obvious, she made note of each turn they took. When she attempted to escape her room earlier—before being so rudely intercepted by the lurking jerk now walking in front of her—she had every intention of making a mental map of the compounds in her head for her eventual escape plan. This place felt like a maze. So, she needed to know every exit and winding hall she might get lost in.

She wasn't planning on being a prisoner again.

They had turned down three hallways so far. Correction: four. Sothenas was turning down another hallway she'd never been down before, which was not at all shocking.

As they walked in silence, they passed one big, beige-colored wooden door after another. Each one had the same black metal X and black hinges along the lengths of the door. There were also floating Light-spelled torches blazing a foot above her eye level against the wall between every two doors that they passed by. The soft, warm lights illuminated the halls as they walked.

From her training growing up, she knew that Fire torches were effective, but Light torches were the safest option. They offered a flameless glow to brighten a space without the risk of setting a fire if flames caught on something. Unfortunately, these floating lanterns were dimmed and did little to light the way. However, they were effective enough for her to see her own feet moving and Kalland walking in front of her.

It was so quiet in the hall that all she could hear were her own footsteps. Sothenas walked so silently that if she wasn't looking at him as he took each step in front of her, she wouldn't have believed that he was even there. It was a mystery how he was so quick on his feet. Now, she also had to add "silent" to the mental list of notable features, joining descriptions such as "faster than should be allowed," "over six feet tall," and "annoying as fuck."

If it weren't for his ability to stand in the sunlight and his lack of dark, lifeless eyes, she would have wholeheartedly believed the male in front of her was a vampire. Then again, he could still be a natural-born vampire. She shook the thought away. He had magic. *Wind* magic, at that. As far as she knew, there was no way for a vampire to have access to Elemental magic.

She tried to mirror his silent steps as they walked. The effort only resulted in her footsteps sounding louder, tripping over her own feet, or thinking so hard about being quiet to the point that she fell behind. While she succeeded in quieting her steps, she was also focusing more on her speed and the pressure of her steps than actually keeping up with the elf.

Frustrated, she gave up as they took a sharp right down another hallway. This one was not quite as well-lit as the last few, with only a single floating torch blazing against the wall for every three doors they passed.

The lack of light casted shadows as they continued. Evenia's breath hitched in her throat as the shadows danced against the corners of the doorframes that lined the hallway. Before she knew what was happening, her whole body stilled. A tightness grew in her chest, suddenly heavy with a pressure she didn't understand, and her breathing became erratic.

Her body was completely still, and yet, her brain was running a mile a minute. Her mind wouldn't latch onto a single thought or the desperate attempt to calm herself.

Mentally, she was screaming. Physically, her only movements were the rapid rise and fall of her chest and her darting eyes, which were scanning back and forth from corner to corner, from shadow to shadow.

She was waiting for them to attack, waiting for them to make their move, so she might make hers. It was impossible to know what exactly that would be, but at that moment, her fight-or-flight instinct was leaning heavily toward flight. That realization only made her heart pound harder. Could she make it away this time?

What were they waiting for? Why weren't they striking? She hated this cat and mouse game—*hated* that *she* was the mouse. The hunted. The vulnerable. *The prey.*

Her brow perspired as her mouth closed to try to gain better control over her breathing. A failed attempt. It was no use, because she knew what was coming, and she couldn't stop it. Her eyes scanned the shadows even faster. It wouldn't be long now, and she didn't know what would happen when they did attack.

Just get it over with, already! If they weren't what did her in, the anticipation would surely give her a heart attack.

And then, it happened. A shadow quickly moved toward her. A *very* large shadow.

She mentally cursed herself for flinching, but she remained rooted to the spot. Frozen. Defenseless. Weak. She couldn't move, couldn't speak, couldn't even scream. It wasn't flight, but it wasn't quite fight, either.

Her eyes closed and she flinched as the warmth of a torch's glow left her face. It was blocked by the shadow that was suddenly hovering over her. It kept her from the light. They were always taking her from the light.

She jumped when she heard a voice. It was a calm voice. A normal voice. The voice of an elf with grey eyes. Not the voice of fear, of darkness, of death.

Her eyes flew open as she stumbled back. The heart pounding in her chest already felt like it might burst out of her with the fear she couldn't contain. The embarrassment now added to that combination made it even harder to get a breath down.

She clutched her chest, trying to place pressure on the pain to calm her heart and the constriction she felt there. Because the shadow standing directly in front of her was not an immediate threat. It was not harming her. Not gripping her. Not choking her. Not dragging her, hitting her, or hurting her.

No, the shadow shielding her from the warm torchlight was attached to a tall elf with beautiful grey eyes that held a shocking amount of genuine concern in them. The being in front of her was not threatening her, not hurting her, not attacking. It just was. And she was having a hard time reconciling that she was safe.

Except...she *was* safe here. Despite the fact that they had attacked each other earlier that night, she somehow knew she was safe with this grey-eyed elf. If nothing else, he didn't slit her throat when he had the chance. He'd also helped steady her when she momentarily lost her balance and her strength.

The shadow moved as the elf it was attached to began reaching out his hand. It halted in midair after she flinched at the movement.

"You're safe here," came a deep, calming voice.

Her eyes shuttered as her head slowly looked up in the direction of the voice. Her gaze met the face those concerned eyes belonged to, and he held her stare.

"You are safe," he repeated. "*No one* will hurt you here." She blinked slowly, watching the words his lips mouthed before they registered with her. "Not even me...for now," he said, mirroring her own threat before.

She blinked rapidly. Her nails dug into the fabric of her sweater while her hand clutched her chest harder. Her cheeks grew hot as humiliation flooded through her, overpowering the fear, inch by excruciating inch.

He slowly began trying to reach out to her again. Her eyes darted toward the movement, and her breath quickened again. She took an involuntary half step back and he retracted his hand once more.

"It's okay. It's just me."

She searched his face and still saw genuine concern and confusion, which only confused her more.

Get it together, Evenia! She mentally scolded herself. She took in a deep breath, held it for a few seconds, and then let it out.

He nodded at her in encouragement as he slowly began trying to reach out to her again. This time, she didn't flinch. Didn't move, but her eyes followed his every movement. Watching, waiting.

The beating in her chest stopped as his fingers grazed hers. Thankfully, she somehow managed to not jerk back this time. After a few seconds, he gently wrapped his fingers around her right hand. His hand was cool and solid against her clammy, trembling one. He squeezed once.

She looked down when he began pulling their joined hands toward him. When she looked up at him, she saw that he was watching her face, watching her reactions. She didn't know what she looked like at that moment or what he was seeing.

Her eyelashes shuttered when he slowly unfurled her right hand and started to bring her now-flattened palm against his chest. Before her hand could make contact with his chest, her body froze again, inches from him, and he stilled with her. Her eyes darted from their hands to his face several times, but his eyes never seemed to leave her face.

Finally, their eyes locked.

A small gasp escaped her when his thumb began gently forming small circles on the inside of her open palm. "*Trust me. Please,*" he Wind whispered to her.

Her lips parted, and she glanced from their hands to his face once more.

She swallowed but managed to muster enough strength to give him a small nod. And in doing so, she granted him permission to do whatever it was he was about to do. It was unclear where this small amount of trust came from. Perhaps because he was there the night she escaped from The Darkness, or that he didn't harm her earlier, despite having every right to after she attacked him.

For some reason, the ice around her heart melted just enough to let him in for this rare, brief moment. Whatever he was about to do, the beast looming just beneath the surface was prepared to kill him if he broke this small amount of trust she was placing in his hands. It was always prepared to kill, no matter how scared she was, or how hard she fought it.

He gently squeezed her hand again, and then brought her palm the rest of the way to his chest. Both his hands were now over hers, not quite squeezing them, but allowing enough pressure for her to feel his heart beating calmly beneath her palm.

"There's no one else here. It's just you and me." The words compelled her to look up at his face once more. "I think you're having a panic attack, but it's going to be okay." He gave her what she suspected was his best attempt at an encouraging nod.

Her breath caught in her throat and her eyes shuttered. Why was he being so nice to her? The man who pinned her down earlier that night was now protecting her against her own inner demons. But it wasn't *only* inner demons, was it? Her body shuddered involuntarily. This must be a trick.

"I'm going to hold you here..." He slowly placed his left hand on her right elbow, and then patted her hand resting on his chest with his right hand. "To ground you as you look around to see that it's just you and me here. Just you and me. No one else."

Her body stiffened and her heart began pounding once more. She didn't want to look. Didn't want to see the shadows again. All she wanted was to run and not look back. Like before. It worked before, and it would work now. It had to.

He must have sensed her hesitation because his thumb began brushing against the back of her hand once more. "You're safe. I mean it when I say I've got you. No one, and I mean *no one,* is going to hurt you here." His voice started off as kind and calm, but his tone became strikingly serious and deep by the end.

She studied his face once more, and seeing no apparent lies, she breathed in and out. In and out. Then, she gave him a slight nod. She'd try. She had to. It was the only way to fight back in this instance, and she'd be damned if she'd give in to the reaction to flee. Thanks to the healing bubble, she had the strength to fight this time, and she was going to, damn it.

A gentle squeeze again in encouragement. She stared at her hand on his muscled chest while trying to work up the courage to look around them. To look at the...shadows.

Not ready to look just yet, she opted for studying her hand. Or, at least, what she could see of it since it was covered by his own big, calloused hand. She focused on what was in front of her. What was happening at that moment.

What did she see? What was real?

Okay, Evenia. You've got this.

She worked up the courage to glance at the shadows that had been dancing against the wall to her left, and her heart stopped when she saw they were still there. Her eyes closed as the fear took over once more.

He flattened his right hand over hers and gently pulled her an inch closer to him with his left hand still at her elbow. Her body didn't resist this time, and he didn't speak. Just waited while she breathed through her emotions and fears.

One breath in, and back out. Then another. And another. It continued until her breathing was relatively under control. She opened her eyes again, and when she saw the shadows this time, her fear didn't consume her. The shadows hadn't inched closer to her since seeing them only a few moments before. Hadn't tried to attack. Hadn't made any move that proved they were anything but ordinary shadows from the torchlights.

Once she felt the truth in those words, she slowly looked to the shadows at the right of where they stood in the middle of the hall.

A wave of relief crashed over her so hard and her eyes started to sting. She was safe. She was actually *safe*.

His thumb resumed brushing her hand as he pulled her in closer to him. Her gaze hadn't left the entirely normal shadows to her right when she felt her breath turning to normal again. Those emotions were settling, and her thoughts were becoming clearer. So clear, in fact, that she realized he was acting as her anchor to reality while her mind was playing tricks on her.

She successfully peeled her eyes from the shadows and looked back at their joined hands on his chest. Her hand was barely visible behind his large one. So, she began to study what she could see. There were small and large scars on the back of his hand. A considerable amount of them, and she could only guess they were all from training and battles.

It occurred to her then that she didn't know how old he was, or just how much action he'd seen. There was no real way to tell how old an elf was, which aggravated her to no end. Well, most things about the elven aggravated her, if she was being honest. It likely didn't help that her biological father was one and he had stayed away...

Thoughts shifting, she found herself wondering why Kalland didn't have a healer tend to his scars and remove them. It was common for those who could afford it. Then again, he was a sentry. It would probably have been tedious and expensive to get every scar of his removed. How many marks in his skin did he have? Had he ever counted them before?

Her hand twitched under his as she felt the urge to run her fingers along the largest one.

All thoughts halted when his thumb gently brushed the back of her hand once more. Her eyes followed the movement. She could see more of her hand now. Hers also had a few scars, but not nearly as many.

At the age of ten, she started training with her uncle, much to her aunt's chagrin. Yes, her Aunt Siersha hated it, but Evenia had begged her Uncle Ensel to train her when she was ten after Lexnim Vonnil and her posse pushed Evenia down and spit on her during her walk home from school. She never understood why Lexnim hated her so, but she refused to be treated that way by anyone, let alone a bully. So, she begged her uncle to teach her how to protect herself.

"These moves are only to defend yourself with, Evenia," he'd said with a stern look. *"Don't go looking for a fight that isn't yours to win, and don't start one because of your own ego."*

She hadn't really understood what an ego was at the time, but she'd agreed to his warnings, anyway. There was a strong determination to get back at Lexnim Vonnil and her crowd. And she had.

Sothenas' moving thumb paused but continued after a minute. The movement brought her back to the present moment.

Right. Be focused on the here and now. So far, she had the sight down in grounding herself, like he'd suggested. But what was she feeling? She felt his calloused hand clutching hers to his chest. Felt his annoyingly muscular chest under her palm.

Her fingers twitched again with the desire to explore more of those muscles, and the pressure of his thumb brushing the back of her hand became stronger and slightly quicker. Her eyes shuttered briefly at the change of pace, and at the shocking display of intimacy in front of her. And even more so because of the one who was on the other end of that action.

Before she could even think about what she was doing, her right thumb jerked under the weight of his palm. The large, calloused hand stilled, holding hers firmer in place.

Her face filled with heat, confusion, and something else, as she realized that not being able to move her fingers was not what she wanted at that moment. So, she pushed against his palm with her thumb once more. Gently, and with only her thumb so as not to remove his whole hand.

He hesitated before relieving a small bit of the pressure on her hand so she could move her fingers freely under his. She wasted no time in mirroring the same movement by gently brushing her thumb against his chest.

His body stilled under her touch, prompting her to look up at his face. Their eyes locked for several seconds before she continued the movement. Neither of them looked away. Another challenge between them tonight, but this was a far different kind, and she didn't know what the stakes were. Even more surprising, she didn't care.

The elf she almost used her dagger against not long ago. Part of her still wanted to... But this new feeling—this desire to stay in the moment—overpowered it, and to her shock, she let it.

She continued watching his face as his gaze moved from her eyes to her lips, lingering there a moment. Her breath hitched under his stare, and her thumb paused for a brief second. Those grey eyes flew back up to hers.

Breathing in, she continued brushing her thumb against his chest. It suddenly became harder for her to keep the movement to a slow, gentle pace.

The heat grew more intensely throughout her body with that one look. The brushing of her thumb against his chest quickened a moment as he began moving his own thumb against the back of her hand once more. Then, his gaze dropped a little lower, to her jaw, and then slowly trailed down her neck. Down to her chest, which was rising and falling rapidly once more, but for a vastly different reason this time.

He glanced back and forth from her lips to her eyes several times. As if he was asking her a question. Whatever it was he was thinking about doing, she found that she did not want to object to it at that moment.

Finally, their eyes locked. After a few seconds, his darkened just a smidge with lust, and that heat she felt in her body was suddenly blazing hot in her core. With one look, her nails gripped his chest instinctively, and her toes curled in her boots. One look. That was all it took. Her body stepped an inch closer to him at the realization.

The hold on her tightened as he brought the palm of her right hand from his chest to his right cheek, and then turned his head to kiss her palm. It was a gentle kiss, and one he'd briefly closed his eyes for. Her lips parted, and she brought her other hand to his shoulder, closing the small gap between them.

Still holding her right hand to his cheek, he gently placed his other hand at the low of her back. They were so close now that she had to tilt her head back just to meet his gaze. This time, she was the one looking from his eyes to his lips several times. She knew exactly what she was asking…and what she hoped his answer would be.

Letting go of her palm on his face, he brought his hand to her cheek instead. He followed the line of her cheekbone, trailing down to her lips, where his fingers lingered a moment. Her lips parted even farther in response, and she felt her body growing hotter. He must have seen it or sensed it in her, because she suddenly felt his arousal against her front. Sheer proof that she wasn't imagining this. The touch only succeeded in heating her core more.

Without dropping his gaze, she brought her right hand from his cheek down to his chest. With her other hand draped around his shoulder, she leaned farther into him. Farther into the finger on her lip. Farther into his arousal against her. His bottom lip parted in response to the pressure, and she had the sudden urge to bite it. She was shocked to realize she would have if he wasn't so damn tall.

He brushed his finger against her lower lip, parting it more. Her chest brushed his as her breathing became erratic. The hand at her lower back drew her in even closer to him, until her chest was pushed flush against his.

In the same moment, with his thumb still on her lower lip, his fingers came to rest under her chin. He gently tipped her chin up, toward him. Toward his face, and toward his lips. And then, he stretched his fingers around the nape of her neck, gripping it firmly, but not enough to hurt her. His eyes were still full of lust, and she imagined her own must be mirroring his.

He paused, glancing from her eyes to her lips once again. This time, she knew what he was asking with the movement, and she nodded once in response. That was all he needed as his lips began to lower to hers.

13

Evenia

There was no denying she wanted it. Wanted *him*, by the heat she felt down at her core.

Inches away. His lips were inches away when a door opened down the hall and laughter filled the hallway. They both stilled. This time, when she looked up at him and their eyes locked, he looked upset. Angry, even.

Those grey eyes looked her up and down, and his lip curled up in disgust as he pushed away from her. Her body suddenly felt cold, and she stepped farther away from him, gasping for air. He was mumbling under his breath as she tried to regain her composure.

Had she really been about to kiss him?

She worked on controlling her breathing as she heard the voices coming closer toward them.

"Sothenas!" a slurred, yet amused voice called. Whoever it was, they were still several feet down the hall.

Kalland's body stiffened and his eyes closed. After a second or two, he released a long breath and turned to face the voice.

"Emil," Kalland said, nodding in response.

His body was shielding hers from the others. She attempted to shift to peek out behind him. He must have sensed it because he shifted to the right, shielding her view once more. Crossing her arms, she stared at the back of his head in response. She hoped he could feel that stare searing into him. Something told her he could. *Good.*

"Shocking to see you here. After all this time, you've finally come to join the party?" the voice—Emil—spoke once more.

Party? This was what the Mirchan sentries did with their free time? Was that why the sentries brought pretty dresses? She felt a twinge of anger forming. No way in hel was she going to a party and letting her guard down while the Mirchan sentries who killed her uncle were still out there.

"No, not tonight," Kalland responded.

He took a small step back, as if to shield her a bit more from whoever was in front of him. The act only angered her more. Was he being protective or possessive? Something told her it was the latter, and she wasn't going to stand for that. But being possessive over her as a woman or for what he really wanted from her was what she had yet to figure out.

"Ah, there's the usual response," came another voice. "That's more like—" The voice stopped, and she saw Kalland stiffen.

Suddenly, a broad-shouldered, completely tattooed beast of a male stepped into her line of sight down the hallway. He was still several feet in front of them, but he'd somehow sensed her there. He had blond hair tied back in a bun and a blond beard. His face wasn't cold, but it wasn't exactly welcoming, either.

Next to him, another elven male popped into view. This one, she knew. *Kaj.* He offered her a small smile and a half wave. "Hi, you."

In spite of the anger radiating off Kalland now, she smiled and waved back. "Hi, Kaj."

Kalland bristled at her response, which only made her smile grow.

"Who's that? Neladrie?" the first voice, Emil, asked.

"Do you really think I'd be waving so cheerfully at my sister, Numb Nuts?" Kaj snapped back.

Numb Nuts? Finally, she peered past Kalland down the hall to the other voice, curious if he was medically impaired. In all the years she'd helped her aunt in treating others, she'd never come across a male with numb nuts before. She imagined that made getting hit in the groin far more manageable, but also more dangerous if they had no idea what level of damage was being inflicted.

Curiosity got the best of her. Clearly knowing it, Kalland sighed before stepping aside, giving her a clear view of those in front of them.

"Well, I'll be damned. Is that who I think it is? How's it going, Cat Eyes?" came the first voice, laced with both desire and...disdain.

Evenia resisted the urge to brush her fingers over the black points winging out from her eyes like a cat's. Instead, she crossed her arms once more. There was an instant dislike for this Numb Nuts. She couldn't pinpoint why; it was just a feeling.

Her eyes narrowed in on him, scanning him to search for any visible reason for why she wouldn't like him. Or for why he would have a reason to look at her like that. Finding none, she came to stand beside Kalland, who didn't look down at her as she did. However, it didn't go unnoticed that he shifted his weight so that he was standing an inch closer to her.

"What are you two doing out this late?" Emil asked, eyebrows dancing. She didn't like his tone.

The tall male tattooed from head to toe reached them first. He glanced from Kalland to Evenia, his eyes quickly searching her up and down, before looking once more at Kalland. Kaj followed.

When the third male finally staggered their way, he greeted her in the same manner. Except, his gaze lingered longer, and whereas the tall male's gaze felt curious, Emil's left her with a dirty feeling. Her eyes narrowed at him as she saw Kalland's fist clench in the corner of her eye. No, she definitely wasn't going to like this guy.

"Look at her like that again, and you might find yourself one eye short," Kalland warned.

Numb Nuts' hand came to his chest in mock horror. "Are you threatening me, Sothenas? It's not smart to threaten a sentry under your command." He had the audacity to look at her again. She gritted her teeth, but the word "command" was not lost on her. This was one of *Kalland's* sentries.

"It's not me you have to worry about," Kalland's voice broke through the tension in her body. He was talking about *her*. She smirked as she saw Numb Nuts look her up and down once more.

"Is that so?" he asked. It took every bit of her self-control not to allow her claws to break through and unleash herself on him.

Kaj's laugh floated through the air before she could say something that might jeopardize her safety in Mircha. "Look at her face! She'd gut you right here and now if she could. Honestly, I wouldn't blame her. Nor would I stop her." Kaj's olive-toned hand slammed into the elf's shoulder, nearly knocking him over and earning a glaring look from the shorter elf. Neither of the two elves next to him seemed to notice.

Kaj waved that same hand toward the tall, tattooed male. "Have you met Alekze? Don't mind the silence. It's nothing personal; that's just him."

Alekze's face hadn't changed from a state of indifference at the interaction, but after a brief pause, he extended his arm toward her. She looked from his hand to his face, and then took his forearm in her hand. It was massive, her fingers not even wrapping all the way around. She took those brief seconds to study his tattoos. It was unclear where the tattoos started or ended on the elf. They trailed from his hand to his arm to his neck.

Looking up at his face, she offered him a smile in return. "Evenia."

She felt Kalland tense next to her as she spoke her name. The name she refused to tell him when he asked during their first interaction. But the secret was already out. So, there was no use in pretending these sentries didn't know who she was now.

"Pleasure," Alekze said as he let go. In the same way instinct told her she'd dislike the shorter elf, she knew she was going to like Alekze. Suddenly, she figured out why he looked familiar to her.

"You were there. The night I... That night," she said. He didn't speak, but he nodded his head once.

"So was I, if we're keeping track," Numb Nuts said in an annoyed tone.

She didn't reward his rudeness with so much as a glance, as she kept eye contact with the tall male in front of her. Alekze seemed to catch onto her act of defiance, and she noticed a twitch of his lips in response. She shrugged and smiled at him. Their exchange only seemed to piss the other elf off more.

"What the fuck is so funny?"

Her head snapped to him then. "I caution you to calm down, Mr. Numb Nuts, or else I'll follow through on Sothenas' promise." Her voice was calm, but internally, her anger was rising.

There was a pause before Alekze huffed a laugh. The first crack in his cool facade. Kaj doubled over in laughter, with one hand on his left knee and the other gripping his stomach. She saw Kalland crack a smile before he managed to don his calm composure once again. His face appeared emotionless, but his eyes were still full of amusement.

"Did you just call him *Mr.* Numb Nuts?" Kaj asked before howling with laughter again.

Alekze slapped his hand against Emil's shoulder, almost sending the elf to the floor with his strength.

She didn't understand why that was so funny. She glanced from Numb Nuts, to Kaj, to Alekze. "Is that not what you called him before?"

"Yeah, minus the niceties. Oh gods, Emil. You're never going to live this one down," Kaj said, wiping tears away from his eyes.

She couldn't help but smile with satisfaction as she saw the anger and disgust on Emil's face. Why did that satisfy her so? She didn't know, but she was quite happy to see him so upset.

"Whatever," he practically spit at her.

Kalland tensed next to her. All the amusement was gone from his eyes. Even Alekze's face dropped back to one of indifference as he seemed to become aware of the exchange. Kaj was the only one still oblivious to the growing tension in the air, just like he was at breakfast.

Emil opened his mouth as if to speak, but he was studying Kalland. Whatever he saw in Kalland seemed to make him think better of saying what it was he was about to, because he closed his mouth.

"What brings you two out here this late if not for the party?" Kaj asked, changing the subject.

The question took her by surprise, despite the fact that she had been expecting it only minutes before. She didn't look at Kalland as she responded, "I needed some fresh air. We," she waved her hand in Kalland's direction, "ran into each other, and he offered to show me the way outside."

Alekze looked from Evenia to Kalland, but it was Emil who responded first. "Is that so? Say, where were you taking her, Sothenas? This isn't exactly the direction of the courtyard." Emil's eyebrows raised one at a time as he looked at Kalland.

Her teeth gritted. She didn't like the male's insinuation, nor did she know what to make of the possibility of Kalland deceiving her and not actually taking her outside. Which begged the question: Where was he taking her?

She watched Kalland from the corner of her eye as his fist once again twitched. Did he possess the same urge she did to punch Emil in the face?

"There are more places for fresh air than the overcrowded courtyard. I didn't think our healing guest would take too kindly to being surrounded by prying eyes and curious tongues." His voice was deep and calm. She didn't know how his clear as day irritation hadn't broken through to his voice.

"Understood," Emil's voice was serious, even that of a sentry receiving a command. But then, he winked at Kalland. This time, it was Evenia's fist that clenched.

Alekze looked down at her fist, then made eye contact with her. His piercing icy blue eyes were full of curiosity. They were brimming with questions she could tell he wanted to ask but wouldn't. He glanced down and his lips twitched again. There was also a glint of respect in his eyes. Yes, she was going to like him.

"Let's go, *Mr.* Numb Nuts. We need to get you sobered up before your watch tonight." Kaj grinned as he spoke the new title.

Emil glowered at the other tattooed male, who clapped his hand to Emil's shoulder, nearly knocking him off balance again. Evenia found herself wondering if Alekze was doing it on purpose or if he really was that strong.

Emil was nursing his shoulder as his eyes burned holes into the back of Alekze's head, who had started walking. He nodded at Sothenas and Evenia as he passed.

"Good to see you, Evenia. I'm sure I'll be seeing you again soon," Kaj said, following Alekze.

"I look forward to it." She nodded, surprised to find herself speaking those words, and even more surprised to find she meant them.

He gave her a grin in response. "G'night, Kalland." Kaj nodded at Kalland as he gripped Emil's arm and dragged the drunk male past them and down the hall. Evenia didn't watch them as they passed, but it was hard not to hear Emil complain while walking by them.

"Hey, get off me!" There was a grunt and a scuffle as the males moved behind where Evenia and Kalland were standing.

Emil's next words came out as what she perceived to be a drunk man's version of whispering. "Sothenas has been such an ass since she got here. We should have just left the bitch of a half-breed to the Urur beasts. I'm sure the dark demon would have a blast getting his hands on her once more."

It wasn't the first time she'd received hate for being a duolvain, but it was his next words that made Evenia's blood turn to ice. "You know what? That's it... We should use her as bait. Maybe then Sothenas will finally go back to normal."

Before her lips had even fully parted, she felt a whoosh of Wind to her left. It was so strong that it blew her double braids up, causing them to slam into her back. She looked over to find there was nothing but air in the place where Kalland had been standing only seconds before.

Kaj swore under his breath behind her. Turning toward him, she saw she was alone with him and Alekze in the hall.

"Wh–where'd they go?" she asked, her eyes searching the newly abandoned hall still full of shadows, but not Sothenas' tall one.

Alekze turned to look at her and placed a finger over his lips in a silent "hush," then pointed to his left ear.

Taking the hint, she honed into her fae senses and listened. At first, she heard nothing. But then...

The blood in her veins turned cold just as Alekze's wide eyes met hers. He must have heard the same thing as her: a faint screaming coming from down the hall.

It was the sound of fear; of terror.

Alekze and Kaj both broke out into a run toward the sound, and she found herself following.

14

Kalland

K alland was going to kill Emil. He was going to do it, and he knew he wouldn't regret it for a second. It was about damn time someone shut the little fucker up.

Emil was already hanging by a thread as a sentry because of the way he treated the duolvain and non-elven they all worked with and helped on a daily basis. Not to mention his overall work ethic was worse than a distracted dog in a butcher shop.

There was a small part of Emil that respected Kalland enough to silence himself when he gave him a warning. Most of the time. However, his comments and general hatred for those that he deemed not "pure" was becoming more apparent and inexcusable. He was starting to voice his disgusting opinions more frequently, but not even Kalland was prepared for what all came out of his mouth.

The final straw was Emil's hatred for who and what Evenia was. It was so strong that he dared to openly hope The Darkness could get its filthy hands on her. Kalland saw firsthand what The Darkness was capable of—what it left in its wake. For Emil to wish that on anyone revealed his true nature.

That was what finally made Kalland snap. He wouldn't allow anyone with so much hatred in their heart to stay one of his sentries. It was either death—consequences be damned—or to make Emil so afraid that he quit of his own accord. Either way, good riddance.

These were the thoughts going through Kalland's head as he held a dangling Emil by the ankle. They were on a balcony in a random room Kalland had shoved them both into, and all he saw was red. He knew he was fast, but he might have broken his own personal record, for he had every intention of pummeling Emil to death in private. It was a happy accident that there was a conveniently open balcony in the empty room he had picked.

Since Emil's already thin thread was snapping, it was only fitting that he be dangling by that nearly nonexistent thread on a balcony three stories up. Kalland might have laughed at what he considered to be poetic justice if he weren't so godsdamn furious with the elf.

A screaming Emil pulled Kalland from his raging thoughts.

"What are you doing?" Emil shrieked.

I'm sure the dark demon would have a blast getting his hands on her once more. Emil's words rang through Kalland's head, and he released two fingers around Emil's ankle. The elf screamed again, but was still secured by Kalland's thumb, forefinger, and middle finger.

"What someone should have done a long time ago," Kalland said, his voice void of emotion.

We should use her as bait. Kalland released his middle finger as the words rang through his head, leaving only his thumb and his forefinger between the balcony and Emil's head meeting the ground below.

"I don't understand, Kal. It's me. It's Emil!" His voice grew shrill with each word that came out of his mouth, and that only got on Kalland's nerves more. "Someone, HELP!"

Kalland waved his hand, taking the air from Emil's screaming lungs. But it was too late.

Alekze, Kaj, and Evenia burst through the door, one by one. The room suddenly felt crowded.

"Kal, you don't want to do this. Just put him down," Kaj spoke first.

"Why, so he can threaten more people? So he can toss them to The Darkness himself? Fuck no. We all know he's outlived his usefulness here," Kalland seethed, not bothering to look behind him.

"That's not true, Kal. I mean...not really," came Kaj's poor attempt at an argument. He heard the male grunt behind him, likely after receiving an elbow from Alekze. "Just bring him back in, and we'll discuss this like civilized sentries."

"Bring him back in? There's no room in Mircha for a sentry who has as much hate in their heart as he does," Kalland said, while the rage boiled inside him.

He looked into the pleading eyes of the elf he shared a homeland with. How could it be that their homes and families were so close to one another, but their morals and beliefs couldn't be further apart? Yes, the line of Kalland's morals could be arguably blurred at times—present moment included—but at least he wasn't a dick to those who weren't fully elven. His behavior was inexcusable and unforgivable.

Kalland had tried to guide Emil as a young sentry—taking him under his wing. Unfortunately, Emil only grew smarter at hiding his cruelty, while he continued growing colder and harder in private. There was no helping someone who didn't want to change. Kalland could see that now.

"He's done here."

"You don't get to decide that." It was Evenia who spoke this time. She was defending the elf who wouldn't think twice about tossing her into the Urur Mountains, defenseless and alone. Why? "None of us do."

Turning around for the first time, he looked into her eyes and saw the unmistakable presence of fear in them. Was it fear for Emil's life or fear of him? Or both? His grip on Emil's ankle tightened for a brief second at the thought of her fearing him. But he caught himself, relaxing his body again. Who cared what this woman thought? Who cared how she felt about him?

His eyes shuttered a few times as he realized *he* cared. Kind of. Just a little. He mentally shook his head. When did that happen?

He racked his brain for the exact moment it started, but he couldn't figure it out. He felt something akin to caring and jealousy when he realized she told Kaj her name but not him. That she knew him and was *friendly* with him. And then, she introduced herself to Alekze without hesitation. Something she wouldn't do with him. Granted, he was livid during their first introduction, and she likely sensed it. No, he wasn't exactly kind to her then.

But those weren't the first moments he felt like he cared about her and what she thought. So, when was? What changed?

Thaïselle.

Yes, it had to be her. She made him mentally compare Evenia to her late daughter, Bryelin, whom Kalland knew. That must be it.

Now having an answer that satisfied him, he looked toward Emil, who wished death upon the woman before him. The same woman who was now fighting to save the ungrateful bastard's life.

"Sothenas..." her voice sounded again as she braved an inch toward him, with her delicate hand outstretched. As if she could simply take Emil from his hand. This feisty, little woman looked so determined and…sweet. Too damn sweet for this world. "Let him go," her soft voice came.

He smirked and met her gaze, those two-toned eyes shining sweetly at him with misplaced hope. "*As you wish, my sweet.*"

He almost cringed when the words he was thinking—about her sweet voice, her sweet lips, her sweet eyes—escaped his mouth.

Instead, he simply released his last two fingers, freeing himself of this burden once and for all. He turned and walked away, feeling 190 lbs lighter, and not an ounce of remorse in his bones as Emil's bloodcurdling screams filled the air.

15

Evenia

I t was official: This guy was fucking nuts.

One minute, Evenia watched as Sothenas held a male elf—someone she thought was his friend based on their interaction—over a three-story balcony, dangling him by his ankle. And the next minute, the grey-eyed elf dropped him, as if Emil was a piece of lint he couldn't be bothered with.

Without hesitation, Evenia ran past Kalland to the balcony railing. The screams from Emil rang in her ears. She reached out her right hand over the ivory stone railing and chanted the words that came to her from memory: "Imin'al tre'eanor clorestul!" She spoke the spell so quickly that she hoped she hadn't slurred the words.

The momentum from running hurled her body into the railing. She leaned over it—Kaj did the same to her left—just in time to see the branch of the large tree in front of them come to life. It extended itself and reached out, looking like the hand of Nature itself. It gripped the back of Emil's shirt just in time before he passed the first-story's windows, right to the lawn below.

The elf was abruptly pulled upright—his head whipping and bobbing from the force of the tree branch grabbing him. Evenia bit her bottom lip to try to keep a laugh from escaping. At the very least, she hoped it gave him a bad case of whiplash.

An elbow bumped into her shoulder. Looking to her left, Kaj's copper eyes were full of both relief and amusement as he nodded in approval. Halfway through the last nod, his chin jutted out toward the now-ascending Emil.

There was an unspoken question in the air. Her only response was a shrug. She wasn't about to let anyone die on her behalf, not even a drunk asshole.

"What the *fuck* is happening? What the fuck is this?" Emil's shrilling voice yelled from below.

Turning her head back over the railing, she saw the tree's hand ever-so-slowly raising Emil up to the balcony ledge. It was moving as quickly as honey sliding down a spoon.

"Just enjoy the ride, Randerjs," Kaj said with a laugh.

Evenia's gaze was averted from the ground as she felt Alekze's presence behind her right shoulder before he finally approached the railing. As bulky as he was, she was surprised she didn't hear him join her and Kaj. He was strangely stealthy for someone whose presence was hard to miss.

"*You're making a mistake,*" a deep Wind whisper came to her ears from behind. The tone sounded disappointed, almost resigned.

She whipped her head around to see Kalland standing in the doorway. His back was to them with his head held high, as if he held no regrets for the choice he made.

"*Then it is my mistake to make,*" she responded, standing taller. He only shook his head, and Evenia could have sworn her semi-pointed ears picked up on the word 'fools.' "*I thought you were supposed to be a peacekeeper,*" she spat out on the Wind.

He chuckled darkly but still didn't turn toward her. "*Was he not disturbing the peace?*"

"Whatever," she muttered under her breath. With eyes rolling in the back of her head, she suddenly remembered what he called her in the same moment he dropped Emil to his almost death. *My sweet.*

Before he could fully cross the threshold into the hall, she Wind whispered, "*And if you ever call me your anything again, I won't hesitate the next time my dagger's to your throat.*"

He paused in the doorway and stood still as a statue for several seconds. His shoulders moved in a silent laugh, and he walked calmly out the door as he whispered, "*There won't be a next time.*"

She was fuming. How could he harm someone for something said about her—when *he* didn't even like her—and then just walk away from it? As if nothing happened. As if he wasn't about to commit murder. The murder of one of his own, no less! Oh, she should have slit his throat when she had the chance earlier that night. What a mess he'd made since then. This could have all been prevented.

"Can this thing go any faster?" Emil sounded angry.

Turning back toward the scene below, she smirked. "Oh? Now you like that it's lifting you?" she taunted and watched as he bared his teeth at her. "I'm afraid not." She shrugged. "He's doing us a favor, and he has every right to go at the pace he wants to." Even if it was practically a snail's pace.

"It's just a fucking tree, you bitch. I could chop it down faster in my sleep than it's moving now," he said through gritted teeth.

The tree suddenly halted, leaving Emil dangling. The elf immediately started coughing and clawing at his throat, as if he was choking. Evenia narrowed her eyes and noticed the collar of his shirt was digging into his throat, constricting his air as the tree held him in place.

"H–help me! M–make it...go!" he yelled in-between coughs.

"It's not me you have to reason with," she called down to him. "Apologize to him, and maybe—*just maybe*—he'll continue saving your life. Then again...he may let go. Not the first time someone's dropped you tonight for your arrogance." She was surprised by her calm and confident tone.

A huge part of her hoped the tree wouldn't let go, putting his blood on her hands. At the same time, she couldn't blame him if he did drop the arrogant asshole.

Emil briefly sneered up at her before his eyes grew wide. His panic rose, as the pressure on his throat tightened more.

"I–I'm sorry! Sorry!" he said, waving his hands.

Everyone's breathing seemed to stall as they waited to see what the tree would do. Several seconds passed before the tree's branch hand started its slow ascent toward the balcony once more. Emil sucked in a giant breath, filling his lungs now that his throat was no longer constricted.

"Remind me never to piss you off," Alekze's deep voice sounded, and the words came out in a quiet tone. She peered over at him from the corner of her eye and smiled.

"Please, as if you'd say enough to piss her off," Kaj joked and Alekze rolled his eyes.

"He's right. You don't really seem to talk much," she said, smiling.

"I speak when I have something to say," his deep voice sounded. His gaze was back on the large tree before them. End of discussion.

"How did you do that, anyway?" Kaj asked.

Turning her head, she studied Kaj's face before deciding to answer. "I'm not sure how Gathéla does it—or the rest of the world, for that matter—but in Enacor, we have schools for witches to hone our skills."

Brows furrowed, he turned to face her.

"Once separated by type of witch—Elemental, Ceremonial, Seer…" She glanced away to not show her nerves as she conveniently left out the most powerful of all: the In-Between witch. "We learn from those before us. As a Light Elemental witch, I practiced healing remedies, studied the dos and don'ts, and learned spells…and more spells."

Her eyes focused on the giant tree in front of them. Its trunk was still rooted in place, and its branch "hand" was the only part of it moving.

"Asking the Element of Nature for help is a common practice among witches. She's our greatest resource, with Her creations spread everywhere in this world. Offering us food, shelter, and protection from the Elements, from the Gods…and from ourselves."

"You called it a 'he,'" Kaj said, nodding toward the tree. She nodded but kept her eyes on the tree in front of her. "How do you know?"

Silence filled the air for a moment, but the secret was already out and visibly moving in front of them. She sighed. "Have you ever heard of a dryad?"

In her peripheral vision, she saw Kaj's white teeth shining as he grinned. "Of course! They originated in Gathéla," he said, his tone full of pride.

"But have you ever seen one? Met one? Talked with one?" He shook his head. "They're intelligent. Wise. Thoughtful. Caring. They care for people more than we care for them, unfortunately. To the point where most have had to actually go into hiding to protect themselves from *us*. Few know they exist, and even fewer know what to look for when they find one."

"You're saying that a dryad lives in that tree?"

"Yes," she said softly. But then, she looked at him, her face grave. "And if you tell anyone, if you risk his life to simply boast about a dryad living in these lands during one of your *parties*…" she spat the word out like it was venom. "I will find you in the middle of the night, slit your throat, and ask him to toss your lifeless body far from here, never to be found."

She kept her face plain, but she felt a jolt of satisfaction as she saw his throat bob.

"I'll take it to my grave," he finally said.

Her gaze went to Alekze next to ensure he knew she was extending the fatal threat to him. She stared, waiting for him to promise the same as Kaj.

His piercing blue eyes finally looked down at her, holding her stare. It wasn't a challenge, but she didn't feel she could back off in this matter. His lips twitched under her gaze, as if amused. Whether he was amused because she would question his silence or because she dared to challenge him, she didn't know. Nor did she care.

The stare-off lasted several seconds before Kaj finally broke the silence. "Of all the people who gossip, this Glacul is the least of your worries."

Alekze physically bristled at the word *Glacul*—meaning Alekze was an Ice elf—but he kept his eyes on Evenia.

She believed what Kaj said, but she still didn't move until he gave her the slightest dip of his chin. That was enough. Silent assurance that he wouldn't tell a soul.

Her shoulders relaxed an inch. "A Glacul, huh?" she asked, resisting the urge to glance at his pointed ears exposed by his blond hair pulled back in a bun. "Is Akvar home for you?"

Alekze's nostrils flared. "Wersves...in Akvar," his gruff voice said. "But Akvar's *not* home." His eyes briefly met hers.

It was obvious he was uncomfortable with the topic, and she had the feeling it was a sore subject. Picking up on his apparent dislike for the Ice Realm of Akvar, she nodded and decided she wouldn't push the discussion further.

"How did you know there was a dryad in that tree? You can just sense it?" Kaj asked, pulling her attention back toward him as he changed the subject for them.

She nodded.

His hands flew up in irritation. "How? I'm a Huymi. A *Nature elf*! Why can't I sense him?" His gaze went to the dryad again.

Smiling, she looked back at the tree. "You have the Element of Nature in your elven blood, yes. However, since witches pull from Mother Nature—since we *have* to respect Her in order to gain access to Her resources—She sometimes grants us more than those who feel...let's say, entitled to Her." Her tone softened with that last bit, trying not to offend anyone.

She offered a small smile as Kaj's jaw dropped. He looked like he might protest her harsh words, but she intensified her stare, daring him to try. His mouth quickly closed again. No one could deny that every elven realm housed those who abused the power of the Element that flowed through their veins. She didn't suspect Kaj was one of those, but he clearly knew some who were like that since he decided not to object.

Satisfied that he wouldn't start an argument he couldn't win, she continued. "Witches have the ability to sense dryads, among other beings in Nature, because She allows us to. The dryad didn't have to answer my plea, but he did."

Evenia directed her attention back over the ledge. The tree's hand was finally bringing Emil up just under the third-story balcony, with his head peeking right under their feet.

Emil mumbled something that Evenia's ears couldn't pick up on. She bit back another laugh as she watched Emil's eyes grow wide when the tree halted once more. This time, the asshole only hovered a few seconds before the tree continued again. The dryad was toying with the elf, and she was enjoying his sense of humor. Honestly, she also respected him for not having dropped Emil yet.

The trio moved aside as the dryad raised Emil onto the balcony. When the large branch hand let go of him, Emil scrambled to the floor, practically kissing it.

Evenia looked back to the retreating tree hand. "Thank you..." she paused. "I don't know your name."

The branch briefly paused. Lifting once more, a leaf on a skinny twig attached to the tree limb gently brushed her cheek and in the warm breeze that accompanied it, Evenia heard the faintest whisper of a name touch the tips of her ears: "Jëka..."

Her hand slowly went to her ear—to where the whisper had touched—while the dryad completely pulled back from the building. She lowered her hand and smiled when the branch went back to its resting spot, unmoving once again.

"What. The. Fuck," came Emil's voice, to no one in particular. "What the *fuck?*" His voice grew louder as his wild eyes frantically looked around. They finally settled on Evenia. "*You,*" he said, his panic quickly being replaced by rage.

Her Light power brimming to the surface, she braced herself as he scrambled to his feet and charged toward her. Kaj and Alekze shifted to stand in front of her, blocking any attack. That irked her. She was perfectly capable of facing off against this sentry.

Emil laughed. "What, are you going to wolf out on me?" His hand waved at Alekze, who didn't take the bait, staying as still as a gargoyle.

Wolf out? Didn't Kaj say he was an Ice elf? She looked at the back of the blond elf, eyeing his *almost* perfectly pointed ears.

"And you? Are you going to throw some dirt in my face?" Emil asked condescendingly. Kaj looked uncertainly at Alekze and then back to Emil.

"Enough of this," Evenia said. Walking in between Kaj and Alekze, she forced them to step aside to make way for her. She felt Alekze's eyes on her but ignored the blond elf.

Raising her right hand, a blinding Light beamed at Emil, sending him to his knees. Blinding assholes was her favorite thing to do, apparently, because it gave her a great sense of joy to see him fall to his knees before her, suffering at her hands.

Alekze rushed forward, surprisingly agile for his muscular frame. She released the Light as the Ice elf pulled Emil's hands from his face to pin them behind his back.

Evenia's gaze was pulled to the door as someone approached it, halting in the threshold. She didn't recognize the male before them.

"Who the hel are you?" the stranger asked. Evenia looked to Alekze's still face, then to Kaj, who only shrugged. "What are you doing in my room?"

Oh, shit.

Alekze was somehow calm, but Kaj looked like a deer in headlights.

Evenia placed a barely visible Light shield over Emil's mouth, silencing him. He narrowed his eyes at her when he realized he couldn't speak, and she smirked in response.

"Um, our friend here had too much to drink tonight, and he just needed some fresh air. Your door was open, and we saw the balcony..." Kaj said. He patted Emil on the shoulder with one hand and with the other, he gestured to the balcony Emil was literally dropped from not long ago. "We'll be off now."

They all awkwardly shuffled out, while Emil put up a fight with each step. The stranger moved into the room and out of the doorway so they could pass.

"Sorry about that," she said, as they walked by. The male glowered at them, but said no more as he shut the door to his room, leaving them all in the hall.

"That was a close one," Kaj said, wiping his brow.

Evenia smiled at Kaj's words, but it faltered when she looked at Emil. She saw rage and pure hatred in those eyes. Why did he hate her so much? She wasn't the one who dropped him. In fact, she *saved* his sorry ass. But here he stood, looking like he wanted to tear her head from her shoulders. Why?

She pulled the Light shield from his mouth, hoping to get some clarity. Instead, her eyes were pulled from Emil's as Alekze shifted so that the angry elf faced the other end of the hallway. The tall, blond elf nodded once to Evenia, and then started dragging the kicking and screaming Emil down the hall. Kaj smiled at Evenia before he turned and followed Alekze.

Letting out a long breath, she exhaled the stresses of the night. On another exhale, she turned back toward the opposite end of the hall. Thankfully, she remembered every turn they made. Her feet followed the mental map she created of the halls that led back to the room she was sleeping in.

While she walked, a certain grey-eyed elf invaded her mind, and her anger grew with each step.

Her quarters were only a hall away when she picked up on the scent of rich bergamot and patchouli. *His* scent. She paused for a few seconds before following the scent to a door that reeked of him.

After fuming down the halls, while imagining everything she'd like to say to him, she now stood outside his door and was not at all sure what to say. Her mind went blank. As she cursed his very existence under her breath and turned to walk away, she heard muttering. Turning back to the door, she placed her ear to it without hesitation. There was no shame as she embraced her sudden nosy side.

The words he muttered were impossible to make out, but his heart was pounding. Was it stress? Regret? He couldn't be explaining the night's events to anyone because she didn't hear another voice or heartbeat in the room.

She stayed there for several seconds and debated on whether to walk away or open the door to make sure he wasn't about to launch himself from a balcony. What if he did jump? She wouldn't blame him after what he just did.

Shit. She couldn't walk away. Not until she knew she didn't save one asshole sentry just to lose another tonight.

Her knuckles rapped once, but there was no answer.

"Damn it, Sothenas. You're going to make me come in there, aren't you?"

Still, no answer. She swore under her breath before turning the knob and opening the door.

Looking around the dark room, she shuddered at the shadows that danced in the dim candlelight by a wooden desk. She ignored them the best she could and focused her eyes, searching. The dim candle only partially illuminated one corner of the big room, where a desk sat.

A voice suddenly pulled her focus to the opposite corner of the room. The side surrounded by darkness. She couldn't understand what he was saying.

"Sothenas?" she whispered normally.

No response.

There was a stinging in her palms as her fingers dug into them. Fucking hel, he was going to make her venture into the dark. At this point, he'd better be standing on the balcony railing. That would be the only thing that could calm her anger and make her fear dissipate. Well, maybe.

Taking a deep breath, she took a step. On an exhale, she took another step.

Another breath.

Another step.

Every muscle froze when movement in the corner of her eye caught her attention. A shadow. Her heart stopped. *Real or not real?*

Counting the seconds that passed, she sighed in relief when nothing happened.

Another step before she finally called forth her Light, creating a floating beam above her head to illuminate the room.

"Of course," she breathed out after she saw where he was.

The elf was lying in bed, drenched in sweat, and muttering nonsense. But he was safe. The voice she heard was only him talking in his sleep.

The male was shirtless, and by the looks of it, pantsless. The sheets were only half covering his legs, with one leg twisted within the sheets and the other not. She stared a little too long at the muscles on his arms, flexing under duress, and his abs. The abs...

She shook her head and silently cursed herself. *Get a fucking grip.* This was the elf who accused her of *commingling* with The Darkness. The elf who almost murdered his companion tonight. The elf who called her *his* sweet. Her lip curled in disgust just as her stomach flipped.

Sighing, she backed out of the room and silently closed the door behind her. He wasn't about to harm himself, like she was initially afraid of. However, he certainly deserved to be haunted by his dreams after what he did tonight.

As she turned and walked down the hall to her room, she only hoped her own nightmares wouldn't also plague her. Especially after the dancing shadows she just saw.

She closed her eyes and sighed. No, there was no use in hoping for that. He would come for her in her dreams, like he always did.

And there was nothing she could do to stop him.

There never was.

16

Evenia

The temperature in the room dropped when the strange presence entered.

"Who—" *Her voice was scratchy.* "Who are you?" *she managed to ask.*

The only response was silence.

It was impossible to see anything through the overpowering darkness, but she knew he was there. Something snaked across her ankle, and she recoiled at the touch.

"What do you want from me?" *she gritted through her teeth as anger seeped in. It wasn't quite powerful enough to overcome her fear yet, but it was there. She held onto it like the lifeline it was.*

Again, no response came. But the looming presence stepped closer.

Her teeth began chattering as the temperature in the room continued to drastically drop. She ground her teeth together to stop the movement and looked within herself to heat her body. There wasn't much strength to reach the full potential of her magic, but it was enough. Her muscles slowly relaxed as the heat worked its way through her bones.

Whatever was floating by her legs retreated after the lukewarm heat flowed through her.

"Interesting," *a voice hissed.*

One word, and suddenly, using her magic was a waste of energy. With one single word, it was as if she hadn't just heated her own body. Her blood felt like ice in her veins, and her skin crawled at the voice. The sound was...haunting.

"What do you want with me?" *Her eyes narrowed, searching for anything. Even with her catlike eyesight, she still couldn't see anything in the darkness surrounding her.*

"Get the spelled chains. I have something else in store for this one." *The way he said "this one" made her want to detach the jaw from his face with her teeth. As if he could read her thoughts, the thing chuckled.* "Oh, I think I'm going to enjoy this."

The fear turned to lead in her stomach. She swallowed down the taste of bile in the back of her throat.

"Let me out of here," *she growled.*

The entire room fell into silence. An eerie silence that caused even the sound of her heart to pause. It was like she was paralyzed. The sensation lasted a few seconds before she regained feeling of her senses, and her heart pounded once again.

He chuckled—a deep noise that sounded more irritated than amused. "The sun will fall a thousand times before I even consider letting you go, Little Dragonfly." *Sharp, white fangs suddenly flashed in the dark. Was that a smile?* "My luck has turned around with your presence."

What the fuck did that mean? And Little Dragonfly? What game was this thing playing? He spoke like he knew her, even calling her a pet name. Except, she didn't know who he was, or where she was, for that matter.

"Who the fuck are you?!" *she screamed, but it was useless. He had already left, the metal door slamming shut behind him. All that remained of him was the ice in her veins, remnants of shadows rubbing against her legs, and the sound of a skin-crawling laugh echoing off the walls.*

His voice boomed clearly through the door. She wasn't sure who he was speaking to. Frantically, she started clawing at the chains around her wrists in a desperate attempt to free herself because the message was loud and clear.

"This one is mine."

Waking, her eyes flew open to see the torchlight was out. Immersed in total darkness, Evenia immediately scrambled toward the head of the bed, tucking her knees into her chest. Her back pressed completely against the wall so that nothing could sneak up on her from behind. It also gave her the best vantage point while she scanned the room.

Something was wrong.

It was pitch-black, and she was forced to blink a few times before getting her bearings. There was the outline of the armoire and the poles of the four-post bed. The balcony doors were wide open, blowing in a chilling breeze through the night. It was cold. *Too* cold.

She shuddered. That icy feeling that prickled on her skin, with the type of cold that seeped straight into her bones, was all too familiar. The chill that never left.

Panic rose to her throat, threatening to cut off her air. The fear was almost paralyzing. *Almost*. Not just yet.

She was on high alert, but she was also at a disadvantage. With the absence of light, the shadows could live and breathe among her without her knowledge. They could slither around like snakes, waiting to strike when she was at her most vulnerable.

Her hand started to go toward her chest to apply weight onto the building pressure within, but she stopped with her hand midair. This wasn't her. This wasn't who she truly was. She was a fighter. A survivor. Not someone who cowered in corners, waiting for someone else to strike.

Instead, she slowly lowered her hand back to the bed and inched it under the pillow. Within seconds, she felt the hilt of the Nulhen dagger that she'd placed under it before falling asleep. Her hand wrapped around the hilt in a death grip as she took a deep, silent breath. A cloud of her breath floated in the air before her, demonstrating just how cold it was.

Yes, something was wrong.

Be with me, Mother, she silently sent out into the universe. She hoped her mother would hear it—wherever she was.

Right hand still gripping the dagger, Evenia lifted her left hand and called forth the Light. What she saw made her blood chill and her breath halt, but her hand instinctively tightened further around the dagger. Not in a show of strength, but from pure fear.

No. No, not again. Not again.

Panic seized her as the gust of a strong, cold breeze blew out her Light.

"Hello, Little Dragonfly."

17

Kalland

Kalland's eyes were closed as he felt the cool breeze of the Wind's kiss on his cheeks, through his hair, and gently embracing his arms and legs. Recognizing that feeling, he smiled. The only time he felt so wrapped up in the Wind's embrace was when he was flying.

He opened his eyes to find himself on Xelfrina's back. Her light grey wings were soaring as they flew high in the sky. It was always so peaceful and quiet up here. He shivered involuntarily. Cold, but peaceful.

"Help," a soft Wind whisper broke him from his peaceful flight. He looked around but saw no one else in the sky. He must have imagined it.

There was a sudden break in the clouds as they quickly departed to reveal a palace below. Kalland smiled at the sight and directed Xelfrina toward the palace gates. He was back home in the Wind Realm of Valoreg. The land of winged beasts, in all shapes and forms. Because weren't they all beasts in a way?

Good intentions or not, there was always something that made good people bad in the eyes of another. It only took one. No matter what you did, there would always be someone who disliked you and punished you for a good deed.

His first encounter with this harsh truth happened when he was fifteen years old, roaming the streets of Viarinen—one of the market towns of Valoreg—with his sister, Camaerin. They weren't supposed to be in the lower towns, or anywhere past the palace gates for that matter. They just couldn't resist exploring the town and all that the market had to offer.

Right before he reached the palace gates, Kalland suddenly found himself transported back to that town square. Back in that market, where the apples were bright green, the spices made his nose tingle, and the freshly baked bread made his stomach grumble. Right on cue, he grabbed his stomach as it let out a loud growl.

He chuckled and glanced down at his hand on his stomach. He did a double take when he realized his hand was...smaller. Younger. Looking at the rest of his body, he looked younger. It was himself from decades ago.

Glancing around, he saw everything was exactly as it had been that day. The voices sounded more muffled now than they had been then, and everyone seemed to be moving much faster this time.

He couldn't focus on any one thing, until he saw an alleyway. It was the clearest image so far out of all of the scenes before him. There was a young girl—not much younger than his sister—surrounded by three guys. She was trying to flee, but one was preventing her from running back toward the market with a hand on the wall of the building she was trapped against.

"Help!" He heard before seeing one of the guys cover her mouth with a disgusting palm.

Without even thinking, Kalland ran down that alleyway. The Wind magic in his bloodline made him much faster than most Wind elves. Because of this, he made it into the alleyway behind the first male in a matter of seconds.

Before the guy even knew of his presence, Kalland grabbed him by the neck and hauled the male against the stone wall adjacent to them. There was a loud crack, but he didn't look as he set his sights on the other two. Kalland paused because the males' faces were blurred, unclear.

Before he could think too hard on it, the training he'd been receiving since he was seven-years old immediately kicked in when the other two bandits rushed him.

There was a wooden crate at his feet. He used the toe of his boot to kick the crate into the air and sent a harsh gust of Wind to smash it into the direction of the male charging closest to him. It made contact but only forced the male to lose his balance.

The third one was too close for comfort now. Dropping to his knees, Kalland threw out his right leg, connecting it with the male's shins and sending him to the ground face first. Kalland grabbed one of the broken pieces of the wooden crate to use as a weapon and faced the second attacker. Without him noticing, the male had already risen and went after the girl again.

The girl screamed, grabbing Kalland's attention away from the male on the ground in front of him. Kalland turned toward her and saw her being dragged farther into the alley by the second male. Acting on instinct, Kalland used the Wind to create invisible shackles on the person on the ground before him, pinning him to the cobblestone.

"What the fuck are you, man?" *the guy grunted, fighting against the Wind shackles.*

"Shut up before I choke you with that invisible rope," *Kalland retorted. With wide eyes, the man wisely shut his mouth.*

Turning, Kalland threw the sharp wooden stake and chucked it at the male who was hauling the young girl away. Her screech filled the air as wood connected, sending the male face first into the ground with the wooden stake sticking out of his back.

The girl screamed bloody murder and threw up on the spot. At the same time, the third male suddenly raced past Kalland, somehow having broken free of the Wind shackles. He cursed at himself. He was still working on perfecting that part of his magic.

The male ran down the alley, past his dead friend—not even offering a single glance to his fallen comrade—and all the way around the corner. Kalland slowly stood and brushed himself off.

"Are you all right?" *he asked, gently.*

Eyes wide, she didn't speak. He started to walk over to the girl, but she took a step back. Her hands and lips were trembling. It was the pure terror in her eyes that made him stop in his tracks.

He forced himself to look around. To look at the male with a stake protruding out of his back, his blood pooling on the ground and staining the girl's skirts. A lump formed in his throat. Slowly, he turned to look at the first male he'd thrown when he entered the alleyway. Kalland's mouth parted as he realized the crack he'd heard before was a skull connecting to the wall, splitting it open.

"But I–I…" *He turned back to the woman, who was also surveying the carnage.* "You called for help. I was only trying to help," *he said, softly.*

She looked back at him, and finally nodded once. "Yo-you—" *She swallowed. Words failing her, she nodded again and stepped away from the pool of blood.*

The gratitude stopped there when half a dozen townsfolk came running into the alleyway, pitchforks and torches raised high. They all halted in their tracks, taking in the carnage before them.

An older woman with a stained white apron wrapped around her waist that had bread sticking out of one pocket was standing toward the front, mouth agape. She looked at Kalland with piercing eyes.

"What is the meaning of this?" *A finger pointed at him.* "Who are y—"

"Louburta," *a male's voice spoke calmly, interrupting her.*

The raging woman rolled her eyes before turning to the new voice. "Randallan, what have I told you about interrupting me when I'm—" *Suddenly, her gaze went into the direction of the male whose head had hit the wall. Louburta's face paled.*

"Les–Lesrat? Lesrat!" *Her hand flew to her chest.* "What is the meaning of this?!" *She whirled on Kalland, but then quickly ran to the man with the lifeless eyes lying on the ground.*

"He and two other bandits attacked this young girl," *Kalland said, but as he pointed in the direction of the girl he had saved, there was no one else in the alleyway. Panic set in.* "She was just right here!"

"Lies!" *Louburta's voice shouted.* "Murderer!" *She was cradling the male in her arms as she pointed at Kalland.* "You murdered my Lesrat!"

"No. No. NO! I swear. There was a girl here," *Kalland pleaded, looking around for help.*

"Lies! You're a liar and a murderer!" *Louburta's face was red with anger and pain.* "You're a beast, and you will pay for your crimes." *She faced the rest of the townspeople who had crowded the alleyway.* "You all saw what he did! Someone arrest him!"

"Help!"

Was that him who yelled out for help? He couldn't tell anymore as the townspeople closed in on him.

"No, please!" *Kalland felt his teenage self breaking all over again. This couldn't be real. This couldn't be happening again. But... It wasn't real. It couldn't be. Not really.*

He shut his eyes hard and imagined his life in Mircha. Imagined his warm bed. Imagined training with Nishara and Alekze at dawn. Imagined talking with Evenia again about The Darkness.

Yes, The Darkness.

Rage built in him as he thought about everything The Darkness took from him and so many. That *was real.*

Before he knew it, his eyes flew open. He blinked a few times, acclimating his sight to the dark and took in his room. *His* room. In Mircha. Not an alleyway in a dream warping a terrible memory. He wiped his brow and squeezed his hands over his eyes. That was the first day he'd killed someone.

You're a beast. The words rang in his head. Yes, he supposed he was. But he was a beast who'd saved a young girl's life.

"If given the chance, I would do it all over again without hesitation, godsdamn it," he breathed into the night.

He raked his hands through his hair and let out a deep breath. It fogged up in the air, which was surprising since it was supposed to be on the warmer side tonight. Brushing it off, his thoughts drifted back to the dream. Ever since that incident, nightmares always plagued him whenever he lost his temper.

Another big sigh escaped his lips as he threw the covers back to slip on a pair of sweats. *"Help."*

At the sound, Kalland stilled. Hands froze on his hips just after pulling the sweats up. Was he still dreaming?

He slowly looked around. The room was exactly the way he'd left it before falling asleep. As a test, he took his thumb and pointer finger and pinched his thigh through his sweats. *Ow!* Nope, definitely awake.

He honed in on his elven senses. There was…a scent. Lavender and…something else. A scent he knew well. A scent that was surprisingly strong in his room.

Eyes frantically searching, he didn't see the owner of that lovely scent. Didn't see two-toned eyes outlined in black wings. The corner of his lip tipped up. What was Evenia doing in his rooms? He'd have to ask her later. To his surprise, it was a conversation he was looking forward to having.

Remembering why he tapped into his heightened senses, he shook all thoughts of Evenia from his head. Honing into his elven hearing, he listened intently to the sounds around him. An owl was hooting outside. He rolled his eyes when he heard Kaj drunkenly telling another story he'd told a dozen times already.

His hearing took him farther. There were low voices in the hall. It was a seemingly innocent conversation about what weapon one of them would pick for training tomorrow. He pushed farther… There was Neladrie and Tasz—

Ew.

Trying to rid himself of the noises and mental image, he shook his head and focused his hearing in the other direction.

After a few seconds…

"No!"

Kalland shot to his feet. It was Evenia's voice. He yanked his chamber door open and raced down the hall toward her room. The closer he got, the lower the temperature dropped, causing his breath to fog up even more as he ran.

Now only feet away from the door, he stopped in his tracks when he saw shadows and dark mist seeping out from under it. His blood chilled and his stomach sank, but it was quickly replaced by his anger and rage.

Not. Again. *Never* again.

With a roar, Kalland advanced on the door. He didn't even shield his face as wooden pieces flew everywhere from him kicking the door in. Looking at the damage, he saw a wooden stake on the ground.

He paused for a split second. Yes, he would do it again. He would gladly do it again. He heard Evenia scream before he snatched the wood and rushed into the dark.

18

Kalland

W ooden stake in hand, Kalland stormed into utter darkness. Even the glow from the hall's floating Light torches was swallowed by the shadows filling the room. It was impossible to see anything, but he could hear Evenia's pounding heart.

"*It's me,*" he Wind whispered to make sure she knew who the stranger approaching was.

"*Ov–over here,*" she responded, and he followed her quavering voice to the edge of the bed that he and Thaïselle sat near only days before.

Evenia didn't make a sound as his left hand found her right one. There was no hesitation as she wrapped her fingers around his in a desperate crushing grip. An action clearly laced in fear.

"*Get ready...*" she Wind whispered to him. He gently squeezed her hand once in response. There was a shuffling sound before her other hand suddenly ignited Light, illuminating the space and all that was in it.

Kalland's blood chilled. The suddenly overwhelming sense of panic thawed the chill in his blood and in the room. With it came an uncomfortable heat that spread from his chest to his fingertips. His palms grew clammy.

What started off as the silhouette of a man grew and grew as the shadows poured off him, cascading like a silent, obsidian waterfall. They spread until the room was filled with nothing but wickedness that broke Evenia's Light, and a coldness that Kalland felt in his bones.

The Darkness.

Kalland was quickly brought out of his trance when Evenia's hand tightened around his after her Light was extinguished by the umbra.

Bastard.

The stake in his hand cracked under the pressure of his fist. Shaking off the splinters, he dropped the remaining pieces to the floor.

Summoning his Lightning to his fingertips, he aimed for the murky tendrils just as they tried to advance on Evenia. He cursed when the bolt missed, hitting the wall between the bathroom and the balcony doors. Instead, it briefly illuminated the outline of the ghastly figure. Kalland was taken aback at the sight. Underneath all those shadows was the outline of a man.

"The middle! Aim for the middle!" Evenia shouted at him, breaking him from his trance.

Lightning danced at his fingertips. He raised his hand and aimed for the middle of the shadows—right where the outline of a man appeared under the shine of his power mere seconds before.

The bolt hit its target, but the shadows merely separated under the blow. The Elemental Storms power hit and splintered a balcony column. Still, the shadows roared from the contact.

Kalland's face fell when the Night-filled waterfall suddenly retreated through the open balcony doors. The moonlight was now shining through the room and the temperature in the air rose to its normal level.

He dropped her hand and was halfway to the balcony when her voice stopped him. "Leave it," Evenia said in-between hyperventilating breaths.

What? She really expected him to just leave that fucking demon, letting him wreak havoc on the world? Kalland half turned to her, the balcony still in his peripheral vision.

"He wasn't real," she said before Kalland could snap at her. "He wasn't..." Her voice trailed off.

"What do you mean?" he nearly growled. "He was right there."

"It was only his shadows. His...powers. It wasn't actually him. You couldn't harm him if you tried."

"I don't know about that. He just screeched." Kalland's shoulders straightened, but he didn't make another move toward the balcony. Didn't move toward The Darkness's retreating form.

His eyes were on her, but she wasn't looking at him. Those beautiful eyes stared past him and at the balcony. She didn't even look scared anymore. Her gaze was...empty.

Sighing, she said, "Yes, you made contact, but nothing you do can inflict any real damage on his shadow self." Slowly, she looked down at her hands, turning them over to look at her palms. Her voice was quiet, calm. Almost *too* calm for someone who had just been attacked.

"No matter what you do to his shadows, I imagine it would only be like feeling a pinprick on skin for him. Or like stepping on a nail that didn't penetrate skin. Painful, but the initial sting will wear off after a minute or two."

Something in her tone made Kalland turn to face her fully now, his fists balled at his sides. "How do you know this?" His tone was dangerously deep.

Except, deep down, he could tell it was true.

Despite hitting and harming the shadowed form, he hadn't smelled that putrid smell seeping from it—a scent of Death itself. There was no mistaking that it wasn't really him. And after all these years of searching, he knew there was no way The Darkness was going to be that easy to get to. He'd been so close for the first time in years, and yet, not.

"Because he used to do that... Real but not real," Evenia's words came out in a whisper as she held herself tightly. Her voice sounded haunted, and although her gaze was averted, he saw tears in her eyes.

Kalland stiffened. His eyes studied her in a different light now. No, she was definitely still scared underneath the shell of numbness.

Rage filled him as he connected the dots of what she was saying. What "real but not real" could possibly mean when a shadow demon visited you in the night and you lived to tell the tale. It explained why she smelled so strongly of The Darkness when they first met. But it wasn't because she was *commingling* with him. Kalland was disgusted with himself for even suggesting such a thing.

Her voice sounded haunted because she *was* haunted by him. The laugh about hurting The Darkness wasn't to mock Kalland, but because she knew firsthand that it was futile to attempt to hurt his form like this. When...

"How many times?" His jaw clenched and his fists tightened, causing his knuckles to turn white.

Her eyes were once again on her palms in her lap. He followed her gaze and noticed a dagger resting close to her right thigh. Her lips parted slightly, but she paused. It looked as if she was trying to decide what to say, or whether to say it at all.

The more seconds that passed—the more he saw the conflict and pain and hurt on her face—the angrier he became.

After a long silence, she let out a deep sigh and closed her eyes. "It doesn't matter." She shook her head from side to side.

"It does to me."

Her eyes flew open and fell on him. His anger was brimming to the surface. He wanted to throw something. To kick something. To *kill* something. Anything. No, not just anything—The Darkness. Before he could stop himself, he let out a low growl, his anger getting the best of him.

Evenia flinched, and the reaction made him take two steps back.

Her head lifted at the sound of his retreating steps, "Sorry. Habit." Her apology over *his* loss of control only made him want to kill The Darkness even more.

Suddenly, his eyes widened as he took in the frightened woman before him. *Really* looked at her. The panic attack she'd had in the dark hall earlier that night. The terror he'd felt coming from her when he first entered her room. The reaction to his anger just now. The way she talked about…what happened to her.

His face grew hard again as the undeniable truth struck him: she wasn't working with The Darkness. She…was hurt by him. Just like his mother. Just like his father. Tonight proved that.

"You have *nothing* to be sorry for."

They locked eyes for several seconds. Finally, she looked away and slowly nodded her head once, but it didn't look like she believed his words.

Eager to get her mind away from her own inner Hel, while still trying to get as many answers as he could, he asked, "Who is he? *What* is he?"

"A nightmare come to life." Their eyes met then. Shaking her head, she said, "I don't know." Her lip quivered, but she raised her chin, and something inside Kalland broke. Was this how scared his mother had been? Did she even have the chance to *be* scared before—

He shifted so that both the balcony and Evenia were within his sights. With one last glance at the balcony doors, he waved his hand to quietly shut and lock them. He looked at Evenia again. One of her hands was now wrapped around her throat and the other pressed down on her chest.

How could he have ever thought this woman before him was capable of being like The Darkness? For fucks sake, she had the power of *Light* at her fingertips. Her very being was the opposite of darkness. But he was an asshole to her. He assumed the worst. Assumed that she would lead him to The Darkness. That she *worked* with The Darkness.

Instead, she was like his mother. Scared, vulnerable, a target. What would have happened if she hadn't called out for help tonight? If he hadn't heard her? Would he have walked in on her, torn limb by limb? Her beautiful, two-toned eyes lifeless, forever frozen in terror? Her—

Thunder grumbled.

"If that's you making all that noise, I suggest reining it in before you anger a lot of people here. Not even you can manipulate the entire sky to do your bidding without consequences."

His eyebrow raised. "No?" She had no idea what he was capable of.

"No," she huffed. "I knew you were arrogant, but you're outdoing yourself right now."

He smirked as a rain cloud silently formed above her head and unleashed on her, drop by drop.

She shrieked and placed a protective shield of Light over her, blocking out his rain. "Nice trick," she said, sticking her tongue out at him. He chuckled at the sight. What, was she ten years old?

"I could say the same for you," he said, gesturing to her shield as his rain cloud dissipated.

Her cheeks grew pink. "Oh, this? It's nothing."

"If you say so."

"I do." Her voice was stern.

He paused, an awkward silence growing. "Sorry about your door..." Kalland gestured toward the door he'd smashed to pieces. "I was in a bit of a hurry."

"Yeah, you got a little carried away there. It was a bit too heroic for my taste." She shrugged and his jaw dropped.

"I'll remember that next time," he joked but immediately regretted it when the words left his lips and he saw the amusement flee her eyes. *Shit. Wrong choice in words, Sothenas.* There wouldn't be a next time. He'd make sure of it.

He cleared his throat and was about to change the subject, but it was too late. Her eyes were blank, as if her mind was already too far away again.

"So, for the sake of your privacy..." He raised his voice a level with the last few words and succeeded in pulling her attention back to the present moment. "For the sake of your privacy, I hear there's now an empty room not far from mine. You can stay there until your door gets fixed."

He omitted the fact that the empty room used to be Emil's. The elf was officially kicked out of Mircha after Kalland reported the night's events to Andira. Of course, he received an earful for the stunt he pulled, but to his relief, she didn't deny that Emil needed to go. *Immediately*.

In the same conversation, she'd also told him a bit more about their guest. Evenia Raldir of Poultom, Enacor. More information than he'd been able to pry out of her. More information than he *deserved* to hear from her that day, really. He recognized that now.

"A room...next to yours?" He nodded. "That depends. Are you going to break that door down, too?"

"I'll use the window next time." He winked at her and she laughed.

"And risk messing up that pretty, little face of yours with shattering glass or by falling? I don't think so. You'd never be so reckless," her tone was light, teasing, even, as she removed her hands from her throat and chest.

"Who said anything about falling?" He smirked. "So, you think I have a pretty face, huh?"

"Oh, shut your face. It's just an expression." She threw a pillow and laughed when he caught it.

"Did you... Did you just try to start a pillow fight with me?" He still held the pillow at arm's length.

"No?" She slowly reached for another one before throwing it at his head.

He dropped the first and caught the second mere inches from his face. She only shrugged when he looked at her, laughter bubbling under his faux cool facade.

"I mean, what else does one do with this many decorative pillows?" She waved toward the weirdly large pile of pillows he could only assume were meant to be *on* the bed.

His toe tapped the first pillow he dropped to the floor. Second pillow in hand, he resisted the urge to retaliate, recognizing she was using humor to distract her mind.

"Luckily for you, I'm going to have to shelve that challenge for now." He tossed the pillow on the bed toward her feet. "So, how about that room change?"

"No, I'll be fine. It'll be fine." It was unclear if she was trying to convince him or herself.

"Do not grow proud on me now. Some things require an army to conquer. He is not something to be fought alone." He tried to keep his voice soft but wasn't sure if he succeeded. He might be stubborn and determined, but even he knew he needed help hunting The Darkness.

She shifted uncomfortably at his words, and he took a step back. "I'll be standing out in the doorway. Grab what you need, and I'll take you to the empty room."

Before he could turn, she pulled the covers off herself, with the lavender and black dagger in hand. His gaze lingered as she wore nothing but a light pink, nearly sheer nightgown.

"You forget, I have nothing of mine here." She stood up and walked toward the door, the dagger still in hand. "Not even this," her free hand waved over the nightgown, "is mine."

"Including that," he said, prying his eyes from her hips and pointing at the dagger. "That's Nishara's." She looked at the dagger, and her expression was one of... Was that guilt he saw? Did she steal it? His walls went up again, remembering this woman was a stranger. "Why do you have it?"

"She gave it to me," her voice was soft, almost distant. "I'm still not sure why she chose *this* dagger, but she said she wanted me to be able to protect myself. To feel safe here."

Kalland's shoulders relaxed an inch. That sounded like something Nishara would do, no matter how precious the dagger was to her. He nodded and gestured for Evenia to continue walking toward the door.

"That's a special dagger, you know. Treat it kindly. Or she just might use one of her other weapons on you, and take that one back." He winked at her and passed her in the hall, leading the way.

"I know how to treat a gift, Sothenas. I'm not a barbarian." He halted and turned toward her at the use of his surname. "What?" she asked. Those stunningly strange light blue eyes and half-green eye stared back at him.

He blinked a few times, cleared his mind in the process, and washed away the thoughts of those plump lips saying his name. He already almost kissed her once tonight, and he didn't need to repeat that mistake.

"Nothing," he said, gruffly. He turned back around and led her to what used to be Emil's room. "Here's your temporary room. I'll clear it with Housing tomorrow to make sure they don't come in and disturb you. If you need anything, my room's two doors down," he said, pointing to the left.

He didn't look at her as he walked away, not giving into temptation anymore tonight.

"Thank you, Sothenas," she said quietly. He almost stopped and turned. Almost walked straight up to her and asked her to say it again.

But he didn't. Instead, he just nodded and kept walking the two doors down to his own room. Before he opened the door, he waited to hear the click of hers shutting. To hear that she'd made it in there safely. He sighed in relief when she finally did.

However, the sound of a door opening further down the hall made him tense. Turning, he saw Tasz pop his head out of his room, with Neladrie following behind him.

"Everything okay?" she asked. "We thought we heard something."

Kalland glanced in the direction of the hall where Evenia's door now laid in shambles. Where The Darkness had been so close but so far away. Where he learned that Evenia was not a threat to him and his family here, but someone who was in danger and needed help. Where he learned a little of what The Darkness did to her... Was *still* doing to her.

With fists clenched, he looked back at his friends. Nodding, he said, "Everything's fine. Good night."

"Okay. Good night, Kal!" Smiling, Neladrie waved and went back into the room, but Tasz stood a moment longer, studying his friend.

"Don't worry, Tasz. We'll talk about it tomorrow," Kalland Wind whispered. Because he was aware the two would likely hear about Emil at the very least from Kaj in the morning.

However, Kalland would have to decide whether to tell everyone the whole truth or come up with a reason for why Evenia was now in the former sentry's room. What she revealed to him tonight was good intel on The Darkness' abilities, but that didn't mean it was his story to tell. What the beast did to her—how he still haunted her—was not for Kalland to share.

With a curt nod, Tasz turned back around, entered the room, and shut the door behind him.

Sighing, Kalland opened his door before quickly shutting it. He walked over to his mini bar and poured himself a shot. He held it in his hand, watching the candlelight bounce off the glass full of amber liquid before he downed it.

The Darkness attacked her tonight. Well, his shadows did. *Real but not real.* Whatever that meant. But he knew. Deep down, he knew. And it made him want to be the one to rip The Darkness to shreds.

His knuckles clenched and before he realized it, the glass shattered in his hand. He swore and grabbed a rag, pulling the glass pieces out of his hand so it could heal on its own, thanks to his elven blood.

A sigh of frustration escaped him because he also knew he couldn't deny that Evenia wasn't working with The Darkness. At least, not anymore. He didn't know what happened to her before—what brought her to this position—but he needed to acknowledge that now...The Darkness wanted her dead. The beast wanted it so badly that he was willing to expose himself here in Mircha.

Kalland wasn't about to let him get what he wanted. Let him get *her*.

He could tell there were secrets she was hiding. What they were, he didn't know, but he planned to find out. Innocent or not, she could still very well be his key to his parents' deaths, and he wasn't going to let her get away.

He also wasn't going to back down from The Darkness. Not ever. He hoped he'd show his face again, and when he did, Kalland would be waiting. Two doors down the hall. He could feel his Lightning zinging at his fingertips, ready to strike.

Yes, he'd be waiting, and he'd be ready.

19

Evenia

Evenia was awake before the sunrays beamed through the balcony doors. She reminded herself these were not the doors that unnaturally cold shadows appeared through just last night. Shadows that could take on a physical form and torment her in ways that haunted every corner of her mind.

She was grateful that last night did not become yet another memory sifting through her mind.

Letting the thought go, Evenia's eyes scanned the room. She felt strange waking up in yet another new room, especially when she was just getting used to the old one. This new space wasn't as big as the last one, but it was still bigger than her room back home in Poultom. Although, this one... There was something off about it, but she couldn't quite put her finger on what it was. It wasn't as bright or welcoming as the last, with the corners of the room seemingly too dark for the morning sun beaming through. A thought that had plagued her all night when sleep evaded her. Or rather, when she evaded sleep. Because not even her dreams were safe from him...

Still laying in bed, her body shuddered as the darkened corners appeared to move. No, it was just her imagination. It had to be, for she'd been observing the natural shadows since she first walked into the room and laid down.

Even after getting free of him, his shadows still haunted the corners of her mind, making her own head feel like a new sort of captive Hel.

She swore he never slept—this nightmare that plagued her dreams—because his presence was there every minute of every day. Somehow, he seemed to always know where she was since she came to Mircha. She could feel him watching her... Beyond the silhouette of a tree. The shadows left behind after a door was opened. Through the dark of night, when the rest of the world was asleep. In the darkest corners of her mind.

He was always there, watching, waiting. Sometimes he made his move, but other days... Other days, he seemed to delight in her squirming, in her growing fear, in her tortured soul. He consumed her terror, seeming to only grow stronger from it.

Evenia's fists balled at the thought. The truth was, he was a coward. A prick. A worthless piece of shit. And someday... Someday, she'd be the one feeding off his fear, delighting in making him squirm, and in being the one who plagued his nightmares. Someday, she wouldn't be the one who was preyed on.

She found a surprising amount of strength and comfort in that thought—no, in that *fact*—as she made her way to the door of the new room to change in the old one. While there was nothing of hers here, she did need to change out of the silk nightgown.

As soon as she pulled the door open, she heard a loud thump and a rather casual "Ouch."

She jumped at the sound and sudden movement of a body quickly coming toward her. When she looked down, she saw Kalland on his back on the ground, with a wooden chair underneath him.

"What the hel?" she asked. "What are you doing?"

"Just dropping by," he said in an irritated tone, as he pushed himself off the chair. With one hand wrapped around the back of the chair, he slowly sat up, the chair raising with him. "What does it look like I'm doing?" He glared at her as he straightened to his full height in the doorway.

"Did you...sleep here?" she asked, looking from the now upright chair to her door. He patted down his trousers and shrugged, the motion smoothing out his white shirt.

"I didn't need that." She straightened her shoulders, too, matching his energy. Sure, she might have called out for help last night, but she didn't need a permanent bodyguard...or someone spying on her.

He gave her a look that said he didn't care. But as if he just realized what she wore before him—still in her nightgown—his eyes suddenly trailed down her body. Down to the deep, lace V of the front of her nightgown. To the hem hitting her mid-thigh and her bare legs.

To her utter shock and annoyance, she felt a heat between her legs at the look in his eyes. Her cheeks pinked from the attention and the reaction to it.

"I know. I did it more for myself than for you," he said, pulling his eyes from her and stretching his back. She eyed him as he twisted, his back cracking, but he gave her nothing more.

"I don't know what that means," she said, sighing. "What is your thing with...you know who? Why did you help me last night, even though you clearly hate me?"

He stopped mid-stretch and fully faced her. She could see a whir of emotions flashing behind those eyes, but she couldn't identify a single one of those feelings before they were replaced by another. Those emotion-filled eyes trailed up and down her body, but not in such a flattering way this time. Still, he said nothing. Not a word.

Grabbing the chair again, he started walking toward his room.

"Don't pull that shit on me," she said, pulling the door shut and following him. "What is your deal with me? With...him? You owe me that much."

He suddenly whirled on her. He was inches from her face, practically seething at her words. "I owe you nothing." His voice sounded like venom.

Surprised, she blinked at the tone. Standing her ground, she stared him down and showed him she was unaffected by his temper.

After only a few seconds, his anger dissipated. He backed away but held her gaze. "Nothing," he repeated. Except, it didn't have the same bite to it as before. He turned and resumed walking toward his door.

"And yet, here you were, busting down my door and sleeping outside like a watchdog." He kept walking, despite the anger in her voice. "Whether you want to tell me or not, *fine*, but don't be an ass when *you* are the one with the issue. Not me."

With fists balled at her side, her short legs moved quickly to stroll past him. She was ready to ignore him for the rest of her time in Mircha, until she saw her family again... Well, whenever she would be ready for that.

Her breath halted when she heard his voice. It was so quiet that she almost missed it. *"He took everything from me."*

She stopped moving. Stopped breathing. Did she imagine that? Did he finally answer one of her questions? Did he finally reveal a secret? She didn't turn toward him for fear of not seeing him, only confirming she'd imagined it. Or, perhaps, making him regret the confession.

There was only one thing she could think to do. So, she closed her eyes and started to walk away from the onslaught of memories she couldn't seem to escape no matter what she did.

⁂

"Moln'shiar! How are you doing this morning?" Neladrie greeted Evenia, who was walking toward them in the chow hall.

Evenia stopped before the chair she sat in yesterday and looked over everyone. Neladrie seemed both eager and concerned. Nishara was just eager. Tasz mostly stared at his plate, but even he gave her more glances with those striking gold eyes than the day before.

Kaj wore a hat that covered his eyes from the sun beaming through the windows. Despite the extra protection the hat gave him, he still held his head, looking hungover. Even so, he stared up at Evenia, waiting for her response. They all seemed even more interested in her than when they thought she was just "Hillrider."

Did they know what happened in her room last night? She shifted uncomfortably on her feet. Just how quickly did word travel here?

She hesitated but finally sat down. An egg scramble and golden mug of coffee immediately appeared before her. A laugh of amazement at the magic in this place threatened to break her facade.

Looking up at everyone around her, she finally said, "I'm fine. How are you?"

Nishara scooted forward in her seat. "Oh, come now. Don't spare the details. We've heard it from Kaj, but we'd like to hear it from a credible source no—" Her eyes suddenly widened. "Ow, Kaj!" Nishara stopped to throw a fried potato from her tray at Kaj. "Kick me again and I'll break your leg."

"Ooh, I ascared," Kaj put his hands in the air, pretending to be afraid of the threat. Nishara only shook her head, probably thinking he was still too drunk to defend himself properly. Evenia could smell the liquor wafting off him.

"What she means to say is that we're curious about your version of the events last night. It's just..." Neladrie paused, drawing Evenia to glance away from her egg scramble to meet her gaze. "It's not every day a sentry gets kicked out of Mircha," her voice was low, so as not to draw attention from other tables.

The night's events. Right. When a sentry was almost killed by another. How was that only last night? And this was the first she heard of Emil getting kicked out of Mircha for what happened. If she hadn't run into Kalland right before this, she would have questioned if he'd been the one to get kicked out for his actions instead of Emil.

Evenia looked around at them all again, and Kaj shrugged in return. "A–ap–appar— Oh, for fuck's sake," he grunted in frustration. *Apparently*, he was drunker than she realized. "My version of what happened wasn't good enough for them." He waved his arm in the air toward the rest of the group and Evenia grinned at him.

"Well, if you told it while half-drunk, I can only imagine how riveting a story it was. I don't know many people who wouldn't love solving a riddle of words to figure out a story," she teased. Tasz suddenly choked on his drink, and a little chocolate milk spilled onto his hand at the movement. "Are you okay?" she asked.

He coughed twice before clearing his throat, commencing the coughs. "Yeah, I just didn't know you were funny," came his deep voice.

She grinned. "Neither did I."

"So? Spill." Nishara prompted as she started eating her fries again.

"Well, *someone* said something rude, which prompted another certain someone to hang him by his foot over a random balcony. We saved him. He's gone, I guess? End of story." Evenia shrugged, wanting to let it go.

"Don't forget about the talking tree." Kaj groaned while holding his head harder, as if talking only made things worse.

Evenia froze. He promised he wouldn't tell a soul about the dryad living on these lands. She glared at the Nature elf.

"What talking tree?" Neladrie asked, her tone full of curiosity.

"It appears someone may still be a little drunk," Evenia said.

Kajarnas whipped his head toward her as fast as he could in his current state. He looked like he was going to protest, but when he saw her face, he stopped himself.

"Oh, was that a dream?" He shrugged and winked at Evenia, whose shoulders relaxed half an inch.

"So, he's really gone?" Evenia asked Nishara, changing the subject. The Moon elf nodded. "Wow. I almost feel bad."

"Don't. He was a jackass," Tasz's deep voice sounded, but he didn't look up from his food.

"That, I won't disagree with. But...you don't feel any sympathy? He was your fellow sentry." Evenia observed all of their reactions.

"You have to understand..." Neladrie paused. "We've dealt with his hatred and cruelty for years. He was good at hiding that side of him from anyone who could actually do something about it, which made it hard to prove."

She sighed before continuing. "We were waiting for the moment he exposed himself to someone of authority, just enough that he'd damn himself. So, no, we don't feel bad. We feel relieved." She shrugged. "It sounds awful, but working with someone like that is taxing. He didn't deserve to wear the uniform."

Evenia slowly nodded. It struck her as odd that they could work with someone and then so easily toss him aside. However, she could imagine how tiring it must have been to work alongside someone like Emil. So, she tucked it in the back of her mind for a later time.

"Where's Kalland?" Nishara asked.

Evenia paused, her next bite hanging in mid-air. "I don't know," she said, shrugging.

"Huh, weird. I feel like he's been glued to you like a lost puppy recently."

Her eyes shot to Nishara's. "What makes you say that?"

Nishara blinked. "You mean, other than the fact that he *has* been following you around like a lost puppy?"

Evenia shook her head when Nishara cracked a smile. "He has been obnoxiously all in my space recently."

"Yeah, like a lingering fart that just won't go away, no matter how much distance you put between yourself and it." Everyone looked at Kaj, who was still holding his head in his hands, shielding the morning light from his eyes. When he finally noticed the silence, he peeked an inch under the brim of his hat. "What?"

Neladrie shook her head at her twin. "Nothing," she huffed.

Evenia laughed. "I'd love to see the look on Sothenas' face when you call him a lingering fart." Nishara joined in the laughter, and even Tasz cracked a small smile.

"I feel like it'll soften the blow coming from you," Kaj said, elbowing Evenia. She elbowed him right back, causing his head to fall from his hands. "Hey!"

She only shrugged and laughed.

Evenia smiled to herself as Kaj stuck his tongue out at her, because gods, it felt good to have a reason to laugh again.

20

Kalland

What a shit night, and the morning wasn't going much better so far. If Kalland was honest with himself, every night since that pretty blonde got here had been rough.

Kalland grabbed hold of his neck and stretched out the kink in it from sleeping in the chair outside of Evenia's door for three uneventful nights in a row. It hadn't been the least bit comfortable, but he held no regrets.

That first day after the attack, he'd informed Andira about an attempt on Evenia's life—excluding details that Evenia shared in confidence. Later that day, the door was fixed and she was now back in her room. Determined not to make that same embarrassing mistake of falling at her feet, he made sure to leave her door and the hall before she woke up the past two mornings.

And now she thought he hated her. That was what she said. And he hadn't had the courage to correct her. Although, maybe it was easier to let her think that. Let her hold onto her own anger.

He didn't know what he felt toward her, but he knew he wouldn't be able to forgive himself if something happened to her. And especially not after he saw the pain and fear from the trauma The Darkness inflicted on her after that night. It was lingering just below the surface if he'd only looked hard enough before.

Real but not real.

That was what she said when talking about The Darkness's shadows. His...illusion. Whatever the fuck that was.

His hands balled into fists at his sides as he walked back to his room to change. He'd hoped to work off the anger brewing inside of him at the training grounds, but it wasn't enough. He'd tried. Hand-to-hand combat with Alekze first, and then a rookie, who foolishly thought he stood a chance against Kalland. Ax throwing, in which Kaj had left during, after complaining about the sound making his hangover worse.

Not even Kalland's favorite—magic combat—was enough to dissipate the anger and bring him even a spark of joy or satisfaction when hitting his mark. Instead, it resulted in half the training grounds strewn about after a particularly nasty tornado Kalland lost control of. After cleaning up, he stormed off the grounds to change and find something else to occupy his mind.

He'd been trying to avoid her and the feelings he felt around her, but nothing had worked.

Every time he closed his eyes, he saw The Darkness's shadows.

Every time he released a bolt of lightning on a target in practice, he saw the distinct figure of a shadowed man from that night.

Every time he so much as blinked, he saw the fear in Evenia's eyes. The pure terror that showed at what she was seeing before her and the memories that undoubtedly flooded her mind from what those shadows did to her in the past.

Real but not real.

A familiar coppery scent made him loosen his fists and unclench his jaw. He felt his skin healing itself from the half-moon cuts in his palms that were bleeding only seconds before from the anger coming through in his grip. He forced himself to breathe in and out a few times, until the tension in his body released some. Not a lot, but enough that he kept his fists from balling up again while his hands healed.

He needed to get his mind off of it all. If the training grounds weren't enough, then a book might help. Or fresh air. Or...

Fucking nothing. He ran his hand through his hair and shook his head. Nothing was going to stop the rage except finding the fucker and banishing him back to the Underworld.

Kalland rounded another corner. He wasn't far from his room now. The plan was to bathe to clean off the sweat and dried blood—none of which was his—from being at the training grounds. Afterward, he would try to distract himself again. Something else.

Anything that might help. Like, maybe taking Xelfrina out for a ride. Something loosened in his chest a bit at the thought.

His gaze found a window to the right of him in the hall. It looked out not at the grounds below but at the clouds in the sky. A smile broke out on his face. There would be enough coverage for him to get some fresh air this morning.

With a new determination setting in, he faced forward again...only to be met with the one person who brought all his rage and anger and pain back. The sudden onset of emotions was unavoidable in her presence. It was impossible to escape the memories when she was near. Not after scenting The Darkness on her that first night in the mountains, and certainly not after what transpired three nights ago.

"Evenia Raldir," he whispered quietly enough for only his ears. He liked the sound of her name on his lips. The name she refused to tell him that first day. A beautiful name fitting for a beautiful woman.

Despite wearing a different outfit than the barely-there slip she wore when she walked away from him mornings ago, that nightgown was what flashed in his head. Then, he remembered what else had happened that morning. First, he fell at her feet. Then, he'd practically poured his heart out to her about what The Darkness did to him and his family. The memories made him cringe.

His eyes caught on the way the black sweater and leggings accentuated her curves. A braid of blonde hair was pulled to the side, trailing down her right shoulder. Strands of pale blonde hung loose in the front, framing her beautiful face.

Those stunning eyes hadn't noticed him yet. Could he turn and escape down the hall before she saw him? It was worth a sh—

Shit. He immediately stopped turning and felt his jaw tense again when she looked up from the other end of the hall and made eye contact. Those mesmerizing eyes were on him, and there was no turning back now. He took a deep breath and kept walking, despite how uncomfortable she suddenly looked, too.

Forty feet.

As he walked, his gaze caught on the ornate windowsill overlooking the clouds. Could he jump out the window?

Coward. Sighing, he pulled his gaze away and faced forward again. His eyes immediately landed back on Evenia.

Twenty feet.

Fuck, she was even prettier up close.

Too close for comfort now.

Her steps slowed and he shifted his feet in anticipation, but neither of them spoke. She refused to meet his stare, which gave him more time to appreciate the way the black attire sat on her body. The way she fiddled with her hands when she was nervous. A strand of hair fell into her eyes, and he had the urge to brush it away.

His throat bobbed when her eyes finally met his. Those stunning eyes, with the light blue and green in one. That mesmerizing combo. The way the blue warred with the green for the spot to claim her eye. It was curious. Unique. Enchanting.

Movement of her chin lifting broke the spell he was under, pulling his attention back to her. A shadow of a smile worked its way onto her face, but he refused to feel embarrassed for admiring her. So, he met her challenging stare and mirrored her expression, which seemed to fluster her.

Shifting on her feet, she asked, "Are you just going to stand there and stare all day, or is there something I can do for you?"

I can think of plenty you can do for me. He had to clamp his jaw shut before the words escaped his lips.

Fucking hel, this woman was going to drive him crazy. No, she already was.

Mentally shaking his head, he cleared his throat before asking, "How is your morning going?" His eyes involuntarily shut for a few seconds. *That* was the best he could do?

She blinked a few times before recovering from the question that seemed to have also caught her off guard. "It's...going okay." She paused. "How is your morning?"

His weight shifted from one foot to the other on the beige stone floor. "Fine, thanks," he grunted.

Where was he even going with this? He should just sidestep her and keep going on with his day. Undress. Bathe. Take Xelfrina out. Ask to borrow Thaïselle's copy of Vardith Viniusauf's most recent book. Train some more. And...whatever else would take his mind off of, well, *her.*

Her brows furrowed, catching his attention. Yes, this just might be the most awkward encounter he ever experienced.

"Okay, cool. I'm just," she gestured down the hall past him, "going to find..." That sweet voice trailed off and her hand quickly fell. Her eyes were wide as she looked at him and he couldn't help but notice a new purpose in her eyes. Could that be passion he saw?

"Oh, actually…" She bit her lip. "Do you know where the library is?" He opened his mouth to respond but she didn't give him the chance. "Well, no. No, of course you *know* where it is. What I mean is, could you point me in the right direction of the library?"

One side of his lips turned up at her rambling. She was beautiful and cute. How had he ever thought she could be working with The Darkness?

Smiling, he said, "I do know where it is, and I'm happy to show you where you can find it."

Her cheeks grew pink, seemingly flustered. "Oh, you don't have to show me." She was fidgeting with her hands once more.

"It's not a problem. I was sort of heading in that direction, anyway," he lied without hesitation, shocking even himself. What the hel was that about? After trying his best to avoid her for days, he suddenly found himself wanting to spend time with her.

It looked like he wasn't the only one feeling that way. Another smile crossed his face when he noticed her looking him up and down. Similarly to that first night in the hall. Was she checking him out?

"Enjoying the view?" he asked, stifling a laugh. Admittedly, he liked knowing she was doing exactly what he did when she first started walking down the hall.

She met his gaze and grinned. "Not exactly. I was just noting how you look like you should be heading to the bath, not the library."

Not expecting that, his mouth parted a few inches. He quickly recovered and grinned. "Astute observation, Raldir," he said. Her eyelashes fluttered at the use of her surname. "I suppose I could just point you in the direction of the library, instead."

Still smiling, she nodded at him. "I'd appreciate that." Her eyes met two healers dressed in cream robes walking down the hall just past them. They were not hiding the fact that they were staring at Kalland and Evenia. Evenia's dainty hand came up to rub her cheek, partially hiding her smile. "And I think everyone else would, too." She wrinkled her nose in a teasing manner.

Kalland scoffed. "No way. I don't smell—" When his arm came up, he caught a whiff of what training did to his body. "Oh, shit. Sorry."

The laugh that escaped Evenia's lips made Kalland's stomach flutter, and he didn't know what to do with that. He'd heard her laugh before, but this sound was different. Happier, lighter. Genuine. The joy on her face made her look like a light in this world, and he suddenly had the desire to give her more reasons to smile in the future.

He cleared his throat, suddenly very aware of the effect she had on him. Her body, her smile, her laugh. All of it. He needed to excuse himself before he acted on his urges.

Get away. The library, right.

Half turning his body, he pointed behind him. "If you take a left, go up two flights of stairs, and take two right turns, then you'll find the Mirchan library." He turned to fully face her again, the smile gone from his face.

"A left, two flights, two right turns. Easy enough. Thanks." She nodded once, the smile still on her face. Her lavender and vanilla scent wafted toward him as she started to walk away, her hips swaying.

Fuck, he needed to walk away. He needed to turn around. And he most definitely needed to stop staring.

When he was finally about to turn and start walking away, he froze as she stopped and turned toward him. Curiosity piqued, his eyebrow raised.

"Oh, and just for the record, I *was* enjoying the view."

21

Evenia

E venia didn't know what compelled her to admit that truth to him, but it was out there and there was no way to take it back now.

Since the night Kalland faced The Darkness' shadows with nothing but a wooden stake in one hand and the other gripping her hand in silent comfort, she'd found herself softening to him. It didn't help that each morning she woke over the past few days, she'd smelled his patchouli and bergamot scent lingering in the threshold of her now fixed door the moment she opened it. As if he'd been there only moments before, watching, waiting.

Plus, she *did* appreciate the view. The way his shirt sculpted his muscles around his arms, his abs, his shoulders... It was clear he had just come from working out, and that somehow made him even more attractive.

She could feel his stare on her back. So, she kept her spine straight and her hips fluid. Because...why not?

Before she could make it down the bright hall and away from Kalland, Alekze rounded the corner, heading straight for her. He was taller in the daylight, and his presence seemed to take up the whole walkway. However, it was the look on his face that made her steps falter.

"What is it?" Kalland's deep voice abruptly sounded by her left ear.

Startled, she jumped a little before recovering. She wasn't used to sudden appearance acts, or how he moved as if he was one with the Wind. The heat of his right arm brushed hers as he stood next to her, sending a tingling sensation throughout her body. To her surprise, she felt a bit of comfort knowing he was right there. When did that start? Her guard coming down a bit, sure. But comfort?

Confused, she blinked at the thought. Her eyes stayed closed for several seconds before opening again. It had to be a result of the events from a few nights ago. Granted, by the scent of him in her doorway each morning, she knew he was still sleeping outside her room. The knowledge of that helped her sleep better last night.

Alekze waited until he was only a few feet from them before responding, "General Elsvarin wants to see us."

"I'll go change and meet you there." Kalland nodded as he turned to walk in the opposite direction, leaving Evenia's side and taking his warmth with him.

Ignoring the sudden cold that she felt from his absence, Evenia nodded in greeting. Those piercing blue eyes seared into her as she advanced, walking just past him.

She only made it two feet before his next words made her stop in her tracks. "She wants to see *all three* of us," Alekze's deep voice sounded.

There was silence except for her pounding heart. She turned to face Alekze, but her gaze caught on Kalland's down the hall instead. All amusement from moments before was gone from his eyes. They were filled to the brim with such intensity and...curiosity. Hel, she was just as curious.

Why her?

"There's something else you're not saying," Kalland said, his eyes assessing Alekze now. Not a question, she realized.

Following the Wind elf's gaze, she found a bristling Alekze. She had to strain her neck to look up at his looming form. His nostrils flared and his pale hands flexed at his sides.

Suddenly, Kalland chuckled, pulling Evenia's gaze toward him again. Her eyes moved back and forth from a pissed-off Alekze to an amused Kalland. What was she missing?

"Fang's here," Kalland mused, "isn't she?" He grinned.

Alekze didn't speak, didn't move an inch, other than another flare of his nostrils. Was that how he communicated more than speech? Little muscle movements like that? How else would Kalland know what was wrong?

"Who's Fang?" Evenia finally asked after neither of them seemed to want to explain.

Kalland looked at her, as if remembering she was there—that she was accompanying them. His grin fell, and that look of curiosity was back.

"She's a vampire," he said, holding her stare. "And an assassin." There was a hint of amusement in his tone again, as if he was hoping to ruffle her feathers.

She looked to Alekze, who still stood stoic in front of her. "Is he telling the truth?" she asked.

Kalland laughed, but her eyes stayed on Alekze. Pale blue eyes silently met hers. Suddenly, she felt frozen to the spot, and it had nothing to do with the fact that he was an Ice elf. Without speaking, she could tell Alekze's bristled stare was silently answering, *Yes.*

She looked back at Kalland. "A vampire...assassin is here? Waiting to meet with," she looked from Kalland to Alekze and back again, "*us?*"

Kalland was smiling slightly as he turned and started walking away. Her feet began moving when Alekze's did, following Kalland's retreating form.

"It appears so. I'm not sure what she wants with you, but whatever you do," he glanced over his shoulder at her, his pearly whites shining, "don't stare at her fang."

She felt the blood rush from her face at the mental image of vampire fangs, but then her brows furrowed. "Fang? As in, a singular fang?" He nodded, with that grin still on his face. "How can a vampire have only *one* fang?" Even with her limited knowledge of them, she didn't think that was possible. Had the other been removed on purpose?

He shrugged nonchalantly. "She was born that way."

Her steps momentarily halted, while his words rang in her head. Vampires were either born or turned. Those who were born a vampire were referred to as natural vampires, or vampyrx. At least, that was what they were called in her textbooks in school.

The textbooks said that vampyrx were born human and lived normal, human lives. Their hearts would beat, blood pumped in their veins, and they had no thirst for blood. They could even mate and have children, creating future vampyrx. That was, until the day they died.

When a natural-born vampire's human lifespan ended, they would come back to life as a true vampyrx. The age they died as a human was the age they would look forevermore—their features never changing.

In death, their hearts no longer pumped and their blood no longer flowed. They had a newfound aversion to the sun and a craving for blood, with four fangs to feed. They were so dangerous once woken that they often unknowingly fed on their own loved ones in their newly undead, blood-thirsty state.

Once their human existence ended, they could live for thousands of years as a vampyrx. They also held the power to turn those of other species into the same creatures as them. Except, an undead creature who was created rather than born as such was simply called a vampire, having only two instead of four fangs.

From what Evenia was told, most fled to the mysterious Vampire Court in the depths of the Urur Mountains after their transition. Not much was known about it other than that it was a place where they could hide from the sunlight and those who hunted them down. However, she also heard rumors that some vampires could still be found in the dead of night throughout the continents of Avlonea.

That rumor was apparently true.

According to the book on mythical creatures from school, a natural vampire was mostly harmless when human but deadly once turned. Now, she was about to meet one. One who was also an *assassin*. As if being a vampyrx wasn't terrifying enough.

"A vampire assassin and a general want to meet with...me?" She couldn't even believe what she was saying. It felt like she was stuck in a weird dream. First, Kalland was being nice to her, and now, this.

She pinched her arm, hoping it would wake her. A groan almost escaped her lips when it didn't work.

The back of Kalland's head was visible once again as a deep laugh sounded from his broad chest.

"Welcome to Mircha, Raldir."

22

Evenia

"What is said in this room shall stay in this room." General Andira Elsvarin's gaze met each individual's in the room, including Evenia's.

"Yes, General," everyone else stated almost in unison.

Not sure what to do, Evenia simply nodded. Fingers twitched at her sides as she resisted the urge to wipe her hands on her leggings from her perspiring palms. She still didn't know what the hel was going on, or why the general requested to see *her*.

With the curtains drawn, the room was fairly dark. Only magically lit sconces and candles offered light. A poorly lit room meant it would be harder to see her sweating. She was thankful for that while she looked around at the others in the room.

Alekze stood in the corner with his arms crossed, looking like an angry bodyguard. The general stood behind her desk, her tall frame demanding attention. Evenia's gaze turned toward a sentry Andira was introducing her to.

"Esral, this is Evenia Raldir. Evenia, this is Esral Volard. They are a Nulhen shifter."

Evenia's ears perked up at the word "shifter." It was not common for fae to comfortably admit they were shifters, as it instantly put a target on their backs. Taking on the form of all sorts of animal species, from canines—not to be mistaken with the born or bitten werewolves—felines, bears, reptiles, and more, a shifter's animal form was twice the size of a normal animal.

This fact made shifters the number one target of trophy hunters for the past century. It was not unusual for shifters to go missing, never seen or heard from again, while their loved ones searched endlessly to no avail.

These days, shifters tended to hide their identities in their humanoid forms, pretending to either be a human, or even a fae of another species if they were a duolvain and could get away with it. The alternative was to seal their own fate—their own deaths. So, it was surprising and yet a great honor that Esral was comfortable with announcing the target that was being a shifter. Something Evenia wasn't willing to reciprocate.

"Nice to meet you," Evenia said as she studied the tall sentry. Their attire was not form-fitting but somehow still flattering on their tall, toned form. One half of their head was shaved, while the other side had pin-straight, raven-black hair laid to their collarbone.

Esral's eyes assessed Evenia, taking her in, and Evenia was doing the same in return. "Likewise." The shifter nodded their head in greeting before facing Andira once more. Esral gave off an air of professionalism to Evenia. This shifter before her was a sentry through and through. A loyal soldier to their general.

While it was not easy to see in the darkened corner, Evenia could feel the presence of another watching her. She had been avoiding looking or making eye contact with them—the one she assumed could only be Fang. However, she could no longer avoid the vampire assassin now that the general was making introductions.

"And this is our guest, M—" Andira started to say, but the vampire cut the general off.

"You can call me Fang. So, you're the new pet," she said, stepping forward. Rich with an undetectable accent, her voice was more pleasant than anything Evenia could have imagined for a vampire. The surprisingly sweet tone compelled Evenia to want to look Fang in the eye. She also didn't want to be rude. Offending a natural-born vampire was *not* on her list of things she wanted to do today. Although, talking to one at all was also not on her list.

Following the sound of the soft tone, Evenia looked up and tried to hide her surprise at the figure who emerged from the shadowed corner.

Fang's shining black hair fell to her collarbone and was cut shorter in the back, tapering down at the sides so that the ends were slightly longer in the front, framing her shoulder blades. Her bangs hung just above eyes that were pure black. Evenia suppressed a shudder as her feline eyesight took in the seemingly endless pits.

A voice broke her from a trance those obsidian eyes put her in. "She's not a pet, Fang," Kalland said. Evenia didn't look his way, but she didn't miss the warning note in his voice. Did he think Fang was a threat to her?

"Oh, no, I strongly disagree. Smells like a pet." Fang dipped closer and flared her nostrils for show. "And looks like a pet." A smile on her face, the vampyrx's eyes trailed Evenia's body up and down, lingering at her hips, and then once again at her chest. Evenia had to will her body to be still so that she didn't shift under the scrutinizing gaze. Trailing her gaze up to Evenia's face again, Fang winked at her.

"I'm *not* a pet," Evenia said. Despite Kalland's warning, Evenia didn't feel threatened by the vampyrx, but she wasn't about to be eyed like an afternoon snack. Especially without knowing what kind of snack the vampyrx had in mind.

"I quite like you," the vampyrx hummed. "We'll settle for describing you as the mysterious new stray, then," Fang chuckled, but she was suddenly eying her warily.

After a moment, the vampyrx leaned in closer to Evenia, who stood her ground. Fang whispered, "Tell me, Kitty, do they know what you are?" She practically purred the nickname as one of her pointed nails—more like a claw, really—traced Evenia's cheek.

Backing away from the touch, a shudder threatened to rack through her body from the deathly cold lingering on her cheek from Fang's touch.

As the cold dissipated, Evenia tensed while the question rang in her head. What was she talking about? Was she referring to Evenia being an In-Between witch? Or being a shifter? So far, she'd only told everyone she was a Light witch, but could Fang see through the lie? At this point, she figured everyone knew she was some form of a shifter, especially after Emil called her Cat Eyes.

She tried to keep her face neutral as the word "kitty" landed. Did Fang know? Could she sense it?

Those she'd met in Mircha might not know exactly what she was, but she had a strong feeling they knew she was a shifter. That theory was confirmed after Esral was casually introduced as one. For now, she told them what she was comfortable with. Told them as much as she could without putting herself in danger. That would have to be enough.

"Yes," Evenia finally said.

There was silence as Fang stared into Evenia's eyes with her own obsidian orbs. It felt like Fang was actually seeing past her face, past her bi-colored eyes, and straight into her soul. To her deepest, darkest secrets held there.

Beginning to sweat once more under the seemingly all-knowing stare, Evenia tried again. "They do."

Still, the vampyrx's stare did not relent. Despite her mind playing tricks on her as her fears exploded internally, Evenia remained physically unwavering under the vampyrx's stare.

"If you say so," Fang finally said, smiling. She held Evenia's gaze for a few seconds longer. It only gave Evenia more time to take in the vampyrx now that she wasn't in the corner.

Fang was slender and of average height, standing a foot shorter than Esral, but also only about half a foot taller than Evenia. The angled cut at her collarbone and her black eyes were a captivating contrast to her pale skin. She wore red-painted lips and skintight, black leathers, with an array of weapons belted to every limb. Including a—

Evenia's lips parted at the sight of a thick leather whip looped at Fang's waist. It wasn't just any whip, as it almost looked like a nailed hammer. Wait... Not nails. It looked as though it had *teeth* sewn on the end of it. *Fangs.*

A laugh pulled Evenia's gaze from the teeth-filled weapon. Fang smiled, with her singular top fang visible.

Don't. Stare. At. It. Evenia felt the blood drain from her face as she remembered Kalland's warning from the hallway.

"You like it?" Fang asked, popping her hip to gesture toward the strip of leather rolled up against her waistband. Evenia didn't know what to say. "I never go anywhere without it." She seemed cheerful. Bouncy. *Lively.* Not at all like the undead creatures of the Night Evenia read about and envisioned from the cautionary tales.

"It's...unique," Evenia managed to say, which elicited another laugh from the vampyrx.

"You have no idea how right you are." She was grinning so much that her singular fang dipped past her lower lip. Evenia heard Alekze shift, and Fang's eyes briefly glanced at him before returning to her. "You see..." She gripped the leather, pulling it toward her. "This little thing right here has a tooth from every," another quick glance at Alekze, "werewolf I've ever had the pleasure of killing."

Oh, shit.

A low growl sounded from the opposite corner that Alekze was in, and Fang rolled her eyes.

"Oh, settle down, wolfie," Fang said over her shoulder in Alekze's direction. Her tone was teasing—almost playful. Alekze didn't seem to share the same sentiment.

This vampyrx had killed werewolves, and she didn't seem to possess an ounce of remorse over it. And Alekze...was a werewolf. No wonder why he was so pissed earlier.

"Their venom is still laced in the fangs, despite having been removed from their corpses." Evenia felt her throat bob at the graphic image. "It comes in handy because werewolf venom is lethal to vampires."

Fang didn't seem to notice Evenia's eyes widened as she continued. "I mean, no one tells you that chasing the speed demons down gets boring real fast. Even when you're centuries older than them. So, I made this guy. Now, all it takes is one scratch from a werewolf fang, and..." She trailed her painted thumbnail along her pale throat in a slicing motion.

Speed demons? She was talking about killing other vampires. Confusion wrapped around Evenia's mind at the thought that Fang killed both werewolves and vampires. An equal-opportunity assassin. Was no one safe around her? Why was the vampyrx here? As a message? A warning?

Evenia glanced toward Andira, who only offered her a small smile in return. "Fang, here, is a guest in Mircha today," Andira said, motioning toward the vampire.

So, not a sentry... Was "guest" codeword for hired assassin?

Evenia's throat bobbed again at the thought. What if... What if Fang was on a mission right now?

The vampyrx leaned against the corner she was lurking in only moments before, but her gaze remained on Evenia. Curiosity etched her features, which Evenia found unsettling.

Pulling her gaze away again, Evenia focused on the last sentry in the room: Kalland Sothenas. He stood similarly to Alekze, though not quite as tall as the blonde Ice elf. His attention was focused on Andira. It was as if he never interjected in the conversation with Fang, as he stood seemingly unfazed by the topic and unaware of Evenia's casual observance of everyone, including him.

In the short time since being here, she somehow became familiar with that face. That chiseled chin sporting reddish-brown stubble in the still-early morning hours, those silver-grey eyes that looked like a storm was brewing in them, and those cheekbones that were so sharp she might cut her finger on them.

Her eyes shifted down to his broad shoulders and the hard-to-miss muscles that laid under his white, long-sleeve shirt. They were accentuated by his arms crossed tightly along his chest, which she also noticed earlier in the hall. It was possible she might have stared a second too long at his muscles then, just like she was now...

She caught on to the movement of his arms flexing further. Heat rose to her cheeks when her eyes quickly looked up to his face, where the right corner of his lip was turned upward into a slight smile. His gaze was now on hers, amused.

"*Eyes forward, Raldir,*" he Wind whispered to her. That shadow of a smile was still on his face.

Cheeks flushed at being caught, she turned her attention back toward Andira, who was standing and looking at some papers laid across her desk. Evenia looked down at the files, attempting to hone into her heightened sight. Her heart started pounding when she picked up on two words: "Urur" and "Missing."

Shit. What was her purpose for being called here?

Andira's gaze met hers. Evenia's heart momentarily stalled, before the general's gaze met everyone's in the room once more.

"As some of you in this room may already be aware of, we discovered an alarming number of shifters going missing in the border along Akvar and the Urur Mountains." Evenia's palms were sweating again. Why was she here? Did they know what she was? "Commander Sothenas, please explain further."

The elf shifted on his feet and his chin stood an inch higher. "After the arrival of our guests..."

Guests? Were they referring to her and Fang, or did they find someone else that night?

His gaze briefly shifted toward Evenia. "I joined in with some sentries to look into Missing Persons and Missing Fae matching Ms. Raldir's description in the hopes of finding her identity.

"In doing so, we discovered a pattern of shifters going missing throughout our continent of Lorathlor. A large number of disappearances over the past few years that have somehow gone under the radar."

Evenia shut her eyes and took a deep breath in. She wasn't surprised but she still hurt for the shifter victims and their families. Too many went missing and were killed simply for being born a shifter, and it was sickening thinking that so many went unnoticed. That this pattern took *years* to find.

She opened her eyes at the sound of Kalland's voice. "Some cases we only heard of because their families wrote to us for assistance. As it is, unfortunately, common for shifters to go missing in both continents of Avlonea, each missing shifter's case has either become a cold case or ended in their bodies turning up months later."

Kalland shifted, suddenly appearing uncomfortable, and Evenia could only guess it was because of the manner in which the shifters' bodies showed up in the end. He probably didn't want to say it in front of Esral and…her, because it was clear they knew Evenia was *something*. Otherwise, why would she be here?

So long as they didn't know what she was, she was fine with them knowing. She didn't like to face her other side, preferring to keep the beast buried deep, deep within…

Her mind wandered to the missing shifters. Were they lying dead in a ditch somewhere? Mutilated? Or, if The Darkness got his claws into them, then likely drained of blood and life for his twisted shifter experiments.

Kalland's eyes went to Esral's, who continued where he left off. "Commander Sothenas came to me with this information, and we decided to look into it further after Nishara and I spoke with the werewolf we found that night. The body we discovered was that of her husband."

Werewolf? What werewolf?

Evenia almost gasped as the sound of howls suddenly filled her mind from the night of her escape. She thought nothing of it at the time, as the biggest threat to her that night was The Darkness hunting her. It never occurred to her that she might run straight into the path of another predator. Getting away from the beast that followed her was all that mattered then.

The howls in her mind faded as Esral continued. "The couple shifted together on the full moon and separated to hunt. After she heard his whines and howls in pain, she said she ran to find him. As we know, she did not make it to him in time to see what happened. However, based on the scent and the scene, we are almost certain it was an act of murder committed by the one who calls himself The Darkness."

Evenia's fists clenched at her side. Why did he go after a werewolf when she was the target that night? She was the one who escaped. Who bested him. Her mind was whirring.

Her mouth parted. Could it be… Could it be that The Darkness protected her from the werewolf, who was out hunting? She shook the thought. *Fuck no.* More likely, he was angry she got away and took it out on the shifted form of that poor woman's husband while he hunted her down…

Evenia's eyes squeezed tightly at the thought of it being her fault for bringing The Darkness that direction.

"The crime scene from the full moon that night matched the murders of a few others we discovered in the files." Kalland cleared his throat and Evenia opened her eyes to see a muscle in his jaw tick.

He continued. "Some of the bodies discovered were in half-shifted forms, with one arm or leg being in their animal form and the rest in their humanoid form. Some, like the werewolf's, were in their animal form when discovered, and others were only recognized from Missing Fae reports and later identified by a family member."

Evenia's mind was stuck on the "half-shifted forms" detail. Flashes of memories were flooding through her head now. There was a dark room with a blinding, white light above her head. Voices she couldn't recognize but that never stopped. A cold table beneath her limp, weak form. Cold instruments splayed across her skin—some dull, some sharp. Feeling drowsy, drugged. The never-ending screaming. The searing pain. The desire to shift to protect herself, but somehow resisting it with every weakened fiber of her being.

Her heart started pounding again. There were so many moments full of so much pain. It was too much.

All breath in her body stalled at his voice sounding in her head: *This one's mine.*

23

Evenia

Heart pounding again, Evenia placed her right hand along her collarbone. She pressed down with slight pressure to remind herself she was no longer there, pulling herself back into the present moment. Back into Andira's office.

"Where'd you go just now, Kitty?" Fang's voice sounded. Besides the use of an unwanted pet name, Fang's tone was not teasing, not taunting. It sounded soft, but also twined with curiosity. As much as Evenia disliked the nickname—wanted to bare her teeth at it—the vampyrx's voice helped ground Evenia further.

The words were out before she could stop herself. "It's him. It's The Darkness." Everyone's eyes were on her now, waiting. "H–he seemed to be obsessed with the fact that I was a shifter, more so when he realized—"

She stopped. How much of her powers was she willing to tell them? They clearly knew she was a shifter, having brought her to this meeting, and then revealing Esral's secret of being one. But Evenia was no meager Light Elemental witch, like she pretended to be for her own safety.

No, she wasn't ready to tell anyone else this detail yet. Being a shifter already made her a target, but being an In-Between witch—one of two born each century who could control every Element—was a death sentence in this day and age.

It was how she was able to use Kalland's own Wind magic against him that night in the hall, and how she survived countless other encounters. But she had to pretend to only be in command of one Element—Light—even among her own coven, because those who feared her wanted to kill her and those who didn't wanted to wield her.

No, some secrets were better left untold.

She straightened her shoulders and continued. "That I am also a Light witch. He seemed intrigued by the fact that I was both a witch and a shifter, but he was focused on shifters there. I'm sorry, I don't remember much from being there, just bits and pieces. But he... *Someone* experimented on me. On us. There were more of us. More...shifters." Her head was suddenly filled with the ear-splitting screams of others.

Roars.

Growls.

Hisses.

Howls.

Screams.

The memories wouldn't stop. There were too many. Others pleading for their lives, begging for the torture to stop. So much pain. So much fear. All hours of the day. It never stopped. And they were still there. She got out, but they didn't.

How? Why? She still couldn't remember much from that night. Just the aftermath of her last session, lying on the cold, damp ground of her cell, when suddenly...a bright light. A nearly blinding light, but it wasn't painful. Just bright for her eyes that grew accustomed to the dark. Next thing she knew, she was running in the woods, escaping her shadows and his hold on her.

She still didn't understand what happened. Everything about being where she was—about being held captive—was still a blur for her. Only bits and pieces broke through the shield. Like now.

One after another, she could hear the other shifters crying, yelling, pleading for their lives. Including the voice of the shifter in the cell next to her. A voice she had to leave behind.

Her body swayed as she spiraled down a rabbit hole of panic, guilt, and fear. There was a pounding in her ears and her vision turned white as the panic built, pulling her further down. It seemed never-ending.

Suddenly, a warm gust of Wind brushed across her face, like the touch of a feather, and she felt a hand pushing down on top of hers that was still laid on her chest. Her eyes started blinking rapidly, trying to regain her vision.

Between the pressure of the hands on her chest—hers and another's—and the touch on her cheek, she was able to blink her way back into the present moment. As her vision cleared, she saw everyone standing in the same spots as before. There was Andira's concerned face. Esral seemed upset. Fang looked full of curiosity. Beyond Alekze's one raised eyebrow, he was still unreadable, and still in his same position.

Then, there was Kalland. His eyes were on hers. The storm in them was calming. Peaceful, even. She stared at that storm until her breathing evened out once more.

When she looked away, she registered that there was still pressure on her hand she had against her chest. When she looked down, she only saw her own hand there, despite the added pressure. The invisible fingers gently squeezed hers before releasing and disappearing into the air, back toward its Wind elf.

If she'd had the mental strength, she would have smiled. Instead, she just stared blankly at the floor while she worked to regain her composure, silently thanking him.

"When you say 'experimented,' what do you mean?" Fang asked, breaking Evenia from her thoughts.

This time, her eyes shuttered as she forced herself to blink away the onset of memories attempting to flood in. She mentally shoved them back into a box in her mind, nailing it down so it wouldn't emerge again right now. It could be dealt with another time. Just not now. Not when she wasn't alone.

Her cheeks grew pink after losing control of her mind. "As I said, I don't remember much. But it's almost like they would torture us until we shifted. I swear, they *wanted* us to shift. I don't know what happened when someone did. I don't know. I couldn't." She briefly paused, taking a breath.

"Once I realized what they wanted, I refused to do it—refused to give them the satisfaction. And it only confirmed my suspicions when I realized they hated me resisting. Hated me fighting back."

A sardonic chuckle escaped her lips as her top lip curled up in a half smile when a specific memory came into play. "And I'm especially not helpful because they started drugging me more during these sessions after I killed one of their...staff." She looked back up to Fang, whose lip twitched at that last detail, and then Evenia looked to Andira. "So, I don't know much."

Andira nodded, her deep brown eyes locked on Evenia's. "It appears you are even braver than we initially thought, Ms. Raldir."

Evenia tensed. "You mistake survival instincts for bravery, General."

Andira's eyes flashed before a shadow of a smile appeared on her face. "Who says they cannot be one and the same?"

Evenia shifted on her feet, not sure how to respond. Brave was not at all how she felt in those moments, or in the moments that followed. Her fists clenched at the reminder of the selfish act. She remembered wanting to help, wanting to fight back. But every time she did—

No, she couldn't think about it. About what happened in the dark. About what happened in the shadows. *Real but not real.* She stopped fighting for a reason. They all did.

"What's the plan?" Kalland asked, pulling the attention from Evenia and giving her a moment's reprieve from her own mind.

Again, she silently thanked the Wind elf, who was being surprisingly kind today after days of not talking. She looked at him again, seeing him in a slightly different light for the second time in that office.

"We need to investigate the kidnapping, and potential torture, of shifters. We need to know what's going on," Esral said, their voice edged with unease.

"And we will," Andira said. "I will assist Esral in sifting through Missing Fae reports from each realm to see what we may have missed and to determine whether a pattern can link them. But there is another manner of business we need to discuss here today." Andira looked up at them all. "We received word from General Noclaf in Nulhe that The Darkness's presence has made its way to their streets."

Evenia's body froze. She'd never been to the Moon Realm of Nulhe before, but she'd heard tales of its lavender skies and silver clouds. Tales of the joy that lived in those streets, and how the city as a whole was made of dreams itself. A little Afterlife in real life. She couldn't imagine The Darkness's presence tainting such a beautiful place.

"The Darkness is there? Now? Why are we just standing here?" Kalland's voice was rough, angry. He turned on his heel and started to reach for the door.

"Commander Sothenas," Andira's voice was laced with authority, a tone Evenia had not yet heard her use. Kalland stopped all movement, with his hand midair, still reaching for the door. An obedient sentry to his general. "I said his presence, not him." She motioned for him to stay.

His eyes flicked to Evenia's at the word "presence," and she had a feeling they were both remembering the shadows from the other night. She shifted on her feet, suddenly feeling even more uncomfortable. His eyes followed the movement and his nostrils flared.

He looked away from her and closed his eyes. Anger was etched in his brows. With his hand remaining still outstretched for several seconds, he finally sighed and returned to the spot he was standing before. "Apologies, General. Go on," his deep voice sounded.

"As I said, The Darkness's *presence* has been noted in the streets of Nulhe by way of a new group of his followers. This group appears to be carrying some sort of symbol to represent him. The message did not reveal much, not even what the symbol is." Her hands clasped in front of her.

"If it was not for General Noclaf knowing of our desire to find this monster, he would not have thought anything of it. Since he is aware, the Commander has requested your presence to investigate the matter further," she said, looking directly at Kalland.

"Of course. When do I leave?" he asked.

"In the morning."

Kalland nodded curtly as the fingers crossed at his hips in front of him started fidgeting relentlessly. Evenia's lip twitched at the sight. She could tell this male was not one for office life; he needed to be in the action, in the heat of it all. It was clear he was itching to get started.

"Furthermore," Evenia's eyes shot back up to Andira's, "we need to investigate these reports of shifters and werewolves going missing in the mountains of Urur and Akvar."

Fang stepped up from the shadowed corner. "I'll speak with my queen about what she's heard, and I'll report back," she said. Andira nodded, and Fang returned the gesture before leaning against the wall once more.

My queen. Could she be referring to the Vampire Queen rumored to reign somewhere deep in Urur? A dozen questions started whirring through Evenia's mind.

"Very well," Andira's voice pulled Evenia out of her thoughts. "We will also need someone to go to Akvar to investigate there."

Evenia swore her semi-pointed ears picked up on Alekze's heart stopping at the mention of the Ice Realm of Akvar.

"As it makes the most sense for Kalland to go to Nulhe to investigate the claims made there, we do need a connection who can get us inside the Palace of Akvar…unofficially. Someone who can get into Akvar, without causing too much attention or appearing as a threat."

Alekze tensed at Andira's words but nodded. "What do you need me to do?" he asked.

"I have sent a letter to Asrynna Vlasca," Andira said.

Alekze's nostrils flared, but he stayed completely still otherwise, like a statue.

"She is in contact with her connection in the palace, looking to secure both you and her a room within the palace's quarters. It is her belief that it will not take long to receive a proper invitation for an...off-duty visit. She said she will meet you on the road tomorrow, and I'm sure she will be in contact with you for where to meet."

Evenia couldn't help her eyes trailing down as Alekze's arms flexed, the veins now visible across his chest.

The sudden silence was deafening. As Evenia slowly looked from face to face, she noticed that the others suddenly found something far more interesting than this conversation. Esral was examining the hilt of their pristinely polished dagger still sheathed at their hip. Kalland was looking up, as if he was reading a coded message written in the ceiling.

Fang, on the other hand, was smiling, her pearly fang visible in her corner of the room. The vampyrx kept quiet, just seeming to enjoy the free entertainment. What that was, Evenia still hadn't figured out.

Only Andira was still enveloped in the conversation, and she was looking right at Alekze, who had gone stiff as a board. Sensing this was no longer a public conversation, Evenia glanced toward the velvet curtains drawn shut over the window, despite the velvet curtains being drawn. Still, she kept Andira and Alekze in her peripheral vision.

The Ice elf only stood there for several moments, the tension in the air palpable. "How should we proceed not as sentries of Mircha?" Alekze's voice finally sounded.

Andira paused, observing Alekze in his corner of the room. "I have received many letters from a one Irenz Fenrusil asking for her son, Alekzeyn Vesely, to have leave to visit home." Alekze's arms uncrossed as his fists balled at his sides. "She has requested many times that you be allowed to visit home for a certain ceremony in Akvar."

Evenia watched as Alekze's knuckles turned white.

Seemingly oblivious to his reaction, Andira continued. "It is Asrynna Vlasca's belief that this ceremony would give you the perfect reason for an invitation to Akvar's Court not as official Mirchan sentries."

The blond elf stood there for what felt like an eternity to Evenia, the tension in the air only growing with each passing second. It was written all over his face and all over his body that he hated this plan.

Curiosity almost got the best of her as she opened her mouth to ask who Asrynna Vlasca was and what ceremony they were referring to. Instead, she paused, realizing she was the only one left in the room who did not have a role.

Esral and Andira were going to look into cold cases in the archives here. Kalland was to go to Nulhe to investigate the "presence" reported there. Fang was going to find out more from her queen, whatever that meant. Alekze would go to Akvar to discreetly gain intel about the rumors spreading there.

But what was her purpose for being here? Why was she needed? Was it just to flaunt another shifter? Try to gain intel on *her*?

As her temper flared, she wanted to voice her questions, but there was an awkward silence in the room ever since the names Asrynna Vlasca and Irenz Fenrusil were mentioned. Evenia's eyes shifted from sentry to sentry, trying to understand what was happening.

When the uncomfortable silence continued without resolution as to if Alekze would investigate The Darkness' rumors, her irritation only grew.

Why were they all just standing here? The Darkness was still out there. He was still kidnapping shifters. He was still hurting others. She wasn't able to do anything to help the other shifters then, but she sure as shit could do something now. Especially with a Mirchan General on her side.

This was her chance to do something. To help. To fight back. And that was exactly what she was going to do.

"Send me."

24

Evenia

The words escaped her lips before she knew it. Her throat bobbed, but she only stood taller, surer in her conviction. This was what she wanted.

"Send me to Akvar," she repeated. If Alekze didn't want to go—because he looked like he would rather walk on glass barefoot than step foot in Akvar—then she would do it. It would be *her* that found out more about The Darkness, and she would help bring the beast down.

Kalland's head whipped toward her. "Are you mad?"

Temper still flaring, she suddenly remembered all the anger she felt toward the elf before he helped her. How he'd accused her of commingling with The Darkness. Treated her like the enemy. Seemed to blame her for something she had no knowledge of. Ignored her since learning her truth that night. How arrogant and controlling he was. It all came flooding back.

"No more than you, Sothenas," she spat out.

"Oh, this just got very interesting," Fang's amused voice came from the corner. "You're just full of surprises, aren't you, Kitty?"

Evenia ignored her—although shocked the pet name didn't bother her as much this time around—and faced Andira. She willed her voice to be calmer. "You want someone under the radar to get you into Akvar without bringing attention back to Mircha. How much more under the radar can you get than someone who isn't even a sentry?"

"Ms. Raldir has a point," Esral stated, a note of approval in their tone.

"She does," Andira said. "Traveling with one not associated with Mircha would certainly bring less attention to those who will recognize you as sentries." Andira's head slowly nodded, as if she was mulling over the idea.

"You can't seriously be considering this," Kalland said, his eyebrows pinched together. "If shifters are going missing, she won't be safe there. She's barely safe here!" His hand gestured at Evenia, whose head whipped toward him, silently willing him to stop before he revealed her nightmare secret.

His gaze met hers and his jaw clenched, but he pressed his lips together. A silent promise that he wouldn't tell her secret. Clearly, he wasn't happy about it. Thankfully, they were only met with shadows that night, but it meant The Darkness was still a threat, even here.

"What does that mean?" Esral asked, suddenly looking alert. A sentry through and through, indeed. But Evenia also couldn't blame the shifter for being concerned if another shifter in the area was in danger.

"Yes, what *does* that mean?" Fang asked, emerging from the shadows. Evenia could feel the vampyrx's dark, assessing eyes and the curiosity practically oozing from her.

"Nothing," Kalland sighed. "We just don't know for sure what danger she's in. So, how can we be certain she's safe? *Anywhere.*" Kalland glared at Evenia before returning his gaze to Andira. "This isn't a good idea."

"I'm perfectly capable of taking care of myself, Sothenas," Evenia said.

Before Kalland could respond, Andira said, "I actually believe that." There was amusement and respect laced in her words. "However, Commander Sothenas is right. It is dangerous for you to go to a place where shifters are going missing. Especially without formal training."

Evenia's shoulders sank an inch as she saw Kalland's chin smugly lift.

The bastard.

"However," Evenia's ears perked, "Nulhe should be perfectly safe for you. General Noclaf and Queen Selaria will make sure of it."

Queen Selaria? Evenia's jaw dropped. In Nulhe? The Moon Realm? The land of dreams? She always wanted to visit but never had a reason to take the long trek there. Now she did, and the Moon Queen would actually play a role in Evenia's safety.

"Yes, thank you," she managed to say. "Also, I do have formal training from my Uncle Ensel Raldir, who was a former sentry for Enacor." She internally winced at revealing that secret about her uncle. Andira only nodded. "What exactly do you need me to do?"

she asked, quickly changing the subject to get clarity on this upcoming and unexpected mission.

"We asked you here because we were curious if you knew why The Darkness would be targeting shifters and werewolves. Why is he kidnapping and killing them?" Andira's voice was calm, but her shoulders were tense. "What is in Nulhe that he might send his cronies there for?"

Evenia's breath stalled. "I don't know. I've asked myself *why* many times. I don't know what he would want with shifters, or why his...followers would be in Nulhe, but I'm willing to help however I can."

"Very well." Andira nodded, a hint of a smile on her face. "You'll leave in the morning with Commander Sothenas."

Evenia froze. *With* Kalland? She took a deep breath in and let it out as she slowly nodded.

Of course, just because she was going did not mean she was taking his place. They still needed a Mirchan sentry there to investigate and deliver the news back to Andira. Evenia would just help him stay under the radar and keep anyone from wondering why there was a commander from Mircha in Nulhe.

An awkward silence hung in the air before Kalland finally broke it. "We'll catch the demon, General."

The breath stalled in Evenia's lungs as one word rang in her head. Emil referred to The Darkness as a "dark demon," but the term hit differently this time.

"Demon?" she asked, looking from Kalland to Andira. Evenia's blood froze when she saw the looks on their faces.

Demons exist, and The Darkness is one, screamed in her head. There was no denying it by the looks she was receiving. How was that even possible?

"You mean to tell me that he's an *actual* demon? That they really exist?" She tried again, needing the words spoken aloud in confirmation to truly believe it.

The general cleared her throat. "Are you familiar with the tale of Nubilnar's Mad Queen?"

Evenia's face contorted in first shock then confusion. The Night Realm of Nubilnar on Druoania—the other continent of the world of Avlonea, far across the Cualisk Sea—was considered the sister country of the Moon Realm of Nulhe. Whereas Nulhe was said to be made of dreams, Nubilnar's story was a proper tale of nightmares told within her coven.

But that was all it was: a tale.

According to the story, Queen Lilene was Nubilnar's first queen. At first, the Night Realm, where the Element of Night—of shadows, of darkness—called home, was peaceful. You could look up at the moon in the night and appreciate the beauty of both. To look without fear. Without monsters lurking in the night.

But then, Queen Lilene took the Night from a peaceful dream to a terrifying nightmare rumored to still be experienced today.

Once a home to all kinds in the world of Avlonea, the Night Realm suddenly found itself home to creatures of the Underworld. With this shift in the realm's nature, so, too, changed Queen Lilene, who was given the nickname of Mad Queen for her actions.

It wasn't known why Nubilnar's beloved queen changed, but once she did, there was no stopping her. Monsters still roamed the land, scaring children all over even long after the queen's death.

That was it. That was all she knew. A ghost story to scare children about monsters roaming the lands, ready to snatch them from their beds. Why were they discussing it now? Wasn't it just a story?

Evenia's throat bobbed. "You're saying that the rumors about the Mad Queen and monsters from Nubilnar are not rumors?"

A faint chuckle came from the corner Fang was hidden in, while Andira simply nodded.

"Rumors?" Fang mused. "What are they teaching you in Enacor?"

Evenia started before turning toward the vampyrx. "Enacor is a human kingdom whose only exposure to magic—other than natives born there—is when others come to us for refuge. People come from all over both continents. So, we hear many stories about the other realms—about others in general—and I've learned to take it all with a grain of salt."

It was difficult to see in the natural shadows of the corner—a corner that felt as though it was wrapping Fang in a shadowed embrace. Despite not being able to see clearly into it, Evenia had the distinct feeling that Fang was smiling at her. Not in a way that was making fun of her, nor in a condescending way. Just...smiling.

Before the vampyrx could respond, the general's voice pulled Evenia's attention back toward the other end of the office. "Fang does make a good point. What do you know about Nubilnar and its...residents? Perhaps we can confirm or deny these rumors for you," Andira said encouragingly.

Facing the general once more, Evenia sighed. She didn't see the point in this, but she'd oblige the general. "There's this old ghost story that Nubilnar's first queen invited demons to live among her people. I don't know why. I don't know what kind of monsters. I don't even think it was true."

Andira held her stare. A look that flipped her stomach.

"But you're saying it is true? That...that The Darkness is one of these demons?" All Evenia's willpower was utilized to keep her voice from wavering as she spoke.

If she was being honest, she could feel the truth of the words in her bones. It suddenly all made sense. The shadows. His powers. His illusions. The way he could torment her in real life and in her nightmares.

Andira nodded. "Your ghost story is correct in that Queen Lilene—as you say—invited demons into her realm. The way in which she did so is what caused the most controversy."

The general straightened her spine. "Before I can go into further detail, I must first inform you that Queen Lilene was one of the first human witches ever born. She and her twin were born as what we now know to be three separate witch types in one. The twins held powers of all three witch types: Elemental witches—with Lilene possessing the power of the Night and her twin, Qelena, the Moon—along with being Seers and Ceremonial witches."

Evenia tried not to show her surprise when In-Between witches weren't mentioned. Not many sought to reveal that part of themselves. The mystery of those who came before her always intrigued her, but it appeared that today was not the day she'd get those answers.

Andira continued. "Legend tells us that the gods approached Lilene and Qelena. They were curious about the magic human sisters possessed. Especially with how their Elemental side was able to request access to the Elements without so much as a drop of elven blood. So, the gods decided to grant them a taste of a different kind of power to see what the mysterious twins were capable of."

Evenia knew some of this. From what she knew, Queen Qelena was both a witch and an elf, but she didn't know she was born a human. There wasn't much known about the Mad Queen. So, she had no idea Nubilnar's first queen was a Ceremonial witch, let alone three different types of witches in one. Or that she was Queen Qelena's twin. And now... Now, Andira was saying that the gods—*the actual fucking gods*—granted humans powers?

The general's voice pulled Evenia from her racing thoughts. "They turned the human twins into elves—with the magic of the Element of Night running through Lilene's blood and the Element of the Moon in Qelena's. This transition augmented their lifespan and abilities."

Eyes wide, Evenia curled her fists to resist fidgeting her fingers from nerves. How was that possible? How could humans become elves? The general must have her information wrong. It had to be a myth.

Before Evenia could fully process the concept, Andira continued. "In addition, the gods granted the twins lands of their own. Thus, the first two realms of our world were born: Nubilnar, the Night Realm, and Nulhe, the Moon Realm. Sister countries, in more ways than one.

"They placed one on each continent for balance. One on each continent as a sign of control. For while the gods granted these witches increased longevity and power, they did not want two extraordinary beings on the same lands, able to dominate the world."

Evenia's heart started racing. This was overwhelming. All of this information about them being twins, three types of witches, and born humans must have been left out of her history courses on witches. Evenia had the distinct feeling that the reasoning for the exclusion had everything to do with the truth behind *why* demons were in Nubilnar and not all in the Underworld. A truth that was about to be revealed to her...

"General," Fang's voice sang as she emerged slightly from her corner. All eyes turned to the vampire. "I don't mean to sound rude, but I am on a tight schedule. May I take over the storytelling for a quicker version?" Her tone was surprisingly polite and respectful at the same time.

"Certainly." Andira nodded and gestured her hand to the middle of the office before kindly responding, "You can speak on it better than I."

Fang stepped forward, careful to avoid the strip of sunlight peeking through the office curtains. Evenia shifted so that she was facing the vampyrx but still had every sentry present in her line of sight.

"I remember it like it was yesterday." Evenia's jaw dropped, and Fang chuckled. "Yes, Kitty, I was alive during the Mad Queen's reign. She was a good woman, up until she became drunk on her power."

Fang crossed her arms, and her eyes narrowed. "Queen Qelena leaned into her Elemental and Seer powers, using her abilities with the Moon and seeing the future to help her people. Whereas the Mad Queen more than embraced her Ceremonial side. Instead of using it for good, she became obsessed with the dark art of witchcraft. Specifically with summoning demons."

Evenia blanched. Dark Magic was strictly forbidden among witches. It was why Ceremonial witches were often monitored closely, with most receiving supervised positions within an assigned realm's palace walls.

"You were right in saying they were *invited* in." Fang nodded. "Yes, the queen was responsible for the demons invading her land. She *welcomed* it. They wreaked havoc on her realm—on her people. All for power." There was a bite in her tone.

Palms turning clammy, Evenia asked, "What does summoning demons have to do with being power hungry? Wouldn't letting them destroy her realm take away her power over the lands the gods granted her?" It just didn't make sense.

The corner of Fang's lip turned upward. "Because *Lilene*"—the name was spoken with such hatred, such venom—"wanted to create a new realm with a new species at the helm."

All the air left Evenia's lungs.

"She became threatened by the success of her sister's realm, which is why she tapped into the one power her sister ignored: their Ceremonial side. Lilene summoned and bedded a powerful demon, later giving birth to the first half-demon of our world—a prince of both the Underworld and Nubilnar."

Evenia suddenly felt sick. This couldn't be real. She hadn't heard so much as a single rumor about this.

Fang's voice turned dark, angry. "During one of her...rituals, a deal was struck. The demons would be allowed access to the above world, and in exchange, they would protect Nubilnar—their new home—where more half-demons have been created since.

"Except, they migrated from Nubilnar to the Gunda Mountains in Druoania. They eventually found their way to our continent somehow. Taking up residence all over, including in the mountains of Urur."

That was why there were so many patrols in Urur, wasn't it? Why everyone back home in Poultom was warned to never wander into the mountains because you never knew what you'd find there... As unbelievable as this story was, it was like puzzle pieces were clicking together in Evenia's mind.

The vampyrx's spine straightened an inch and she cleared her throat, as if attempting to regain her composure. "Once it started, it seemed like there was no way to stop her or them. At least, not without a war. And a war was exactly what the Mad Queen got." There was no mistaking the anger Fang felt around the topic.

Snarling, she continued. "The outcome of which brought about a treaty of living in harmony with these demons, so long as they strictly remained in Nubilnar and the mountains." The bitterness in her tone had returned, and Evenia had the distinct feeling that the history of Nubilnar and the history of Fang intertwined somehow...

Andira chimed in. "The war also resulted in the creation of the Peacekeeping Realm of Qeregroth on Nublinar's continent of Druoania," her gaze met Evenia's, "and the Peacekeeping Realm of Mircha on our continent of Lorathlor."

Evenia had to pick her jaw up off the floor as the words sank in. *That* was why the peacekeeping realms were created? Demons. Half-demons. Mad queens. War. All of the above. She never thought it could be possible, but the truth was far worse than the ghost story of lurking monsters she was frightened by as a child. Never in her life would she have imagined something like this to be real.

Uncle Ensel used to say there was always a price for peace. In this case, the price was forcing people all over the world to live with demons and their spawn. That didn't sound peaceful at all if you asked her. The urge to never step foot in Nubilnar—to never even gaze upon its lands—slammed into her like a ton of bricks.

The feeling only deepened when something else Fang said clicked in her mind. *A new species... More half-demons have been created since...*

Her feet spun her toward the general. "You think he's one of these half-demons?"

"It is possible." The general sighed. "No one is born with that much darkness in their being. We believe something must be influencing it," Andira said.

Holding in her frustration and waning patience, Evenia asked, "How do you know? There are plenty of dark and evil people out there." Gods knew she had witnessed enough to last a lifetime.

"A person isn't born evil, but a demon is."

Evenia wasn't convinced. She'd met some pretty shitty people over the years.

Andira held Evenia's stare for several seconds before continuing. "As for your question, it is hard to know whether The Darkness is a demon who has been summoned or a demon who has been created."

"What's the difference? Full or half, they're both demons." Evenia was still processing this information, but she couldn't understand how they were being so calm about it.

The general cleared her throat and straightened her shoulders. "The difference is one can only be banished back to the Underworld—free to be summoned once more—while the other can be vanquished for all eternity."

A full body shiver racked Evenia as the words hit her. If a demon could be banished, someone like Lilene—a Ceremonial witch—could re-summon it. But...if he was only a half-demon, then if they figured out how to kill him, he'd never be able to return. Never be able to hurt anyone else. Never be able to hunt or torment her again.

Fists curling at her sides, Evenia asked, "So, what do we do?"

"What we're doing now," Andira said with a small smile. "We go to Akvar and Nulhe to investigate these reports. We all do research and find out as much as we can on him—what exactly he is and what he's doing. Of course, it might not hurt to talk to a Ceremonial witch to be as prepared as possible."

Kalland shifted on his feet, his white-knuckled fists hanging at his sides. She felt his anger. Felt his urge to get moving—to get to Nulhe.

And whatever they all discovered, it'd better be enough to bring the demon down.

25

Evenia

T aking a look around at everyone in the office, the general cleared her throat and said, "I have occupied enough of your time as is."

Clasping her hands behind her back, she took a step toward her desk and the energy in the office suddenly shifted. "Sothenas, Vesely...Fang, you are all free to go. Volard, please wait outside for me," Andira said.

Kalland. Alekze. Fang. Esral.

No dismissal for Evenia. *Great.*

Alekze didn't waste any time before he high-tailed it out of there, still white-knuckled and grim-faced from the conversation before.

Fang followed. Her eyes lingered on Evenia, the curiosity still there. "Until next time, Kitty." She winked.

Evenia rolled her eyes, but she was surprised when a smile graced her own face. It quickly fell when Fang turned into a small bat, her leathery wings flying off into the hall.

Mouth agape, Evenia stood staring at the door for several seconds. Vampyrx could turn into bats. Okay... That was a new bit of information to tuck away in her limited knowledge on them.

Blinking, she regained her composure as she realized who hadn't moved yet.

Kalland met Evenia's eyes with his own that were full of anger and...something else she couldn't identify.

"General," he finally said with a curt nod before he walked out the door behind Fang and Esral, shutting it as he went.

Now, with just the general and herself standing there, the large office suddenly felt rather small. It felt like the walls were caving in on her as the anxiety built.

Was she ready to go on a mission to research a *real demon* with a *Mirchan sentry*? And not just any sentry, but Kalland. The grey-eyed elf who seemed to boil her blood with rage one moment and heat her body with desire the next. To go on a hunt of one monster of the Underworld in the company of one who served a different type of monster—Mircha. With arguably even worse to face...

Was she really ready for this? Ready to explore a lead that might take her straight to The Darkness? To risk exposure and possibly see him again?

No, that wouldn't happen. Because *he* wasn't in Nulhe. His followers were. With some sort of symbol. Andira wouldn't risk her safety otherwise. Right?

"There is another matter I wish to discuss privately with you." The general's voice broke Evenia from her thoughts. "We discovered a few details in our search for your identity." Swallowing air, Evenia slowly nodded as Andira continued. "According to the Missing Fae report your aunt filed, you went missing over six months ago."

The room was spinning. *Six months.* She was in that helhole for six months. Six months of—

"Do you remember how it happened?" Andira's voice was calm, hopeful.

Blinking, Evenia strained her memory to try to recall that night. She'd tried time after time to no avail. Again, nothing came to her. All that ever appeared when she tried to think of that night were the events that happened after—the memories of which now plagued her nightmares.

Sighing, she shook the dark, unhelpful memories from her mind. "No."

"It will come in time." Andira nodded. "And when it does, just know that the Vice President of Mircha and I will be here to learn all that we can about The Darkness. I've held him off for now, but he'll be eager to gain more intel on this being and his followers."

Evenia's throat bobbed. The Vice President of Mircha? Fucking hel. Could she just take up permanent residence in Nulhe, never returning back here?

Andira's voice broke Evenia from her thoughts. "You also mentioned your uncle was a sentry for Enacor." Not a question.

Evenia did her best to hold her features still at the mention of her uncle, but she didn't know if she succeeded. "Yes," she said, keeping her chin raised. Where was this going?

Andira nodded and looked down at some of the papers on her desk. She grabbed the corner of one folder, pulling it free from the pile. "He passed away ten years ago." Again, not a question.

Evenia tensed. "How do you know that?"

Andira held a folder in her hands as she met Evenia's stare. "The name 'Ensel Raldir' appeared when we did a background check on your family." That made sense. The tension in her shoulders released half an inch, but she was still on alert. "As did his death."

Shit. She was fighting the tears threatening to spill. Whether from anger or grief, she didn't know. Likely both.

"I thought you might want to know that we caught the men who murdered your uncle, with the exception of one individual involved."

Evenia's eyes shot to the folder in the general's hands. "The sentries?"

Andira's face contorted. Her brows scrunched together and her lips pursed.

"No, the imposters. They are part of a group of humans who murdered and stole from many of our fine sentries over the past decade. They kill our people, steal their uniforms to gain the trust of others, and defile our name and reputation with their diabolical acts." Her voice rose in anger. It was the first time Evenia had seen the general lose control of her emotions and resolve.

Evenia gasped. "They... No." Her head was shaking from side to side, but she hated to admit that it made sense. Why their uniforms didn't fit. How they were randomly in the woods and not on the town road that the Mirchan sentries who frequented town took. Why her uncle was on alert the second he spotted them. He noticed what she had not. He knew, and he sent her and Émeriah home to safety.

Sighing, Andira walked around her desk, with the folder still in hand, and slowly approached Evenia. "Forgive me. They killed someone dear to me..." Her face fell, and her tone dropped. "My niece."

"I'm sorry for your loss," Evenia said, and she meant it. She understood the pain that came with the loss of someone you loved. Understood how it never went away, no matter what you did.

Andira nodded with a sad smile on her face. "And I'm sorry for yours."

With shaky hands, Evenia accepted the folder Andira offered her. The folder that undoubtedly had a portrait of her uncle. That held his name and information of service and...death.

Another wave of grief suddenly hit her, suffocating her. It was short-lived, being replaced by guilt at the thought of thinking that any one of these sentries could have played a part in the murder of her uncle. Their comrades were murdered for their uniforms and false titles for ill deeds. They were just as much victims as her uncle was.

"Thank you," she managed to say. Her voice sounded so small, even to her. Not having the strength to open it yet, she clutched the folder to her chest as the general made her way back to the seat behind her desk.

"Of course," Andira said. The general paused when the folder slipped in Evenia's hands, revealing there was more than one the general handed her. "There is something else." Andira nodded her head at the second folder.

A small gasp escaped Evenia's lips when she placed the second, thin folder on top of her uncle's slightly thicker one. In black ink, the name "Nioma Brohn" was on both a side tab and on the front cover.

"What is this?" she asked, her voice trembling.

"You mentioned your mother's name before, and something compelled me to look if we had any information on her, as well." The general's eyes swept over the folder. "The information is scarce, but if it was me, I would want to know."

Anxious. Panicked. Hopeful. Numb. Evenia felt all at once before feeling nothing at all. She didn't know what to say.

Part of her wanted to tear open the folder right then and there, but the other part was terrified to see what was in there. To see if they had a record of her mother's death, something her aunt and her had secretly feared for years. Or worse...record of her life, which would confirm she left Evenia as a baby of her own accord. That she didn't want her.

Evenia swallowed down the lump forming in her throat. She didn't trust herself to speak at that moment. So, she blinked away the tears forming and nodded.

A small smile graced the general's face. "Now, regarding this spontaneous trip of yours, should I send word to your family in Poultom that you need a few more days?" she asked, seemingly unaware of Evenia's downward mental spiral of anxiety. Or, at the very least, politely pretending it wasn't happening.

My family.

She sighed. How did she forget? *Again.* No, she knew exactly why she forgot. She was purposefully putting them out of her mind—putting off facing them and the questions she wasn't ready to answer. The shame she felt at the thought of having to share what happened to her.

Evenia's eyes briefly shut. The sting and the sudden bright light that came from squeezing them so tightly was welcomed. When she finally opened them again, Andira's eyes were still on her as she just sat there behind her desk, waiting patiently.

Evenia nodded. "Please. I'm just... I'm not ready yet. I don't know what to tell you all about what happened, let alone what to tell them. What to... I'm just not ready." She sighed. "But I know I must. I suppose the day I get back is the day I'll face them."

"I understand," Andira said. She briefly looked at the papers on her desk before speaking again. "I will not pretend to know your situation or your family dynamic, but I do have a question."

Not knowing what would come out of the general's mouth, Evenia's throat bobbed, but she nodded at the general to proceed. Was it going to be about The Darkness? About what happened to her? How she ended up there? Or the quiet life they've had to live to protect her and her cousin?

"Could it be that you are not giving them enough credit? Might they be more understanding and patient with you than you think?"

Evenia felt her shoulders drop an inch as her fists relaxed. Her knuckles stung from the sudden release of pressure at the general's thoughtful questions.

"Forgive me for asking. It is not my place," Andira quickly added.

"It's fine." Evenia slowly shook her head.

Yes, her aunt and cousin would be understanding of her...situation, as Andira kindly put it. And yes, they would be patient with her. However, knowing that did not make her any more ready to face them right now. No, she couldn't even face her own thoughts about what happened. Couldn't bring herself to face her own inner demons.

She wasn't ready to continue resurfacing it all by having to relive these memories over and over again. And that was exactly what she would have to do to explain to her family why she was now so jumpy, so scared, so *angry*.

Her eyes shuttered, blinking away the tears once again forming in them. She cleared her throat, shoving down the ball of emotions forming in it. "Of course, they would be. My aunt and cousin are wonderful, kind. The fault lies with me, not them."

Andira looked down as she slowly stood and walked toward Evenia again. An oak and honey scent grew stronger with each of the general's steps. Not sure what to do, Evenia waited with bated breath, until the general stood only a foot in front of her.

"I do not know what happened to you. I can only imagine what it is you were put through these past months, and what you are still being put through. You see, you are quite skilled at hiding how you feel, but it is your eyes that give you away, Evenia."

Breaking eye contact, Evenia looked away. Her own eyes betrayed her?

"There is a truth shining there that, even though you escaped, you are still fighting every day for your freedom." Andira's eyes were assessing her face, as if she could see that Evenia's mind was her own personal hel right now.

Evenia was struggling to keep her chin up as her eyes stung with tears she refused to release. Silence had shrouded the room, but her mind seemed louder than ever, with memories threatening to spill into the present moment. Finally quieting her thoughts, she pushed her chin up and met the general's kind gaze.

"What fuels your desire to travel to an unknown land to seek this monstrosity is a mystery to me. However, as wild as my imagination may be, the truth is, there is no one who knows your journey the way you do," Andira said, pausing before laying a hand on each of Evenia's shoulders. The gentle touch made Evenia bite her lip in a last, desperate attempt to contain her sob.

Swirling shades of brown stared back at Evenia as Andira's voice broke the silence. "One thing I do know for sure is that *none* of the fault lies with you."

Evenia's breath caught. Her eyes searched Andira's, looking for any sort of lie, any pity. Any inkling of desire to fib instead of tell the truth in the hopes of protecting Evenia's feelings.

But there was none. No lie. No pity. No deception in the form of kindness. All she saw was Andira's clear, kind eyes. All she saw was truth.

And with that, she could no longer fight the sob climbing up her throat as her hand went to her mouth and her legs gave out from under her. Andira caught her and held her as she let out all the fear and the pain overwhelming her. With each sob, she released herself from it, little by little.

There was no telling when she would begin to believe the words Andira spoke, but something in her heart told her this was a start.

26

Evenia

"Please send Esral back in on your way out," Andira said from behind her desk as Evenia stepped in the threshold, exiting the general's office. "And Evenia?" She looked back toward the general, whose eyes were kind, patient. "Trust in the commander. And be safe."

With dry eyes and the folders still clutched to her chest, Evenia dipped her chin as she motioned for Esral in the hallway. The sentry didn't hesitate to enter the room. When the door closed, Evenia closed her eyes and took a deep breath, her chest caving in on half an exhale.

This was really happening.

She was really going to help investigate The Darkness.

She was going to play a part in bringing the monster down. The *demon* down.

Suddenly, the scent of patchouli and bergamot filled her senses. She couldn't resist rolling her eyes, knowing what was coming. Ignoring the inevitable, she started walking down the hall.

"You really do have a death wish," he said from beside her, keeping pace, which probably wasn't difficult to do with his long legs versus her short ones.

"Considering I *just* ran from death," she side-eyed him, "I think you have that wrong."

"No, I don't. Why else would you volunteer yourself to investigate The Darkness?" There was so much anger in his tone, which only irritated her more. What gave him the right to be angry with *her* decisions? It was her life, not his.

"Why do you do it as a sentry? You didn't hesitate once when Andira mentioned The Darkness in Nulhe. In fact, you were more than ready to run there on foot until she stopped you." Evenia's hands were waving in the air, showing herself just how angry and worked up she was over this. His eyes briefly followed the folders in her hand, now waving in the air, but he met her gaze again.

A slow inhale because he wasn't worth it. Yet, she still couldn't stop herself.

"It's my *job!*" he half-yelled, trying to keep his voice down in the hall full of closed doors.

Before she could respond, there was a gentle pressure on her arms as she was suddenly whisked down a hall in a dark corner.

"What the—"

Darkness. There was nothing around her. No warmth. No light. Nothing. Her heart started pounding.

"Don't worry. Use your Light," his voice said gruffly, a stark contrast to the gentle pressure he held on to her wrists, grounding her.

"Wha–what?" There was nothing but darkness. Where were they? What happened?

"Your magic, Raldir," he said. "Light this place up." Despite the bite in his tone, his thumb started gently tracing her wrists.

Lifting her hand not holding the folders, she flicked her wrist, creating an orb of Light hanging in the air above them. The pounding in her heart slowed as the space around them became clearer, the natural shadows retreating from the Light. Kalland stood before her, still holding her, still grounding her.

Looking around, she saw they were tucked into a stone pathway. The farther down the path, the darker the tunnel became and the harder it was to see the grooves of the stone walls and floor.

What the fuck? Her eyes met his again. All warmth left her wrists as he removed his hands from her, seeing she was okay now. She wouldn't have needed that stability in the first place if he hadn't messed with her.

"Where are we? What did you just do?"

"Later," he growled. "Why are you putting yourself in danger?" He wasn't touching her, but his eyes were pinning her down, with her back against the stone wall. Her Light illuminated his silver eyes and the anger in them.

Unwavering, she held his gaze. "Later? You get to ask me question after question, expecting me to answer, and all I get in return is *later*?" She was seething again. This self-righteous asshole just didn't stop.

His eyes assessed her face before his mouth opened again. "It's part of my powers. There. Now, it's your turn. *Why*?"

She rolled her eyes. That wasn't much of an answer, but what else did she expect from this elf?

"That's not helpful," she said, narrowing her eyes at him. "If you want a real answer from me, you'll have to give a real one in return."

His eyes were hard, but he finally sighed, giving in. "It's called evanescing. A form of teleportation, if you will. Now, it's your turn. Why are you insisting on putting yourself in danger?"

She knew of evanescing. Witnessed it before, in fact. But Kalland's powers seemed to be...more than just that. However, she would let it go this time since it didn't seem like a lie.

"Why do you care?" Her voice was low, having reached the point of her patience.

His jaw clenched, but he released his breath. "Forget it." He stepped back. "I'll see you tomorrow morning." He started to walk toward a large tapestry hanging up, which appeared to be the opening of the tunnel.

"That's it?" she asked, pulling his arm to make him face her before he reached the entrance. "Question me tirelessly, throw me in this weird hallway—wherever the fuck we are—and then simply, 'Forget it, I'll see you tomorrow'?" Her arms were waving in the air, and the folders slapped against her left thigh.

"No. No, we will not forget it. Why do you care what I do with my time? With *my* life?" Using her free hand, she pointed a finger at her chest to emphasize the word 'my.'

He turned toward her. "Because you fucking survived! Do you know how few come in contact with The Darkness and *survive?* No one else got to do that. You're throwing your second chance away. Walking face first into danger the first chance you get." He paused, hands raking through his hair, and his face suddenly looked sad and pained. "You already got away. So...why? Why risk it again?"

Because you fucking survived.

No one else got to do that.

His words rang in her head. She stood there, blank-faced, with her mind whirring. Who did he lose? Who didn't survive? Who didn't get to walk away?

None of them did. She closed her eyes. Everyone she left behind was still there. That was why she was doing this.

"That's precisely why I have to do this." He rubbed his brow in frustration, but she continued before he could interrupt. "I got a second chance, but as far as we know, no one else has. That's not okay. We need to stop him so that all of his victims can be freed, whether in spirit, in mind, or in body. Or all three." She sighed. "I'm doing this *because* I survived, and so many others did not."

He turned away from her, his hand supporting his weight against the wall. His head slowly nodded, and she could feel the anger in the air dissipating between them. "Andira's right—you're braver than we gave you credit for. Than *I* gave you credit for," he said, softly. Turning, he met her gaze.

Cheeks flushed, she broke eye contact.

His eyes landed on the folders in her hand. "Is that relevant to the mission? Anything I need to know?" He gestured toward the folder.

"No." Shaking her head, she resisted the urge to grip the folders tighter. Resisted drawing attention to her uncle's life and death, or to the mystery of her mother.

To her relief and utter shock, he nodded his head and dropped the subject. Just like that. No questions asked. Was he... Was he beginning to trust her?

She looked away and rubbed her temple with her free hand before meeting his gaze once more. "Look, think what you want, Sothenas, but I have to see this through. If he's out there, kidnapping more shifters, and doing gods only know what else, I owe it to his other victims and myself to do what I can to stop him."

"I understand your reasons, but what makes you think you can stop him?" Kalland asked, his voice low again. A question from the sentry who had to rescue her three nights ago, when she froze in the presence of only The Darkness's shadow self.

"Why else do you think he wants me so badly?" she asked, giving a challenge of her own. The thought plagued her for a long time while in captivity. She obviously couldn't reveal the whole truth of her magic, but she had to reveal enough to convince Kalland to let her go with him. "There's something he wants with *me*."

"All the more reason for you to *stay*," Kalland growled. She could see he didn't want to budge on that, and that pissed her off. He stopped, his eyes assessing hers. "But you won't."

"Astute observation, Sothenas," she said, using his own words from earlier that morning against him.

His lip twitched, and her stomach fluttered at the sight. But she couldn't get distracted. Couldn't let him keep her from her goal.

"Listen. You lock me in a cage, and I'll break free. I proved that already." She took a step toward him. "You can take me with you from the start, or I'll find you on the road and continue the journey with you. Either way, I'm coming." The stubborn determination to prove him and herself wrong tamped out the flicker of fear threatening to grow and consume her.

There was a long silence as they stared at one another, neither of them turning away from the other's challenge.

Finally, he relented and blinked. "You really mean that, don't you?" She nodded and he let out a breath on a long exhale. "Fine. If this is what you want, then we'll figure it out."

She might have stopped breathing. Was this a test?

"But you'll have to follow my lead, or else I'll cut you from the mission and have you sent right back here." His tone was firm.

There it was—the catch. Resisting the urge to roll her eyes and risk upsetting him after getting what she wanted, she bit her bottom lip and nodded.

His eyes dipped down to her lips at the movement before meeting her gaze again. "Good. Rule Number One: Don't do anything stupid, like put yourself in unnecessary danger. Deal?"

Fighting the urge to smile, she responded, "Deal."

He stared into her eyes, as if expecting to find some sort of deception. But she meant it. Why put herself in danger if she didn't need to? He seemed like the impulsive type to do that enough for them both.

Not seeing whatever he thought he might find in her eyes, he shook his head and sighed. Without looking at her, he grabbed the edge of the fabric in the doorway of the tunnel and said, "I'll see you at first light tomorrow."

Before he could fully lift the fabric, she closed the distance between them. Her hand wrapping around his wrist, she jerked him back. The fabric fell again, taking the light from beyond the entrance with it. His grey eyes pinned her to the spot again, but she met their challenge.

"That's it? All of *this*," she motioned in the air to the tunnel and the tension between them, "for you to just walk away?" she asked.

Warmth radiated from his wrist to her palm. The opposite position of what they were in when he first brought her into the tunnel. Instead of letting go, she tightened her grip, which resulted in his eyes darkening and her feeling things she shouldn't at the sight.

Her eyes caught on the movement of the corner of the tapestry flapping from him dropping it and her throat bobbed. "I don't even know where you took us, and you're just going to leave me here?" Her voice was quieter than she meant for it to be, and she silently cursed herself for letting him have an effect on her.

His eyes briefly looked back at the dark, stone path behind her. Those grey eyes shined as his face was mere inches from hers. "You're the one who seems to want some adventure in your life," he said, his tone playful. His eyes assessed her face before he winked, and with that, he was gone. It was as if he vanished into thin air. The tapestry flapped again from his departure, the movement momentarily leaking bright light into the tunnel.

What was going on?

Did he make a joke? And he actually stopped yelling at her? Stopped questioning her? He...gave up.

What. The. Fuck.

She stood there, breathing in and out and trying to get her emotions under control. She let out a small laugh. What was with him today? He was acting so hot and cold. And yet, she liked it. Liked this side of him.

On an exhale, she gripped the edge of the tapestry and eliminated her Light. To her relief, when she lifted the fabric, she saw that the exit led to the hall General Elsvarin's office was located on. Thank the gods. She was nervous that he was serious about that "adventure" comment.

A small smile on her face, she shook her head. He really had made a joke. Seeing no one around, she stepped through the doorway and quickly replaced the tapestry back in its rightful place. A smug sense of satisfaction hit her at knowing a secret passageway in the Mirchan headquarters. Had he thought that through when he brought her in there? And why a secret tunnel? Why not pin her in the hall?

Because he wanted to do it in private. To get me alone. Her stomach fluttered at the thought.

With each step down the hall she took, the lower her confidence fell. What was she thinking by volunteering to go? She didn't know. Yet, it felt right. Like Kalland said, they would figure it out.

And she *would* figure out the rest later. How to tell her family what happened. How to face them. How to relive the trauma she experienced. Somehow, she would figure out how to go back to her daily life. Help her aunt as a healer, help keep herself and her cousin under the radar, and help keep food on the table. If there was a way to get back to that life—that Evenia that once existed—she'd find it.

But right now…she had a temporary way out. A way to not have to go back to that. To not have to relive the trauma. To not have to see the sadness, pity, and fear in her aunt's eyes, or experience her own sadness, pity, and fear.

To not have to answer the endless questions from the neighbors back home in Poultom. Sure, they would likely give the obligatory kindness and sympathy when someone experienced something out of the ordinary. However, after a day or two, the nosiness and questions were bound to come out. An interrogation rather than a welcome home.

She rolled her eyes at the thought. How could people thrive on gossip and bothering others? Those who were in need of kindness, without strings attached. Not judgment. Not endless questions that were no one else's business.

Her aunt was one who usually hung around the gossip mills, unashamedly so, but Evenia took after her uncle more in that she felt gross whenever she was involved in any sort of gossip. Talking about someone behind their backs when they weren't there to defend themselves felt…wrong.

She could only imagine the gossip that would surround her when she made it home. Maybe they would say that she faked her abduction and made it up for attention. Or that she ran away because she got pregnant. Something absurd that they would come up with. Who fucking knew with those villagers she called neighbors. Granted, they weren't all like that, but there were enough to make her hate it there.

Most of her coven would accept her back, but even they would have questions for her. Questions she wasn't ready to answer.

So, no, she was not ready to go back and face them all. She was not ready to go back to hating her life around such deceptively nice people, who really only cared about themselves and the village gossip. No freaking thank you.

She rounded the corner of the hall, going right—the way they came when Alekze led them to Andira's office. She was not entirely sure where she was going because she had been nervous as hel when Alekze walked them to the general's office, not knowing what would happen when she got there.

Evenia suddenly stopped in the middle of the hall, just shy of the next four-way walkway. That previous turn was the last direction she remembered.

She was lost.

In Mircha, of all places.

Surrounded by people she feared. Except, she didn't need to fear them according to the folder in her hand. If she was to believe General Elsvarin's words, or what was in the file. The one that apparently contained evidence that these people weren't as bad as she'd been led to believe.

Clutching the folders closer to her chest, her eyes shifted frantically from hall to hall. Which direction should she go in? Straight ahead appeared to be a hall with more rooms. To the right looked brighter because it was filled with more windows than the rest. To the left was a bit darker, not having many windows in it, and since it was still daytime, the floating lanterns weren't lit.

Whatever the right choice was, the shadow-filled hallway was not even an option. She couldn't do it.

Shit. This was not the time to get lost. Her nerves were already shot. Her fears were already high. Her anxiety? Through the roof. What was she thinking, agreeing to go to Nulhe? Despite how beautiful it sounded, she had never been before. Going to a strange place, with a strange fucking sentry, to what? Search for the fucking Darkness.

Her hands went to her forehead, the folders hitting her in the face, but she didn't care. She really was out of her fucking mind. Was it too late to back down? Surely not. Maybe she could just turn right back around to Andira's office and tell her she would not be going, and then ask for directions back to her room. Then, back to Poultom. Her tail tucked between her legs, so to speak.

She shook her head, her hands still clasped on her forehead. There was no way she'd be able to do that.

You couldn't walk away even if you wanted to, she thought to herself. A groan escaped her lips as she dug the palms of her hands into her eyes, trying to alleviate the pounding in her temples. What a mess this was.

Her chest was heaving again. A sensation she was getting sick of at this point, but it was out of her control. So much of this was out of her control. What was she thinking? *Why?* Why did she feel the need to do this? Why couldn't she just walk away?

The pressure in her palms stopped.

Because she wouldn't walk away from the shifters who didn't make it out. Because she couldn't walk away knowing that she would still be hunted, that she could still be dragged back to that helhole.

Even if she couldn't fully fight for herself right now, as she was still seemingly fighting her own body and mind through all of this, she would at least fight for the others. The ones who didn't make it out of this alive. The ones who didn't escape that building. And the ones who would never be free if The Darkness was allowed to continue kidnapping shifters.

She would do it for them. If not for herself, then for them.

Deep down, she knew that someday...someday, she would be able to see she was also doing it for herself. For her future self, who would need the security of knowing she didn't have to look over her shoulder everywhere she went. For a future where she wouldn't have to worry about whether shadows were natural or unnatural.

A deep breath, with the palms of her hands still on her eyes. She slowly straightened her spine on the exhale, dragging it out as she went vertebrae by vertebrae. Breath by breath, she would pull herself out of the darkness.

"*Evenia?*"

Bergamot and patchouli.

Her body stilled, and she quickly lowered her hands from her face. Instead of calming, her heart only beat faster from embarrassment when her eyes laid on familiar faces. Those grey eyes filled with regret and then lavender eyes full of concern. Both sets only feet away from her.

"Evenia?" It was Nishara's voice this time. The Moon elf held her hand out, slowly reaching out to her.

"*You were never alone,*" Kalland Wind whispered to her. "*We've got you. I made you a promise you'd be safe here, and I meant it.*" His eyes met hers, and he looked like there was more he wanted to say, but he closed his mouth, not saying another word.

She didn't have the chance to process his words or thank him before he was gone again. Vanished into thin air. Evanesced? He'd let her try to figure this all out on her own—to give her space—and then brought someone she actually trusted when he realized she needed help. But how did he know?

"Evenia?" Nishara repeated, pulling her attention away from the empty spot where Kalland stood only seconds before. "Can I help?" The kindness and sincerity in Nishara's voice was the breaking point for Evenia, who could no longer hold back her tears.

What started as a stinging in her eyes at the sight of Nishara and Kalland quickly grew to full on sobs. She couldn't stop it from happening. And before she knew it, she was kneeling on the floor, with Nishara's arms suddenly wrapped around her.

"Shh, it's okay. You're okay now," Nishara whispered, with one hand brushing through Evenia's hair and the other rubbing her back. The act of kindness only made Evenia cry harder.

People caring for her wasn't something she was used to. Neither was panicking or crying all the time. And she certainly wasn't used to people being nice to her for no reason. And what was with these panic attacks? Would it always be like this? Would she always be scared? Haunted by her past? Would she never be free again?

This was too much. Too much.

It was getting hard to breathe with how much she was crying. When the sobs became so frequent that she couldn't get a breath in, her survival instincts kicked in, forcing her to swallow the next sob and calm her own breathing. She wasn't about to go through all of this just to die from the lack of oxygen thanks to the tears.

A new sense of determination flaring through her, she wiped her face. She was determined to breathe, to fight, to win—in whatever way that meant—in order to survive.

As her breathing finally calmed, she felt Nishara's soothing touch slow. Evenia pulled away from the hold to sit up and regain her composure.

"Sorry," she managed to get out on a breath as she wiped her damp face. The sides of her hands were now drenched in her tears, leaving her cheeks still wet. She pulled the hem of her shirt up to soak up the rest of the tears on her face.

"For what?" Nishara asked, her tone full of confusion.

"For *what*? For making a fool of myself in front of you. In the freaking hallway, no less. For drenching your shirt in my tears. Oh, gods, your shoulder is practically soaked." Evenia grimaced at the sight, suddenly full to the brim with embarrassment for breaking down.

The Moon elf only shook her head. "Evenia, emotions exist for a reason. We are meant to feel them, to embrace them, and then to release them. That is how we heal. That is how we are able to move on in a healthy manner."

She grabbed hold of Evenia's hand and squeezed. "Suppressing those emotions will only harm *you* more than anyone else, and will likely lead to your internal destruction. I have seen it happen one too many times and do not care to see it again." Her voice went from soft to stern, seemingly unrelenting on the subject. "The more you ignore how you feel, the more damage you will do to yourself. So, let it out. Always, and especially around me."

Evenia's eyes shuttered, blinking back the emotions Nishara's words stirred inside her. Unable to speak, she swallowed down the lump forming in her throat and nodded her head.

"Do you want to talk about it?" Nishara asked.

Evenia started to shake her head 'no' in response, but she stopped.

Suppressing those emotions will only harm you *more than anyone else, and will likely lead to your internal destruction.*

She took a deep breath and dragged out the exhale. "Okay," she nodded, "but not in the middle of the hallway."

Nishara cracked a smile. "If you're up for some fresh air, I know where we could go."

Evenia swallowed her pride, swallowed the embarrassment of showing her emotions in public, and nodded. "I'd like that."

It surprised her to realize she meant it. What was Mircha doing to her?

27

Evenia

fter leaving Evenia's room, where she hid her parents' folders in a drawer to deal with later, Nishara led Evenia through the halls of Mircha and to a courtyard. Her eyes closed the second they stepped outside, and she felt the warmth of the sun on her cheeks.

Without forcing conversation, Nishara continued to lead the way. A fork in the road lay ahead of them. One trail led toward a maze of hedges and the other toward an open path with the training grounds in the far distance. Evenia let out a breath when Nishara took the open trail, the maze entrance now behind them.

Relief washed over her because she didn't think her anxiety could take feeling trapped and lost again, especially in a place where her short frame would be a disadvantage when it came to seeing over the hedges. She'd already felt trapped by her own mind, and she didn't need to feel physically trapped, too. Her frazzled emotions couldn't handle that right now.

Nishara eyed Evenia and then the maze as they passed it. "It's for training," explained her soft voice. "It's heavily spelled, and there are obstacles within the maze that make for great training."

Evenia nodded and eyed the maze once more as they continued on the path. No way in hel would she be caught dead in there.

The two continued to walk in silence, with only the sounds of their boots crunching on the beige and light grey stone path. Gratitude toward Nishara filled Evenia for her not forcing any conversation or small talk, which allowed her time to find the words to express how she felt.

As they strode along the stone path, her eyes scanned over the lush green grass and hills beyond, where she could hear the sentries on the training grounds.

The sentries who didn't kill her uncle, but who helped bring down the murderers who did. She shook her head. Everything she thought she knew was a lie.

A twinge of guilt twisted her gut for even thinking that Nishara or the others could be associated with murderers like that. They had only ever been kind to her. Present moment included, when the Moon elf next to her—the very same who held her while she sobbed in the middle of a hallway—now walked by her side, somehow offering both space and support at the same time.

Exhaling on a deep breath, Evenia straightened her posture, finally ready to talk. Nishara kept her gaze in front of them, but Evenia caught on to the slight change in her pace, slowing down in anticipation.

"I volunteered to go to Nulhe," Evenia said, not sure where else to start.

Nishara's brow raised and there was a hint of a smile on her face as she asked, "Is that a bad thing, going to Nulhe?" The amusement in her tone was evident, but Evenia couldn't mirror it. Not with what she had to discuss next.

She started fidgeting with her fingers in front of her. "I volunteered to go to Nulhe to investigate a lead on...The Darkness," she managed to get out.

This time, Nishara's steps faltered, but she kept pace with Evenia. She remained silent, letting Evenia talk at her own pace. The tension in Nishara's body didn't escape Evenia, and she remembered that Nulhe was the elf's home realm.

"He's not there, according to the message," Evenia said quickly, and some of the tension visibly left Nishara's body. "But there are reports of a...group associated with him that's in the streets of Nulhe." She ran a hand through her hair, and her front pieces that framed her face got caught on the slight point of her right ear.

Still, Nishara stayed silent.

Evenia couldn't hold it back anymore, not now that she had opened the wound. "I don't know what I was thinking at that moment. I don't know. It felt like Alekze didn't want to go to Akvar, because of something to do with someone named Asrynna, and his reluctance stirred a fire in me." She knew she was rambling, but she didn't care. Now that she started, she couldn't stop. It needed to come out.

"I decided I should go, because what else am I going to do? I can't return back to the life that I had in Poultom. *How* can I? Not now. Not when I know that there are more shifters going missing—*dying*—at the hands of that monster. But then, how do I go? How do I..." Her rambling stopped and her voice trailed off as her fear and anxiety suddenly felt suffocating again.

Clearing her throat, she tried again. "I can't not help, especially when it's something as simple as traveling to Nulhe to check out rumors of a group. Not actually him. On the other hand, how do I work up the courage to go toward something associated with the very monster I just fled from?"

Nishara nodded in Evenia's peripheral vision. When she didn't speak, Evenia turned her head toward her, waiting.

"What do you need? Are you needing to vent, or are you seeking advice?" Nishara asked, and Evenia wasn't sure how to respond to the words.

She opened and closed her mouth twice while she mulled over the question. "Both, I think."

"Okay," Nishara said, smiling. "First, I'm going to need you to clarify a little something." Evenia nodded. "Is the lead in Akvar or Nulhe? Because you mentioned both just now."

Evenia huffed a laugh. "Sorry, I didn't mean to ramble so much. There's a lead in Akvar, Nulhe, *and* somewhere in Urur. All are being investigated. Alekze is going with someone named Asrynna—"

"That's his sister. And she prefers Asryn. 'It's less stuffy,' is what she always says." Nishara eyed her, a smile on her face. "I think she'll like you."

His sister. Then why did he seem so angry when her name was mentioned? "Does Alekze not get along with her?"

Nishara laughed. "Just the opposite. Those two are cut from the same cloth, literally and figuratively. Once they're in the same room, you can't keep them apart." Nishara smiled at her. "Why?"

"Oh, nothing. He just seemed so angry when Andira mentioned her name and that she would be accompanying him to Akvar."

Nishara nodded her head slowly. Her gaze forward again, she said, "I see. It's not what you think. Asryn is a Mirchan sentry, and she's very good at what she does." Nishara didn't elaborate, and Evenia knew better than to ask, but her curiosity was piqued.

"Alekze has been trying to get his little sister away from here for years now. Not because he doesn't like it here, but because he's protective of her. He wants a different life for her."

Evenia nodded, but she didn't fully understand. If he liked it here, why would he not want his sister here, too?

Nishara continued. "She recently got herself a position with the healers, working to become one, and she's hoping to create a whole team of healers for shifters among the Mirchan sentries. For werewolves and others who don't otherwise have access to many healers with knowledge of fae in animal forms. It'll be exactly what Mircha needs—a way to help more fae throughout the lands," Nishara said, pride in her voice.

"But for now, she's still a sentry...with a very specific skill set. As much as Alekze hates it, she comes back whenever General Elsvarin calls on her."

It all suddenly made sense. Why Alekze was so tense, why he didn't seem to be pleased to hear about Asryn going, and why he refused his *general*. It was for his sister. She felt her heart swell a little at the thought, knowing just how protective she was over her own sister-cousin, Émeriah.

"I can understand that." Evenia nodded. "Well, she and Alekze are going to Akvar to investigate reports of shifters going missing on the border of Akvar and Urur."

"Yeah, he's going to hate that..." Nishara sighed. "He loathes Akvar."

"Why's that? Isn't he from there?" Evenia asked.

Nishara paused, and Evenia suddenly felt like she asked the wrong question.

"Sorry, it's not my place. He told me he doesn't call it home..." Evenia's voice trailed off, thinking about the icy blue eyes that were common among those born of Akvarian descent. Especially Glaculs—the Ice elves.

"He's right. Just because your lineage and magic come from a certain place does not make it your home, or a place you necessarily feel the urge to visit...or revisit." She gave Evenia an apologetic look. "Sorry, that's all I can say, as it's not my story to tell."

"Of course," Evenia said, nodding. "Anyway, they're going to Akvar. Andira gave the order and Alekze protested, hating the idea, especially after Asrynna—sorry, Asryn—was mentioned. So, I... Well, I...volunteered."

Evenia shrugged before rambling from suddenly feeling the need to defend her actions. "I don't know why I did it. I was angry, thinking he was refusing to go after The Darkness, refusing to follow a lead—to help. And before I knew it, I was telling Andira to send me. To send *me*. What an idiot..." she muttered.

Yes, she felt the need to defend herself. Not to Nishara, who had zero judgment in her body language or expressions, but to herself. She was doubting her decision, the actions she took, and the whole ridiculous plan.

What compelled her to volunteer to go to Akvar in the first place? The coldest realm on the continent, not just in weather, but in the people who resided there. It was rumored that they were some of the most stuck-up, cruel people you would ever meet. Evenia had experienced enough coldness to last a lifetime.

And yet, she volunteered, anyway. Decided to open her mouth and tell Andira to send her. To send *her*. A duolvain who wasn't even a sentry. On a mission. To seek The Darkness. Alone.

Nishara chuckled. "I bet Alekze felt relieved at that offer."

Evenia side-eyed her. "If he did, I didn't notice, because Kalland immediately denied the suggestion." Nishara's eyebrows rose. "Yeah, he keeps trying to control what I can and can't do."

"What do you mean?"

Evenia paused, suddenly feeling self-conscious. She was opening up to Nishara now, but was she ready to tell her about her real-life nightmare? Of The Darkness haunting her both in sleep and in life?

No.

She shook her head. "He's just not a fan of mine, that's all." Nishara nodded, seemingly satisfied with that answer. "Anyway, General Elsvarin was on my side, but instead of Akvar, she suggested I go to Nulhe...with Kalland."

Nishara suddenly stopped walking and started laughing. "Oh Qelena," she said between laughs. Evenia noted the exclamation of the first Moon Queen, Qelena, who was now considered a goddess among many in Nulhe. And, as she now knew, was the twin to the Mad Queen.

Seeing Evenia's face, Nishara stopped laughing and slowly straightened up to walk again. "Sorry, it's just...now, I understand."

Evenia rolled her eyes, a smile on her face, and bumped Nishara with her elbow. "Yeah, so, whatever advice you have for going with him, I'll take." Her smile faltered. "And for, you know, preparing for possibly finding out something about The Darkness."

Nishara cleared her throat. "Okay, we'll deal with Kalland in a second. First, you're going to love Nulhe. When you get there, go to Duloar, the blacksmith who crafted that dagger," she pointed toward the dagger sheathed at Evenia's side, "and tell him I miss him.

Please. Oh, and that he should make you something, per my orders." Nishara's voice was full of happiness, with a smile to match that reached her eyes.

"Second, I'm assuming you heard from Noclaf?"

"Yes, I believe General Elsvarin mentioned a General Noclaf." Evenia nodded.

"Not surprising, he and Kalland are good friends. He'll take good care of you while you're there. So, don't worry about that."

Kalland's friend in Nulhe would take care of her while she was there? Evenia didn't know whether that was a good thing or a bad thing, being that she wasn't sure if Kalland even liked her.

As if sensing her hesitation, Nishara bumped Evenia with her elbow, copying the act from only a few minutes prior. "I wouldn't steer you wrong. He has a soft spot for women and children. He turns into a watchdog. Not to mention that he's responsible for all patrons who come into Nulhe, which would include you. It's his job, and he's good at it. You'll like him."

Evenia nodded, a small sense of relief flooding her. She wouldn't be alone there, she had to remember that. She wouldn't be alone. Not when it came to The Darkness—or, rather, his followers   and not when it came to being in an unfamiliar place. Or with Kalland. Although, she wouldn't mind having a little alone time with—

She mentally shook her head. Where did that come from? *Focus, Evenia.*

"As for the rest..." Evenia tensed at Nishara's words. "You do not have to go if you do not want to."

Shaking her head, she answered, "As scared as I am, not going is not an option. I have to do this." She met Nishara's eyes, showing her the sincerity and determination she felt.

"I understand." Nishara nodded, not looking at Evenia but ahead of them, her gaze thoughtful. "From what you've said, fear is the venom in your veins. You must find your antidote. Find what it is that cures you of your fears and helps you to heal properly, so that you may live without that fear."

Evenia blinked as the words sunk in one by one, echoing in her mind.

Fear is the venom in your veins.

Find your antidote.

Heal properly.

Live without fear.

As vague as it was, it also sounded annoyingly simple. And yet, the verbal puzzle made some sense to Evenia. Somehow, she found comfort in the plan. Perhaps it was the fact that it was a plan—a way for her to take charge over herself and her life again—and something she could control in all this mess.

Since being here, her fear was proving to be her weakness. The sudden panic attacks. The crying. No, the *sobbing*. The inability to defend herself from The Darkness. Not in…months, really. She couldn't deny she was allowing her fear to consume her. Here, and everywhere, since she was taken.

But not anymore.

Her fingers went from an anxious fidgeting to tightly intertwining with one another as her fear was replaced by rising anger. Was that to be her antidote? Her anger? Determination? Revenge? If not forever, it would at least do for now.

Nishara nodded. "I happen to have good connections in Nulhe. While Kalland will do everything to protect you with his life—"

Evenia scoffed. Not meaning to express the emotion out loud, her cheeks flushed.

Nishara playfully bumped Evenia's arm with her elbow. "I know it might be hard to believe, but it's true. He may be stubborn as a bull, but he will always put his own pride and…differences aside to help an innocent. He might not seem like the type, but he is. Trust me. And that includes for you. Between General Noclaf and Kalland, you couldn't be in safer hands while in Nulhe. Truly."

Evenia let the words sink in. She already saw firsthand how Kalland put his dislike of her aside in order to save her from The Darkness's shadows, and she had a feeling he would do it again. Perhaps even put himself between her and The Darkness's true form, not just his shadows.

She shuddered at the mere thought of seeing them again.

"Okay, that helps a little. Thanks." She meant it.

"Good, that's a start, at least." Nishara smiled. "I can make sure you have some added protection, if you'd like."

"Added protection?" Evenia eyed her warily. That almost sounded like a bodyguard, and she didn't like the idea of being watched. Monitored. Controlled.

Nishara nodded, smiling. "My sister and cousins live in the palace. If I ask, my sister will keep an eye out for you."

Her sister. Some of the tension released from Evenia's shoulders. "Oh, thank you."

"Of course. She'll be happy to do it." Nishara smiled, but her eyes quickly grew sad. "Beyond that, I'm afraid this is a journey you must travel alone. As scary as it may seem right now, it sounds like it is what you need in order to continue to heal. Am I wrong?" she asked, her voice soft and kind.

Evenia sighed. "No, you're not wrong."

"I know it's easier said than done, but if this is what you need to heal—to move forward, to grow—then you must see it through. I'll do what I can to help you, while also making sure you're safe and supported. Even from realms away." She gripped Evenia's hand, squeezing it once before releasing it.

A stinging in her eyes and nose started at Nishara's kindness. Looking at her with blurry eyes, she shook her head, at a loss for words. Nishara only smiled warmly back.

"Thank you," Evenia finally managed to say, finding her voice again after successfully blinking the tears away. "Seriously."

"Don't mention it. It's about time I bug my sister, anyway." Her toothy grin made Evenia smile.

"Thanks for—" Evenia stopped. Her senses were suddenly on fire all at once. The beast inside of her was screaming at her, warning her. But after years of ignoring it, she had no idea what that side of her was saying—what its instincts picked up on that her heightened fae abilities had not.

All she knew was something was seriously wrong, and her beast was fighting to come out. To protect herself.

She started to turn to take in her surroundings of the path, when Kalland suddenly appeared before her. An arrow was gripped in his hand, with the sharpened metal point hanging mere inches from Evenia's face.

Taking a step back, Evenia blinked a few times, still taking in the arrow as her mind tried to process what was happening. With wide eyes, she looked to Kalland. There was pure rage filling his swirling, silver irises.

"Kalland?" Nishara's voice sounded from behind her, but Evenia's eyes were glued to the grey storms in front of her.

"Seize him!" Kalland's deep voice boomed, the anger oozing off him, but his eyes never left Evenia's.

Those words broke Evenia from her trance. A group of sentries were running toward a hooded figure on the hillside. Kalland waited by her side, as guards tackled the hooded assailant, but they were too far away for Evenia to see who they took down.

"Are you okay?" Kalland asked, his voice low.

Peeling her eyes from the hillside, she saw he was looking over every inch of her face. The look in his eyes—rage mixed with concern—caused her stomach to flutter.

Evenia nodded her head. "Y–yes." Throat bobbing, she glanced down at the arrow and back up as Kalland looked at her. "How did you know?"

No response.

Heat grew in her cheeks as he continued to silently hold her gaze, as if he was deciding for himself if she was okay. She didn't know how long passed before he finally broke eye contact to examine the arrow.

"This is one of ours. And I know the coward who loosed it is." He grimaced and handed the arrow to an on-duty sentry in full armor.

Evenia's eyebrows raised. She didn't even notice the sentry had approached until Kalland addressed him.

Those grey eyes grew dark again. "Ferlant, take him to the cells," he motioned toward the arrow, "and take that with you." Kalland's authoritative tone left no room for question.

"Yes, Commander." The sentry nodded before walking away.

"Who is it?" Evenia asked, looking toward the retreating sentries before glancing back at the tall elf before her.

Kalland looked at her again, a storm still raging in those grey eyes. Somehow, she knew that anger wasn't directed at her for once.

"Emilzorn Randerjs. Apparently, the elf would like to see you dead." Evenia's head whipped toward the masked figure, now being dragged by sentries, before returning her gaze to Kalland's again. "Do you know why that is?" Kalland asked, his eyes studying Evenia's face for her answer.

"What? No! I only met him the other night. Hel, I saved his life!" Now putting the pieces together, Evenia's anger was rising, mixed with her nerves of almost being pierced by an arrow finally settling in. "Why me? I don't understand."

Kalland grunted. "I told you, it was a mistake to help him. He's always been impulsive. Reckless."

Evenia's anger tipped dangerously close to the edge.

"Unfortunately, those like Emil do not need a reason to fuel the hatred that resides deep within their hearts." His voice was sharp and his gaze trailed toward Emil's back, his feet dragging in the ground while he tried to fight off the sentries.

As if sensing her eyes on him, Emil turned his head toward her. Her heightened hearing kicked in and she heard him yell, "You're dead, you fucking bitch!"

She bristled, but before she could even think of what to do next, Emil was suddenly choking. Evenia honed into her catlike eyesight to see what was wrong, but he was choking on…nothing. It was like the air was being pulled from his body, his lungs robbed of—

Her head whipped toward Kalland. "*Stop it*," she Wind whispered to him. His hard eyes met hers and she didn't falter from the anger in them. She held his gaze, her own eyes pleading with him. "*Please.*"

His nostrils flared, but she suddenly heard Emil coughing as he sucked in air once more. The breath stuck in her chest escaped her own lungs, but her eyes were still on Kalland's.

"What is his problem?" Nishara asked, stepping up to stand beside Evenia, both of them now facing Kalland.

Kalland slowly tore his eyes from Evenia to look toward the retreating sentries and Emil. He shook his head. "Fuck if I know." His eyes narrowed on Emil. "But I'm going to find out," he practically growled.

With one last look at Evenia, he turned and started to walk away, following the direction of the sentry who took the arrow from him.

Evenia's jaw dropped. That was it? That was all from him?

"Where did you come from?" She didn't mean for the words to sound so…bitter. But she was irritated with the elf.

He stopped walking. After a few seconds, he finally faced her again. "I forgot. I was coming to tell you that Asryn Vlasca arrived early. She's only staying for a bit before heading out to scout for us, and we'll meet her at a safe house."

His weight shifted. Was he nervous? Evenia's eyebrow lifted in question.

"I—" He grimaced. "*We* wanted to know if you're okay with heading out earlier than we'd initially planned to. I was volunteered to ask you."

His hands flexed at his sides, anger suddenly etching his brow again. "When I came to find you, I saw Emil's arrow from the hill while approaching you two. And, well…" He shrugged, suddenly erasing the anger from his features and feigning indifference.

"Thanks," she said. As for the other thing… She sighed. "And sure. I don't want to hold you guys up." Was she ready? No. But she never would be. It was now or never. Nishara squeezed her shoulder, but Evenia didn't take her eyes off Kalland.

He held her gaze a moment longer and nodded his head. "We leave in an hour."

An hour? Panic threatened to seize her, but she breathed through the bubble of anxiety forming in her chest.

"Where are you going?" she blurted before he fully turned, but she already had a fairly good idea of what he was going to do. So, why did she feel the need to ask? Her cheeks flushed.

His grey eyes held her stare, looking unsure of how to respond. Her breath stalled. Why wasn't he answering? That wasn't a good sign. But his eyes told her everything she needed to know.

Nodding his head, he said, "See you at the stables in an hour." With that, he turned and walked toward where the sentries were taking Emil.

Part of her wanted to beg him not to go. To not do what he was planning. But the other part... The other part wished she was the one about to make Emil scream. Wished she was the one about to make his life hel, to steal his air, to hear from his lips why he hated her so much.

Nishara's words suddenly played in her head again.

Find your antidote.

Straightening her shoulders, she held onto her anger, donning it like armor. Yes, it looked like her antidote was to be anger, and her purpose, revenge.

28

Kalland

Kalland was ready to commit murder. An overwhelming instinct he felt another time this week, and both instances were directed toward one elf. One fucked-up elf who didn't deserve to breathe the same air as the woman he chose to take his anger and hatred out on.

His fists uncurled at his sides, releasing the tension in them. He needed to get a grip on his emotions. What was it about the blonde woman with the two-toned eyes that drove him crazy? That made him see red. Made him ready to kill someone who was once under his command.

He had to figure it out before he did something he couldn't take back. At the same time, his only regret was not ending Emil's life before, snuffing the air from his lungs. Forever.

With a clenched jaw, he approached the metal door of the interrogation room that Emil was being held in. With a nod, the sentries standing guard on either side of the door stepped away. One of them was a Metal elf—a Zeorlan—who tapped into his powers. In a matter of seconds, the solid metal door vibrated with the Zeorlan's power as it lifted away from the doorframe, allowing Kalland to enter.

Before he even stepped into the room, Kalland's anger turned to pure rage when he heard Emil stop shouting. Taking a deep breath, Kalland took a step into the threshold and heard the metal door falling loudly back into place behind him. With Emil's gaze now on him, a sick smile replaced the scowl on the asshole's face. It took every ounce of strength Kalland possessed to not unleash himself on the smug male.

"Look what the cat dragged in," Emil said. He laughed at his own joke, finding himself hilarious. No one else in the room joined in.

Yes, his nickname for Evenia: Cat Eyes. What was it with Emil and her?

Realizing no one would indulge his antics, Emil's smile fell as he leaned against the metal table. The spelled chains around his wrists that were blocking his Wind magic—practically making the Wind elf before Kalland a human—clinked at the motion, the sound echoing through the metal room.

Kalland stepped through the threshold and took in the scene before him. Next to Emil stood Alekze, his eyes glowing yellow instead of icy blue, telling Kalland just how close he was to letting the wolf inside of him loose. Kalland could only imagine what was said that brought Alekze to the brink of shifting and unleashing his wolf.

Next to Alekze stood Asrynna's tall, pale frame, her platinum white hair half-pinned up, showing off her sharp cheekbones and pointed ears. Despite Kalland's entrance, her pale blue eyes didn't peel away from the chained elf, but unlike Alekze, she looked more amused than angry.

Twirling her knives in her hand, she looked ready to strike at any moment. Ready to make him talk or simply squeal, whichever she felt inclined to do. Ready to finish the job, if she was granted permission to. It was no secret she always hated Emil, and she looked ready to see him finally get what he had coming to him.

She wasn't alone in that desire. There were three of them in this room alone.

"I knew you'd miss me," Emil said, his smug tone grating on Kalland's last nerve, which was already barely hanging on by a thread. "I told them you can't turn your back on family."

"You're not family. You're not even a friend." Kalland's voice was gravely low. He bristled before peeling his eyes from Asryn and turning to face the sorry excuse of an elf.

Emil's face went slack at Kalland's words, but he quickly recovered, steam coming out of them again. "It's okay, you don't mean that. You're only saying that because of *her*."

"What is your fucking deal with her, Emil? Why are you so bent out of a shape for a woman you don't even know? For a woman who represents the people you took an oath to serve and protect?" Kalland kept his voice calm, but he was ready to explode just under the surface. He had to stay calm.

Emil shrugged with his jaw locked tight, not offering anything for Kalland's questions. That nerve was dangerously close to snapping. If it did, Alekze's wolf would be the least of Emil's worries.

"Why did you come back after General Elsvarin graciously offered you reprieve from your contract? Why did you try to kill Evenia Raldir?" Kalland tried again.

Another wordless shrug, but there was no missing the flash of hatred that appeared in Emil's eyes at the mention of Evenia's name. What was it with this woman that made Emil hate her so? Sure, she got under Kalland's skin, too, but not like this. In fact, it was the complete opposite of this.

Emil was hot with hatred toward her, only focusing on her eyes and semi-pointed ears from being a duolvain at their first introduction. On the other hand, Kalland was hot with desire, lusting over those curves and two-toned eyes that practically put a spell on him the moment he saw them.

The woman who had been through so much already. So much that Kalland wanted to ignore initially. Begged to ignore. Tried his hardest to look the other way and call her the enemy. To use her to get The Darkness. But after what he witnessed the other night, after what he heard her say... The confession of "real, not real" that she revealed to him...

Kalland didn't realize his fists were balled at his sides until he smelt the metallic tang of blood hit his nostrils. Blinking a few times, he uncurled his fists, allowing his crescent-shaped cuts to heal immediately.

Emil was smirking in his seat. "What's the matter, Sothenas? Cat got your tongue?"

Oh, how he wanted to take these fists and wipe the smile off Emil's face. Not yet. But soon.

Unclenching his jaw, Kalland cleared his throat and tried again. He had to try again. For her sake. If she wasn't safe here, he needed to know. He needed to know how to protect her. After treating her the way he did, after assuming she was working with The Darkness, he owed it to her to help her.

At least, that was what he told himself that he was doing it for. To make it up to her. But that wasn't entirely true, was it? After seeing what The Darkness did to her in her room, he found he couldn't deny he didn't want anything bad to happen to her. Ever.

So, he would calm himself down and try again. And again. Until Emil broke down and gave them something.

Kalland cleared his throat, a new sense of determination flooding him. "We thought releasing you from Mircha as a free man would be enough. Clearly, we were wrong. You not only decided to come back but attempted to murder an innocent woman. But you knew you'd never get away with it. You had to know. Archery was never your sharpest skill. Apparently, neither is attempting to be an assassin. So, why? Why risk it?"

Throwing salt into the wound, Asryn grinned and Alekze grunted at the mention of the amount of times Emil failed the qualifications to such a school. A school Asryn aced but Emil never had the balls to even try to get into.

Emil's brown eyes flashed a darker shade with anger as they flickered from Alekze back to Kalland, but he managed to force a smile on his face as he said, "I have unfinished business."

Finally, a fucking answer. Sort of. "With Raldir? What business?" Kalland asked, taking a step toward Emil.

The elf leaned back in his chair, his cuffs clinking together as he crossed his arms against his chest. It was clear he would be keeping his mouth shut and didn't have a care in the world about the situation he was in. He was a little too relaxed...

When Kalland first approached the room, he expected that Emil wouldn't answer any of his questions. That didn't stop him from still wanting to smash that smug face until Emil's skull caved in.

Kalland didn't understand why he felt this protective edge toward Evenia Raldir, or why Emil's words and actions toward her made Kalland want to kill the elf he once tried to help. He couldn't let Emil get under his skin. Or let Evenia worm her way to his heart. Because something had shifted between them.

Taking a deep breath, he suppressed the urge to rip Emil to shreds. Because there was a bigger threat to Emil than him at this moment. His lip twitched at the thought. Emil caught the motion, and Kalland saw a bit of fear flicker in and out of Emil's eyes. A deep sense of satisfaction flashed in Kalland at the sight. Even if it was only short-lived, this asshole was finally about to get what he deserved. For once.

As if the Fates intervened and sensed it was time, the metal door suddenly started vibrating under the control of the Metal elf guard opening it. Catching sight of Alekze's grin, Kalland stepped farther into the room and away from the doorway so that their guest would have more room to work.

Emil's hands uncrossed as the door fully opened and Ozepinia—Ozi—walked in, her dark green curls bouncing with each step. Her petite frame was deceiving for the amount of power she possessed in her being.

With her silver, round glasses perched on her nose, she took in everyone in the room. Most elves had perfect eyesight, with their bodies able to heal most imperfections, but some inherited genes, like astigmatisms, could pass from one elf to another. Ozi was one who had to wear glasses and she embraced it. Honestly, the look made her seem even more innocent and incapable of hurting a fly.

Unfortunately for Emil, that was not the case. With the elven magic that coursed through her blood, she was capable of taking down Alekze, Asryn, Emil and Kalland at once.

And Emil knew it.

The color drained from Emil's face at the sight of her. Before them stood an Aeslige—an elf born of both the Moon and the Sun, possessing the rare power of both, which allowed them to enter one's mind, controlling what they would see and believe. Some called them Dream elves. Or, depending on who you asked, a Nightmare elf, because the images they planted in your mind weren't always pleasant.

In this case, Emil was about to face nightmare after nightmare for the next hour, until Kalland got what he wanted from him. Because in an hour, he would be setting off for a mission with the woman this elf was hunting. In an hour, he would have some fucking answers as to why Emil was targeting her.

And the clock was ticking.

29

Evenia

An hour. That was all he was leaving her with? Ugh, why did she agree to do this? The early departure. Going to Nulhe. Going with him. Going to search for The Darkness. The whole damn thing.

She was silently cursing her past self for agreeing to leave early and her past-past self for agreeing to any of it. Pulling herself out of her never-ending anxiety spiral, she followed Nishara, who was guiding her to the stables to greet Kalland and her horse for the road.

"How are you feeling about leaving?" Nishara asked, giving her a soft, knowing smile.

"I can't decide," Evenia sighed deeply. The packed bag hanging on her back sagged an inch from the movement. "I don't think I've had enough time to process leaving, let alone figure out how I feel. Although, with what just happened with Emil, I'm kind of glad to be going..."

"Fair enough." Nishara chuckled. "So, I guess moving up the deadline was a blessing in disguise?"

Evenia side-eyed her, glaring. "I wouldn't take it that far." Both women broke under the other's glare, as a small laugh escaped from Evenia's lips and Nishara grinned from ear to ear.

Evenia's laugh died and her stomach twisted in a knot when she saw they were approaching the stables. Each of the two massive cream-colored buildings had to be sixty yards long. Their double doors alone were taller than Evenia's whole house back home, with the largest horseshoes hanging just above the entrances of the doors. There was no way a real creature could have worn the horseshoe, but there was also no way an ordinary-sized horseshoe would serve as a noticeable decoration above such large doors.

Only a few feet away from the largest building, the doors opened. As if on cue, Kalland walked out of them with the reins of a horse in each hand. To his right was a light grey horse. The almost silver-colored coat was speckled with white, matching a white mane and tail. A beauty of a horse.

In his left hand were the reins to a horse that practically glowed in the light. Its hide looked like captured stars stuck in this horse's body, sparkling in the sun like a galaxy twinkling on its back. It was mesmerizing.

"Oh!" Nishara said, clapping her hands together in delight. At what, Evenia didn't know. "Oh! Ven, you're in for such a treat." Evenia had to laugh, because Nishara looked like a little kid who just learned her parents brought home a puppy. In the same breath, Kalland's glare toward Nishara gave her pause.

"What? What am I missing?" she asked, glancing back and forth between the two sentries having a stare-off.

Nishara finally rolled her eyes and sighed, but she turned toward Evenia again, smiling. "You'll find out later. Don't worry, it'll be amazing." Evenia couldn't figure out why Nishara sounded so excited after seeing two horses come out of the stables. "Just hold on tight," she whispered normally to Evenia, eliciting another glare from Kalland.

Not understanding what was going on, she shook her head, but responded, "Oka—"

She was interrupted by Nishara pulling her in for a big hug. "Be safe. Keep an eye out for my sister, Shiavari, and remember that if you need anything, anything at all, she'll be there." Nishara squeezed her, and Evenia did the same in return.

The pack on her back started to fall from the hug, but she ignored it, leaning further into the embrace. "I will," she said, clearing her throat.

The two women separated, and Evenia resecured the pack on her back.

"Don't think you're exempt from this," Nishara said, walking up to Kalland and pulling him in for a hug. To Evenia's surprise, he returned the embrace, wrapping his arms around Nishara's toned frame. "Come back to us in one piece, you hear?"

"Always," Kalland said.

They broke their embrace and Nishara hugged her once more, which made Evenia laugh. "Okay, okay, I'm going to head back now. Just be safe, you two," Nishara said.

"You don't have to worry about us," Kalland said, his voice kind. And Evenia nodded in agreement, even though she wasn't sure if she completely believed the words.

Seemingly satisfied, Nishara nodded and started walking away. Her strides only took her about five feet before she turned and started waving again.

Kalland laughed and said, "You're like a hovering parent, Nish." Evenia laughed when Nishara stuck out her tongue at him and kept walking back to the palace. "She's really taking a liking to you," Kalland's voice was suddenly deep again.

Evenia turned toward him. An inner battle ensued to keep her emotions intact because she realized she was starting to like being this close to him. "It's a good thing, too, because I like her," she said, smiling. As good looking as Kalland was, the horses pulled her attention again. "Who are these beauties?"

Kalland beamed at her. "Evenia, I'd like you to meet my horse, Xelfrina," he said, raising the reins in his right hand, belonging to the grey horse, "and your horse for the road, Rianore." The reins in his left hand lifted, pointing to the shimmery tan horse.

Evenia's jaw dropped in amazement, but it didn't mean that her heart didn't catch on the words "for the road." Because this was not her horse. This wasn't even her home. No, back home, she didn't have a horse. Not for the road, not for fun, not for anything.

But here, in Mircha, *this* Evenia did. Even if it was just for this mission, she would enjoy every second that she got to be around this beauty, Rianore.

Graciously, she took Rianore's reins from Kalland. "Thank you."

Xelfrina's reins in his hand, he started walking. Without encouraging her, Rianore immediately started following, prompting Evenia to do the same. She guessed they were going to where Alekze and Asryn were waiting for them.

"So, it's Ven, now?" Kalland asked.

Her head whipped to his, eyes glaring. "Call me that and you'll find yourself with a broken nose."

Chuckling, he said, "Well then, I guess it's a good thing elves heal quickly, even from a broken nose." He winked at her, and she felt equal parts arousal and irritation.

"Well then..." she started, mimicking him as she tried to keep the arousal at bay and let the irritation shine through. Yes, the irritation was the better emotion to act on right now. "I guess it's a good thing there's more than one way to break a nose," she said, winking back at him.

She was expecting another smart-ass reply. Another sarcastic comment. Another dark chuckle, half-laced with amusement, half-laced with a hidden "I wish I could just kill you now" tone. She was expecting something to come out of his mouth that would make her want to act on her threat.

What she wasn't prepared for was the sudden growing grin on his face, or her reaction to seeing it. It was a smile that reached his eyes and brought symmetrical dimples on each side of that panty-dropping-worthy smile.

Gods, panty-dropping smile? She peeled her eyes away from his dazzling white teeth. *Get a grip.* She was acting like a hormonal teenager.

The thought reminded her of growing up with her cousin, who was only a few years younger than her. When they both reached maturity, they realized they tended to have the same taste in boys, but the rule was to never fight over one. Never. Not even the cute, young professor who came to teach them about botany. Mr. Owernin Remiast. More commonly referred to as—well, what Émeriah had nicknamed him—Mr. Make Your Ovaries Explode.

Yeah, *panty-dropping smile* reminded her exactly of being a hormonal teenager. To her further irritation, she was shocked to discover that she preferred the reaction her body had experienced thus far in response to Kalland more than she had to anyone in the past, including Mr. Make Your Ovaries Explode...

The realization made her cheeks pink. She turned away, looking toward the horse next to her, so that Kalland wouldn't see her face. That would only make her feel even more embarrassed in that moment.

As she turned to her horse, her eyes caught on those twinkling stars again. She was mesmerized as she guided Rianore along with her on the path. Although, the horse seemed to actually be guiding Evenia by following Kalland with every step she took. It didn't seem to feel one way or another about Evenia's presence.

Now that she was closer to it, she realized that the stars looked more like glistening gems. Or like one of those shining rocks with hundreds of tiny crystals in it that she used to find by the lake in Poultom, just past the ferynmin berry field.

"This coloring, how does her coat shine like that? Is that why Nishara was so excited?" she asked, her face turning toward Kalland's once more. His smile faltered, and her curiosity only nagged at her more over what Nishara was talking about, and why he seemed so dead set on Evenia not knowing why.

"Rianore's a Seinoradt—a breed of horse native to Valoreg. I trained her as a foal back home and brought her here with me when she was old enough. She's been with me for many years." There was no mistaking the fondness in his voice when speaking about the horse. There was also no denying how it made Evenia's heart melt a little. Just a little.

Damn it. No, damn *him.* He was so fucking cheery and kind of all of a sudden. She didn't know what to make of it. But...she also liked it?

As if he could sense the war of emotions and thoughts inside her mind, his smile turned upward again. There was a glint in his eyes that made her want to both grab his face to kiss him and, well, break his nose.

Reluctantly, she turned back to the horse, admiring her coat once more. But then, a question came to mind, and she found herself looking at Kalland again. His eyes were still on hers. Seeing that glint this time, she felt less like punching him and more like kissing him.

Before she could act on either feeling, she asked, "Why Rianore? Why did you pick that name?"

"It's a name that means 'beautiful' in Valoregan." He smiled at Rianore, his pride showing through. "And she is a beautiful horse."

A fitting name, then. Evenia nodded, understanding why he chose his native tongue for such a beautiful name.

"How do you say it properly in Valoregan?" she asked, and her cheeks flushed again when he looked at her with surprise. "The Common Tongue is the only language I know. Unless you count the Witch's Words, which I don't use often. Well, no, I mean, yes, but no," she rambled.

Her lips clamped shut as she realized that she was giving away that she didn't practice her witchcraft much. The truth was, she didn't need to. Not really. Not as an In-Between witch, whose powers from the Elements came to her as naturally as breathing. Granted, general spells required her to speak them, but Elemental magic did not.

"Like what you did for Emil?" he asked, an edge to his tone.

Her ears perked. Was he finally ready to talk about it? About what happened that night? Likely not. But she nodded anyway. "Yes, I'd always wanted to use that spell. Truth be told, I had never been in a position to ask for a dryad's help before. Seen one, yes. Many, actually. Especially in the springtime, coming back to Enacor from their hibernation in the south. But I had never used the spell, and I didn't know if it would even work." She sighed at the confession.

"I'm almost a little happy it did work. *Almost,* if only for you to experience that," he said. His voice was grave, angry, but she knew it wasn't directed at her anymore. Not when it came to this matter.

She huffed a laugh. "Yeah, I know. That's an experience I will never forget. The dryad was nice. Funny, even." She smiled at the memory of the dryad, at his humor. What an honor it was that he chose to answer her plea and reveal himself to her upon her request for help.

"I didn't realize a dryad could be funny," Kalland said, intrigued.

"Oh, very. You should have stuck around and found out," she said, elbowing him the way she and Kaj had done just that morning at breakfast.

His eyes widened, seeming like he wasn't sure how to respond to the playful act.

She shook her head. "Part of me wishes I hadn't saved him, wondering if it would have saved us unwanted trouble, like what happened today. But then...I wonder what would have happened if I hadn't." She glanced at him, the unspoken words of whether Kalland would be arrested and tried for murder as a consequence of her not helping. Not to mention whether she could live with herself if she hadn't done all she could to help before someone was killed.

He only stood taller in his stance as they walked, not a sign of remorse on his face. "What about the other part of you?" She cocked an eyebrow at his question, not sure what he meant. "One part of you wishes you hadn't helped, but what about the other part of you? Do you fully regret it?" Despite the questions, his deep baritone had a calming effect on her body.

She shook her head. "No. In fact, the other part of me thinks not helping him would have been one of the greatest regrets of my life. As cruel and unkind as Emil may be, he is still a living being. I couldn't just...walk away." She glanced at Kalland, who had done just that.

He shrugged. "It wasn't difficult to do." His tone was hard.

Shock filled her at his words. "You mean, you don't regret dropping him? Not even a little bit? Not even a second of regret?"

"Not even for a millisecond." Her breath caught and her steps halted. He stopped with her, the horses following suit. "Knowing who he is, what he's said, what he's done, and now knowing what he planned to do today," he took a small step toward her, "my only regret is not dropping him before you entered the room."

"You can't possibly mean that..." Her mouth hung open in shock.

He took a bigger step toward her, looking so deeply into her eyes—switching from her left to her right eye—that her heart stopped. "I do, if it means he wouldn't have come as close as he did to cutting the light out of these eyes." Her breath caught as his stare intensified. "The wholly, piercing blue or the one split in two, like blades of grass bleeding into the ripples of a lake." His voice was soft, just above a normal whisper.

The world might have stopped. Surely, she hadn't just heard those words. No one, absolutely no one had ever talked about her eyes in such a way. In fact, she was always teased for having one two-toned eye, with jokes about how she didn't stand a chance to fit in because not even her eye color could choose to be normal.

Even *she* hated her eyes. It helped knowing that she shared the blue of her eyes with her mother, but with no one else in her family possessing pale green eyes—not her aunt, not her grandma, not her grandpa—she had a suspicion that the two-toned eye of hers was a result of her biological father's genes.

Yes, she hated them. To her, the green represented the roaring beast inside of her that she inherited from him. It was visibly fighting with the serene blue she inherited from her witch mother. Just another painful reminder that her biological father would never be there, never wanted to know her, but still plagued her very existence with the genes he left her—her shifter side. The genes that fought with her day in and day out, making life difficult. It put her very existence in danger, not to mention made her a fucking target for The Darkness in the first place.

She took a deep breath, flushing down the anger brewing at the thought of her biological father and what his shifter genes left her with. Maybe if he had wanted to be part of her life, she would have a reason to not care. At least, that was what she told herself.

It was what her younger self imagined when she would picture her father showing up on her aunt's doorstep and apologizing for not coming sooner, wanting to make up for lost time. But at twenty-six years old, she now knew that was a pointless dream. He was never coming. He never cared to before, and he certainly didn't now.

Shaking her head, she focused on Kalland's words again. While she heard many things about her eyes over the years, no one ever talked about them so poetically. Or about her that way, for that matter. She didn't know how to respond, since it was a compliment for her eyes, not her. Or not really a compliment. Just...his thoughts? She wasn't sure how to categorize his words.

So, she chose to comment on the topic at hand, not the poetry Sothenas was suddenly spouting. "But he's your friend. Surely—"

"*Was* my friend. Was," he interrupted, correcting her. "And only barely. Truthfully, he attached himself to me as his Wind elf mentor, and I tried so hard to help him be a better sentry—a better person—but there's only so much you can do if the person does not want to change or better themselves."

Evenia nodded, not sure how to respond to that.

"I'm sorry for what he's done. For what he said to you, and what he tried to pull today. It won't happen again." His eyes searched hers again.

Wanting to comfort him, her hand instinctively reached toward his. Thankfully, she realized it and stopped before her skin touched his. "It's not your fault. Like you said, you can only help someone so much." Shrugging, she turned to start walking. Her eyes met his again when a warm Wind suddenly enveloped her, stopping her in her tracks.

"I mean it, with every fiber of my being, that he will never harm you." He took a step toward her, and she didn't step away, didn't put distance between them as his delicious patchouli and bergamot scent permeated around her.

The witty comeback on the tip of her tongue escaped her, her mind going blank, as her breath caught when she saw the look in his eyes. "What did you do to him?" Her voice was soft, as if she was uncertain she wanted to know the answer.

"Not enough." His eyes slowly searched her body, landing last on her face that was almost impaled by an arrow an hour ago. "And nothing he didn't deserve."

How comforting. Her throat bobbed. "Did you find out why he did what he did today?"

"No." His brows furrowed and his fists clenched at his sides. Sighing, he said, "He had some sort of mental block we couldn't get past. Something far beyond what I thought him capable of."

Those grey eyes suddenly seemed far off, as if he was lost in thought. She shifted on her feet—the warm Wind still enveloping her, moving with her. The movement drew his attention back to the present moment.

Clearing his throat, he continued. "But we have sentries watching him, and he'll be under their...care until they break that mental barrier. We'll learn more soon enough."

Not wanting to know what these sentries would do to Emil—what *Kalland* did to him—she opted for letting it go by starting to walk again. After a few steps, the warm Wind left her, and she suddenly longed to feel it again.

30

Evenia

"Ah, there's my favorite sparring partner!"

Evenia's head popped up at a woman's voice. Kalland faced toward a red-haired woman in a beige Mirchan tunic walking their way.

Kalland smiled. "Yeah, just in time for me to be leaving. We need to do a better job of coordinating our missions."

"How do you know I'm not staying away on purpose?" the woman asked, winking at Kalland before he pulled her into a hug. Evenia had not seen the woman before, and she was trying her damndest not to let jealousy interfere with her impression of her.

"Bullshit," he huffed a laugh into her wine-colored hair, making Evenia's stomach twist in knots. "You always miss me too much for me to believe that."

"I miss fighting with you, is more like it," she said, slapping his arm as she released him and went to hug Alekze. "Hey, big man. Missed you." Even at an average height, she was so tiny in his arms, practically swallowed up by his tattooed arms.

"Hey, Red," Alekze said as they broke up their hug.

Trying not to break eye contact under the pressure of a social interaction, Evenia stood there awkwardly, as the beautiful woman now approached her and Rianore.

"Hi, I'm Marensha, Mircha's resident Fire witch," the woman said, sticking her arm out to Evenia in greeting. She took her forearm, shaking it once before releasing it.

The woman's porcelain skin bore faint freckles on her cheeks, nose, and forehead, and her eyes were hazel. Now that they were closer, Evenia was surprised to realize the woman was human—a witch—and looked to be not that much younger than her Aunt Siersha.

A human witch wearing Mircha's symbol?

"I'm Evenia," she said, suddenly self-conscious in the presence of another witch. It was hard enough to keep her In-Between powers hidden from these perceptive elves, let alone having to hide them from another witch, who would easily be able to spot an In-Between witch's powers if in use. Was she coming with them to Nulhe? Evenia's palms started sweating at that thought.

"I know who you are, and I've heard you've been giving this one shit," Marensha said, a toothy grin on her face as she cocked her head in the direction of Kalland.

Fighting the heat wanting to rise to her cheeks at everyone here seeming to know her damn business, Evenia casually shrugged the irritation away. "Trust me, it's a mutual thing."

"Is it now?" Marensha asked, her eyebrows raised. Her gaze flicked from Evenia to Kalland, and back again. "Interesting."

"What is?" She crossed her arms out of habit, but she didn't like the witch's tone.

"Oh, nothing, just that it's not every day someone can get under Kalland's skin, and especially not for him to *like* it." Her tone was playful, and her words caused the heat to rise to Evenia's cheeks again. Evenia resisted the urge to send Ice throughout her body to cool off the reaction.

"Fuck off," Kalland laughed as Marensha joined in.

"Right back at you, lover boy," Marensha winked at him, and Evenia's stomach dropped.

Lover boy? First the big hug, and now the pet name? She looked to Kalland, who was rolling his eyes and smiling, while leaning up against his horse. He made eye contact with her, his smile big enough to reach his eyes and show his dimples. She held his stare, searching, as if hoping she could read his thoughts. Could it be that she got this all wrong? Was the woman in front of her his girlfriend?

Before Evenia could process everything, Marensha was talking again. "It's a shame you're leaving, when we've only just met. It would be a nice change being around another witch, who isn't a healer." Marensha smiled and Evenia did her best to return it. It wasn't this woman's fault that Kalland played them both, if Marensha and Kalland were even a couple.

"It's a welcome break from all these pointy-eared bastards." The witch grinned as her voice raised, but the two elves only smiled and shook their heads. Her eyes returned to Evenia's, taking in her slightly pointed ears. "Well, sort of a break from them."

"I'll take 'sort of.'" Evenia's lip twitched upward. "And I agree, but I think being around another witch would kind of make me miss my coven."

Marensha grimaced at the word *coven*. "I wouldn't go that far. But it would be nice not being the only one here."

"What do you mean?" Evenia felt her brows furrow.

Covens were meant to be like a witch's second family—their first, in some cases. It was a community where a witch learned about their powers, grew in their craft, and could rely on their coven to do what needed to be done. So long as the coven agreed, of course.

"A story for another time." Marensha's tone left no room for discussion, but her smile was sad.

Evenia nodded, respecting the Fire witch's wishes. It wasn't her business who was or wasn't in a coven, or why.

Marensha shifted on her feet, her head gesturing in the direction of Sothenas. "Don't let this one boss you around." Her voice was loud enough for him to hear. Then, her voice went low as she focused on Evenia and said, "But don't get any ideas. He might be a prick, but he's our prick."

The Fire witch's irises started to burn with flames, a bright red in comparison to the deep wine color of her hair. It was mesmerizing. One could get lost in those embers. But just as quickly as the flames ignited, they extinguished, with her hazel eyes visible once more.

"Who are you?" she whispered. Marensha's wide eyes focused on Evenia, and her red lips slightly parted in surprise.

"Wh–what?" Evenia stammered. Her heart was pounding. She couldn't possibly know her secret after only a short interaction, and Evenia was certain she hadn't used a lick of her magic.

Sucking a deep breath, Marensha recovered quickly and seemingly dropped the subject as she looked to the two elves, who were finishing up packing their saddles. Those wary eyes briefly flickered back to Evenia, but her words were directed toward them all. "Take care of each other, or I'll have to come out there and kick your asses," she yelled.

Nodding to no one in particular, she began walking away backward. Her eyes lingered a bit on Evenia before she fully turned toward the palace. Her red hair whipped in the wind behind her.

That was weird, Evenia thought to herself.

"Bye, Marensha. Try not to piss too many people off while I'm gone," Kalland called after her.

The witch raised her hand in the air and flipped him off before turning her head and smiling at him. Evenia's stomach flipped again at the flirting, and she silently cursed the unwanted reaction.

"I see she tried the flame trick on you. Did it work?" Kalland asked from behind her.

"What?" she asked, without giving him the satisfaction of looking at him. The deceptive asshole. This was going to be a long journey.

"It's a trick she uses to intimidate others. I heard her threaten you. So, did it work?" Kalland's tone was playful, only succeeding in irritating her further.

Evenia wanted to call forth *her* access to Fire and send the flames to her own eyes. Hel, she wanted to light his ass on fire. But doing either of those things would give her away as being more than just a simple Light Elemental witch, and she couldn't risk that exposure.

So, she turned toward him and narrowed her eyes, letting her anger—a formidable enough power on its own—come forth. "Do I look intimidated?"

The corner of his mouth twitched. "You look fired up," he said. "*Hot,*" he Wind whispered.

Fired up? Hot? She didn't take the bait. She knew she hadn't called forth her Fire. There was no way she had flames in her eyes or at her fingertips. Instead of rising to the bait, she calmed her breathing. He was just trying to get a rise from her, and that wouldn't happen. He wasn't worth it.

"Just eager to leave," she finally said, resigning a bit. He blinked a few times, as if he was not expecting that answer from her. As if he expected her to play along. But fuck him. She turned back around to grab her sack.

"Here, let me." He reached for her bag, and both of them now held one end of it.

She pulled the sack toward her, attempting to free it from his clutches. "I'm perfectly capable of packing my own horse," she scoffed.

"Are you?" He looked her up and down, slowly. "Shall we get a step stool out here for you?" His lip twitched again.

Bastard.

She felt the Fire simmering again, waiting to be unleashed, but she refused to let it win. Refused to let herself be exposed to him. Maybe she'd use his own Wind magic on him? She needed some sort of an outlet for all this anger. The thought reminded her of Marensha calling Kalland her favorite sparring partner. Kicking someone's ass would be a great outlet for her anger right now.

Smiling at the mental image, she said, "It's a shame we never got to take to the training grounds, Sothenas. Laying you flat on your ass sounds like the best way to start a trip."

Alekze chuckled ahead toward her right. Kalland's eyes briefly flickered to the blonde male's, which only resulted in a deeper chuckle from Alekze, before Kalland returned his gaze to Evenia.

"My mother raised a gentleman and taught me not to hit girls." He smirked.

Seriously? "She must not have done a very good job, if Marensha's your sparring partner," Evenia shot back, the jealousy she couldn't shove down peeking its way through. She soon realized her mistake in her words.

Kalland tensed and Evenia felt the air shift. He took a step toward her, propping an arm on either side of her horse's saddle, boxing her in without laying a finger on her. But she held her ground, chin raised.

"Rule Number Two: Don't. Talk. About. My. Mother." His tone was rough and his eyes were void of humor. A sign to her that he would make good on his threat of kicking her off the mission if she didn't tread carefully.

Still, Evenia didn't falter. She could take this grey-eyed elf any day. To be fair, he was the one who brought up his mother first.

Before she could respond, Alekze cleared his throat. She watched Kalland blink a few times, washing away the anger from his eyes and face. He looked at Evenia, as if just realizing how close they were now, and slowly stepped away without a word.

"Good start to the trip, no?" Alekze looked at her, teasing. She gave him a half smile and returned her gaze to Kalland's before he turned away, walking to his horse.

The urge to tell off his retreating form quickly escaped her as she turned and sighed into her saddle. She recognized that anger. Knew that overwhelming feeling of grief in his eyes.

He took everything from me.

That was what he said to her after The Darkness's shadows attacked. Could that be referring to his mother? His family?

Suddenly, she understood why this unpredictable elf was so invested in The Darkness. In *her*. And to her annoyance, she found she couldn't blame him...if she was right.

She finished with her pack, careful not to crumple the still-unopened folders inside. Chancing a look at Kalland, she knew he was pretending to do the same, because he'd already finished securing his bags before Marensha left. He was tugging at the straps along the saddle. His gaze had remained averted from hers ever since she spoke about his mother.

Looking at his tense back as he stood next to his dapple-grey mare, she sighed and pulled her eyes away to Alekze, who was standing next to his chestnut horse, who Evenia had found out earlier was affectionately called Pork Chop.

When Kalland and Evenia met up with Alekze after leaving the stables, Evenia had been expecting to meet the infamous Asryn, but she wasn't there. Alekze informed them his sister decided to forgo a horse and leave early in her wolf form, claiming it would be faster and freer, as well as give her some time to catch up with their mother—the owner of the safe house they were going to.

Evenia felt a little disappointed, having looked forward to meeting Asryn, but she couldn't blame anyone for wanting to spend time with their mother. She would do the same if she could.

Wouldn't she? The thought took her by surprise as guilt flooded her. She would like to think she would if her own mother were around, but she did turn down the opportunity to see her aunt and cousin before leaving for this trip. So, could she really say she would do the same?

The sight of Kalland mounting his horse pulled her from a downward spiral of guilt and shame, bringing her attention back toward the brooding elf.

"Ready?" he asked no one in particular, as he still was not looking at her.

Alekze nodded in response, mounting his horse.

Mounting her own horse, *without* a step stool, she nodded at Kalland's back. "Ready."

She wasn't sure how true the word was as she spoke it, but there was no turning back now. She was really doing this, and she would figure out to prepare for what lay ahead for her. Whatever that may be, she would be ready.

31

Kalland

The clearing of a throat cut through the sounds of hooves clopping and birds chirping, pulling Kalland from his thoughts.

Two hours passed since they left Mircha. Two hours in which they rode silently. Peacefully. It was inevitable after the awkward way they left the conversation. A small part of him felt bad for snapping at her. It wasn't her fault she didn't know about his past, about his mother and father.

Closing his eyes, he let out a long exhale. He shouldn't have lost his cool like that. Still, he wasn't complaining about the quiet ride.

Then again...

His eyes opened, falling on the blonde riding Rianore feet from him. While the silence was peaceful, he also didn't mind the sound of this petite blonde's voice. A realization that both surprised and pleased him. Especially in moments like these, when she gave him a look that said she wanted to talk to him. To say something that was only for his ears.

Smirking, he obliged. *"What can I do for you?"* he Wind whispered to her, offering her the current of connection she needed to speak with him. He had tried to prevent the smile from reaching his face, but his self-control dwindled more and more in her presence. The thought that she needed anything from him—*wanted* anything from him—did something strange to his chest.

"I have a question," Evenia's soft voice traveled through the Wind and caressed his ears.

His brows furrowed when he saw her eyes widen and lips part after the words left her plump lips. Something fluttered in his stomach at her words. Curiosity got the best of him. So, without fully looking in her direction, he quickly dipped his chin in a sign of permission to carry on.

In his periphery, he saw her spine straighten. She looked confident. Beautiful. *"Are you and Marensha together?"*

Whiplash wouldn't be a shock as a result of the speed at which his head whipped toward her. Shocked by his reaction, her reins slipped an inch in her hands, as she fumbled to regain her hold. Quickly recovering, she rolled her eyes at the slow smile working its way on his lips, and he could tell she regretted asking.

Were Marensha and him together? Abso-fucking-lutely not. Never were, never would be. He loved Marensha, but he had never been *in* love with her. Never felt any sort of intimate feelings toward her at all, in fact.

They teased one another, and she was the first one he would walk up to at one of their parties back in Mircha, if he even attended. Except, that was mostly because she was fun to be around and would never judge him for not enjoying the gatherings like everyone else.

The mere fact that Evenia seemed to be bothered by the encounter he had with Marensha made him feel an alarming amount of satisfaction. Did she feel for him more than she let on? His mind briefly wandered to their encounter in the hall that morning when she admitted to checking him out.

The corners of his eyes crinkled as his smile grew. It only deepened when she scoffed in annoyance at his reaction.

"Raldir, if I didn't know any better, I'd say you're jealous," he Wind whispered back to her.

"You wish, Sothenas," she shot back, but there was too much of a teasing element in her tone for the words to sound as harsh as they were probably meant to be.

She was flustered. In more ways than one? He shook his head for enjoying this far more than he should be.

"First, you admit to checking me out, and now you get...territorial. Is there something you'd like to confess?"

A flood of regret doused every ounce of amusement and joy he felt. He took it too far.

If looks could kill, he imagined his guts would be spilling out of him the second the humor left her eyes. "*You know what? Fuck you.*" She flipped him off as she tapped her toes into Rianore, catching up to Alekze in front of them.

"*Now you're just threatening me with a good time.*" Bright stars shined from the force of shutting his eyes closed as the words left his lips. Why was he like this? Why couldn't he just keep his mouth shut for once?

His eyes flew open again, but she wasn't looking at him. Instead, she was staring at his best friend, and the look in her eyes made his stomach flip.

The large elf nodded at Evenia, with a strand of his blonde hair slipping out of its low bun. "Get tired of the silent treatment back there?" he teased her.

Kalland's grip on his reins tightened. Was Alekze actually...flirting with her?

Her shoulders shrugged. "You're definitely the fun one."

Someone needed to come pry his jaw open. There was a chance it was permanently shut, as molars grinded against molars.

Alekze's deep chuckle brought a smile to her face. "If I'm the fun one, then there really is a problem." His bun bounced as he shook his head before facing forward again.

"Come now, Alekze, haven't you heard that the quiet ones are always the most fun?" She winked, and he swore he saw Alekze's cheeks pink above his blonde beard.

The heat that was coursing through Kalland right now was a different kind than the one he had experienced previously in Evenia's presence. It was a dark feeling; a dangerous feeling. All he could think about were the ways in which he would like to torture his best friend for even looking at her like that, while wanting to punish Evenia for teasing him like this. There was no doubt in his mind she knew exactly what she was doing to him.

A smile spread on her face as she opened her mouth to start talking again, but he took that opportunity to strike. "*Are you trying to drive me mad, Raldir?*" He didn't know it was possible to growl in a Wind current, but the words weren't coming out any other way.

He caught sight of the goosebumps that graced her flesh at the sudden Wind current, but she didn't look back at him as she continued trying to make small talk with Alekze. Kalland smiled to himself, knowing that trying to make Alekze social was like trying to pull teeth from a dragon.

He did his best to try to ignore the blond who was driving him crazy. Except, it was a different kind of feeling toward her now, one he didn't much care for.

Or did he?

He shook his head. They still had at least five more hours of riding before they would get to their usual campsite when riding toward the border of Akvar. It was not the original direction Kalland and Evenia were meant to be heading, but the detour was welcomed, knowing who would be on the other end of that journey.

When Kalland and Evenia had made it from the stables to Alekze and Pork Chop, the elf told them that his mother, Irenz, had confirmed they would all stop by her home—and their unofficial safe house—before going to their individual destinations. Asryn had already left in her snowy white wolf form by the time they reached Alekze and Pork Chop, which wasn't surprising because Asryn always preferred her wolf to any other form of transportation. She had been like that since a young pup.

Their detour did mean his and Evenia's arrival to Nulhe would be delayed by a day, but that was fine by Kalland. He never looked forward to being in the snow, but he loved Irenz—who took him in as part of her family the second she met him/ And he had a feeling that being around someone as calm and caring as Irenz would be good for Evenia right now.

He hadn't missed the way her heart pounded in fear whenever she saw shadows dancing in the corners, or the anxiety attack she experienced the night they ran into each other in the hall. He recognized the signs from his own experience with them after his parents' deaths. And then, there was the panic attack she had just that morning.

After the meeting, he pulled her into the secret alcove down the hall from Andira's office. He didn't know why he chose to pull her in there instead of having a conversation out in the open. A part of him just felt compelled to be...alone with her.

And since she was so determined to go off an adventure, he left her there to find her way back on her own. The truth was, he hadn't gone far. He didn't stalk her, per se, just...kept an eye on her. And it was a good thing he had, because his heart nearly cracked when he saw her breaking in that hall.

The second she started crying, he wanted to cradle her in his arms and wipe the tears away. Instead, he sought the one person he could think of to help comfort her considering she'd already given Evenia a gift. Evanescing to Nishara was out of the question, because he would have had to know her exact location in order to find her. Sure, he could have evanesced to random locations in the hopes that one of them would be right, but it was not the most effective solution and would take far too long.

Thankfully, with the type of Wind magic that flowed through Kalland's blood from his family line, he was able to search for Nishara's aura on the Wind and travel straight to her. Being used to his sudden appearances, her surprise passed quickly and she didn't hesitate when he told her he needed her help. In a matter of seconds, he pulled her from the training grounds, and brought her straight back to Evenia.

It was instinct at the time. When he thought about it later, it was because he knew Nishara wouldn't just give her dagger to anyone. So, he took a chance on who to bring to her. It seemed to have paid off, since Nishara was by her side during Emil's attack, and again when she took Evenia to the stables.

A muscle in his jaw ticked at the thought of Emil. That bastard. How dare he try to hurt her? He not only threatened to use her as bait for The Darkness the night before, but then he tried to *kill* her.

The sound and pressure of his molars grinding brought Kalland back to reality. On a deep inhale, he released the tension in his body, imagining it flowing out of him.

Neither Alekze nor Evenia seemed to notice the sound. In fact, Evenia was trying her damndest to find a topic Alekze seemed interested in, and the grump looked ridiculously uncomfortable.

All because Kalland asked if she was jealous.

He sighed. This was going to be a long fucking trip.

32

Evenia

lekze was a good sport. It was clear he wasn't interested in talking, but he still let her go on and on about Enacor and the sights there.

It started off as a way to make conversation and pass the time, but the more she spoke, the more she realized that Enacor no longer felt like home. That it really never did after her uncle passed... Speaking about the good of her hometown with Alekze was her desperate attempt to find something she did like about it. So far, she was failing.

At least Alekze was nice to her. The truth was, he wasn't the elf she wanted to talk to. Not that he talked much to begin with...

"If you're trying to make me jealous now," a familiar deep voice growled, *"then you're about to make me do something I don't want to do in front of my brother."* A shudder of pleasure skated up her spine at the threat and the voice that came with it. In the same breath, a warm breeze snaked around her waist, feeling like a strong arm embracing her. *"And don't think I won't,"* he added.

Her breath stalled as the Wind's invisible hand moved down to her thigh, stopping for a few seconds, as if waiting for her to tell him to fuck off again. But to her surprise, she didn't. Whether due to curiosity or desire, she didn't know, but she wanted to see how this would play out.

A thought occurred to her as his power embraced her. Besides when he pinned her after she put a knife to his groin, when he helped her with her panic attack in the hallway, and then that stunt in the alcove, he barely touched her with his physical body. Instead, his Wind was always caressing her ears, weighing down her chest, grounding her.

"Funny how you're not willing to touch me with your body, but you have no problems touching me with your magic," she teased.

Everything stopped. There was no more warm embrace on her, and she no longer felt his presence. Shit.

Her eyes briefly flickered to him. *"That wasn't telling you to stop. Just an observation of your touch."*

She sucked in a breath as an invisible hand started caressing her thigh again in slow, soothing circles. The movement silenced any response from her, and she felt a wetness pool as the sensation moved to her inner thigh.

"Hmm. So, the fun one, huh?" His voice was deep, sending a wave of heat pulsing through her core. *"Are you trying to drive me crazy, vhi'aiorhi?"*

Who was the jealous one, now? And what did he call her?

She straightened her spine, trying to hide the way her body reacted to the pet name and his touch. *"I don't know, is it working, lover boy?"* she snapped back down the Wind current, as the memory of a different pet name came to mind.

The invisible hand clutched her inner thigh before releasing it. Her breath stalled in anticipation, waiting to see what it would do next, and if she could hide her reactions from the unaware Alekze riding calmly next to her.

The invisible hand inched closer toward her center. *"Is that really what this is about? Are you jealous, Evenia?"* When the hand cupped her center, she clamped her mouth shut, silencing a gasp. She turned her head toward the trees to her right and away from Alekze.

She started to pull back on her reins—pull away from Alekze—when the pressure tightened on her clit. Eyes wide, she snapped her gaze to the grey-eyed elf diagonally behind her.

"Uh-uh. Where's the fun in that?" Her eyes rolled in the back of her head as he started a gentle rhythm on her clit. *"If you want me to continue, you have to stay exactly where you are. Where the fun is."*

Curse this bastard of an elf. But fuck, as embarrassed as she was to be touched next to someone else—practically in public—and by an elf she wasn't sure how she felt about at the moment, her body wanted this. The wetness pooling between her legs was proof enough.

"But if you want me to stop..." The hand momentarily stopped its rhythm, and she shot her gaze to his. *"Just say the word."*

Maintaining eye contact, she shook her head. A silent demand to not stop. With a heat in his eyes, he continued the rhythm. Biting her lip to suppress her delight was her response.

"How...am I...supposed to be...quiet...when you're...touching me...like this?" she asked him, struggling to get the words out in-between breaths.

"Then don't be quiet."

She would have glared at him if she could, but she was afraid glancing at him too much would give their communication away to Alekze. So, instead, she discreetly flipped him off behind her back.

"Feisty. I like it," he said, increasing the pressure.

Her hands were squeezing the reins, and she couldn't hide her heavy breathing. Not even through her tightly closed lips.

Sensing a change in her breathing, Alekze looked over at her. "You good?" he asked, assessing her face. His gaze moved lower, down to her slightly heaving chest.

Shit.

"Choose your next words carefully, vhi-aiorhi," Kalland Wind whispered. *"The quiet ones are the most fun, remember?"* She wanted to smack him and tell him not to stop all at the same time.

"Fine," she managed to get out on a breath. "Just...feeling...anxious," she lied. That had to be believable considering where they were headed, right?

"Oh, right," Alekze said, rubbing the back of his neck, suddenly looking uncomfortable. Thankfully, comforting others didn't appear to be Alekze's forte, as he averted his gaze forward once more.

Ugh, men, she thought to herself, rolling her eyes. In the same moment, her eyes got caught in the back of her head as the invisible hand slipped a finger inside her.

"Good girl," he Wind whispered, and she about lost it at the unexpected praise.

"Fuck...you," she responded.

She felt a deep chuckle come down the Wind current. *"Is that what you'd like to be doing right now?"* She flipped him off behind her back again, but her fingers quickly ended up digging into her low back as the invisible hand stuck another finger in her. *"Fuck, Evenia, I can feel how wet you are all the way over here."*

If she kept hearing that deep voice caressing her ear, she was going to lose it. *"Kalland..."*

The fingers faltered for half a second before increasing in speed.

"Say it again."

She squeezed tighter on the reins. That fucking voice. It was deep and dripping in desire for her.

"Kalland..." His fingers picked up speed inside of her as his thumb continued rubbing her clit. *"If you...don't...stop...I'll..."*

"You'll what? Come for me?"

Fucking hel. She nodded once, and he sent a Wind barrier to her mouth, constricting her air flow. She silently thanked him for the privacy, but knew it was partially for selfish reasons, because he'd still be able to feel her reaction to coming against his Wind barrier. That somehow made it even hotter.

Now, she could make noise and still be quiet. Halfway turning her body in her saddle, she faced the trees passing by instead of seeing Alekze next to her. One hand clutched her chest and the other on the reins, as she decided not to deny her body the release it so desperately wanted.

The next thing she knew, Kalland appeared on horseback next to her, blocking her line of sight from the trees. His eyes were instantly locked on hers. She heard Alekze say something next to her, but she couldn't make out the words over the pounding of her heart.

Kalland said normally, "I've got her." His voice sounded husky as his eyes remained locked on hers.

"That's it..." he Wind whispered to her, increasing the rhythm on her clit. *"I'm not going to stop until you come for me. I want to look into your eyes as you do."*

Fuuuuuuck. That was her undoing. The look in his eyes. The heat. The lust. The desire. More importantly, the way he seemed to want to pleasure her. Her eyes stayed on his as she felt her inner walls clench around the invisible fingers. She moaned into the Wind barrier, knowing her sounds would be silenced. His eyes shuttered, likely feeling it all against the barrier.

No longer able to fight her powerful release, she broke eye contact when the last wave hit.

"That's it." He coaxed her through it, until the last wave of pleasure passed.

As she came down from her high, her breathing going back to normal, he slowly released the Wind hand on her center and the barrier around her mouth.

She locked eyes with him once more, only to see that his had suddenly hardened. There was still heat deep down inside them, but there was clearly something else on his mind now.

"*How's that for an answer as to if Marensha and I are dating?*" he Wind whispered to her. "*I may be many things, but a cheater is not one of them. I belong to no one.*" His eyes bore into hers before he slowly retreated back to his spot behind Alekze and her.

A different kind of heat flushed to her cheeks, embarrassed for asking, and even more embarrassed for giving into temptation and coming next to Alekze. The emotion was accompanied by anger at his reaction and reasoning for pleasuring her. *Asshole.*

She adjusted herself in the saddle, hanging back from Alekze to ride in-between the two elves, rather than next to either one. She didn't want to talk to anyone the rest of the trip.

But *damn*. She smiled to herself because she also didn't regret letting him in. Her body was calmer and more relaxed than she had been in a long time. He might be an ass, but at least he knew how to put his hands to good use.

Her bottom lip bit into her teeth as she suppressed an incredulous laugh. The tension in her shoulders stayed away and the shadow of a smile remained on her face for hours after.

33

Evenia

A breeze ever so gently caressed her face, and she leaned into it. Slowly, her eyes closed as she created a mental image of this exact moment and how it made her feel: the sounds of crickets chirping; the smell of crisp, fresh air and pine needles; the feel of the warm breeze across her face—

A *warm* breeze. Evenia's eyes flew open. She looked over at Kalland, who was smiling at her from the other side of the now-dead campfire.

"Shouldn't you be sleeping?" he Wind whispered to her.

Her eyes rolled in the back of her head as she pulled the blanket closer to her chin, suddenly feeling even colder with the absence of his warm magic. The closer they got to Akvar, the more faux fur blankets she had to wrap around herself.

When she grabbed the last one, Kalland explained to her that the reason Mircha exclusively used faux fur was because of the hunting and treatment of shifters and werewolves. It made her appreciate the Peacekeeping Realm just a little bit more.

"Shouldn't you?" She glanced at him from the corner of her eye.

This was the first time they'd spoken to one another since she asked if he and Marensha were together, and he...proved his point. She couldn't help herself after the use of the pet name "lover boy" did something to her stomach that made her feel like she'd held an eight-minute plank and ate bad fish at the same time. She hoped finding out the answer would make the feeling go away. Instead, she ended up embarrassing herself and giving him more fuel to use against her. Although, it wasn't all bad...

With full bellies from the food they packed for the trip, they were now laying down not far from the dwindling campfire and doing their best to soak up every ounce of warmth it had left to offer. It was also helping a bit with her sore muscles from riding for hours.

He shrugged and shifted onto his back, his gaze turning toward the night sky. *"I like looking at the moon on nights like these."* He paused for a moment, his eyes never leaving the sky. *"The stars might be hidden behind the clouds, but the moon's light can't be dimmed."*

Shifting onto her side, she propped her head in her hand. A mirror image of what he looked like only moments before, when he sent the warm breeze her way.

"I didn't take you for a poet, Sothenas," she teased.

"That was hardly a poem, Raldir." He rolled his eyes, but he didn't shift his focus from the sky. *"You can't look at that and tell me you don't think it's beautiful."* His voice was soft, even for a Wind whisper.

She studied his relaxed face a moment longer before shifting onto her back once more to look to the sky. No, she couldn't disagree with him, for above her was one of the most picturesque night skies she'd ever witnessed.

The moon was poised high in the sky, and around it laid three rings. Closest to the moon was an ethereal circle of milky white, with a yellow-orange ring around that, and a lavender outer ring surrounding both. Watching the glistening stars on a clear night could be beautiful or even fun, but this was one of the most mesmerizing and magical things she'd ever seen.

As she studied the sight, she noticed that the clouds were moving quickly in front of it. Yet, no matter how many clouds passed over the moon and its circles of beautifully blended colors, she could still see it shining brightly. High in the sky, with its perfect, unwavering round circles of light surrounding it.

It almost looked like a shield around the moon. A shield of Light. Evenia knew all too well how powerful those could be. Her chest warmed at the thought, calming her cold, tense body for a moment.

There was no resisting the smile that bloomed on her face at the sight that made her think of her mother. Well, the image of her mother her young mind had created and held onto all these years. A sense of peace washed over her as she watched the clouds pass by the unfaltering circle and the beautiful, strong force at its center. Yes, she could stare at this all night.

It would be even better if she could stop shaking from the cold. She was concentrating on keeping her body calm and still from the chilly night when another warm breeze was sent her way. This time, Evenia didn't roll her eyes. It would have been easy to warm her own body with a flash of heat, but she didn't mind it.

Her nose crinkled at the realization that she wanted Kalland to use his power for her. She could take care of herself just fine, but that didn't mean it wasn't nice to have him looking out for her. Or touching her, like earlier. What a strange change from when they first met...

Shaking all things Kalland from her thoughts, she took in the sky now, slowly looking at each section from left to right to capture a mental image of the peaceful night. It was then that she noticed dark clouds suddenly moving at an increased speed to the right of the moon and its "Light shield." They were the only clouds in the sky that were moving at a different pace than the others.

Her eyes widened in shock and amazement as she saw the first break in the moon's light shield, as the dark clouds broke through.

But then...

Her breath stalled as those dark clouds transformed into what looked like a shadowed hand, stretching and growing in volume. It reached its sharp claws out for the moon. Where the night sky was a deep navy—almost black—this claw stuck out in contrast, like an obsidian void. The color of shadows. The color of The Darkness.

Her stomach dropped at the thought.

She could only watch in horror as what looked like a long arm with a sharp-clawed hand—that closely resembled The Darkness's claws—closed in on the beautiful view and peaceful night.

All air caught in her chest, sitting there like a metal ball in her sternum and preventing her from breathing. Her body was no longer allowing her to will it into stillness against the cold air. It crept across her skin in an unwelcome caress—like cold claws raking down her arm, just waiting to dig in—piercing its icy cold depths straight into her bones.

Her heart was racing, and despite the chill, her palms began to sweat. For a moment, she forgot where she was, or what she was doing here. Everything in her peripheral went black.

That shadowed claw stretching for the moon and its rings was all she could focus on. It was so close now. As the hand reached out for the moon, penetrating its rings, that little ball of metal was rising from its spot in her chest—up, and up, constricting her throat. It was so high that it felt like she might throw it up at any moment.

Then, the claw shifted directions. While the circle of rings had been penetrated by the seemingly shadowed claw, only the bottom portion of the outer lavender circle was compromised. The rest of the "Light shield" surrounding it was still intact. Strong. Unfaltering.

Stunned, she watched as the outer ring surrounding the moon slowly replaced its lower half, repairing itself into a perfect sphere again. Evenia felt a strange sense of relief at the sight.

That feeling was quickly replaced by fear once more as she watched the shadowed claw continue to move across the night sky, fleeing from its bright, shining target. It was moving so quickly in comparison to the other clouds. As if it had a place to be. As if it was on a mission. Her eyes stayed watching until it finally disappeared into a sea of clouds, no longer haunting the once serene scene before her.

She didn't know how much time went by before she finally risked releasing a breath.

Another breath. And another. Until her chest suddenly started heaving. She didn't care if she was surrounded by hyper-sensitive hearing Fae. She didn't care if the sound woke them. No matter how many breaths she took, it felt like she couldn't breathe in enough air.

It wasn't real.

It wasn't him.

It wasn't his hand. *His claw.*

That shield of light was only a reflection of the moon's light, not Evenia's magical Light shield surrounding her. Shielding her. Protecting her.

The moon wasn't her. The moon was an unmovable force in the sky, not a confused, broken duolvain.

Then, her breathing stopped altogether. That stupid metal ball had found its place in her throat once more.

Because, what if... What if it was a warning?

A warning that even The Darkness can pierce the light.

A warning that he could reach her anywhere, anytime.

A warning that he found her, and he was coming.

Evenia jumped to her feet and made it four trees deep into the forest before losing her dinner all over the forest floor.

When her body finally stopped hurling, she slowly backed up until she felt the strength of a tree trunk behind her. Eyes still closed, she leaned the back of her head against the tree, wiped her mouth, and let out a deep breath.

A few seconds later, she heard a twig snap. But she didn't react—didn't so much as open her eyes—because she recognized that presence. Not only his physical scent but his aura.

"You okay?" Kalland asked, concern in his voice.

Did he not just see what she saw? How could he not be panicking right now?

"No." She immediately regretted opening her mouth. Eyes still closed, her hand clasped tightly over her mouth as another round of vomit threatened to escape her throat. She squeezed her eyes shut and willed it to stay down.

She didn't speak again until the feeling had passed. "No, but I will be." Because she had to be. There was no other choice. No other path.

She'd find a way out of The Darkness' clutches. Someday.

"Do you want to talk about it?" With one eye open, she peeked long enough to spot a canister of water now sitting next to her and Kalland leaning against a tree to her right. He seemed calm. Had that all been in her head? Or a warning for her eyes only?

"No," she sighed.

Her hand drifted from her mouth to her chest. She pushed a small amount of weight into her palm against her chest. It was as much as she could muster in this weakened state, to try to offer her body some sense of comfort. That ball in her chest was now stuck in her throat. With each passing second, it felt like it was slowly moving down to her chest again. As she calmed her body, she relaxed the knot.

"Anything I can do, vhi-aoirhi?"

It was hard to know what annoyed her more: the fact that he called her something she didn't know, or the fact that she was beginning to like it. Because there was that word again. All she could think of was when he called her "my sweet," and she told him to never say it again. Instead, he started calling her this term she'd never heard of. Was he trying to mock her? Luckily for him, she didn't have the strength to fight about it.

She opened one eye again. "No," she sneered, whether in response to the unknown term or her reaction to it, she didn't know.

Still leaning against a tree, he took a small step back. The movement wasn't out of fear or hurt, but out of respect, she realized.

Her expression softened at his reaction and she sighed. "But...thank you."

He offered her a small smile. "Of course."

In a brief moment of her stomach feeling somewhat settled, she risked it and reached for the water jug he brought her. Taking a small sip, she swished the water in her mouth before spitting it out again.

She took one small sip after, in an attempt to wash down the acidic feeling. Not thinking she could brave another, she closed the jug and slowly set it back down. Leaning back against the tree, she rested her head on it and peeked one eye open again.

The grey-eyed elf was still there. He shifted so that the tree he had been leaning his shoulder on was now against his back. Slowly, he slid down it, sitting opposite her in the clearing. His knees were bent in front of him, with his clasped hands casually draped over them.

"What are you doing here?" Both of her eyes were open now, if only barely, and locked on him. Now that the question crossed her lips, she wanted to know the answer. Why *was* he here?

"Just getting some fresh air." He took in a deep breath, looking around at the trees, with their leaves blowing in the wind.

"Really? Getting some fresh air while we're camped outside." Her hand clamped over her mouth again. Speaking that many words at once made her feel nauseous again. Breathing in through her nose, she let it back out, again and again, until the feeling passed. "Makes sense." The words came out more like a whisper as she spoke through the spaces in between her fingers.

The corner of his mouth turned upward. "There's campsite air, and then there's fresh air. This," with his eyes closed, he motioned to the clearing, "is fresh air." Suddenly, his nose twitched and he made an unpleasant face, as if his elven smelling took in all of the scents in the air around them. "Well, it *was* fresh air."

Grabbing a pinecone that was sitting on the forest floor next to her, she launched it at the elf. Weakened in her current state, the pinecone was practically moving in slow motion as it soared right for his head. He ducked before it even came close to hitting him. It bounced off the tree and landed in front of his feet.

Removing his gaze from the downed pinecone, he narrowed his eyes at her, but there was a hint of amusement in them.

Truth was, the smell was bothering her, too. Especially since she was still nauseous, but she wasn't about to give him that satisfaction.

"There's an easy solution to the fresh air dilemma, you know." He stood and casually walked over to her.

"What's that?" she asked, looking from his face to the hand outstretched toward her.

"We go back to bed."

Her eyes rolled in the back of her head when she saw the corner of his lip twitch, but she took his hand and he helped her to slowly stand. To her surprise, he didn't let go of her hand as he guided her through the trees, back to the campsite. Back to—

All her muscles froze, her body not wanting to go back, just in case the hand in the sky really had been a warning. Kalland turned to look at her still form. So many questions were swarming in those grey eyes, but he resisted, opting to squeeze her hand in comfort instead.

That touch helped a bit. Maybe because *he* had helped her before. When he saw The Darkness's shadows after he bursted into her chambers, he helped run them off when she was paralyzed with fear. By the way he reacted in Andira's office at the mere mention of The Darkness's presence in Nulhe, he seemed just as invested as she was in sending the demon back to the Underworld. Or vanquish him forever. Her vote was on the latter.

And if her suspicions were right, Kalland's reasoning for being invested had to do with his mother...

So, she nodded and followed him back to camp.

When they got back, she heard Alekze snoring loudly enough to wake the creatures that undoubtedly roamed the forest. Her hand shot to her mouth to stifle a laugh and the inevitable wave of nausea that would have followed. Kalland grinned at her, clearly also finding amusement in his friend's ability to sleep soundly here.

They reached the fire, which was now just barely embers. Still, he didn't let go of her hand as he laid down next to her sleeping bag, gently pulling her hand to encourage her to return to her spot. She hesitated for only a split second before curling up under the faux furs once more. She would be fine. These were two trained sentries sleeping around her, with Alekze sleeping to her right, and Kalland now to her left, lying down—

Oh. Her body tensed, but she quickly relaxed into the warmth Kalland's body offered her as he curled up behind her, with her back flush against his chest.

"*Is this okay?*" he asked her.

Yes. Yes, it most definitely was. Instead of saying that out loud, she simply nodded.

"*And this?*" he asked as he wrapped one arm around her, pulling her closer to him.

Unsure of what to do, she felt the rise and fall of his chest as she finally relaxed into his warmth and comfort. She nodded, and he gave her a gentle, brief squeeze in response.

"*You're warm,*" she whispered to him, while her body acted on its own to snuggle closer to his body heat. Her movements stopped when something hard hit her lower back and she felt his body tense around her.

"*If you don't stop wiggling against me, you'll find out just how warm I am.*" The huskiness in his voice caused her cheeks to flush and her body to heat for an entirely different reason.

Lips parted in shock, she debated between continuing to move closer, or settling for the warmth he'd provided her so far. How far was she willing to go with this Wind elf she'd almost castrated and then nearly kissed the first time she'd run into him? What good could come of giving into temptation with this sentry?

Shaking her head, she Wind whispered, "*Very tempting, but I don't think your sleeping friend would like that.*"

"*Very tempting, you say?*" Her elbow met his ribs. He chuckled and nuzzled his nose into the top of her head. She leaned into the touch as he said, "*He'd appreciate that you considered his feelings over your own.*"

"*Bold of you to assume I have any feelings for you, Sothenas,*" she quipped.

"*Hmm,*" he hummed, the vibration of it caressing her ears and sending a pleasant shiver throughout her body. "*Perhaps, but the fact that you didn't pull away or tell me to fuck off when you felt me against you says a lot.*"

She smiled. "*Yeah, it says that I'm fucking cold.*"

His chuckle floated to her ears before he lifted his head from hers, choosing to rest his cheek on his bicep slightly above her.

With each second that ticked by, she felt her body stop shivering and her muscles relax one by one. She focused on his breathing and on the way his chest rose and fell against her back. The way his thumb lightly brushed her forearm, and how his breath innocently caressed her neck. Everything about it brought her peace and comfort.

Allowing herself this moment to feel safe, she fell into it. Her breathing slowed as exhaustion finally took her under in a dreamless sleep.

34

Evenia

They made their way through the snow on horseback, which was probably now up to Evenia's knees if she'd been on foot. Thank goodness for Rianore, because even with all her Fire power, she'd certainly freeze to death in that much snow. Up until that moment, she'd always said she enjoyed cold weather. Now, she knew she meant chilly weather in autumn, because this—*this* cold—was something else.

It was around late afternoon when they approached a small village with candlelight and smoky fireplaces. If it wasn't for the frostbite she was surely acquiring, she'd think it was almost picturesque.

As they neared the village, she heard laughter and singing and fires crackling from what looked to be a town market. There were fluffy dogs running after kids in the road, narrowly missing the horses' hooves. Parents and guardians were yelling at the children to be careful, which only seemed to make the kids more defiant and determined to play in the road.

The sight was nerve-racking. Rianore might be a well-behaved horse so far, but how would she react to kids and dogs running so closely to her?

In her peripheral vision, she saw Alekze's right wrist flick, and an unevenly built snowman next to the cabin to their right suddenly came to life. With one stick arm shorter than the other, the snowman jumped in excitement and waddled like a penguin in the snow to the kids, who were now screaming with pure joy. More importantly, they were also now staying out of the road and away from large horse hooves.

Evenia thought she heard Alekze chuckle, but the sound was drowned out by a sudden wind chill.

"That was kind of you," she said.

Without looking at her, he merely shrugged, his expression blank again.

The hairs on the back of her neck raised, pulling her attention from Alekze and the animated snowman. Now on alert, her eyes scanned the crowd. It felt like someone was watching them, but she didn't see anyone.

Looking over her shoulder, she continued scanning the market and buildings, but stopped when her eyes fell on grey ones looking back at her. There was a small smile on his face, and she was suddenly reminded of his warmth wrapped around her last night.

Turning forward once again, she only hoped her pink cheeks could be played off as frostbitten.

As they rode farther into town, the light of day was slowly leaving them, but there was enough for her to notice the houses slowly started to grow in size. Just as the sky turned a deep magenta and orange during the Sun's descent, the trio reached a small village with a sign that read "Welcome to Wersves, Akvar." The houses were average-sized, and the snow was brighter and nearly untouched here except for the main road.

Suddenly, Alekze sped up slightly, taking the lead in front of Kalland, before slowing down once more at a cabin four homes away. Evenia's nerves shot, as she realized they must be approaching his family home.

The large, wooden door suddenly opened. Light trickled onto the wooden steps from inside as a woman stepped past the threshold.

Besides the big, warm smile on her face, there was no mistaking the resemblance between her and Alekze. Her hair was a dirty blonde, with silvery grey streaked here and there. Knowing werewolves had longer lifespans than humans, Evenia couldn't tell the woman's age, but she looked fairly young and was certainly beautiful.

She was covered in multiple faux furs that would have weighed down any normal woman of her frame, but the woman moved faster than should have been possible under all that weight as her arms wrapped around Alekze. It looked to be a big, bear hug that made Evenia long to hug her Aunt Siersha.

Evenia felt a pang of guilt as she thought about how she evaded her aunt and cousin by going on this mission, instead of seeing them after months apart. She shook the feeling off as Alekze pulled away, and the woman pulled Kalland in for a hug. Alekze had the biggest and warmest smile Evenia had ever seen on his face. Even bigger than the night she made him laugh when she called Emil "Mr. Numb Nuts."

A warm sensation spread in her chest at the sight of this happy Alekze. Before she could take it all in, a tall, elven woman with platinum hair emerged from the cabin door and pounced on Alekze. The two rolled around in the snow, a blur of blonde hair and furs as they laughed and tried to pin the other to the ground.

"My apologies for my pack of goblins. I gave up trying to wrangle them years ago." The woman chuckled fondly as she approached Evenia. "I'm Irenz."

"Pleased to meet you. I'm—" Before Evenia could finish introducing herself, Irenz had pulled her in for a warm embrace. Yes, she was right—Irenz gave great bear hugs, and Evenia leaned further into the embrace, not realizing how much she'd missed her aunt's hugs.

"I'm Evenia," she finally said as they broke away from the hug.

"Of course, you are. I've been told you've had quite the journey to us." Evenia tensed. Irenz wrapped her surprisingly warm hands around Evenia's right hand and squeezed gently. Her voice was soft as she said, "I know nothing else beyond that. But I do know that if anyone can find and bring down whomever you're after, it's my two goblins." Evenia laughed at the statement and felt her shoulders relax half an inch.

"Thank you." Evenia hoped the smile on her face showed her gratitude at the woman's kind words and for respecting her privacy. She resisted the urge to look at Kalland or Alekze, wanting to silently thank them both for not sharing her story without her permission, but also not wanting to bring attention to it at that exact moment.

Irenz mistook Evenia's long pause of hesitation as fear. "Oh, sweets. You have nothing to fear. Not under this roof of mine." Irenz's hands closed over Evenia's. As she looked into the older woman's eyes, she saw truth and warmth in them.

Her teeth pulled on her lower lip as her eyes filled with tears. Blinking them away, she simply nodded, a smile on her face. A loud grunt suddenly pulled her attention back to the scuffle on the ground. Evenia grinned as sister finally bested brother, with Alekze trapped under his sister's arm pushed against his throat.

"Ha! Who's the big, bad wolfie now?" Asryn teased. Alekze bared and snapped his teeth, but Asryn only laughed as he pushed her into the snow, causing her to fall butt first. "Don't be such a sore loser, Alekzeyn."

Alekze grunted in response, but there was a shadow of a smile on his face as he stood up and brushed the snow off himself.

As if she hadn't just been wrestling for minutes, Asryn stood up gracefully. Her breathing even, she jumped on Kalland, wrapping her arms around him. "Missed you, Thunderbird."

"Missed you, too, Little Pup." He rolled his eyes, but he hadn't hesitated to return the embrace. One that went on a bit longer than she'd expected.

Evenia felt her cheeks pink at the sight. Was that jealousy she felt? *Nonsense.*

Then, the tall, blonde elf was standing in front of Evenia. Her movements...it was like she was a ghost. There one moment, and here the next. Evenia started to understand why her skillset was needed.

"And you must be Cat Eyes."

Evenia blinked a few times. "Pardon?"

"Asrynna Ivonria Vlasca! You were raised better than that," Irenz's voice sounded from the doorway of the cabin she had started to walk back into after Alekze recovered himself.

"What?" Asryn shrugged. "It's not like I came up with that nickname."

Irenz's eyes narrowed at her daughter. All sorts of unspoken motherly threats loomed in that one stare. Evenia resisted the urge to wither under the stare that reminded her of a similar look her Aunt Siersha used to give her and her cousin one too many times during their rebellious stage. Two teenagers at once? Her aunt was unbelievably strong.

Evenia found herself biting back a laugh when Alekze stuck his tongue out at his sister while she was being silently scolded. Seeing her smile, he winked at Evenia, and she didn't know what to do with this new Alekze that stood only a few feet away from her.

"Yes, Mother," Asryn groaned after a moment.

Satisfied, Irenz's face immediately returned to its warm glow from before as she turned and walked into the cabin.

"I'm Asryn, and you're Evenia. The reason we get to have a family reunion." Not sure how to respond to that, Evenia paused, but Asryn grinned. "Breathe, Cat Eyes. I meant it as a good thing. We actually like each other. Was it not obvious when I pinned his sorry ass to the snow just now?" Her voice raised an octave with the last sentence, her head slightly turned toward the door.

"It was a pity win, Little Pup," Alekze's deep voice sounded from inside the cabin.

Asryn's grin fell as her head whipped toward the cabin. She was gone again in the blink of an eye. Their arguing voices were cut off by the howling wind biting at Evenia's ears and nose. Starting to pull the furs tighter around her, she stopped as the icy air was suddenly met with a warm gust of Wind on her cheeks. She opened her eyes and saw Kalland standing a few feet from her.

"You didn't have to do that," she said, though grateful for the relief from the cold.

"I didn't do it for you. Your teeth were chattering. It sounded like an army of horses trotting into town," he said, sounding bored. "If I hadn't intervened, the townsfolk would soon come out of their homes with pitchforks and torches, only to be greeted by an army of one."

"That has to be the longest insult of all time, Sothenas. Not to mention that complaining about loud noises is rich coming from the elf whose snoring woke half the forest." She thought she saw his lip turn up for a split second.

His hand went to his chest as his face twisted in mock horror. "*My* snoring? I think you're confusing me with the other elf," he said, pointing at the doorway, where Alekze's voice could be heard faintly.

Her smile faltered when she saw he was holding something back. He was waiting to tell her something. *Shit, what now?* "What is it?"

His eyes widened for a moment before recovering. "Before we go in, we should talk about tonight's sleeping arrangements," his deep voice sounded. His eyes darkened, sending a wave of warmth through her again for an entirely different reason.

"Oh?" she asked.

"Alekze and Asryn will stay here—a family reunion, as Asryn put it—and you and I will stay at the inn in town." He jutted his head in the direction of the heart of the village. While his eyes watched her face for any reaction, her breath caught when they suddenly trailed to her lips.

"An inn?" He nodded. "You and I?" He nodded again, and her throat bobbed.

"Easy, Raldir," he said playfully. "We'll have separate rooms. I'm just letting you know ahead of time so you don't get blindsided when we have to head out."

Her shoulders seemed to deflate an inch of their own accord. Part of her was relieved, the other part entirely disappointed. She nodded. "Right. Okay, then."

He assessed her face again before gesturing toward the cabin door. Not looking at him, she walked to the door, and he followed behind her. Hearing laughter from within, she hesitated in the doorway again. Seconds ticked by as she stood there, waiting for her feet to move.

"Did I upset you?" his deep voice rattled behind her. She turned, and he looked both uncomfortable and annoyed.

"What?"

"I'm just trying to figure out why you stopped walking toward the warmth." His gaze switched back and forth from her eyes to her lips. On instinct, she licked her lips, and his eyes darkened.

With his attention on her, she responded, "It takes a lot more than a long-winded joke and a bed at an inn to upset me."

"Then, what is it?" Evenia hesitated as she heard another bout of laughter. "Today, Raldir. Preferably before I get frostbite."

She narrowed her eyes at him, all warmth gone from the look she gave him.

"I'm fine," she said, and she used her anger and annoyance to search for the courage to walk into the cabin toward the laughter and joy she could no longer feel herself, no matter how hard she tried. But here, the light and love showed through each of their faces. Even Kalland, the normally pessimistic jerk, seemed to glow with love and light in Irenz's and Asryn's presence moments before.

My darkness will break that light, Evenia thought to herself. She only hoped it wouldn't come to fruition.

But the truth was, wherever she went, darkness followed.

35

Evenia

Finally mustering her courage, Evenia stepped over the threshold of the cabin. It was...warm and cozy. She instantly felt a pound lighter, until she sensed a presence behind her. Her body shivered as a chilled breath from the cold brushed against the slightly pointed tip of her left ear.

"Want to talk about it?" a deep voice sounded near her ear.

Instinctively, she leaned into the warm body mere inches from her back for an escape from the cold breath—*his* cold breath. Feeling his chest tense underneath her in response, she immediately straightened again, taking a step forward and away from him.

"Nothing to talk about," she lied. *Again.*

He grunted, clearly not believing her, but he didn't push the matter. "Then, let's go cook."

She followed Kalland into the house as he led her to the kitchen, where Irenz, Asryn, and Alekze were sharing the responsibility of cooking. Each took on a different task, while Asryn was relaying what sounded like a fond memory. Laughter and savory aromas filled the air, and Evenia took a few deep breaths as she decided to try to relax into it.

It was weird seeing Alekze smile even once, but here he was, with a massive grin on his face and joking with his sister and mother. As if he knew she was watching him, he looked up at Evenia and winked. An incredulous laugh escaped her. Who was this elf in front of her?

"In this kitchen, everyone cooks," Irenz's cheerful voice sounded as she handed Evenia an apron.

"Oh, no, you don't want that." Evenia waved one hand—the apron in the other—and shook her head side to side. "I'm a horrible cook."

"Yeah, that won't work. I've been trying it for decades. No luck," Kalland said as he grabbed his apron and kissed Irenz on the temple before she turned back to her task of cutting onions. He turned to Evenia slowly, one eyebrow raised. "How is it that a witch, who is taught to brew potions, could possibly be a bad cook?" Those grey eyes narrowed on her, but his tone was playful.

"Easy," she said as she secured the apron around her. "Potions don't have to taste good."

Irenz chuckled. "I can teach you a thing or two," she said, winking, and handed Evenia a potato to cut. Evenia looked up and saw the woman's smile reach her eyes as she turned and looked at her son. "We have to make sure you're all fed before the ceremony tomorrow." Alekze tensed, but Irenz gently slapped his tense back with the end of a dish towel that was next to her hands only seconds before. "Oh, it'll be fine. You know it," she said, encouragingly.

He simply nodded but didn't turn around or look away from his task of cutting what looked to be a variety of vegetables.

"Um..." Evenia cleared her throat and asked the question she'd been wanting to ask since Andira first mentioned Alekze's reasoning for getting into Akvar. "What type of ceremony is this, exactly?" Irenz's smile faltered a little, and Evenia immediately wanted to take the question back. "I'm sorry, it's just...I don't know anything about Akvarian culture or its ceremonies."

"It's all right, deary." Irenz nodded, a kind smile on her face.

Asryn attempted to casually wrap an arm around her big brother's shoulders. Despite her tall frame, she was still just a few inches too short to not be practically hanging off the elf like a sloth on a tree limb.

"He's dropping his asshole bio father's name and taking my father's name," Asryn said, grinning. "Hey!" she exclaimed when Alekze pushed her arm off his neck, making her lose her balance.

Irenz nodded slowly, while Alekze stayed silent. "Yes, that is one way to put it." She turned to Evenia. "You see, I thought having Alekze take—"

"Don't say his name in this house," Alekze's deep voice rumbled, interrupting his mother.

"Alekzeyn Iorack Vesely, I will say whatever I want in my own house," Irenz huffed before turning back to Evenia. "Let me start again…" she said, smoothing the creases of her apron. "Werewolves are not treated well *anywhere*. Sadly, all forms of shifters in general are not safe in our world."

Evenia nodded, as she knew that all too well.

"However, werewolves have it a little worse than normal shifters, since we don't have the ability to control our shifts. The second the full moon rises in the sky, we're out there…in excruciating pain as we go from human to wolf to bay at it."

"She gets it, Mama," Asryn groaned. "Ma met an Ice elf," Asryn pointed to Irenz, "Jokull Vesely, who is a dick."

The sound of a carrot snapping in Alekze's grip at the name spoken aloud drew Evenia's attention.

"Asrynna Ivonria Vlasca!" Irenz scolded.

"What? He *is* a dick. I'm not going to protect him, and neither should you." Asryn shrugged as she turned back to Evenia. "He was a dick to Ma and Alekze, to put it plainly, but his elven blood is what keeps Alekze from having to shift every full moon."

Irenz sighed and faced Evenia. "As I was trying to say, when a werewolf has elven blood, they can control their shifts. I saw an opportunity for a better life for my future children, and I took it." Her eyes were sad. "You see, I'd always wanted to be a mother, but I didn't want my children to go through the life I went through. This seemed like the least selfish way to make both those wishes come true."

Asryn kissed her mother on the cheek before saying, "After ditching the asshole, she met my father, Vincentin Vlasca, who is also an Ice elf. He's actually pretty great, if I do say so myself."

The pride in her father struck a chord of jealousy and pain in Evenia's chest. She wondered what it would be like to feel that way about your birth father.

"He took Alekze in as his own in the Akvar Court. Decades ago, he offered to legally adopt Alekze, even though he and Ma aren't together. It sounds like Alekze's finally accepted, and he'll be a Vlasca soon enough!" Asryn said, slapping her hand to Alekze's shoulder the same way Alekze had to Emil the other night. But unlike when the big Ice elf almost knocked Emil over, Alekze's strong form barely moved under his sister's touch.

Evenia nodded while she processed all the family information. So, the ceremony was an adoption of some sort. A way to invite Alekze into the Vlasca family. Like how Uncle Ensel gave Evenia his last name and he and her aunt took her in as their own after her mother left her. And again, when they legally adopted Émeriah, her cousin, after her parents were killed at sea. Evenia felt a stinging in her eyes and nose at the thought of her family. She looked down at the potato as she blinked away the tears.

"The ceremony gets us into Akvar for our mission, but seeing Father take Alekze in as his own is also something Mother's been waiting to see for years now," Asryn said.

Irenz nodded as her daughter hugged her gently. "I just want the best for you both."

Alekze stopped chopping carrots at the words and slowly turned to face his mother and sister. Sighing, he wrapped his big arms around them both, practically covering both of their heads with his muscles.

"*You* are the best thing for us, Ma," Alekze's deep voice grumbled.

***

After dinner, they played a card game called Tulipins, which Evenia found out she was terrible at, and drank spiced cider Asryn had secretly brought with her. When Irenz's back was turned, Asryn pulled out a flask from her jacket and spiked Alekze's and Kalland's drinks.

Evenia shook her head when Asryn offered the booze, while simultaneously stifling a laugh over the rebellious act. Although, having her own heightened shifter scent, Evenia suspected that Irenz could smell the potent alcohol and chose not to reprimand her adult children.

She was finding it hard to want to leave the warmth, not only from her body but from her heart. With each passing hour spent with Irenz and her *goblins*—as she called them—Evenia felt like she could let go a little. The cold hardness around her chest was chipping away inch by inch with each moment spent here.

Irenz's first hug.

Chip.

The playful sibling rivalry between Alekze and Asryn.

Chip.

How Irenz made sure Evenia was included in everything. Despite how close the four clearly were, she somehow made Evenia feel like part of their family.

Chip.

The way Kalland looked at Irenz like she was a mother figure, and the respect and love each one of them had for the other.

Chip.

The smile on Alekze's face and the happiness radiating from the male who usually looked like the world was out to get him.

Chip.

But more importantly, the way Evenia was able to forget, even if just for a little bit. They made her feel happy and light enough that she was able to momentarily forget why they were here. Forget what happened to her, and the anxiety of what might happen next.

Chip.

Right now, that was what she felt the most grateful for.

The moment Kalland gave her the look—the *'time to go'* look—that warmth and happiness and lightness left her body. It was quickly being replaced by the reminder of why they were here—of what they were on a mission to do. That ice brick constructed of fear and pain bordered itself around her heart once more, as if she never had this moment of reprieve. A shield for survival.

When Kalland stood up and announced they were leaving, Irenz immediately pulled Evenia in for a big hug, one that she chose to lean into this time. *Chip.*

"I wish you luck, little one," Irenz whispered into Evenia's ear, squeezing a little tighter with each word. "You are always welcome here, Evenia."

"That's enough, Mother. You'll end up suffocating her with your love," Asryn said, her tone playful.

Chuckling, Irenz pulled away. A split second later, Asryn immediately took her spot, wrapping her slender, toned arms around Evenia.

"Oh!" Evenia let out in shock as Asryn practically fell into her. Platinum blonde hair slapped her in the face in the process.

"Oops," Asryn said, chuckling, her breath smelling of booze, before nuzzling her nose into Evenia's neck. "Oh, you smell good, Cat Eyes. What is that? Lavender?"

"Okay, that's enough, Pup," Kalland said as he gently pried Asryn off Evenia, who gave him a smile of gratitude. "You'll see her in the morning." Kalland patted Asryn's shoulder and she hugged him next.

Alekze was up next, and in his relaxed, booze-filled state, he wrapped his arms around Evenia in a hug that swept her feet off the ground. A laugh escaped her lips as she hugged him back.

When he put her back down on the ground, he patted her head twice, and then dropped down on the sofa, sprawling his large form out on the deep-cushioned couch.

"We'll see you all in the morning," Kalland said as he ushered her out the door in an attempt to evade Asryn's third hug of the night.

In the doorway, Evenia looked back once more at the cozy cabin and the lovely people who called it home. She only hoped she'd be able to see it again. Her heartbeat shuttered as she turned and walked out the door.

36

Kalland

Kalland was laying in bed at the inn in Wersves, struggling to sleep. The fourth layer of faux fur blankets he just pulled over himself for more warmth was not helping the way he'd hoped. His body wasn't built for the cold. A fact he denied as much as he could for someone who often flew high in the sky.

Not to mention that being in the snow all today brought back painful memories. The combination of the dastardly mental images of his dead parents on an endless loop and the cold making him uncomfortable was doing wonders for his mood.

Trying for about the hundredth time that night to use his sentry training of being able to fall asleep anywhere, he took a deep breath in through his nose and held it for a few seconds. When he finally released the breath out through his nose, it was white and foggy, creating shapes in the night air. He knew he was in trouble when the idea of the shapes in his breath was more interesting to him than sleeping.

Groaning, he rolled over.

While trying a different approach of closing his eyes while breathing, he was interrupted by a faint sound. It sounded like a whimper, but he couldn't be sure over the sound of his teeth chattering. With an embarrassing amount of effort that made him despise the cold more, he stilled his jaw and honed into his elven hearing.

Thump, thump. Thump, thump. Thump, thump.

A heart beating too fast. *Evenia.*

He shot out of bed and closed the distance between his bed and their adjoined room door in a matter of seconds. When he swung the door open, he saw Evenia sleeping in bed, the room well-lit in the candlelight.

His jaw ticked as he realized the significance of the light. He noticed she hadn't yet lit a candle at night in Mircha, no matter how many nightmares she had. But here...she didn't know how close the inn was to where she'd been held captive. Being this close to the Urur border no doubt made her fears worse.

He looked around, but there was no darkness to be found. No creepy shadows crawling all over her. No...danger. Scanning the room once more, his eyes finally fell on Evenia, who was somehow sweating through her sheets in this freezing air.

The sound of her heart pounding hadn't stopped. Was it a bad dream?

"E–Ev—?" His voice broke as his teeth began chattering again. Willing his body to stand completely still, he tried again, sending her name out into the night with a whisper. "*Evenia?*"

She stopped writhing, but her pulse quickened even more. He took a tentative step forward. He didn't want to scare her, but he didn't know how to help her if he couldn't see the danger she was facing in her dream.

His footsteps stopped when she whimpered and began moving again. A *very* subtle movement as her inner thighs rubbed against one another. Slowly, so slowly.

Now, he was the one breaking out in a sweat.

He half laughed, half sighed and shook his head. Evenia let out another one of those whimpers. This time, instead of setting his body on alert, he felt a twitch in his pants.

Fuck, he needed to get out of here.

When he took a step back, a floorboard croaked underneath him. She stirred as he stilled. Her heartbeat quickened again. This time, he knew it was from fear, not pleasure.

"It's okay, Ven. You're safe. It's just me." Her pulse slowed with each word that caressed her cheek. He couldn't help but smile when her lips twitched upward as those words fell over her. Nor could he help the sudden throbbing in his pants. He had to get out of there.

Trying again, he made it two feet before another floorboard croaked. A groan of frustration died on his lips, not wanting to risk waking her. One hundred six fucking years in this world, and he suddenly forgot all of his stealth training?

Another creak, and her eyes opened. He froze. What should he say? Should he leave on the Wind, or should he stay?

She blinked a few times, as if she might still be sleeping. When her beautiful eyes fell on him, her gaze softened, almost in a dreamlike state.

"I'm sorry," he whispered normally this time. "I heard you, and I thought something was wrong."

Those mesmerizing eyes looked from him, to his wide-open adjoined bedroom door, and to the sweat-soaked sheets. As her eyes trailed lower, and lower down her body, her cheeks grew pinker. It took everything in him to not smile as he realized she must have just noticed the wetness between her legs. He silently cursed himself for wanting to know what that felt like. What *she* tasted like.

Her eyes flew back up to his.

"I'm sorry. I was just leaving." And yet, he still wasn't moving. She must have realized that, too, because her face turned from embarrassment to curiosity to...lust. There was so much heat in that stare. Oh, he was definitely sweating now.

And he needed to leave. He needed to retreat to his cold-as-fuck bedroom, and maybe only place two layers of faux fur blankets on himself until he completely cooled off.

Then, she bit her lower lip. Just the smallest, tiniest nibble. *Fuuuuuuuck.* No, no blankets. No clothes for that matter. At this point, he might have to go butt naked to the snow outside and just sit down to cool off. What the fuck was wrong with him?

"Are you okay?" she asked him while sitting up a bit in bed. The outline of her plump breasts was showing through her sheer nightgown, her nipples peeking through. He allowed himself to look a second too long, and he knew she was watching. *Fuck.*

Think, Kal. Think. Her voice...she'd asked him something. What was it? *Oh.* How the hel was he supposed to answer that? He knew she was asking because he wasn't moving toward the door. And for all he knew, she could have seen the sweat or heard his pounding heart or, gods, even sensed his arousal.

Shit. Not sure how to answer, he swallowed and nodded.

There was a teasing grin on her face and her eyes twinkled. Those plump breasts raised an inch, bouncing slightly with her small laugh. "Don't lie to me, Sothenas."

This time, he didn't stop himself from looking that second too long. Her breath hitched under the heat of his gaze. When he looked back up at her face, she was biting her lip again. It wasn't nearly as subtle of a gesture as before.

He smiled back, his tense shoulders easing an inch, and then another. "I wouldn't dream of it, Raldir."

Still smiling, she inched lower on the bed. Those surprisingly toned legs moved inch by inch, the sheets moving down with them, until the top of her hips were peeking through the sheets. All the air might have left his lungs when he saw the nightgown had risen above her hips, exposing the tops of her thighs. When he looked back up at her beautiful face, he saw her eyes watching him, waiting for his move.

The words escaped before he knew what he was saying. "But *you* were dreaming of something," he said. The tops of her cheeks pinked slightly, but she nodded slowly, as if prompting him. Encouraging him. "What were you dreaming about?" His voice sounded gravelly, but he didn't give a shit. He took a step closer, not even realizing it until her gaze trailed over his body.

"Do you really want me to say it?" she whispered normally. Breathily, but normally.

His cock was throbbing in his pants again. Pants that were tightening around him even more now. He'd need to undo them soon, whether to cool off, or...

"I do," he challenged. He hoped. He *wanted*.

"*Are you sure?*" she asked. The words caressed his cheek, setting his heart pounding while sending a sense of peace throughout his body. Their eyes locked for a moment longer, inching the sheet even farther off her, exposing more of her legs.

Staying rooted to the spot, not wanting to move until he knew for sure, he said, "*Yes.*"

She didn't speak until he looked her in the eyes again. There was desire. Need. Want. A mirror to his own.

"*You.*"

37

Evenia

She didn't know what she was doing, what *they* were doing, but it felt right. So fucking right. All she knew was that she wanted him, and that she needed his body on hers at that moment.

The grey-eyed elf was in her dreams only minutes before, gripping her ass as he pounded into her, and kissing her neck as she climaxed. Then, as if the Fates were granting her this wish—this dream—he appeared in her room. She needed that dream to be reality. She wanted it. Wanted *him*.

This was what she'd hoped for when he first told her about the inn. Granted, part of her had hoped they'd be sharing a bed, but him ending up in hers during the night was good enough for her. In fact, it was exactly what she dreamed about.

It was clear as day that his resolve was breaking, but she could also see the hesitation. He respected her too much to act without her wanting him to. So, she offered him a small smile and nodded, letting him know this was what she wanted. That *he* was what she wanted.

That confirmation was all it took, and he was at the foot of the bed in a split second. Her breath hitched. Not at the movement, but at the proximity. At the prospect that her dream might actually become reality, and at the realization that that reality may never live up to that dream. That after, their relationship would never be the same. Was it worth the risk?

We'll figure it out later, she told herself. All that mattered now was them in that moment.

He was still standing at the foot of the bed, clearly unsure of what to do next.

Smiling, she said, "Don't tell me this is your first time, Sothenas. Then I'll really know you're lying to me." Teasing him worked, just as she knew it would.

He smiled at her, but it wasn't the playful one he'd given her only minutes before. No, this one was full of desire, as his eyes grew dark. The heat between her legs only grew more intense, more demanding.

He placed one knee on the bed, and then another. She sat up a bit more on the pillows, willing him to come closer to her, to close that gap between them. To show her this was also what he wanted. Inch by inch, he closed the distance between them. She tucked her legs underneath her and sat down in front of him. To her surprise, he cupped her cheek in his hand and brushed a thumb against her cheekbone. Closing her eyes, she leaned into the touch.

"I'm happy to inform you that it is not my first time."

She smiled into his hand as he continued caressing her cheek. His other hand brushed hers. A simple movement. Instinctively, her hand opened in invitation, and he gently wrapped his fingers around hers.

He slowly removed his hand from her cheek, and she opened her eyes after a minute of no movement. She was met with swirling silver. A brewing storm of desire and...concern.

"I just don't want to hurt you or do anything you'll regret." By the tone in his voice, he meant it.

Copying him, she placed her hand on his cheek, and it was his turn to lean into the touch. He gently grabbed it and kissed her palm. A warmth spread through her chest at the touch and the sight. At the sight of him holding the kiss for a few seconds, that warmth traveled lower, until it was a full-blown, tense heat. When he finally released the kiss and looked at her again, there was still nothing but concern in his eyes.

That ice around her heart melted a little. "You could never hurt me." As the words left her lips, she felt them so surely, so confidently. He wouldn't. And even if he tried, he couldn't. "As I recall, you promised me you wouldn't."

He huffed a laugh. Still, his reservation was clear as day. As if he didn't believe her, his eyes closed at the words.

"Kal," she Wind whispered. His eyes flew open, and the desire in them was back. *"Kal, I want you."* She saw his throat bob. She waited a few seconds, and he held her gaze the entire time. "Please, don't make me ask you twice."

"Never," his voice was gravelly, and he let out this low, aroused growl that instantly had her growing wet again.

A soft sound escaped her lips and, with a satisfied grin on his face, he devoured that sound with his mouth. When their lips touched, her whole being felt like it was melting and being engulfed in flames at the same time.

Her hand raked through his dark hair as one of his hands wrapped around the back of her neck, and the other started kneading her breast. She groaned in his mouth at the touch, and he responded by biting her lower lip, which only drove her crazier. Her breaths were coming out in pants now.

The smile of pure desire was on his face as his mouth moved lower down her body, kissing her cheek ever so gently, with featherlight kisses down her jawline. They only deepened, becoming more passionate as he moved down her neck, to the hollow spot behind her ear. Another moan from her lips, and she felt a chuckle of a breath on her neck from him.

Her back arched as he made his way to the peak of her breasts. Both hands in his hair now, she gently pulled, urging him to lift his gaze. His lust-filled eyes met hers. The look in them promised a night that might rival her dream. At the sight, she let out another whimper. Her thighs rubbed together to ease the throbbing between her legs as he lowered his mouth to the peak of one breast. Another moan as he nipped.

He chuckled. "You like that?" She nodded, and there was another breath of a laugh against her breast. He bit down on one as he lightly pinched the other. Her hips bucked as her hands dug deeper into his hair. "And that?" His voice was breathy, *sexy*, and knowing it was because of her only turned her on even more.

She tried to say yes, but only a whimper came out.

"Sorry, what was that?" he asked, teasingly.

She could hear the smile in his voice and knew he was enjoying every second of torturing her. Her hand quickly moved in-between his legs, gripping his cock through his pants. It was meant as a way to tell him to stop teasing her and get on with it—*with her*—but instead, she found herself growing even hotter at the feel of him in her hands. The sheer size of him. Her mouth watered as she felt the urge to unlace his pants and wrap her lips around him.

"Uh-uh-uh." He grabbed her hand, releasing her touch. Eyes wide, she tried to protest, but he only brought her hand to his mouth and kissed it in response. "This is about you, vhi-aiorhi."

Shit. How was she supposed to argue with that? *Vhi-aiorhi?* There was that term again, but she couldn't deny the tingling sensation it brought her in this setting. She'd have to dissect that feeling later, but damn if it didn't do something to her body.

"Deal?" he asked her, his tongue lightly teasing her nipple once more.

Leaning back onto the bed, she leaned further into his touch on her breasts. He sucked on her breast again in response, causing her hips to arch again. Her hand once more found its way in his hair.

One hand gripping the breast his mouth was on, his other began caressing her body, going lower, and lower. Exploring every inch of her. Touching her stomach, the place where her ass escaped outside of her hips, having nowhere to go when her body was laying flat. He nudged her hips up, her breasts falling deeper into his mouth, and he gripped her ass. She felt him moan against her chest. Gods, that wetness was pooling between her legs now.

His hand lingered on her ass for a few seconds before grazing lower down her thigh. Holding her hips against his chest, he shifted arms so that his other hand gripped her other breast. Giving one last nip, his mouth released her and she let out a groan. He chuckled before teasing the nipple of her other breast with his tongue. Her hips bucked again, but this time it was right against his groin, and he let out a deep, deep moan that reverberated through her body.

Grinding her hips into him even harder, she felt a bit of satisfaction as he released her breast, trying to get his breathing under control.

"You like that?" she teased.

"If you do that again," his mouth trailed up to her ear, nipping it as he whispered, "I'll have to stop." She stilled. He nipped the sensitive spot under her ear before he pulled away from her. "And I don't think either one of us wants that."

Nope, definitely not. She shook her head.

"Glad to hear you agree, because I would hate to end this..." He held her hips in place in the air as he slowly moved his body down and down, until she felt his breath on her wetness. His eyes meeting hers, he said, "Before we really get started."

The sight of his desire in his eyes, of the anticipation of where his mouth was... Another moan as she could feel herself dripping down her inner thigh now.

"It's Valoregan, isn't it?" she asked, breathless. "Vhi-aiorhi?" Eyes locked on one another, with his peeking over her hips, he stopped moving at the word. But she wanted to know. "What does it mean?"

Several seconds passed before he finally answered, ever so softly, "My sweet." The words caressed her in the most sensitive parts, melting her further into the mattress and closer to him.

He held her gaze while he kissed the inside of her right thigh. Gently at first, with one hand on her hip, the other on her ass. Gradually, his kisses turned deeper. Her hips bucked again when she felt his breath at her wetness once more, and she sucked in a breath. Unable to breathe. Unable to move in anticipation.

He chuckled, the breath and sound traveling straight to her core, teasing her. Eyes still locked on hers, he only grinned before slowly moving to kiss the other thigh. She let out a small groan and he playfully bit her thigh in response.

Not being able to withstand the torture anymore, she looked away. Several long seconds passed before she felt his kisses trail back up her inner thigh, to her center, and her eyes flew to his once more.

"Are you sure you're ready?" he asked.

He couldn't be serious. Without thinking, her hand went to his hair once more, raking through it as she gently urged him down. "Yes, Kal," she breathed out.

Biting his lip, he let out a low growl again, one she felt in her core, and her hips bucked up in response. His mouth caught hold of her most sensitive spot, sucking, and her head flew back as her hand gripped his hair harder.

Letting go, his tongue swiped, separating her before entering deep. As if he was enjoying himself just as much as she was, she felt him moan inside of her, and she couldn't resist the natural rock of her hips in response. One of his hands pushed on her abdomen, simultaneously teasing her and steadying her movements, while the other came up to caress her breast.

He was so gentle. His tongue went deeper, deeper in her, and she let out a moan. The grip on her breast tightened as the hand on her abdomen pushed down harder, trying to keep her from moving too much. And then, that hand inched lower, and lower, still steadying her lower stomach, but his thumb reached to her clit, brushing against her most sensitive part. That coil of heat tightening, her hips bucked and moaned again. She was losing her will.

He slowly pulled away, just enough to release his tongue, but his mouth was still against her, feeling his breath at her center, teasing her again. Pulling his hand from her breast, he eased one finger in her, slowly pumping in and out as he used his tongue in unison with his finger. Every one of her muscles was shaking from desire.

He nipped her clit, urging her to look at him. She did.

"There's something I want you to do for me, Ven." She moaned at the sound of her nickname on his lips, or maybe it was at the sight of him looking at her while between her legs.

Her grip on his hair tightened with her growing desire. "Anything," she managed to say on a breath.

As he inserted another finger, with his other thumb still stroking her clit, he held her gaze as he pumped harder and harder. "I want you to come for me."

The words alone were enough to drive her crazy, but his tongue entering her after he said it? *Fuck,* he was good. That request while in-between her legs was her undoing.

Her head flew back as her nails dug into his scalp, pulling him closer, harder, as her hips rocked with his movements. He devoured her the way he had devoured her moan with their first kiss tonight.

He must have sensed she was close, because his hand on her stomach went to her hip, raising them higher and giving him better access to her. That same hand smacked her ass, and her restraint was gone.

There was a sudden humming sound, and she felt a shield go up around them as her body shuddered with her release. She moaned and whimpered loudly with each shudder. His mouth stayed on her, prolonging each second of her release, and devouring her orgasm just as he had her desire. He didn't stop until she sighed and her body relaxed in his hands.

Lifting his head, he gently sat her hips back on the bed. That wicked tongue licked his lips, and she felt another sudden flare of desire at the sight. Gently, he kissed her stomach, trailing kisses from her abdomen to her breasts, flicking one nipple with his tongue, and continuing to kiss up to her jawline. She couldn't take the teasing anymore. Her hands found their way back into his hair, and she pulled his head up so she could kiss him.

He moaned as their tongues met. The kiss was full of passion, gratitude, and need. His leg slid in-between hers, and she wrapped one leg around his hips. Breaking their kiss, he moaned as he nipped and sucked her bottom lip before releasing it. Instead of kissing her once more, he rested his forehead on hers.

Smiling, she brushed her thumb against the nape of his neck as their breaths intermingled. She didn't know how long they sat like that, but she stilled when the sound of teeth chattering filled the air. Her eyes flew open, and she realized he was shivering.

"Are you okay?" she asked. She shifted so that his leg wasn't in-between hers anymore. Wrapping both legs around him now, she offered him her warmth. Her hand went to his cheek while the other hand rubbed his back, hugging him close to her.

"Y–yeah, j–just cold," he said.

She looked at him for a minute before laughing. With ease, she flipped their bodies so that she was the one on top, with her hips on his. His eyes were wide with shock at the sudden reversal.

"Why didn't you just say so?" she asked as she placed one hand on his chest.

"W–we were a b–bit p–preoccu–u–pied." He smiled at her before kissing the palm of her other hand still on his cheek.

Leaning down to kiss his forehead, she sent a wave of heat through the hand on his chest. He abruptly ended the kiss on her palm, his eyes growing wide as he looked at her.

"What was that?" he asked, the shivering and chattering gone.

She shrugged. "I just sent a little heat...ed Light through you." She removed her hand from his chest and hoped he hadn't caught her slipup of her In-Between powers, since Light magic didn't heat the same way Sun power did. Yes, she'd allow him a night with her body for pleasure, but that didn't mean he had the right to know everything about her yet.

He looked down at his now still body and sighed. "Thank you."

She smiled at him, but her eyelids suddenly felt heavy from her release. It was as though she'd just taken a sleeping draft. As if sensing how tired she was, he pulled her in close to him. With her head on his chest, she quickly fell into a peaceful slumber.

38

Evenia

First thing in the morning, they ate breakfast with Alekze, Asryn, and Irenz before separating again, the trio now heading farther into the cold toward the palace of Akvar.

For some reason, Evenia found it difficult to say goodbye to Irenz a second time. To try to appease the surprising emotions that built in her chest, she promised Irenz they would visit again on their way back from Nulhe. Kalland had raised his eyebrow in silent question, but he didn't deny her the request. Especially not after the way the promise made Irenz's face light up and she hugged Evenia once more, telling her she looked forward to it.

After finally separating from the tight-knit family, Kalland and Evenia were now officially headed toward Nulhe. The ride was quiet so far, and Evenia wasn't complaining about it. There were worse places to be than on the back of a horse on a peaceful forest path, with birds chirping, leaves rustling in the wind, and squirrels racing up trees. Not to mention the memories from the night before...

"What's made you so happy?" Kalland's voice and playful tone startled Evenia, making her smile falter.

"Nothing," she said, shrugging. She hadn't realized the peaceful view had made her smile.

He chuckled and faced forward again. "You're a terrible liar, you know?"

Evenia couldn't help sticking her tongue out at the back of his head. She stifled a laugh, the act making her think of memories with her cousin, Mer.

"You don't know me," she said, regaining her composure.

With a smirk on his face, he half-turned to her. "Don't I?" Her mouth fell open, resembling an *O*, as he winked at her before facing forward again. Was he referring to their night together?

Who was this new Kalland she was traveling with?

"What is your deal?" Lightly tapping her heels into Rianore's sides to pick up her pace, they were now side by side with Kalland and Xelfrina.

"What do you mean?" He side-eyed her.

"Seriously? You're being nice. You're joking. You're flirting... And last night..." The night they seemed to be ignoring happened in the first place, despite the fact that they woke up in each other's arms. She shook her head as she felt her cheeks pink under his gaze. "I hardly recognize this version of you," she said, waving her right hand in the air. Ever the dramatic talker. Something she got from her aunt.

He shrugged, some of the amusement visibly gone from his demeanor, as if mentioning it dampened his spirit a bit. A twinge of guilt pierced her, but her annoyance won out. He'd been an ass to her up until they left Mircha, and she wasn't soon to forget just because he was suddenly being nice. And sexy...

"It's probably Nulhe," he said, facing forward. "Thanks for ruining the fun by pointing it out." He side-eyed her again, but there was amusement twinkling in his eyes.

She rolled her eyes. "It wouldn't be so noticeable if you hadn't been an absolute ass to me up until recently."

He scoffed and his hand raised to his chest in mock horror. "I resent that, Raldir," his tone sounded angry, but his eyes told another story.

Back to surnames, then...

She sighed, suppressing a smile. "Hmm, maybe it's a good thing I know the effects Nulhe has on you, Sothenas." He turned to her, and she stopped fighting the smile as she faced forward. "A weakness of yours. I'll be stowing that away for future reference." With one eyebrow raised, she looked at him.

He paused, his eyes assessing hers, and she felt a flutter in her stomach at the look in his eyes. The same lust from last night. "Is that your way of saying you plan on keeping me around, Raldir?" His voice was deeper than before, and she had to adjust because of the tension it sent to her core.

"Hardly," she shifted her thighs in the saddle, "but it's good to keep that knowledge in my back pocket, just in case my future is cursed with your presence." She smiled and, to her surprise, he returned it.

"Lies, again," he chuckled. "But let's hope for all our sakes that our paths won't have to cross again after all this." Without warning, his words cut deep, like a knife to her gut, stealing her breath.

Why did she care whether Sothenas was in her life or not? He was an asshole. Case in point.

Blinking the hurt away, she straightened in her saddle again. "Yeah," she managed to say, not sure how else to respond.

He turned to her, and she could see in her peripheral vision that he was assessing her again. The next thing she knew, Xelfrina was next to her and Rianore, and an invisible hand lightly tapped Evenia's thigh. A gasp fell through her lips from shock at the unexpected touch.

"If I didn't know any better, Evenia, I'd say you almost dislike the idea of not seeing me again." His tone was playful, and a shadow of a smile graced his face.

She rolled her eyes and huffed a laugh. "Keep dreaming, Sothenas." But part of her was annoyed to find he was right.

A deep chuckle sounded from his chest as he pulled Xelfrina away again so that the horses were about six feet apart from one another again. *"It's okay. I'd miss you, too,"* he Wind whispered.

She didn't look at him, only smiled to herself as the words warmed something in her chest. The reaction made her internally groan. Talk about fucking annoying how her body was responding to him today. It had to be because he was being strangely kind and how he was with her last night.

"I didn't deny that I'd dislike it...a bit, but no one said anything about missing you." She turned to him, a big smile on her face, but when their eyes met, her breath caught. The desire she saw in his eyes stirred the heat in her core again. "What?" The question came out breathy under the intensity of his stare.

Just as quickly as it appeared, he blinked it away. "I don't think I've ever seen you smile so much. It's mesmerizing," he said, his voice suddenly husky.

Her cheeks grew pink, immediately feeling self-conscious. "Oh, thanks." She gave him a small smile.

"No, your real smile," he said right as a warm gust of Wind caressed her cheek and gently pulled her chin toward him. "Not the courtesy laugh or the polite smiles you give to us all. The genuine one, the one that shows you're allowing yourself to enjoy life. Those brief, fleeting moments when you show us the real you."

The invisible Wind hand gently squeezed her chin before releasing her as she blinked away the stinging in her eyes. Facing forward once more, she steeled her spine, not succumbing to the emotions wanting to surface. She was not used to compliments from anyone, let alone him.

"I've made you uncomfortable, I'm sorry." She didn't look at him, just continued facing the path ahead. "You're only protecting yourself, and I recognize that. But you do have a beautiful smile. The real one, and the fake one."

She shook her head, eyes closed. "Stop, I can't take another nice thing from you," she said, her emotions reaching their limit.

"What?" His tone sounded so shocked that she couldn't help but look at him. His eyes were scanning her face. "Have I really been that much of an ass to you?"

She stared at him for a few seconds before laughing. "Well, yes." She smiled wider at the surprise in his eyes. "And no. I'm just...not...used to..." She sighed, annoyed at herself for struggling to get the words out.

"Regular asshole or not, I'm not used to compliments. They make me...uncomfortable." As the last word left her lips, she sucked in a deep breath. A sudden sense of pride in herself for getting the words out filled her, but she was also a bit embarrassed by the confession.

Slowly, she met his gaze again. He looked almost...angry? But he quickly hid the emotion. *Shocking.*

"We'll be working on that," he said. She blinked at the words, but before she could respond or react, he continued, "But if it makes you feel more comfortable in the meantime, I think asshole Sothenas can be arranged." He smirked at her.

She rolled her eyes, but there was a smile on her face. "Not for this trip, he can't be. You're Happy Kalland right now," she teased him. "What is it about Nulhe that changes you so?"

Looking like he was deep in thought, he stared ahead for a few moments. "I don't think I could put it into words. It is a place you have to experience to fully appreciate." His eyes met hers. "I hope it brings you some happiness and peace, too."

She smiled at him and the thoughtful words. "Okay, where's the Asshole Sothenas at?" she teased.

He grinned. "He's on vacation."

She laughed at the joke. A laugh she felt in her belly, which she clutched until the cramp died down. "Oh my gods, who are you? I didn't know you were funny."

Sending a gust of Wind toward her, he tousled her braids, making them whip on her back as they came back down. "Keep it up, and I just might send you toppling on your ass."

"Hey!" she said, grabbing a braid. When she met his gaze, the whites of his teeth were still shining. "There he is. Welcome back, Sothenas." She winked at him, but he only rolled his eyes in response.

"Gods help me," he mumbled, but a small smile was still on his face.

"Oh, hush your face, you know you like it." So did she.

The look in his eyes told her exactly how he felt, while simultaneously sending butterflies to her core. Shooing the imaginary butterflies away, she sobered up by remembering the conversation at hand. The place they were going to on a mission. A place that seemed to make him happy, despite their task.

"Tell me more about Nulhe—what I can expect going into the Moon Realm. I've only heard and read stories about it," she said, changing the subject.

His eyes lingered on her for a moment longer, before facing forward again. "No book can prepare you for the beauty of Nulhe and its palace. Or its queen," his voice went from serious to wistful.

"Queen Selaria?" Evenia asked.

Kalland nodded. "Yes, Queen Selaria." He turned to her, smiling. "She'll like you," he said, and Evenia's cheeks flushed again as she broke contact. "Come on, that was hardly a compliment."

"Give it a rest. It's just uncomfortable being told nice things," she managed to say.

"That's going to change," he said, his tone serious. "Who made you feel like you're not worthy of kindness?" Her eyes shot to his, his gaze intense.

"Is that really any of your business?" she snapped back, feeling embarrassed and defensive all of a sudden. This line of questioning made her feel way too vulnerable.

"That depends." His voice was deep, with all humor lost as he searched her face. For what exactly, she didn't know.

"Seriously?" she scoffed. "On what?" Her anger was brimming to the surface under his scrutiny and entitlement to her life.

"On whether or not someone hurt you," he growled.

Oh. Not ready for that conversation, she couldn't hold his gaze anymore. "It just...is. Okay? Let's just drop it," she said, embarrassed and irritated. "What's your favorite thing about Nulhe?" It's the only question she could think of to change the subject.

They sat in silence for a few moments, and with each passing second, her irritation was quickly being replaced by embarrassment and sadness. His question made her think. Why was she like this? Why couldn't she accept a compliment from another? Why couldn't she accept a compliment from herself?

She had a very good idea of the answers to those questions, but she wasn't ready to face them yet.

She sighed and looked at him once more. "Summoning Happy Kalland?"

He looked as if he just snapped out of a trance when his eyes dropped the anger and focused on her. "I thought you preferred asshole me?" he joked, trying to match her mood.

"Apparently not." She shrugged.

He smiled, shaking his head. "It's hard to keep up with your brain, Raldir," he said.

She grinned. "Try living with it," she joked, but her smile faltered, thinking about how hard it actually was to live with her brain. It seemed to delight in tormenting her with memories of the past and making her see things that weren't actually there.

"What is it you asked me before?" he asked, pulling her from her thoughts.

Clearing her throat, she straightened her spine, willing herself out of her thoughts and back into the present moment. "What is your favorite thing about Nulhe?" she asked him again.

His gaze swept her face once more. "Easy, the palace," he said.

"Why?" Her head cocked to the side, curiosity overcoming her. Of all the places to go and see there, why the palace?

"You'll see why." A smile lessened the intensity of his stare, replacing it with genuine excitement. "The artistry that went into every crevice of it. The history that's marked in each stone. The beauty etched into the designs of each pillar. The murals on the walls and ceilings. The colors everywhere you look. The clouds beckoning to you from every room," he rambled. His gaze was fixed in front of them, but his vision appeared lost in a memory elsewhere.

"It sounds beautiful," she said.

He looked at her then, a dreamy smile on his face. "It is."

She was starting to get concerned with her body's response to his gaze and words today. With what they did the night before...and with what she hoped they would do again tonight. She broke eye contact, willing the relentless flutters in her stomach to stop.

"I've heard stories of how many steps adorn the palace. What is it, one hundred steps?" she asked, changing the subject by trying to remember what she learned in school many moons ago.

"Try four hundred steps, with one hundred steps for each child Queen Qelena, the first Moon Queen, bore," Kalland said, not looking at her.

What a way to honor your kids, I guess. She shook her head in amazement at the thought of having to walk up four hundred steps. Or even having to *create* that many steps.

Pausing, her head whipped toward him. "We're going to walk up all of those steps to the palace?" She almost didn't want to know the answer to that. Grimacing in anticipation of the answer, her thighs already burned just at the thought of it. "I'll need an ice bath and a nap before we even meet anyone."

"You can get to the Moon Palace by foot, but that would take hours. I don't recommend it," he said, nonchalantly.

"You don't *recommend* it? What does that even mean? What other way could there be?" she asked. Her mind whirled with possibilities, but nothing came to her. Wait, maybe evanescing—the way elves could travel? That would mean he wouldn't have to walk up the steps, but she didn't possess that elven power. She resisted the urge to roll her eyes at the elf and his mysterious powers.

He pulled on his reins, stopping Xelfrina. Rianore followed the movement, bringing Evenia to an abrupt halt. It was evident he really had trained Rianore. Glancing from her horse up to him, her stomach dropped at the emotionless expression on his face, except for the pure amusement in his eyes. Suddenly, she felt like a deer in a wolf's sight.

Shit.

"What other way is there, Kalland?" she asked, though part of her was afraid to hear the answer.

"I would hold on if I were you," Kalland said, amusement laced in his tone. He gestured his head toward her reins.

Eyes narrowing on the much-too-excited elf, she instinctively grabbed the reins tighter and sat straighter in the saddle. Suddenly alert, she braced herself as her eyes briefly scanned their surroundings, looking for any threat, before falling on Kalland once more.

His eyes scoured her body, assessing her, as he instructed Xelfrina to step a few feet farther from Evenia and Rianore, who didn't move an inch. Now facing Evenia and her horse, Kalland smiled again. Seemingly satisfied, for whatever unknown reason, he spoke a command in a language Evenia wasn't familiar with, "*Inojk'l.*"

Before she could even attempt to decode the term, she felt Rianore's body vibrate under her. "What the fuck?" she asked, her voice a scared whisper.

Mouth agape and eyes wide, she suddenly understood why Kalland handpicked her horse and why Nishara was so excited, as both Xelfrina and Rianore sprouted wings upon his command.

Dumbfounded, Evenia just sat there as giant wings appeared out just in front of her thighs, spreading so wide that the wingspan had to be longer in length than either horse. Rianore stretched her wings, the champagne feathers rustling and taking on hues of gold and silver in the sunlight.

Slowly looking up, Evenia saw that Xelfrina's wings were light grey and somehow looked bigger than Rianore's massive wings.

She forced her jaw closed as Kalland chuckled. Xelfrina flapped her wings once, likely in anticipation of putting them to use. The sound jarred a memory in Evenia.

The faint flapping of wings, almost like a melody. The warmth of the Wind surrounding her cold, frail form, and the Wind whispering of a certain grey-eyed elf—assuring her that she was okay—over the sound of wings soaring.

Her eyes landed on Kalland. "I did hear wings that night!" she exclaimed.

Not saying anything, he only grinned enough for a single dimple to appear in his right cheek. She rolled her eyes at that damn dimple.

"How?" she asked, resisting the urge to touch Rianore's wings.

"Winged horses are native to Valoreg," he said, smiling.

Images of paintings of the Wind Realm of Valoreg from her school's textbooks popped in her mind, but winged horses were never mentioned. That was definitely something she would have remembered.

"They're rare, but they are just as much a product of the Wind as my kin are. It sort of means we share a bond." He shrugged, as if horses sprouting wings was as normal as a fly with wings. Then again, she guessed that for someone from Valoreg, who also owned a winged horse, it was normal for him.

She shook her head in disbelief.

"If you're done gawking, are you ready to see the Moon Palace? Without the need for an ice bath." His eyebrows danced and he grinned, a boyish excitement written all over his face. "We're still about a day and half's ride away, but traveling this way will shorten that time a bit."

Her head was shaking again. She looked around at their surroundings and back to the unbelievable magical creatures in front of her. Was this real? Or were they already in the land of dreams? Someone better not pinch her, because this happy, excited Kalland was unrecognizable to her. Add in the winged horses, and yes, this all was most definitely what dreams were made of.

"Is that a no?" he asked, his smile faltering a little. Those grey eyes scanned her once more, as if he was making sure she was okay. "Are you afraid of flying?"

She huffed a laugh. "No, I'm ready. At least, I think I am. Just...processing," she said.

He smiled again. "Good, because we were going to be flying either way." She scoffed in response. "Hold on tight." He barely got the words out before his toes dug into Xelfrina and she spread her wings wide, taking off.

"Whoa!" Evenia grabbed the reins tighter and leaned into Rianore's mane a little as she took off in the air, following Xelfrina's lead once again. Evenia felt her stomach jump as adrenaline flooded her system at the sudden rush. "Holy fucking shit," she whispered with equal parts excitement and nerves.

As they cleared the tops of the trees and the wind blew through her hair, her body slowly released its tension, inch by inch.

Resisting the urge to look down, she glanced toward Kalland. She wasn't at that point of courage to enjoy the view just yet. Not like him. It was impossible to stop the grin spreading on her face from seeing Kalland atop Xelfrina, with his arms outstretched, enjoying every second of this freedom. He looked so...happy up here. So free.

There was a fluttering in her stomach again, but it didn't look like they were gaining any more altitude. She ignored the feeling as his eyes met hers, watching her with a smile on his face as the clouds passed by.

39

Evenia

Soaring through the sky on a flying horse was something Evenia never knew she would want to do before she died. But now that she had experienced the freeing feeling of soaring near the clouds, she realized she wanted to fly as often as possible.

They decided to land for the night shortly after the sun descended. They had set up camp a little over an hour ago, with dinner now in their bellies from leftover food Irenz packed for them. The stew they all made was just as good a second night in a row.

This version of Kalland—the way he had been since they left Mircha—was fun to be around. He was light, funny, caring, carefree. Conversation came easily, and the laughter came even easier. If she had the courage to say it out, she might even admit she...liked him. Her eyes squeezed shut at the thought and the swarming butterflies in her stomach.

Sitting on the cold ground, she brought her attention back to the present moment, to the folders from Andira resting in her lap. A few minutes ago, she watched the fire start to die down and felt uncharacteristically brave, prompting her to feel ready to grab the folders and read them for the first time.

With a flick of her wrist, she sent her Fire to the flames, keeping them just low enough so she could read without the light waking Kalland. The embers danced as she let out a breath and opened her uncle's folder first, leaning it toward the little firelight. This folder would be the easier one, as she already knew what to expect. Tears welled in her eyes as she saw a photo of her Uncle Ensel on the first page.

Ensel Igoran Raldir

Species: Human

Home: Poulttom, Enacor

Occupation: Sentry of Enacor

Marital Status: Husband to Siersha Brohn Raldir

Family: Father to Émeriah Raldir;
Uncle and adopted father to Evenia Raldir.

Status: Killed in the line of duty.

She wiped away tears with the back of her hand as she read about her uncle's life and death. The next page listed the names and photos of the men suspected in killing her uncle, including the one who managed to evade Mircha's capture. She recognized him as the one whose tunic didn't fit his belly. *Brudon Rolpher*. His name and face would be seared into her memory forever now.

The edges of the folder crumpled under her frustrated grip. Letting go, she closed the folder and took a deep breath in and out. Another breath, in and out, before she opened her mother's folder.

She sucked in a breath at the sight of her mother's photo. Looking at it, she could see a lot of herself in the image. The blonde hair. The pale blue eyes. Her mother's nose. Her smile.

Closing her eyes, she opened them again on a long exhale before braving it and reading the folder.

Nioma Brohn

Species: Human, Light Elemental Witch

Home: Poultom, Enacor

Occupation: Healer of Enacor

Marital Status: Engaged to █████████

Family: Mother to ████████
Sister to Siersha Brohn Raldir

Status: Missing

Every sound in the forest stopped, leaving her in utter silence inside her own head. Not even the pounding of her own heart could be heard. It was a good thing the folder was already in her lap, because she would have dropped it otherwise.

Engaged? To whom? Could it be Evenia's biological father? If that were the case, why wouldn't her mother have left her with her father? Aunt Siersha told her before that her mother got tied up in the wrong crowd, which her rap sheet in the folder supported. Could that mean...

Was Evenia's father responsible for her mother's disappearance? That would mean leaving Evenia with her aunt was the best way to keep her safe, right? Maybe even from her father... And why was *her* name redacted? Could her birth name have her father's last name tied to it? Would it tie her back to him?

Question upon question flashed through her head, and her frustration only grew more as she realized she didn't have an answer to a single one.

What the hel was this?

Breathe in, breathe out.

Reading on, she saw her mother had been arrested by sentries of Akvar for trespassing the year prior to Evenia's birth. According to the records, Nioma Brohn also filed missing shifter reports in the region. *Many* reports.

Evenia stilled. Could this be relevant to their mission? To *all* of their missions? Did it have something to do with The Darkness?

A glance at Kalland's sleeping form next to her kept her from blurting out her new theory to the night sky. Her theory that The Darkness had been taking shifters not just for the past few years, but for decades now. She didn't have any evidence to support it, just a gut feeling. A terrible feeling.

That's enough for tonight, she told herself, shaking her head. Taking one last glance at her mother's photo—engraving her face to memory—she closed the folder and tucked it safely in her bag. She would tell him tomorrow, and when they got back to Mircha, she would ask him to help her search through records to find out more. This couldn't be everything. It just couldn't be.

The sleeping bag crumpled under her as she laid down on the ground, which wasn't nearly as cold as at the campsite that first night of traveling. Kalland informed her they were closer to Nulhe than the Ice Realm of Akvar at this point, and thanks to their new way of traveling, they were only about half a day's flight from the Moon Realm.

A different kind of fluttering took over. Nerves from excitement and anxiety over going to a new place. She was excited to see a place she had only ever dreamt about, but also nervous for multiple reasons.

One, she had always been an anxious ball of nerves, ever since she was little. Two, she was going to a place where she didn't know anyone but the grey-eyed elf she was traveling with. Three, she, Evenia Raldir of Poultom, Enacor, was to meet a *queen*. Four...for the reason they were going to Nulhe in the first place: The Darkness.

Shudders racked her body. Was she really ready for this? Bright stars were taking over her vision from how tightly she was squeezing her eyes shut. Letting out a breath, she slowly opened her eyes. The night sky through the naked tree branches was now the only thing she could see.

The sky was a deep navy, while the clouds hiding the stars were a mixture of white and lavender, indicating just how close they were to Nulhe. The moon was nowhere in sight, hidden somewhere behind the clouds.

Suddenly, she heard one of the horses whinny as she felt a pinch in her neck. Instinctively, her hand reached for her neck, but it fell limply, as if there were no muscles in her arm. She must be more tired than she realized after the day's events.

Still staring at the night sky, her body rapidly grew limp with each passing second, but her mind fought it. Her vision was suddenly hazy, as the view of the trees above her swayed slowly, turning from leaves dancing in the wind to branches that took on a grim, almost hand-like appearance. The branches were suddenly crowding the once peaceful sky above. It was like they were alive as they reached out, grabbing down, down, down.

No, her exhaustion was playing tricks on her mind. Her eyes shuddered as the calming effect the lavender clouds had on her wore off. No matter how hard she fought it, sleep pulled Evenia under, as images of lavender and silver skies in her mind were replaced with sharp hands and hushed voices.

40

Evenia

"Where are you taking me?" Evenia asked in a teasing tone. Glancing to her left, she saw Bunard Cralins, the blonde-haired, blue-eyed boy who stole her heart.

She wasn't sure when it had happened, but he had officially claimed all that she was, and as far as both of them were concerned, all she ever would be. It was clear in the way he talked about how he wanted her to stop working with her aunt so she could stay home and look after their future children.

"You'll see..." he whispered. His lip pulled up in one corner and there was a mischievous look in his eye. A look that made her suddenly excited for their little excursion and grateful for the cloak of night to hide their...activities.

With their fingers linked, she playfully bumped his shoulder as they walked. Resisting the urge to smile back at him, she focused on where they were to hopefully find at least one clue as to where they were going.

They were walking in a part of the forest she didn't recognize. It was far past where she would have been allowed to go as a teen. Past the spot she wished she never had to see again: the ferynmin berry patch where her uncle was killed.

An angry shudder racked her body, but she resisted the numbing grief that wanted to consume her at the memory of her uncle's murder.

She forced herself to continue looking at their surroundings—forced herself to continue looking for a clue—as Bunard guided her through the trees. They weren't following any man-made path. In fact, she couldn't figure out a pattern to his madness. With linked hands, he appeared to be weaving them both in and out of trees without any path or clear direction.

Nothing. She recognized nothing. They were too far into the woods to see any sort of path. There were no sounds of horses, no cows mooing, not even the sounds of the dogs in town barking. They must be too far. That was the only explanation for the absence of Poultom's regular nightly sounds.

A pit formed in her stomach. Nothing good would come from being too far away from town.

"Seriously, where are we going?" Evenia tried to keep her tone light, but her nerves were too high. When there was no response, she looked up at him. He wouldn't meet her eye as he continued guiding her through the path.

Eyes flying to their linked hands—the only thing pulling her any farther away from home—she started to unlink their fingers and regain control of her hand. As she released his fingers and tried to pull hers away, his grip tightened to an alarming intensity.

"Ow! You're hurting me." Nothing. "Please, let go." Again, nothing. Her chest was heaving as her panic set in from the instincts of the beast beneath wanting to come through. What was happening? She had to show that side of her that nothing was wrong, that she was safe. Otherwise, it might risk coming through and hurting Bunard. That couldn't happen.

Digging her heels into the dirt ground beneath them, she tried to gain traction to free her hand. His grip only tightened further as she fought to be freed. It was almost crushing the bones in her hand at this point. This wasn't right. But surely he wouldn't hurt her? Her nerves were just on edge from being too far into the forest, making her scared for no reason. That's all this was.

Suddenly, he whipped his body around to meet hers.

"Stop it! Stop—" Something flashed in Bunard's eyes then. Instead of the kindness and heat she'd experienced these past several months, she only saw anger and... Was that remorse? "It'll be easier if you'd just..." He let out a breath and shook his head. "Fuck it. Here. A few feet farther. What does it matter? They'll find us either way."

They? She stopped pulling. Stopped moving.

"Wh–who? Who will find us?" She tried not to cringe at the sound of her voice trembling in fear.

Before he could answer, the sounds of leaves rustling and twigs snapping caught her attention. Her head snapped from side to side, but she couldn't pinpoint where the sound was coming from.

To the right of her first...

The left...

Her neck cracked as she whipped her head around at the sounds coming behind her. It was almost like it was in every direction.

Like *they* were coming from every direction.

Fear screamed at her as she fought to keep it in.

"Wh–what is this?" she asked, her claws coming dangerously close to releasing. One more second of this, and she might lose her entire control over her shifting. Something that hadn't happened in years, and she wasn't ready to have it happen again.

A gasp escaped her lips when she felt a pinprick at her neck. She blinked a few times as her vision began to blur and her brain became foggy. Her free hand slowly went to her neck and felt something sticking out of it. Before she could pull out whatever was making her feel this way, strong, calloused hands roughly grabbed her arms and pulled them back as a burlap sack was placed over her head.

She screamed. She screamed like her life depending on it...because every instinct in her body told her it did.

"I can't be taken again," she breathed out.

But wait...

This moment, this feeling...she'd felt it before.

Everything stopped. The voices. The taunts. All she felt was the fear overcoming her, drowning her. Without the bag over her head, her vision would already be darkened with terror.

She knew what was coming. Knew *who* was coming next.

Her chest was heaving as she struggled to get air down. "I can't be a prisoner again."

The dirty, icy cell. The cold seeping into her bones. The tests. The experiments. The pain. The needles. The desire to shift, to protect herself, but giving it her all—what little she had left in her—to refuse them what they desired most. Those yellow eyes. The...shadows. The late-night visits, whether she was dreaming or not. The—

Her vision turned white from the panic and fear gripping her, pulling her down, down. *No.* "Not again. Not again. He can't take me again."

"*Evenia...*" a strange voice caressed her ears.

It went ignored as those terrifying yellow eyes came into view in her mind again. As the shadowed figure they belonged to took up space in her cell doorframe. Step by step, he would approach, and with each advancement, she'd curl herself farther into a corner. Farther away from the inevitable obsidian waterfall, as pitiful and useless as an attempt it was. Away from—

"*Evenia...*" the voice sounded again.

Her ears perked up when she realized it was a Wind whisper. Except, this was...different. It was nothing like Kalland's warmth as a current of Wind caressed the tips of her semi-pointed ears. Nothing like hearing his deep voice in a hushed whisper for only her to hear.

In her experience, Wind whispering had been a warm sensation for her. But this...this was something entirely different than she'd ever heard or felt before.

Or... No, that wasn't true. She *had* heard it before.

That night she fell off the cliffside.

The night she got away.

The night she fought back.

This voice—not quite cold but not quite warm either—had touched her ears once before. It had said to her then: "*You made it out, Evenia. Now, you must prepare.*"

She didn't know what it meant, but when she focused on Wind whispering in that moment, she was reminded of swirling silver irises staring back at her. Silver that she'd grown fond of. Her body and mind had been too out of it that night Kalland helped her that she didn't remember the strange voice or the words spoken. But now...

The fog she'd felt moments before—the abyss of terror-filled memories attempting to drag her down—lifted as that memory became clearer in her mind. The knowledge that she'd made it out—that she'd saved herself that night—struck her like a drum she could not ignore. *Would* not ignore.

The fog continued to dissipate as the image of Kalland standing there, waiting for her that night in a different set of woods became clearer in her mind. *That* was where she needed to be. Not trapped in the past melding with the present. Not being consumed by her fear.

Blink.

As if by magic, the burlap sack atop her head was no more.

Blink.

Away went the harsh grip on her arms, holding her down.

Blink.

The image of the boy she'd once loved—the boy who betrayed her—vanished into thin air.

Blink.

A short breath of disbelief escaped her lips. She wasn't in The Darkness' clutches, and wasn't about to be taken to him. It had all been an illusion. A dream. And yet, it was a memory at the same time. Not only a memory of what she experienced when she was captured for The Darkness but *how* she was captured before.

And... She was suddenly struck with the realization of how she had been captured again.

Her hand slowly went to the right side of her neck. She winced as her hands were pulled back down with such a force. Almost like...she was chained again. Was it too late?

She couldn't let herself think like that. Keeping the panic at bay, she focused on the stinging in her neck. Her brows knit together as her lips pursed. It had to be some sort of drugged dart that pierced her skin. Back then...and now. Suddenly, the image of swirling silver came to mind and panic set in. If she was hit, then so was he.

He was also in danger.

Her fists balled at her sides as she willed her mind—her body—to wake. To fight.

But...The Darkness. What would she see when she opened her eyes again? Was she already back there?

No, she couldn't think like that. There was no way in hel they were going to take her again. No way was she going to be dragged back to that helhole, back to *him*.

"You will not take me." As she spoke the words, a sense of peace wrapped around her like a warm blanket welcoming her home. It all became clear to her as the voice sounded once more.

"*Evenia,*" the voice Wind whispered to her, "*it is time.*"

41

Kalland

K alland stirred as he heard birds chirping nearby. That should have signaled a relatively peaceful morning camping during their travels. Instead, his senses were dulled and his head felt like he'd drunk nonstop from Tasz's secret wine stash back home.

He groaned and tried to lift his hand to rub the ache, but his eyes flew open as his hand was instantly pulled back to the ground with great force.

Squinting from the harsh sunlight, he blinked a few times to make out his surroundings. He looked to his right, at the hand that had been thrown back from his face, and saw his shackled wrist secured to a tree trunk. *What the hel?*

Faint voices sounded in front of him. Blinking a few times, he looked up to see a crackling fire farther into the clearing with six human men sitting around it. Kalland watched as one stood up and walked past the tree line. None of them seemed to notice he was awake yet.

Flashes from the day before broke into his mind. *Saying goodbye and good luck to Alekze, Asryn, and Irenz. Riding off with Evenia on their journey to Nulhe. Surprising her with flying, then camping for the night in their final hours to Nulhe. Then...*

Nothing. They must have been attacked at night. Kalland silently cursed himself for not being better prepared.

Based on the discomfort in his neck, he guessed these men used some sort of a sleeping dart on them. His hand instinctively went to touch his neck, but it was yanked back down by the chain before he'd moved even a few inches.

Bastards. Who the fuck were they?

Kalland heard metal clinking on metal and murmuring next to him. Head moving ever so slowly, he looked to his left and froze as he saw Evenia chained to a tree about ten feet to his left. She was staring at the ground, whispering to herself. She didn't look injured, but she looked scared out of her mind.

"Evenia? Are you all right?" He had meant for it to come out as a Wind whisper, but his voice was raspy from a parched throat and at a normal level.

"I can't be taken again." She was muttering to herself so quietly that Kalland could hardly hear her, even with his matured elven hearing. He could see that her chest was heaving. "I can't be a prisoner again."

"They're just humans. We're going to be fine," Kalland tried to assure her. Again, the Wind whisper failed. Something told him his words didn't matter, as she looked like she was beyond hearing, overwhelmed by fear. She was spiraling into a panic attack, and he couldn't help her.

He pulled at the chains again in frustration, attempting to pull free to get to her.

"Not again. Not again. He can't take me again." Her voice was breaking next to him, coming out no more than a whisper under her breath.

He? Kalland's blood chilled. His head whipped back to the bandits, studying them. They looked like ordinary fuckheads to him. He didn't smell The Darkness on them. They weren't—

No. The one in the middle, the biggest bandit with the mohawk...there was a faint trace of The Darkness's scent on him. Kalland bared his teeth.

The bandit who had vanished into the tree lines returned. As he walked back toward the fire, he saw Evenia muttering with her head down. "Oi!" he shouted. "Wot ya going on about thur?" His accent was thick, and Kalland couldn't place it.

She whispered something even Kalland couldn't hear, which only angered the bandit further.

"Wot?" He walked closer and kicked dirt in her direction. Whether to torture her further or get her attention, Kalland didn't know, but the act irked the shit out of him.

"Leave her the fuck alone," Kalland spat at the bandit, pulling so hard on his chains that he felt a stinging pain and smelled something metallic as the chains cut into his skin. The bandit broke out into a cruel grin as he looked from Kalland's chained hands to his face.

As if chains could stop me. Kalland grinned at the thought. He tried to call upon the Wind to knock the ugly fucker on his ass...but She failed him. His lips parted as he looked at his shackled right hand. What was happening?

"You will not take me." Evenia's voice was clearer and calmer than it had been only moments before, but it sounded...different. Kalland realized that everything in the clearing had grown eerily quiet. The leaves had stopped rustling, and even the birds that woke him had stopped chirping. He looked around, but saw no explanation for the quiet, and no one else seemed to notice the sudden shift in nature.

"Wot?" The bandit laughed again. "Yer fuckin' chained do'n, ya bisch."

"Yeah, with some strong-ass spelled chains," a voice from near the fire pit chimed in, causing more laughter from around the pit.

"Fuckers," Kalland said under his breath as realization dawned on him. Spelled chains would cause his Wind whispering to fail. It also left him unarmed. His anger rose.

"Evenia? It's going to be okay," Kalland's quiet voice sounded in question next to her, but as he studied her, he realized she'd still heard nothing from him.

Her gaze slowly fell to the chains bound to her wrists and linked to the thick tree trunks beside her. Her eyes trailed back up toward the voice, and she grinned at the man sitting by the fire pit. Despite the smile on her face, her stare was blank.

He searched her face, but her eyes were odd. He stared at them and saw...nothing. It was as if her eyes were not her own. Not even her voice was that sweet sound he'd come to enjoy hearing.

"Even in these chains..." She paused as she gripped each chain link securing her hands, loosening the tightness around her wrists and holding the chains and dangling them from the tree trunks in the process. "You will not stop me."

Her eyes, normally a bright blue, with one eye a two-toned bright blue and green, were now turning wholly grey—the color of fog, of mist, of nothing. With her hands still bound on either side of her, she effortlessly rose to her feet, as if something had lifted her up.

"Maybe you don't know what 'spelled chains' mean, girl, but you're not going anywhere," one of the men around the fire pit said as he used his pocketknife to pick at the dinner remaining in his teeth.

The bandit closest to him started walking toward Evenia, his eyes locked with Kalland's with each step he took, taunting him. Kalland growled, which only made the asshole's grin grow wider.

The bandit stilled and his smile fell at Evenia's next words.

"You will not take me. I will be his prey, no more." Her voice sounded hollow. "You will fail, human." Her chin rose, her gaze locking onto the bandit in front of her.

"I don't know, it looks like we've already succeeded," the bandit with the mohawk spoke from the fire pit. A few more snickers came from the other four bandits sitting around the fire. "You're fucked, blondie."

She only grinned, but her eyes were void of emotion, of all feeling. "I am the ground that lies beneath your feet." Her voice was cold and warm all at once. It sounded unrecognizable, yet hauntingly beautiful to Kalland.

His eyesight narrowed as the dirt around her and Kalland started shaking, causing little pebbles to vibrate on the ground. He blinked a few times to make sure he wasn't hallucinating after his head injury. Looking around, no one else seemed to notice what he saw. Was she casting a spell?

"What the fuck is she saying?" yelled the bandit with the pocketknife. "And what the hel is he grinning at?" The same bandit directed the point of his knife at Kalland.

"Somebody shut her up!" yelled the man with the mohawk.

"I've got the little bitch." The bandit closest to them stepped toward her.

"Don't. You. Dare," Kalland's smile fell and his voice was gravely dangerous as he fought against his chains.

"Oh, yah, and jus' wotdoya think yer gonna do 'bout it?" The bandit looked at him, then down at his chains again, and grinned, showing his two front teeth missing. He raised a hand in the air, as if to strike Evenia, but a gust of Wind in the shape of a small twister had suddenly surrounded her, blowing dirt into the bandit's face.

What the fuck?

Taken aback, Kalland looked down at his chains to make sure the miracle Wind hadn't come from him. Seeing that his spelled chains were still intact, he looked back up at Evenia, who was somehow glowing white in the grey of the small twister surrounding her. Her long, blonde hair was blowing in the wind behind her. The only sign the twister was affecting her.

Without even so much as a muscle twitch, her chains burst free from her hands. With eyes still closed, she looked up to the skies.

"Wot da fok?" yelled the bandit who had almost hit her. "Rolpher, wot da fok is dis?" His arm was raised above his head, shielding his eyes from the debris as he looked back at who must be the head bandit—*Rolpher*—the one with the mohawk. He was still sitting by the fire, his eyes wide, mouth agape.

Without her even so much as glancing in the direction of the bandit closest to her, a tree root slithered to the bandit's feet, wrapping around his ankles and rising to his shins. He tried to run, but it was no use.

Up and up it rose, until it had quickly curled itself around his entire body, squeezing his neck and covering his mouth, cutting off his air supply. His eyes bulged as the root strangled him like it was a boa constrictor sprung from the earth. Still, she didn't look. As the bandit fell, unmoving, the tree root slithered back to its resting place in the ground.

All the bandits around the fire suddenly jumped up, alert and reaching for their weapons. Kalland tried to prepare for a fight out of instinct, but he swore out loud as he was jerked back down by his chains.

"I am the air that you breathe." Her voice came again as Kalland realized her eyes had filled wholly with that grey color.

Now on alert, another bandit who had been sitting by the fire seconds before attempted to come toward her, his pocketknife in hand. Before he made it even a foot from the fire pit, he fell to his knees, holding his throat, choking on nothing.

The twister suddenly picked up speed. Kalland's own hand instinctively went to raise above his brows before the chains pulled his wrists back down again. He was growing tired of that shit.

However, attempting to shield himself was pointless as he noticed that no debris was even coming toward him. When he looked closely, he realized she'd placed a Light shield up so that he was protected. Just like the one that she summoned when he put a rain cloud over her head in Mircha, and the one that appeared that night in the Wersves Inn during her orgasm. He shook his head, an incredulous smile no doubt on his face.

"I am the Moon that you bow before." The grey twister of wind surrounding her was quickly accompanied by sparks of purples, reds, blues, greens, and the deepest black, but she was still glowing like a beacon of light in the middle.

Kalland's breath caught as the words and swirling colors registered with him. She was listing all of the Elements. No, not just listing them, but *calling* upon them. All of them. Not just any witch, then.

He let out an unbelieving breath. He'd never seen an In-Between witch in action before. A witch who could command every Element, having access to each, but never one more than another, operating in the In-Between. He smiled as a sense of pride and awe filled him.

Weapon in hand, a bandit with brown hair and a nearly toothless grin rushed her, stepping over the now-lifeless body of his purple-faced companion. Suddenly, he stopped mid-step six feet away from her.

"I am the Sun that burns you endlessly," she said as the brown-haired bandit started screaming, gripping his arms, his chest, his face as vicious boils and burns appeared all over his skin. His misery lasted less than a minute before he laid motionless and unrecognizable on the ground.

"I am the Water that flows within your veins." The twister picked up speed again as a bandit running to her right suddenly froze in place. His raised arm dropped the ax he was holding and came down as both arms were pinned, unmoving at his sides. His eyes suddenly bulged as veins started popping in his head. Within seconds, he fell to the ground. Dead.

"Vertim!" yelled a male voice from the other side of the fire pit. He unsheathed a second sword before stepping around the fire pit. "That was my brother, you bitch!"

"I am the Fire that warms your bones." The fire that was calmly crackling moments before was now blazing six feet tall as it captured the bandit within its grasp, engulfing him in its flames.

"What the fuck are you?" It was the head bandit, Rolpher, who spoke this time, his eyes glued to the fire blazing. He was the last one alive.

She looked at the head bandit in front of her. "I am the dark of Night you love to serve."

Kalland's stomach dropped as the air chilled and the sunny day was suddenly met with unnatural darkness, both robbing and heightening his senses at once. His heart was pounding in his ears. It couldn't be.

"I am the Light that will set you free." Just as quickly as the darkness had come, it fled, being replaced by warm, bright light. He saw the panic on the human's face as the darkness—*her* darkness—retreated.

Her eyes were still on the head bandit, who reluctantly met her gaze after he looked at her unshackled wrists, where the spelled chains lay broken and useless on the ground next to her. There was pure terror on his face.

"I am nothing," she took one step forward, that colorful twister following her movement as she glowed within, "and I am everything."

The man standing in front of her started coughing as the dirt entered and burned his lungs. Forgetting about the shield of Light, Kalland's own hand instinctively went to raise above his brows before the chains pulled his wrists back down again.

Narrowing his eyes, he saw it was directed solely at the bandit in front of him. It was choking Rolpher and cutting him with dirt and sharp pebbles.

"I am a daughter of the In-Between." At that, she burst into Fire, the flames cascading down her petite frame to the ground in front of her.

No, not flames. *Lava*.

42

Kalland

Kalland couldn't stop staring at her. She was magnificent.

The molten fire was slowly swirling throughout her curves, becoming one with her until her pale skin was undetectable under the lava. Her clothes were gone—whether melted or covered, he didn't know, and he didn't care. Because of those curves. He'd always thought she was attractive, but seeing her now, embracing her power, and basically naked...

He blinked, reminding himself to look away. To. Look. Away.

Now.

Kalland stirred within his cuffs as he tried to bring himself back to the present moment. The movement caught her Fire-filled eyes. She looked up at his face, searching it. He met her stare, but he didn't know what to do. Yell at her for not letting him help? Smile with all the pride he felt in her right now? Bare his fucking teeth for not telling him what she was? Travel back in time to two nights ago when he should have fucked her until dawn?

He sighed, allowing all the anger and sexual tension brimming to the surface to release with that breath. Truthfully, she didn't owe him anything, and if he was honest, up until a few days ago, he trusted her just as little as she probably trusted him with such knowledge. But he *did* trust her now.

Whatever she saw in his face made her shoulders relax an inch. She held Kalland's stare as the chains around his wrists unlocked before turning her head back to the head bandit, Rolpher.

Kalland immediately felt the Wind's power rush into his body, coursing through his veins again. That alone made him feel more alive and less vulnerable. That power was a part of him, a part of his body and soul, and without it, he'd felt almost...human. Not that there was anything wrong with being human, but there was something very wrong with blocking out part of your soul—your very being.

Rubbing his sore, bleeding wrists, he felt them beginning to quickly heal. He looked down at them as the elven magic in his veins worked to heal himself from where he fought to be freed.

Slowly, he stood, but looking at the scene in front of him, he wasn't sure how close to step. The colorful twister had stopped the moment she'd embraced the Lava and was immediately replaced by a river of molten fire surrounding her. Evenia was holding Rolpher in place with tree roots. The bandit was on his knees, fighting the hold on his wrists as the Lava slowly worked its way toward him.

"I will only ask this twice before I allow it to reach you, Brudon Rolpher," Evenia said his name with such disgust in her voice. She was referring to the molten fire spreading toward Rolpher.

Kalland's eyes shot to hers. How did she know the man's full name? Rolpher was sweating, panic written all over his face, but he somehow managed to respond with a sneer.

"What does he want with me?" His eyes went wide for a brief second, but he shook his head.

Kalland knew better than most that the nightmare Rolpher was facing now was nothing in comparison to The Darkness. Evenia seemed to have the same thought as she made the tree roots slither farther up his arms, twisting more.

Before Kalland even had the chance to blink, there were shadows slithering toward the man. Rolpher's panic heightened as he started trying to break his hold on the roots, which only made them tighten further. The shadows slowly made their way down his throat, taking his air in a way Kalland hadn't seen her do yet in this clearing. He understood why she chose that method, but the sight of unnatural shadows still made his skin crawl.

"You have one more chance," she warned. The bandit's eyes were wide, but despite the panic and pain, Kalland could tell how this would end.

Before the bandit could shake his head again, Kalland took a step forward, still keeping his distance from the Lava moat surrounding Evenia. "Rolpher, was it?" In his periphery, he saw Evenia tense a few feet away from him, but she didn't look at him as she eased her shadows away.

After coughing and catching his breath, the bandit looked from Evenia to Kalland and gave him a half nod. "Hypothetically speaking, Rolph," Kalland interlocked his hands behind his back, "what do you think he'll do to you if you return to him without us? Without *her*?"

"They'll k–kill me," the man stuttered.

They? Kalland paused for a second. Out of everything she had done and was doing to this man now, the thought of The Darkness was still what scared the man the most. But who were *they*? Could it be the group found in Nulhe? Kalland's anger rose at the thought of that monster holding such power, but he tamped it down.

"Oh, that's not the complete truth, now is it?" He gave the man a cruel grin, letting that anger and urge to kill something show through. "You and I both know this is merciful in comparison to what he'll do to you." Kalland gestured to the river of molten fire ever-so-slowly making its way to the bandit. "And I'm half-inclined to let her go through with it."

Evenia's head whipped toward Kalland's at the word "let." He only winked at her. It was impossible to tell for sure since her face was swirling with Lava, but he could have sworn her nostrils flared in response. Oh, he liked this fiery side of her.

"Do it." Rolpher raised his chin. "Like you said, it's better than what's waiting for me back at—" Evenia's gaze flew back to the bandit, but he had stopped talking of his own accord, shutting his mouth at the slip up.

"Don't grow shy on us now, Rolph. Back where?" Kalland asked. "Back where *they* are waiting for you?"

Rolpher shifted uncomfortably, causing his worn, leather vest to shift open a bit. The movement caught Kalland's eye. He sent a gust of Wind to flap the vest open further, revealing a strip of fabric that had been sewn into the bottom inside of the vest. The fabric depicted a picture of a black hourglass with red sand. The symbol looked familiar to Kalland, but he couldn't figure out why.

"What is that?" he asked.

Rolpher's eyes followed Kalland's gaze. He stilled but remained quiet.

Evenia raised her right hand, and out of everything that he'd witnessed today, what he saw her do next made his jaw unhinge. Her Lava-swirled fingers transformed into claws, but her hand remained a human hand. *Claws.* He knew she was a shifter, he'd always known, and gods, he wanted to know what she was. He wanted to know it all.

She took one slow step at a time toward Rolpher, each footprint leaving behind charred grass in her wake. As she neared the bandit, he started squirming, to which the roots around his arms tightened further, until he was unable to move anything but his head.

He started to spit in her direction, but she waved her left hand—the hand that still had normal-shaped fingers—placing a shield of Light to block it. She gave him a tight-lipped smile as she dropped the shield and held the flap of his vest with her left hand. With her right, she used her sharp claws to cut the scrap of fabric from his vest.

"What the—" Rolpher was quickly shut up by shadows choking him again. This time, Kalland didn't feel quite as much disgust at the sight of them.

Once it was cut, she tossed the fabric at Kalland and returned to her Lava moat, facing the bandit. Kalland caught the fabric. Studying the hourglass for a few seconds, he definitely recognized it, but he couldn't place why. He tucked it into his pocket.

She pulled her shadows back as her claws retracted, being replaced by her slender, normal-shaped fingers again. "You will answer him," Evenia said. The bandit spat at her feet, and she called forth her magic to take the air from his lungs, sans shadows this time. The bandit made no sound as she held him like that for several seconds. When she finally released him, he started coughing.

"I–I'm dead e–either way," he said in-between coughs.

"Might as well make your death count for something, then," Kalland's voice was bitter, and the bandit just glared at him.

"Piss off, Pointy," Rolpher sneered.

Kalland laughed. "You've got spirit, I'll give you that." His face fell. "But you're also a fucking moron for aligning yourself with that monster."

The bandit huffed out a laugh and glanced at Evenia's right hand, where the claws had been only moments before. "He's ridding us of vermin." He looked up at Evenia's face before speaking his next words. "But I'm not sure he knew he was hunting a creature as equally as monstrous as himself. If he had, he probably would have come to finish the job himself. I wish he had. It's no less than you deserve," he sneered.

This time, it was Kalland's Wind choking the man. He stole his breath from him until the bandit started squirming. "One more fucking word," Kalland increased the pressure of his magic, "and I'll make sure this will be as slow and painful as possible before she finally ends you." Evenia took a step forward into the Lava, her river of molten fire inching closer.

After a long coughing spell, the bandit took in one last, long breath, filling his lungs before grinning. "Just do it already," Rolpher grunted.

"*We can't let him go,*" he Wind whispered to Evenia. "*I want to. Gods, I want to. Let him get what's coming to him. But the punishment he'll receive for failing is not worth The Darkness gaining more intel on you.*" She took another step forward, smiling.

"Then we make him suffer just as much," she said in her normal voice. Oh, yes, he liked this side of her very much.

"Agreed." Kalland grinned as the Lava finally reached Rolpher, and his screams filled the clearing.

43

Evenia

The bandit who killed her uncle sat before her, quaking in his boots from fear. She'd recognized his photo and name then, and while she felt murderous at the time, she wasn't now. The Fates granted her this closure today. Closure in the form of another kidnapping, but it was closure, nonetheless.

The fear was evident in his face. Whether it was because of her or the threat of what The Darkness would do to her, it didn't matter. Rolpher wielded no weapon, his arms still trapped by roots. There was no murderous note in his eyes, like the others who had attacked her. This man before her wasn't a danger to her anymore.

Looking around, she saw no more threats. There were no more threats. Not the bandits, and not the ghost of the past with her ex who sold her out as a shifter. The memory of him leading her to be drugged and carried off made her shudder involuntarily. Did he know what was in store for her? How was he connected to all of this?

Closing her eyes, she allowed herself to breathe and not think too harshly about what she'd done in this clearing.

It was necessary to survive.

It was necessary.

Find your antidote, Nishara's words rang in her head.

Anger. Revenge. Those had been the formula for her antidote thus far.

She remembered the paralyzing fear when she woke in the clearing this morning. The scent of The Darkness on the one bandit—Rolpher—sent her into a spiraling panic in the form of a memory merging with reality. Distorted memories and reality played tricks on her, melding the two together and making it difficult to decipher the past from the present. It led to the thought of being caught in his claws again. Of being trapped in that room, vulnerable, defenseless, weakened. Of being tortured and...

No, she was not going to let that happen again. She had been flooded with the overwhelming need to flee. But as she envisioned The Darkness again—his yellow eyes, his cold claws, his cruel shadows—that need to flee was quickly replaced with a need to fight, to survive, to win. And that's exactly what she did.

After the strange Wind whisper, she remembered her entire body going calm as she allowed the Elements to take control and help her. They'd spoken to her many times over the years, but she'd never let them in for fear of exposure. Then, when she was kidnapped—held prisoner—The Darkness kept her heavily drugged so that she wouldn't be able to use her powers.

This time, she knew she needed to embrace her magic if she had a chance to escape those spelled chains. Chains that only the In-Between itself could grant her the power to be free of.

She had been in control the entire time, fully aware of every action—of every death at her hands—but she'd allowed her magic to respond. Fighting based on instinct alone, she felt fucking powerful. There was no other way to put it. She'd never felt such power before.

As an In-Between witch, she'd always had to hide that side of her, for fear of someone catching her and hunting her down. There were even some witches in her coven who believed that In-Between witches were too powerful and should be exterminated. Because of that, there were few she could trust her secret with, which meant she'd never been able to test the extent of her true power. But fuck, if it didn't feel incredible to finally embrace her gods-gifted power.

And then, it was over. Her face fell as she remembered the In-Between leaving her and everything going red. There was a heat that rose in her, stemming all the way from her gut, rising to her chest, her neck, her face, her arms, and her hands, until all she saw was red.

The Lava.

It was more powerful than the Fire's heat she'd felt from her In-Between side. More relentless. That simmering heat had always flared deep within her bones—within her very being—all her life. Recognizing it as separate from her In-Between side, she shoved it down every time it threatened to surface. It was the side of her, her father must have left for her. The elven part of her that was responsible for her semi-pointed ears.

She looked down at her hands, at where she'd allowed her claws to slip through. Yet another curse from her father, and she'd embraced both today. She suddenly felt sick.

"Evenia?" asked a voice beside her.

She looked up to see light grey eyes. Those calm eyes. She stared into them as her breathing slowly began to even out. He held her gaze and he wrapped an arm around her, lifting her. Looking down, she realized she'd been sitting on the ground. When had she fallen? There was charred ground all around her, and the smell of burnt flesh suddenly slammed into her like a ton of bricks. She felt a wave of nausea as her chest started heaving again.

His hand gently squeezed her shoulder, pulling her attention back up to him. *"I've got you,"* he Wind whispered as they locked eyes. *"You're safe."* His voice was calm, soothing. *Safe.*

Yes, safe. The same words he'd said to her the night she escaped. She leaned into his arms as her body suddenly felt weak, so very weak. His stance didn't even falter as she unintentionally placed all her weight on him. He wrapped his second arm around her, holding her into his chest. Gods, that felt good. Safe. How many times had she said that word since making it to Mircha? How many times had she *felt* safe since she first fell at this elf's feet?

"What do you want to do about him?" Kalland asked, his chin jutting toward the silent bandit still trapped but very much alive.

He was giving her a choice in protecting herself from The Darkness potentially learning more about her. It was sweet, because he didn't know that there was little about her The Darkness hadn't already learned. During her time under his watch, he'd manipulated and pulled every little piece of her. He just took and took, attempting to bend her to his will, while exploiting her biggest weaknesses for his gain.

She shuddered at the memories threatening to hit her. A warm, invisible sensation touched her chin. Being pulled back into the present moment, her eyes lifted as she met Kalland's gaze again.

A scowl crossed her face at the realization of what she must do. "He lives," she said normally.

Kalland stiffened at her words. "Are you sure?"

She held his gaze for several seconds before she looked the murderer right in the eyes. "Brudon Rolpher," his eyes went wide at the mention of his full name, "killed my Uncle Ensel, and he's going to pay for it. The proper way." She looked back to Kalland as silver lined her eyes, threatening to spill past her lashes. Blinking them away, she Wind whispered, "*It's what my uncle would have wanted.*"

That invisible warmth brushed her cheek in response. "*He'll come to Nulhe with us,*" he Wind whispered. "When we're done, we'll bring him to Mircha so that he can answer for his crimes," he said normally so that Rolpher heard him.

The bandit scoffed. "It's funny that you think I'm safe in Mircha. You really have no idea how far their reach is." It was clear he'd meant to have some bite in his words, but the fear possessed him too much. If anything, it actually made him sound more menacing.

Kalland's body stiffened around her as he looked at the murderer before them. "What do you mean?"

Rolpher shook his head. Eyes wide again, he squeezed his lips tightly together. A sign he wasn't going to say anything else.

"*He's really starting to piss me off with all his cryptic messages,*" Kalland Wind whispered to her. She grunted in agreement. There was no way of knowing when he would or wouldn't offer useful information. She didn't have the mental capacity to deal with it right now. He might not be a physical threat, but he was most definitely a threat to her mental health at the moment.

Without thinking too hard so as to not talk herself out of it, she slowly lifted her right hand. Her still trembling fingers briefly danced as she released the branches wrapped around his arms and spoke the spell, "Paasiou n'clorestul."

A loud thump followed by a cloud of dirt made her flinch in Kalland's arms. His chest shifted, shielding her face and eyes from it as Rolpher landed face first into the ground.

Once the dirt cloud dissipated, Kalland loosened his grip on her and looked toward the indisposed bandit before meeting her gaze. "Remind me never to piss you off," he said. There was both amusement and weariness in his eyes.

A small laugh spilled from her lips. "Alekze said the same thing when I asked the dryad for help." She smiled weakly. "Marensha was right; Mircha could really use more witches."

Kalland grinned. "*Or maybe we just need more of you,*" he Wind whispered to her. The breath caught in her throat as his words enveloped her.

An involuntarily groan escaped her as he released one arm from around her. He chuckled, and she felt the vibrations from his chest throughout her body. He partially twisted away from her as he let out a high-pitched whistle. It reminded her of a bird sound. Slowly, she glanced up at him.

"It's for the girls. They're not here, which can only mean they fled before allowing themselves to be captured." His voice was full of affection. "They're smart girls."

Smarter than us, apparently, she thought to herself.

She didn't fully understand what he was saying, but she nodded into his chest anyway as his other arm remained holding her. In her weakened state, she somehow couldn't make the movement of her nodding head stop. It wouldn't stop. She sent the signal to her brain once, twice, three times, but it continued. It didn't stop until he placed his hand on her chin, stilling the movement and guiding her gaze up to his. His thumb brushed gently over her jaw.

He looked from her eyes to her lips, lingering there a moment as he traced them with his thumb. "You were incredible," he said. It was like her entire body blushed.

His lips parted, but she never found out what he was going to say. His grey eyes looked up at the sound of large wings flapping in the distance. That dimple was back as he grinned when Xelfrina—that beautiful horse—landed in the clearing a few feet from them. She stamped her hoof as she retracted her large grey wings.

"Hello, old friend." Kalland's voice had a loving tone to it as he spoke to Xelfrina, which made Evenia's heart melt. The horse whinnied in response.

The sound of more wings flapping made Evenia's eyes shutter open again, and relief flooded her at the sight of Rianore landing a few feet from Xelfrina.

"Hi," she whispered at the sight of the golden-winged horse here and safe with them. Rianore whinnied in response, pulling a small smile from Evenia.

Kalland went to place his free hand under Evenia's knees, but paused. "May I pick you up?"

"Yes," she said. In the next breath, he lifted her up as if she weighed nothing, pulling her in close to his chest. They started moving toward Xelfrina, walking around her to the side closest to the trees.

He placed her upon Xelfrina's back. "Is that okay?" he asked her, his voice soft.

Evenia started to nod but stopped herself in fear of the uncontrollable movement starting again. Why did she feel so weak after having felt so powerful moments before?

"What's happening to me?" she asked. It came out as almost a whisper.

He brushed his thumb across her cheek. "You just expelled a lot of power at once. The In-Between probably did not exhaust you too much, but you used more than that today.

Based on this reaction you're having, I'm guessing that it is a power you've never allowed yourself to use before."

His movement on her cheek stopped as her body tensed, so he cupped her cheek instead. "Whatever it is you're afraid of with your magic, it's not worth denying yourself this side of you. You are part Aesthï—a Lava elf. That is an undeniable fact. Your Lava is a part of you—your heart, your soul, your blood. That power is always with you, coursing through your veins as we speak."

No. She didn't want it. It was too much. She tried to pull away from the conversation, which resulted in her accidentally physically pulling away from his touch. The second he released his hand from her face, she missed it.

Her eyes locked with his again. "My biological father... He left. He never even wanted to meet me. But he left me with this–this..." Her hand twitched along Xelfrina's neck, not quite strong enough to fully lift it and point it to herself. The tears started to flow. "An–and with..." her voice trailed off, the words not being something she could bring herself to speak.

All the breath in her lungs stalled as he focused on the black marks in the creases of her eyes. "Your shifter abilities?" Slowly, she nodded. He made eye contact with her again. "*What are you?*" he Wind whispered.

Eyes wide, she shook her head to the side once. *Not yet.* That was a part of her she wasn't sure she wanted to fully reveal. A beast she didn't want to release into the world again. If they talked about it—if she had to breathe life into that part of her—it would make it too real. It would become a part of her she could no longer hide from. No, she wasn't there yet.

Seeming to understand her hesitation, he nodded. "Whatever it is, you must learn to master it, Evenia." She shook her head with such force, she almost knocked herself off Xelfrina. He was there in a heartbeat, arms securing her from falling.

"I don't want to," she whispered, looking up at his face.

"I know, I can tell," he placed a hand on the back of her neck, supporting her head, "but you must."

She avoided his gaze as he continued talking. "You must learn to master each and every skill. We will train you in private so that no one beyond those you choose will know the power you hold. If you so choose, those of us in Andira's circle will help you to master each Elemental skill. Tasz for the Sun; Nishara for the Moon; Andira for Nature and Metal;

Asryn for Ice; Elham for Water; and Caerdwyn Von Narra for Fire and Lava. You haven't met Caer yet, but I think you'll like her. I'm sure we can find someone for...Night."

Darkness, he meant. Shadows. His hesitation with the Element was understandable, given its association with the shadowed beast they were searching for information on. The one who seemed to still be hunting her, based on the nightmares she still experienced and Rolpher's words.

She looked up at Kalland, her gaze softening at the fact that he was willing to find someone to help her control and master that side of her. Except...it wasn't necessary. She didn't know how to tell him that it was part of her.

Yes, she was an In-Between witch, and the use of the Elements came naturally to her—almost like they lived within her. However, the darkness that resided in her now was a result of being trapped by the demon. A monster grew inside of her in order to help her deal with the demon monster who plagued her mind, her body, and her soul.

He succeeded in creating a darkness of inner demons that lived within her. First spreading in her blood, her veins, was a sickness that became a blessing, as it allowed her to fight back. It allowed her to break the chains he'd put around her—both figuratively and literally. She was still fighting to break the mental restraints holding her back—the fear, the panic attacks, the memories—but she would get there.

Now, the Lava side...that almost consumed her. That pull was somehow stronger than the other Elements, making her think his assumption that she was part Lava elf was correct. Which meant that her biological father was an Aesthï... He confirmed what she always suspected. It was the very reason she'd denied herself that side for so long.

Kalland's voice pulled her back from the inner turmoil she was spiraling down. "Me, with Wind and Storms." Oh, she liked the sound of that. "And Alekze with your shifter abilities." *That,* she didn't like. She didn't say anything—didn't react at all—and he seemed to understand. "The truth is, you'll be at your strongest when you can fight in any form and can use your shifter abilities while still in your human form, like you did today."

She glanced down at her hand, where there had been claws earlier.

Not looking up from her hand, she whispered normally, "What if I'm done fighting?"

He lifted her chin to look up at him. "You proved you are a warrior, and you will never be able to resist a fight." She looked away, but he kept his hand on her chin. "Your spirit won't allow you to walk away from protecting the defenseless, or keep you turning from prey," she locked eyes with him, "to predator."

I will be his prey, no more. The words she spoke in her trance earlier passed over her.

"*You are powerful, Evenia. Embrace your power—embrace your fire—and you'll burn them all to Hel,*" he Wind whispered to her.

"My...darkness..." He tensed, but she continued. "Please don't fear it. Don't fear me." No, this was too much. She backtracked. "It will always be there. No matter how hard I try to deny it, my power of Night—my own darkness—is just as much a part of me as my Light. But I am *not* him. I will not let it consume me. I will not let it consume others around me. Especially not you."

She held her breath, waiting for his response.

"I know. I'm not afraid of you, Evenia. Never you," he said, looking into her eyes so she could see the sincerity there. After a few seconds, he released her chin and took a step back.

Blinking away tears, she asked, "Where are you going?"

His eyes never left hers. "I'm going to secure him to Rianore's back," he gestured toward Rolpher's sleeping form, "and then I'm going to give these dickheads a proper sendoff and erase our scents from them. Care to give me a little hand?" His eyebrows danced as he gestured toward her hands, to her power.

Fire. He meant he was going to burn their bodies. It was a test. One she didn't care to pass. So, she shook her head once.

He only nodded and squeezed her hand. "Stay here and rest. When I'm done, we're going straight to the healers in Nulhe."

She almost nodded again but stopped for fear of the uncontrollable movement taking over once more. Instead, she closed her eyes, sinking deeper into Xelfrina's back. Quickly succumbing to the exhaustion and weakness seeping into her bones, his words played over and over in her head: *You are powerful, Evenia. Embrace your power—embrace your fire—and you'll burn them all to Hel.*

Again, and again, they played in her head, until sleep washed over her.

You are powerful.

Embrace your power.

Embrace your fire.

And you'll burn them all to Hel.

A small smile escaped her because that was exactly what she planned to do.

Epilogue

Unknown

F**our weeks later…**

"Beware the black and red," his voice came out in a sing-songy Wind whisper as he walked along the streets of Akvar. *"For here come the dead…"*

It was the night before a full moon, which brought all sorts of creatures in its wake. Especially in the mountain town of Wersves in Akvar, where the Moon was seen as a goddess to those who woke in her glow. In other parts of the continent, some would see the full moon and run in fear of what monsters would awaken in its light, but others…others saw it and felt more like themselves.

The latter was the case for him, even if he wasn't a Moon elf of Nulhe or one of those who…changed in the Night.

His lip curled in disgust at the thought of those whose blood wasn't elven, and how many of them walked these very streets with him.

There were many people out tonight in the market. Some human, some elves, some duolvain. And others…unknown. It was hard to tell what species one was at first glance, especially with some being wolves in sheep's clothing. Thankfully, no wolves roamed tonight, marking one less threat to achieve his mission tonight.

"Hi, Resena," he heard a soft voice sound from the left, catching his attention as he walked. His gaze shifted to two women, one of whom had semi-pointed ears and the other just looked human. But he knew better; no one was ever only as they appeared in the world of Avlonea.

"Hello, Irenz," the other woman responded.

He stopped walking. *Irenz.* The name tugged at his memory, but he couldn't quite place it. He turned to look at the two women one more time, but he didn't recognize her round face or dirty blonde hair. She was no one to him.

His eyes slowly dragged away from the two women greeting one another as he picked up his pace again.

Names were a funny thing. Full names. Surnames. Nicknames. Names given to you in the Night after ill deeds done. He smirked as his thumb began absentmindedly tracing the hourglass shape in the pocket of his coat.

He no longer held a name, just a purpose.

A very big, very special purpose.

He smiled at the thought.

"*One queen's reign will cease to remain...*" he began singing on the Wind again. "*As another takes the crown to watch the world drown.*"

A dog peeked its head up at him, ears perked, as if he'd heard the words, which was impossible.

Filthy beast. He shook his head, not understanding how anyone could take in pets when so many around him were practically animals themselves.

Booth after booth went by on his walk, as the market was crowded with people taking advantage of the moon's light to sell their goods. He'd seen better markets in other parts of Akvar, where there were polar bear tamers and ringmasters who tamed the shifters inside their cages. But this one was about as boring as its endless, snow-covered surroundings. And yet, people seemed to be enjoying every second of it, as if this was the most exciting day of the year for them.

No one paid him any attention, with the exception of some smiling his way as he slowly passed booth after booth, pretending to be interested in each merchant's stand.

"*She'll sit upon the throne made of bone and stone, to watch her people fight over what's wrong and right,*" he sang, while plucking a black feather from a dead raven on a hunter's stand.

"Oi! Take one more feather and you'll be buying the lot!" yelled the merchant.

Putting one hand up in defeat, the feather now hidden in his closed fist in his pocket, he smirked.

"Cover your ears, for she'll prey on your fears..." he sang while not using the Wind, giving the merchant a big, toothy grin in response to the red-faced anger before him, "and use your desire to bring herself higher." He turned, feather still in hand, and continued walking.

"Freak! Why do they always come out in the moon's presence?" He heard the merchant yell.

He froze, contemplating turning around and cutting the hunter's throat. Blood would spill all over the white snow on the ground, bringing some color to the monochromatic view. He was tempted. So very tempted.

Flexing his fists, he forced himself to put one foot in front of the other. The half-breed scum would get what was coming to him soon enough. They all would.

"*She claims love and peace, but will only bring chaos to these streets,*" he started singing on the Wind again, determined to finish the song. The words succeeded in drowning out the screams of children building snowmen and annoying laughter all around.

Despite the chaos around him, his smile only grew as he reached the last stand in the market, where the streets were beyond dark, save for the spots the moon's light touched the cobblestone paths and the flickering of lanterns on every three or four houses.

"May the Goddess be with you tonight!" a woman called to him from the last stand, showcasing paintings on dishes.

When he turned to look at her, her smile was bashful as she dipped her chin. The movement caused her hair to fall forward, and the semi-point of her ears peeked through. He sneered when he saw they weren't sharp-pointed ears. Not a true elf. These streets were littered with duolvain.

And then, he remembered her words. She was referring to the Moon goddess, but his own goddess was waiting for him. Yes, *his* goddess. He needed to ignore this distraction and fulfill his purpose. So, that's exactly what he did as he turned and continued walking.

He smiled again when he saw his destination. Just past the third house after the market's booths laid seven brown barrels with hay strewn all over them, half hidden in the snow. Casual, out of the way, unsuspecting barrels. To those walking by, it would look like nothing, but to him, and to the others in his cause, it was a way of sending a message.

He wondered how she would react to this plan he came up with. He was certain The Darkness wouldn't like it, but he didn't give a damn about that.

Head shaking, he never understood the fear that surrounded the shadowed figure. And now that he'd met him—now that he served alongside him—he just found the half-demon to be annoying. Just another demonic shifter to him.

Not to mention all the trouble his obsession with the girl was causing. The Darkness called her his little dragonfly—*his good luck charm*—but all she seemed to be bringing them was bad luck. He'd tried to get rid of her—to put an end to the ridiculous waste of time—after she suddenly showed up in Mircha, but his plans had been thwarted.

He cursed before regaining his composure. No matter. Soon enough, he would be rid of both The Darkness and that little obsession, and then he'd take his rightful place next to his queen's throne.

As he approached the barrels, he whisked the stolen feather he snatched out of his pocket. His fingers ran over the length of the soft bristles before he lifted the feather up, straight into the first hanging lantern's flickering flame. Eyes forward, he pulled the feather back after he smelled the smoke billowing from the tip a few seconds later.

Six more paces.

His heart skipped a beat. *"Beware the black and red..."* he sang again, bringing his Goddess's song close to its end as he walked toward the barrels. There was one small box laying next to the barrels. One that would...snap the second any weight was placed on it. But no one else knew that.

Four paces.

He held out the feather, the flames slowly building on it, working their way down. It wasn't a strong flame with the cold, but thankfully, the wind chill wasn't blowing. Another sign to him that this was the night. He was doing what he was supposed to do.

One.

His bottom lip caught in his teeth in his excitement as he dropped the feather above a bit of unsuspecting dry hay by the barrels. Feather now free of his physical hold and being controlled by his Wind, he kept on walking. His head shook in amusement that no one thought it odd fresh hay was laid down. No one found it suspicious or caught on to it. Just another sign to him that these imbeciles didn't deserve to share the same breath as him, let alone his queen.

With his thumb, he once again started tracing the hourglass symbol embroidered on the inside pocket of his jacket and sang the final line as he waited for the feather to float toward the hay behind him. Waited for it to bring chaos to these streets, just as his Goddess—his *queen*—would want.

He smiled as he sent a final small gust of wind toward the feather, hitting its target.

"For here come the dead."

Glossary

1. Aeslige (s)/ Aesliges ("ay-ss-league"): A Dream (or Nightmare) elf.

2. Aesthï ("aye-ess-tee"): A Lava elf.

3. Akvarian ("Ack-var-eee-en"): Native to Akvar, the Ice Realm.

4. Common Tongue: Sometimes referred to as Lorathish, is the language spoken commonly all around the continent of Lorathlor.

5. Deuri (s) / Deurix (p) ("Durr-eee"): A Wind elf.

6. Duolvain: Someone who is part fae, part human. Mostly identified by slightly pointed ears or other physical characteristics of fae that are inherited and difficult to hide.

7. Elndish ("Elle-nnn-dish"): Native to Elndion, the Sun Realm.

8. Enacoran: Native to Enacor, the Human Kingdom.

9. Evanesce: Transporting from one place to another.

10. Fae: Someone who is born of one or more types of magical species (e.g., elf, shifter, werewolf, dryad, siren, mermaid, witch, etc.).

11. Gathélan ("Guh-they-len"): Native to Gathéla, the Nature Realm.

12. Glacul (s) / Glacules (p) ("Glah-cuhl"): An Ice elf.

13. Huymi ("hugh-my"): A Nature elf.

14. Imin'al tre'eanor clorestul ("eee-min-yal tray-ay-nor cuh-lore-res-stuhl"): A witch spell to wake nature. Roughly translated to: "From my lips to Nature's ears."

15. Inojk'l ("inn-oh-kull"): Valoregan for "let's go."

16. Lunrea (s) / Lunreas (p) ("Lune-ray" / "Lune-rays"): A Moon elf.

17. Nulhen ("Null-hee-en"): Native to Nulhe, the Moon Realm.

18. Mirchan: Someone from Mircha, the Peacekeeping Realm.

19. Moln'shiar: "Good morning" in Gathélan.

20. Moragaink ("more-uh-guy-ink"): A master healer of not only the body but of the land.

21. Seinoradt ("sin-ore-at"): A breed of horse with wings that is native to Valoreg.

22. Soluxen ("Soe-lux-en"): A Sun elf.

23. Valoregan ("Vuh-lore-uh-gen"): The native language of Valoreg, the Wind Realm.

24. Vampyrx ("Vam-peer-ex"): A natural-born vampire.

25. Vampire(s): A vampire who is turned. Sometimes vampyrx are referred to as vampires as a whole species.

Acknowledgements

To my love, Andrew. No words can do justice to the level of gratitude I feel toward you. For the endless love, support, and encouragement. For the multitude of brainstorming sessions that lasted until two a.m. For being my guinea pig and reading my words before anyone else. For shouting my book out to the world, even before it was done. For never doubting me. For never letting me doubt myself. Thank you. I love you, *vhi-olnjk*.

To my lovely editor, Callie. Thank you for falling as hard for Kalland and Evenia while editing PNM as I did while writing it. Thank you for all your kind words of encouragement, and your willingness to brainstorm when I was stuck or feeling discouraged. Thank you for taking such good care of PNM and me. This book wouldn't be what it is without your love and encouragement.

To my sweet friend, Anaïs. Thank you for encouraging me to write this story since day one. For not allowing me to give up. For being willing to read it in its rawest stages, and helping me brainstorm when needed. For the love and support you always give no matter what.

To my chaos babes. There are so many of you to name, which makes me one incredibly lucky woman. Without you, I never would have finished writing this book or started on the rest of the series. You not only push me to be the best writer I can be but the best person I can be. You're my family, and I love you all dearly.

To my Mager family. I don't know if you ever could have predicted the little girl who created stories based on illustrations from her journals would turn into a published author, but here we are. Thank you for allowing me to be that imaginative, wild child, and for supporting me every step of the way.

To my Lightfoot family. Thank you for never making me feel insane for pursuing writing. For being just as excited as me at every turn, and for the support along the way. Your joy, love, and support mean more than I could ever express.

To the little girl I used to be. We did it. You didn't give up. You didn't stop dreaming. You didn't let your spark dull, and instead, you let it shine. I'm so proud of all you have accomplished. Even if it didn't seem big at the time, you helped lead us here.

To my darkness. I set you free.

About the Author

Stevi lives in the U.S. with her husband and dogs. Her mind lives in fiction, and her heart in fantasy. If she's not writing, she's daydreaming about it.

A deep love for writing encouraged a passion for editing, which inspired her career as an editor to help other authors bring their words to life. When she's not at her computer, she can be found getting lost in a book, trying a new recipe, or on her tippy toes at a rock concert.

Find out more about Stevi and her books at www.stevimager.com.